Enemy Sighted

CW Browning

Book Cover by DissectDesign / www.dissectdesigns.com

Book design by Clare Wroblewski

1st edition 2024

ISBN: 978-1-963466-35-5

Author's Note

"The gratitude of every home in our Island, in our Empire, and indeed throughout the world, except in the abodes of the guilty, goes out to the British airmen who, undaunted by odds, unwearied in their constant challenge and mortal danger, are turning the tide of the World War by their prowess and by their devotion. Never in the field of human conflict was so much owed by so many to so few."

Prime Minister Winston Churchill spoke those words to the House of Commons on August 20, 1940. Since July, the Royal Air Force had been steadily losing pilots and fighter planes over the North Sea and English Channel as the Luftwaffe confined its attacks to shipping convoys. But the world knew that it was only a matter of time before Hitler attacked his last remaining foe.

On August 13, 1940, the German offensive against Britain, codenamed Adlertag (Eagle Day), began, with the mighty Luftwaffe under orders to "smash the Royal Air Force." Reichsmarschall Hermann Göring was so confident that his Channel raids had already decimated the RAF that he assured his commanders it would not take long to wipe out the Royal Air Force. He calculated that the coastal defenses would be knocked out within four days, and Fighter Command crippled and destroyed within four weeks. At that time, Operation Sea Lion, the invasion of Britain, would commence.

Air Chief Marshal Hugh Dowding faced this attack with a diminished air force, knowing that it was solely up to his pilots to defend all of Britain and keep the Nazi jackboots at bay. What was asked of the pilots, ground crew, and support personnel was impossible. Pilots were asked to fly against overwhelming odds without break, without leave, and many times with injuries that would otherwise have left them grounded; Ground crew were asked to work around the clock to repair aircraft and keep the landing strips viable; Support personnel, many of them part of the Women's Auxiliary Air Force, were asked to maintain stressful twelve to sixteen hour days and work through raids, bombings, and destruction. They were all asked to sacrifice themselves in a fight for freedom that was being watched by the entire world.

They took an impossible task and not only made it possible, but saved all of Britain from certain invasion.

It is to those men and women, to whom we owe so much, that this book is dedicated.

FROM REICHSMARSHALL GÖRING TO ALL UNITS OF
AIR FLEETS 2, 3, AND 5. OPERATION EAGLE. WITHIN
A SHORT PERIOD YOU WILL WIPE THE BRITISH AIR
FORCE FROM THE SKY. HEIL HITLER.

Telegram from Reishmarschall Göring to his pilots, August 13,
1940

Prologue

Bordeaux, France

E isenjager bent his head to light a cigarette as a burst of raucous laughter erupted from the table beside him. The group of noncommissioned officers were several pints in, enjoying a respite from the hard work of installing gun batteries and organizing the defensive positions along the coast. The German forces had lost no time when they occupied the city in June, and now the ports were almost unrecognizable. The swastika was prevalent throughout the city, leaving no doubt as to who was in charge. Checkpoints had been established, housing seized for the troops, and chateaux commandeered for the ranking officers. Engineers were doing surveys along the coastline to begin planning for a proposed U-boat pen, one of several slated for construction along the Atlantic coast. Bordeaux had become a bustling, military stronghold. The Nazi war machine had come to stay.

Another burst of laughter rang out as he tucked his lighter into his pocket and reached for his beer. His eyes shifted to a table in the back where a group of locals sat with bottles of wine. The one seated in the corner commanded his attention, his dark hair just long enough to make him appear slightly disreputable. However, his mustache was perfect, and so were his gleaming teeth, one of which sparkled gold. While the group at the table outwardly appeared careless and none too sober, Eisenjager noted the occasional sharpness of the man's gaze. He was far from inebriated. In fact, Eisenjager had the distinct impression that, aside from himself, he might be the most dangerous man in the bar.

His name was Captain Jacques Beaulieu, and he had the enviable position of owning this establishment. While the Germans could simply take over the café-restaurant as spoils of war, in this instance, the good captain had managed to convince them that it was better to allow him to retain complete control of his business. In return for that honor, he guaranteed they would have a place to relax and drink where they were protected from any form of retaliation by the locals. The captain ran a loose establishment indeed, and the locals who frequented it were of a very dubious character. Yet they never even looked sideways at the German soldiers who reveled there nightly, a circumstance that had not gone unnoticed. Captain Beaulieu exerted an iron control over the local patrons, and as long as the Germans didn't start anything, nothing occurred to mar the evening's entertainment. However, if, as occasionally happened, a German soldier became too obnoxious, the atmosphere shifted drastically. On those incidents, both Captain Beaulieu and the ranking German officer in the bar would step in, and it never ended well for those involved.

Eisenjager sucked on his cigarette, considering the captain. It was due solely to that man's control that they had no problems with the rough and ready crowd. It was said that he was a smuggler, but when the local general had searched his ship, there had been no evidence of smuggling to be found. The captain claimed it was a fishing vessel, and after the single, cursory search, the general had agreed to allow him to continue his fishing on one condition: that 75 percent of what he caught went directly to the German forces. The captain had agreed.

Quite the feat, that, Eisenjager reflected, tapping his cigarette into the ashtray. Not only had Captain Beaulieu managed to retain control of his restaurant but he was also allowed to keep his ship, which was large for a fishing vessel. There were rumors that the agreement with the general involved substantial cash payments as well, but they were, of course, unfounded. All that was certain was that the captain held a very unique position for a Frenchman in Bordeaux, and that was all Eisenjager was really interested in.

Well, that and the Frenchwoman.

He knew the captain had whisked his target away to England at the end of May. He had watched them board the ship after his bullet missed her and instead hit her companion. Eisenjager's lips tightened grimly. That was twice, now, he'd missed his opportunity to kill the Englishwoman. The first was in Oslo when someone had attacked him from behind. Then, in May, her associate had seen him just as he pulled the trigger, pushing her to safety. The captain and his crew had surrounded the two before he could try again, and his second attempt had gone the way of the first.

Yet Eisenjager didn't blame Beaulieu. He'd been hired to carry her to safety, and that was what he'd done. The captain was merely an incidental actor in this play that he and the English spy known as Jian were engaged in. He bore him no ill will for the part he played that day.

No. His interest in the captain was far more practical.

Eisenjager reached for his beer. If Jian knew the captain, then so must the woman who accompanied her on her flight south across France. He'd caught her name that day on the road, when the Stukas made such a mess of the refugees. Jeannine was what the man had called her, and that was who Eisenjager was waiting for.

Sooner or later, the captain would lead him to Jeannine.

And Jeannine would lead him to Jian.

Chapter One

F lying Officer Fred Durton wrinkled his nose and peered up at the overcast sky.

"Not likely to see anything in that soup," he muttered to the pilot next to him, "much less hit anything."

"Maybe Jerry will stay home today," the other man said hopefully. "Seems like we're up all the time these days. I could use a few hours' break."

"Not bloody likely." Fred stretched and got up from his chair outside the dispersal hut. "They'll be along soon enough. Too many ships trying to get supplies through the Channel. They can't have that."

"I heard that they knocked out the radar towers yesterday. The bloody cheek."

Fred grunted and felt in his pockets for his cigarette case.

"Not surprising, really. They're not exactly hidden, stuck out there along the cliffs like beacons."

"Yes, but how will Group HQ know where to send us with them out of commission?"

"Haven't you heard? They're back up already. Old Charlie told me." Fred lit a cigarette and tucked his lighter back into his breast pocket. "Only Ventor is still out of action."

"Oh! Well, that's a relief." His companion yawned widely. "What time is it, anyway?"

"Just gone twelve, I should think." He looked up as a ground sergeant ran towards the landing strip with bright flags in his hands. "What's that, then? Why is young Pierson running about with grounding flags?"

"The Poles are coming back," a new voice said, joining them. "Where's the rest of the squadron?"

"In the hut, listening to the news on the wireless," Fred said, turning towards the newcomer. "Don't the Poles have radios in their kites?"

"They do, but there's some sort of flap on. Call came in from Group saying to get them down immediately."

"Charlie, you really are a wealth of information. How do you know that?"

"I'm the intelligence officer. It's my job to know things like that." Charles replied calmly. "When they come in, Pierson's to get them off the landing strip without delay."

Fred frowned. "That sounds suspiciously like Group knows something we don't."

"That *is* rather the point. It's their job, you know."

"Explain to me again why the Poles don't have to fight along with the rest of us?" The other pilot demanded, peering up at Charles and Fred. "They're pilots. They flew over there. Why aren't they fighting over here?"

"Because they haven't been made operational yet. There's some debate as to whether or not they'll be more hindrance than help."

"Don't see why they should," the pilot muttered. "Enough of our own blokes are getting thrown up there with only a few hours flying time. The Polish squadrons have more hours than they do!"

"Yes, but they don't speak English, Terry," Fred pointed out.

"I don't see what that has to do with anything. We're not up there having a conversation with the Jerries. We're shooting them, and you don't need to know English to do that."

Fred tilted his head to the side and considered Terry thoughtfully.

"Have you been consorting with the Poles?"

"'Course not!"

"You sound suspiciously sympathetic towards them. How do you understand them? I tried to have a drink with one at the pub the other night and could only make out one word in ten!"

"No rules against fraternizing with the Polish officers," Charles pointed out cheerfully as specs showed up on the horizon. "Why shouldn't he get to know them? They *are* on our side, you know."

"Never said he shouldn't," Fred said with a shrug. "I'm just trying to learn his secret for understanding them!"

Terry opened his mouth to say something, but before he could get it out, the window to the dispersal hut flew open as the rest of their squadron began pouring out of the little hut.

"SCRAMBLE!!!"

Fred stared at the yelling corporal in astonishment while Terry jumped to his feet.

"Are you serious?" Fred demanded, looking up to the sky where the Polish squadron was just coming around to land.

"Don't stand there gaping!" His CO bellowed as he ran by him with his Mae West in his hand. "You'd be up there fast enough if it was a real raid!"

Fred gulped and threw his cigarette away, turning to run with the rest of his squadron towards their Hurricanes.

"Another drill, then?" Terry gasped beside him.

"Lord knows!"

Fred rounded the nose of his Hurricane and clambered up onto the wing where his ground crew sergeant was waiting for him.

"You'll have to take off that way, sir," the man told him as he helped clip on his parachute. "303 squadron is coming in from the other direction. Is it really a raid?"

"Lord knows, but if it is, then it explains why they're being waved down."

Fred climbed into the cockpit as the sergeant leapt off the wing. He shook his head as he fastened himself in and reached for the ignition. Terry was right about one thing: there was really no reason for the Poles to have to sit these things out. They could fly and they could shoot, and as far as Fred was concerned, that was all that mattered. Who gave a damn if they were still learning English?

And if this was the beginning of Hitler's attempt to invade England, they were going to need all the help they could get.

RAF Coltishall

Flight Lieutenant Miles Lacey looked up as a shadow fell over his book.

"Reading at the ready, Miles? Haven't you got anything better to do?"

"Oh yes, but the RAF seems to think I should sit out here instead," Miles murmured, closing his book. "Where'd you come from? I thought you were up with the old man."

"We were. We landed twenty minutes ago." Robert Ainsworth dropped into the empty deck chair next to Miles. "You didn't hear us come in?"

"I wasn't here. I've just come out. The bone crusher dropped us off a few minutes ago."

"Oh? Where're Chris and young Thomas?"

"In the hut, harassing the corporal. Did you see anything while you were up?"

"Not a damn thing." Rob pulled out his cigarette case and opened it. "It was thick as pea soup up there this morning. Wouldn't be surprised if we don't see a Jerry all day."

Miles pursed his lips together and was silent. The waiting was getting on all their nerves, and he hadn't missed the annoyance in Rob's voice. They all knew an onslaught was coming. The radar towers along the coast had been bombed the day before and it didn't take a genius to realize why the Jerries would do that. They were coming, no doubt about it. The only question was when.

"Have you heard from m'sister lately?" Rob asked suddenly.

"I had a letter the other day, but nothing since. Why do you ask?"

"How did she seem to you? All right?"

"Yes, I think so. Why?"

"The last letter I had from her sounded, oh I don't know, off somehow. Not like her usual self." Rob blew smoke up into the air and watched it dissipate on the breeze. "I know she's on a holiday, and I suppose I expected her to be more cheerful than she was."

"Perhaps she will be once she goes back to Ainsworth," Miles said with a shrug. "I got the impression that she's rather tired of London at the moment."

Rob made a sound suspiciously like a snort.

"Evie? Tired of London? Not likely. She thrives on society, y'know." Rob glanced at him and grinned. "You'll learn soon enough. She gets restless in the country. High-energy, that's what Evie is. Always was. M'father used to say she could dance until dawn and then go shooting and bag a pheasant as if she'd slept the night through."

"And did she?"

"On more than one occasion." Rob chuckled. "I remember once in France, we were staying with my uncle, in Paris y'know, and she went to a nightclub with our cousins. They came back just before dawn without her. When I asked where she'd got to, Gisele told me, gay as you please, mind, that she'd loaned her the Bugatti as Evie decided she wanted to drive down to the chateau and do some shooting."

"In the middle of the night?" Miles stared at him. "After dancing all night?"

Rob nodded. "Precisely. So off she went and bagged three pheasants before ten o'clock in the morning!"

"My word. She's a good shot, then?"

"Lord, yes. Well, we both are. We've got a knack for it, or so the groom's always said." Rob stared up at the overcast sky. "I wasn't surprised in the slightest when she told us that she was joining the WAAFs. Neither was my father. All this, of course, is to say that if Evie's getting bored with London, then she's worse off than I thought. I wonder what's got to her?"

Before Miles could respond, the window to the dispersal hut behind them flew open and the corporal shoved his head out.

"SCRAMBLE!!!"

Miles and Rob started and jumped up, turning to look at him in astonishment.

"Are you sure?" Miles demanded, reaching for his Mae West on the ground by his chair as Rob threw his cigarette away.

"Yes, sir!"

"So much for not seeing Jerry today," he called to Rob as they jogged towards the Spitfires lined up along the landing strip. "Are you sure you didn't see anything earlier?"

"As God is my witness!" Rob waved to their squadron leader, who was running from the other direction. "Scramble, sir!"

"Yes, I know. Get moving!"

"Where the hell are my pilots?" Miles demanded as they covered the ground to their fighters.

"Right behind you," a distinctly American voice gasped. "Tomcat tripped over his feet in the door and slowed us down."

"I say!" Poor young Thomas exclaimed, passing Miles with his longer stride. "That's not true! You're the one who tripped, Yank!"

Miles rounded the nose of his Spit and nodded to his ground crew sergeant as he leapt onto the wing.

"Do you think this is it, sir?" Jones asked as he helped him on with his parachute.

"Lord knows! Thanks."

Jones nodded and jumped off to grab the chocks from the wheels as Miles climbed into the cockpit. A second later, he started the engine and motioned to Jones that he was pulling out. Taking a deep breath, Miles steered onto the landing strip. Chris Field, the American pilot, was starting his engine as he pulled by, and Miles motioned to him. He nodded and motioned back, then Miles turned into the wind and opened up the throttle. The fighter responded immediately and hurtled along the grass until, all of a sudden, the wings caught air. The wheels left the ground as the Spitfire lifted effortlessly into the sky. Miles reached down to retract the undercarriage with one hand, then reached up to slide the canopy closed.

"Blue Leader, airborne," he said calmly as he banked and glanced down at the landing strip below him. Chris was already hurtling down the strip, with Thomas turning into the wind behind him.

"Blue Two, airborne," Chris said a moment later.

Miles arched up into the clouds and flew steady until Chris and Thomas joined him on either side.

"Fibius Blue Leader to Cowslip. Blue Flight airborne. Where are we going?" He said into the radio.

"This is Cowslip, Blue Leader. Is Red Flight with you?"

"This is Red Leader, Cowslip. We're here."

Ashmore's voice was steady, and Miles twisted his head to see Ashmore, Rob, and one of the new pilots joining him on the left side.

"Roger that, Red Leader. Steer Angels 2-4-0. Bandits, 100 plus."

Miles blanched as his stomach lurched, feeling as if it were dropping out of the cockpit.

"Red Leader to Cowslip. Sorry. It sounded like you said 'bandits, 100 plus.' " Ashmore's voice was sharper than before. "Confirm number of bandits."

"Yes, Red Leader. Number of bandits confirmed. Steer Angels 2-4-0 to intercept bandits, 100 plus."

"They do know there's only six of us, right?" Chris demanded.

"Roger, Cowslip. Red Leader received. Steering Angels 2-4-0."

Miles looked over to Chris, flying close off his right side. The Yank held up a hand and pointed his fingers like a gun to his head. Miles swallowed and fought the irrational urge to laugh. Chris had it right. This was suicide.

"You heard him, lads. Bandits, 100 plus," Ashmore said, his voice more steady now. "We'll be joining up with the rest of the Wing, Field. You all know the drill."

Miles tightened his lips and glanced to his left. Thomas was already looking above and below them, searching for enemy fighters. Good man. He'd come to the squadron a few weeks before with exactly zero hours flying a Spitfire. He'd gone into the Channel once but had learned faster than any pilot Miles had flown with yet. He was extremely grateful to have Chris and Thomas at his side.

This had to be it. If HQ was correct, and there were really over a hundred enemy airplanes flying over the coast, then it could only mean that Herr Göring was launching an attack against Britain at last.

"We're coming into range. Keep your eyes out for enemy cover," Ashmore said tersely.

"Cowslip to Red Leader. Watch for friendly squadron joining on the right."

Miles' headset crackled again, and he turned to scan the skies to the right.

"I see them!" Chris called a moment later as three flights of Hurricanes came into view on the horizon. "That makes me feel a little better about these odds."

"Cowslip to Red Leader. Steer Vector 0-4-5 to join Big Wing."

Miles glanced at his instruments and adjusted his bearing, taking a deep, calming breath. Even when the multiple squadrons had joined together, they were still going to be heavily outnumbered. Over a hundred enemy airplanes?

"Red Leader to Cowslip. Joining now."

They flew through a cloud bank and Miles blinked before refocusing on the four squadrons ahead of them.

"So what they're saying is we're looking at odds of four-to-one here," Chris said as they joined the other squadrons. "In the Krauts' favor."

"Never mind the chatter," Ashmore snapped. "Just do what you do best, Field."

"Oh, don't you worry about me, sir," Chris replied cheerfully. "I'll be shooting like they're rabbits at my cousin's farm in Ohio."

"Good man," Miles murmured to himself.

Then he looked down and saw them. He swallowed a sudden lump in his throat as he stared at the waves of enemy aircraft below. It wasn't 100 plus. It was a lot more, plus their fighter escort.

"Holy shit," Chris said, his voice shaking. "That's more than a hundred."

"At least we're above them," Miles managed to choke out. "Close up, Blue Three. We're in for a fight."

"Red Leader to Cowslip. Bandits spotted. 150 plus. Repeat, 150 plus."

"Roger, Red Leader."

Miles took another deep breath and glanced over at Chris. He was shaking his head and Miles didn't blame him one bit.

"All right, lads. Let's go. Watch those fighters!"

"Tallyho!"

Chapter Two

London
August 14

Evelyn Ainsworth unlocked the front door and stepped inside, turning to look out onto the street. The short walk from the post office to the house on Brook Street had been uneventful, but disturbing, nonetheless. There seemed to be a heightened sense of urgency as civilians, along with men and women in uniform, hurried about their business. The morning newspapers were filled with accounts of the enemy raids that took place all over the south of England the day before, and the amount of activity in the skies above indicated that the RAF expected the same today. It had begun at last.

Evelyn closed the door, blocking out the busy residential street. The massive barrage balloons that floated high above the city had seemed a little redundant in the past weeks, but now she admitted to herself that she felt a bit better for their presence. The enormous floating devices were meant to protect London from the attacks of low-flying aircraft, , forcing them within range of the anti-aircraft guns dotted all over the city. At least London would be spared the horrors of the Stuka dive bombers, if nothing else.

Walking down the hallway towards the kitchen in the back of the house, she remembered the hordes of bombers flying over France towards Dunkirk and knew that it was only a matter of time before she saw the same over London.

And the only thing standing in their way was the RAF.

She paused next to the hallstand against the wall and removed her hat, setting it down next to the telephone before removing her gloves. Miles, Robbie, Fred, Chris, and all the other pilots were up there defending them every day, but would it be enough? Could it be enough? They were outnumbered four to one at the last count, and that was going to change considerably as pilots were killed and planes were lost. Well, it had already begun to change. The number of planes lost over Dunkirk had started the ball rolling, and they'd been losing more in defense of the convoys. Aircraft production was increasing dramatically, but she didn't see how the factories could possibly build as many fighters as they needed in such a short time. It would take a miracle.

The silence in the house was shattered when the telephone rang shrilly, making her start, and Evelyn exhaled, reaching for the receiver.

"Hello? Ainsworth residence."

"Evie? Is that you? Are you still there, then?"

"Robbie!" Evelyn exclaimed. "Yes, I'm still here. How are you?"

"Tickety-boo. How are you? Why are you still in London?"

"I'll be going back to Ainsworth soon. I'm just finishing up some errands here." She cleared her throat. "Is everything all right? No one's hurt, are they?"

As much as she tried to keep her voice light, Evelyn was aware that it came out with a sharp edge to it.

"Good Lord, no. Nothing like that. I just thought I'd ring up to check on you. Your last letter sounded a trifle off."

"Did it?" Evelyn sank down onto the chair next to the telephone. "I can't think why."

"Miles thought perhaps you're growing weary of London. Is that it?"

"Perhaps I am, a bit. Robbie, you really wouldn't believe what some of our old acquaintances are like these days. It makes me wonder how on earth I've changed so much."

"You *have* changed," Rob said unexpectedly after a moment. "I can't quite put my finger on it, but you're different now. Well, it's to be expected, isn't it? We're all changing as we do our bit."

"Speaking of doing our bit, how is it up there?"

"Rather anticlimactic, to be honest. No doubt that the Jerries have turned their sights to us, but I think the chaps in Eleven Group are the ones having all the fun."

"I doubt they consider it fun, Robbie."

"No, I suppose not." Someone spoke in the background and Robbie exhaled. "I have to ring off, Evie. We're off to the ready again. When are you going to Ainsworth?"

"Soon. Tomorrow, perhaps."

"Good. I'll feel better when you're out of the city. They'll try for London soon enough. Go home and keep Mother company for a few days."

"Robbie. . .take care of yourself."

"Piece of cake," came the flippant answer. "Give Mother and all assorted aunts and uncles my love. Bye now!"

The line went dead, and Evelyn laid the receiver in the cradle, her throat tightening. Rob had sounded like his usual self, but she knew he would never let her hear the strain he must be under. It was enough to hear his voice and know that, for now, he was all right. When she'd first heard him, she'd been afraid that he was phoning with bad news about Miles. Thankfully, that wasn't the case, but for how long? How could she expect both of the men in her life to make it through this war? How could she expect herself to? Would any of them survive the coming months? Or years?

Rob was worried about her because of the tone of her last letter, but he had no idea what she really did, or why her last letter had been so "off," as he put it. She'd written it the day after she discovered that several of their peers were Nazi sympathizers actively plotting to help overthrow the government and monarchy. She'd thought that she'd managed to send off letters to both Rob and Miles without giving away her upset, but apparently her brother knew her too well.

Evelyn got to her feet and continued down the hallway to the kitchen. Hopefully, she'd managed to set his mind at ease a bit. The last thing she needed was Rob popping up unexpectedly to check on his little sister! It was bad enough that she had to worry about Miles showing up at Northolt without warning.

She was just entering the kitchen when the front doorbell went, and Evelyn frowned, looking at her watch. Now what? Who on earth could that be? Who knew she was still here?

"At this rate, I'll never have my cup of tea," she muttered, turning to retrace her steps to the door.

A moment later, she opened it to find Sir William Buckley standing on the step, an umbrella in one hand and a briefcase in the other.

"Bill!" she exclaimed, opening the door wider. "What are you doing here?"

"I should ask you the same," he replied, stepping into the hallway. "You're supposed to be on holiday, and I thought you were going back to Ainsworth Manor."

"And so I am," she said, closing the door behind him, "eventually. Here, let me take your hat and umbrella."

Bill handed them over with a murmur of thanks, his eyes taking in her appearance with a swift glance.

"You've been out. Shopping?"

"The post office, to mail some letters." She laid his hat next to hers and set the umbrella in the stand. Turning, her lips curved in amusement. "Why are you so curious about my whereabouts this morning?"

"I've had some rather unsettling news, as a matter fact. It's why I'm here."

The smile faded and Evelyn nodded briskly.

"I should have guessed as much," she said. "Come into the kitchen. I was just about to put the kettle on. It sounds as if we'll need it."

Bill followed her down the hall to the large, sunny kitchen that took up most of the back of the town house.

"I understand Anthony Marrow was pleased with the package you recovered," he said as she waved him into a seat at the table. "Fitch had lunch with one of his aids yesterday. Your package is the talk of the Security Service."

Evelyn frowned and glanced at him over her shoulder as she filled the kettle at the sink.

"Wesley didn't give me away, did he?"

"Of course not." Bill sat back and crossed his legs. "He was at school with the man, and they have lunch regularly. All he had to do was listen."

"And you? Were you as impressed with the information?"

"Impressed isn't quite the word I'd use, no. Appalled would be closer to the mark. Did you see the names on that list?"

"Yes." Evelyn lit the burner under the kettle before opening a cabinet and pulling down a tin of tea. "I'm afraid I don't have any sugar here."

"That's perfectly all right. Just a spot of milk is all I need. You sound very calm about the whole thing. Are you sure you examined everything in that packet?"

Evelyn's lips twisted wryly, and she nodded.

"Yes. I've had a few days to come to terms with it."

"Hm. I don't feel that I'll ever be able to look at them the same way again. Thank God I don't go about in society much these days." Bill cleared his throat. "Montclair was very pleased. Even though he was quite opposed to you working with MI5, he admitted that, under the circumstances, you did an outstanding job."

"I didn't do anything very much, really. I was able to take the package, but even that was a messy business." She pursed her lips thoughtfully and leaned against the counter. "We really must find out who this Henry is and put a stop to all this business. He's the one who blew my cover, you know. Lord Gilhurst told me a man had given them the information. It had to have been Henry."

"Yes, well, that's part of the reason I'm here. Henry may know a bit more than we already suspected."

She raised an eyebrow. "Oh?"

"Sam, the fellow who flew you in and out of Switzerland in May, is in town. Well, not London. He's in Bedfordshire at the moment. I went to see him last night, at his invitation. He had some information for me that he managed to smuggle out of France and wanted to hand it to me himself. During our conversation, he told me something rather alarming."

"Do stop being so dramatic, Sir William," Evelyn said when he paused for a long moment. "It doesn't suit you, you know."

Bill was surprised into a short laugh.

"It wasn't intentional. Rather, I was trying to decide the best way to tell you."

"I've always been partial to directness myself." The amusement was back in her voice. "Really, Bill, it can't be that shocking. Just spit it out."

"I believe that Henry contacted Sam last week. Oh, he used an assistant and went through hoops to ensure that Sam didn't know just who was asking, but I've no doubt that it was Henry. Sam was told that they needed to complete a form for the archives, and Sam had no reason to doubt it. Apparently, he's had legitimate requests from us like this before."

"If Henry is as well established in the government as we believe him to be, then it's hardly a surprise that he would know that," Evelyn said slowly. "I assume he was looking for information on Jian?"

"It's more serious than that. He was asking after a passenger that Sam flew into Switzerland two months ago. A young woman."

Evelyn stared at him, her mouth going dry.

"How the devil did he know that?" she demanded, her voice much sharper than she intended. "*I* didn't even know that I was going until I received your coded message in Paris!"

"Precisely, and I can assure you, Evie, that he was *not* tipped off by me." Bill's voice was grim. "No one else knew anything about it."

Evelyn frowned and turned as the kettle began whistling on the stove top.

"The radio operator who sent the message?"

"Doesn't have access to the codebook. They have no idea what the messages they send are."

They were silent as she warmed a teapot with a bit of boiling water before scooping tea leaves into it.

"Well, he found out somehow. Who *is* he? Really, Bill, this is getting to be absolutely ridiculous. Why can't we find this man?"

Evelyn carried the teapot to the table and set it down before turning to pull teacups and saucers from a cabinet against the wall.

"You know how delicate the situation is, Evie. We must be patient. Eventually, he'll slip up and make a mistake."

"Yes, and in the meantime, he continues to learn more and more about me!" She looked over her shoulder as she lifted down two cups. "What did Sam tell him?"

"Not much, thankfully. He didn't know anything other than that he'd been instructed to fly a passenger to and from Bern."

"And he didn't question why someone was asking questions so long after the fact?"

"No, he didn't. That's our fault, I'm afraid. Because we have no idea who Henry is, we haven't alerted anyone to the fact that there's an internal investigation in progress. Sam had no reason to doubt the story of a desk clerk needing to dot some i's and cross some t's."

"Then why tell you about it at all?"

Bill's lips twisted ruefully as he accepted the cup and saucer from her.

"I told him that there was a bad apple among us. He's been grounded in England ever since he barely made it out of Spain in one piece. There's no possibility of his being Henry, so I told him that we're investigating a mole. That's when he told me about the contact. Henry tracked him down in Barcelona the day before he left. He thought absolutely nothing of it at the time, but after hearing about a mole. . ."

"He realized it probably wasn't as innocent as it appeared." Evelyn sighed and sank down into a chair across the table and handed Bill a tea strainer. "Well, it could certainly be a lot worse. I was going by the name of Geneviève in France, but Sam didn't know that. We used the code word, and that was it. No names."

"Quite." Bill poured a little milk from the small jug into his cup, then poured tea through the strainer. "However, he did give Henry a description of you."

Evelyn paused in the act of reaching for the milk, her eyes locking with Bill's.

"He knows what I look like?" she asked softly.

"I'm afraid so." Bill cleared his throat. "Not too terribly detailed, but close enough. Sam told him you were young, blonde, and very beautiful."

Evelyn's eyebrows flew up and she let out a choked laugh.

"Thank you, Sam," she murmured.

Bill grinned and lifted his cup.

"Sam didn't give him your eye color, but I'm not happy with the rest. It seems likely that he already had a rudimentary description of you, but now we know for certain, and I'm not comfortable with you coming and going from Broadway anymore."

"You really think he's watching Broadway?"

"I would if I were him. Wouldn't you?"

Evelyn finished pouring her tea and sighed.

"Yes, I suppose so. What, then? I'm not to go at all?"

"I'd rather you didn't, but that's hardly a solution." Bill drank some tea, then set the cup down with a clink. "If you must come to the office, I'd suggest a disguise."

Evelyn stared at him, torn between amusement and annoyance.

"A disguise?" she repeated. "Here in London? Really!"

"I'm not suggesting full makeup," he assured her, "but perhaps something to cover your hair and, I don't know, some way of changing your appearance somewhat. Perhaps different clothes. Something that won't draw attention."

"Plain Jane in a mousy wig and spectacles?" Despite herself, Evelyn felt a laugh bubbling up. "Oh Bill, that's ridiculous. Why should I have to slink about like I'm the one who's the criminal? It hardly seems fair!"

"Think of it as being cautious. It's what we trained you to do on the Continent."

"Yes, on the Continent. Not here in London!" She shook her head and lifted her cup to her lips. After sipping her tea in silence for a moment, she sighed again. "Very well. If I must go to Broadway, I'll take every precaution. Thankfully, the description matches half the women in London."

"Yes, but I'll still feel much happier when you're out of London altogether. Go home to Lancashire and relax. You still have over a week of holiday, and I'd rather you took it at Ainsworth Manor. Given the onset of the Luftwaffe's attacks on England, I don't want you anywhere near an airfield at the moment."

"It's true, then? It's begun?"

"Oh yes. Göring's sending over half of everything that he's got. They're trying to take control of the skies, just as they did in Norway, Belgium, and France. A bit of a challenge now, though. They can't send their tanks in right behind them."

"Thank God for that!" Evelyn shuddered. "The sight of that Panzer division racing across France isn't one I'll forget in a hurry."

Bill's face softened. "I know. You've seen things no one should ever have to see, Evie. There are days when I regret that luncheon in Neuilly-sur-Seine."

"Don't be silly," she said briskly. "If you hadn't recruited me, someone else would have. We both know that my skills are much in demand, and they wouldn't have gone overlooked for long. I much prefer that it was you, and I'm sure Daddy would have as well."

"Would he? I'm not so sure about that."

She raised her eyebrows and studied him over the rim of her cup.

"Aren't you? Whyever not?"

"Robert had some funny reservations at times," Bill said slowly. "He didn't always agree with our methods. I'm afraid your father was a bit of an idealist at times."

Evelyn was silent for a moment, then she set her cup down.

"I'd say that we're all a bit of an idealist at times. Why else would we take the risks that we do, if not because we believe in a future different from the one presented to us?"

"Perhaps." Bill shook his head. "It's all a moot point now, in any case. You're in it, for better or worse, and Robert is not. When will you return to Ainsworth?"

"I suppose I'll go home in the next day or two. I want to take care of a few things here in town first."

"Well, please take care of them quickly. As I said, the sooner that you're out of London, the better I'll feel."

"I will."

"Before I go, I have some news for you. From Norway."

Evelyn felt her gut clench. "Yes?"

"It's not bad news," he said hastily, seeing the look on her face. "Quite the contrary. We've determined that Erik Salveson is alive and well. You were right. He remembered the incident with the rifle and was able to recount the event exactly as you said. He and Anna have taken refuge in the mountains and are continuing to build the resistance that you began."

Relief flowed through Evelyn, making her feel an almost uncontrollable urge to laugh.

"Anna's with him? She's all right?"

"Yes, at the last transmission." Bill cleared his throat. "They're not in for an easy time of it. The Germans have taken over completely and are working hard to ensure that no one will aid a resistance."

"It's the Germans who won't have an easy time of it, not with them," she said with a wry smile. "Erik will run that resistance just like the army. What's more, he'll make sure all the members are properly trained and armed. The Norwegians are a fiercely determined people. If they want to resist, they will, and woe betide anyone who tries to stop them."

"I do hope you're right. Montclair is in agreement that they must be helped at all costs. We'll do what we can to get them supplies, but the rest is up to them."

"I think they'll surprise you. I really do."

Bill nodded and got to his feet.

"Now, you'll leave in the morning?"

She laughed and stood.

"Yes. I promise that I'll go home to the pile and spend my days practicing my aim with my rifle and riding my horse. All right?"

"Good show." Bill picked up his briefcase and turned to leave the kitchen. "I never knew anyone who required so much arm-twisting to take a holiday!"

"It's your own fault, you know." Evelyn followed him down the hall and watched as he picked up his hat and umbrella. "You introduced me to excitement and intrigue. I'm afraid the rolling hills of Lancashire are a very poor substitute for fleeing from advancing German armies and assassins!"

He turned to face her, shaking his head.

"Well, after that training course, I'm ordering you to rest. Whether you think it or not, you need the break."

"And so I shall," she promised him.

Chapter Three

August 15

E velyn closed her suitcase and secured the straps, looking around her bedroom to ensure that she had packed everything she meant to. She always left a few articles of clothing for the occasions when she came to town unexpectedly, as did Rob and her mother. Her eyes fell on the open wardrobe, and she considered the frocks still hanging inside. She missed wearing her pretty dresses and casual, wide-legged pants. While she was on station at RAF Northolt, appearances had to be maintained. That meant living in the drab and uncomfortable WAAF uniform with the perfectly appalling sensible stockings and shoes. These few days in London had allowed her to return to her civilian wardrobe, and she had enjoyed every moment.

Evelyn lifted her case off the bed and carried it over to the door, ready to go with her in the morning. Everything was packed. Her eyes went to her toiletries case sitting on the vanity table and her lips tightened. Well, almost everything. Crossing the room, she opened the case and removed the tray and the few boxes containing jewelry. She ran her hand along the inside edge until her fingers caught the hidden clasp behind the lining. There was a faint click and the false bottom released, revealing a sheaf of papers and four sheets of microfiche. This was what her father had left for her in Zürich, along with instructions not to entrust it to anyone. He'd known she was working with MI6 and had been very clear in his directions to keep this from them. He hadn't trusted their agency, but he hadn't said why.

Evelyn picked up one of the sheets of microfiche and stared down at it pensively. She'd taken it that very afternoon, along with the other three, to the largest newspaper in London. After spending weeks trying to determine the best way to read the blasted things, she'd suddenly remembered Uncle Lenny. He wasn't an uncle at all, but she had called him that for as long as she could remember. Her father had been great friends with him, but then, Daddy had been great friends with most people that he met. She never knew how her father had become acquaintances with Uncle Lenny, for they certainly didn't move in the same circles, but she had spent many an hour playing in his cramped and untidy office at the newspaper while he and her father discussed international business and politics. When she called him yesterday to ask if they had a microfiche reader, he'd been thrilled to hear from little Evie.

And her visit that afternoon had certainly not disappointed.

She smiled faintly. Uncle Lenny was still the same as she remembered, with gray hair that stuck up at the back, rumpled suit jacket, and ink-stained fingers. He was an editor, quite high up now, and the cramped office was much larger and better appointed than the one she remembered. He'd accepted her story of her father leaving her photographs on microfiche without question, remarking that Robert always was a strange, old dog, God rest his soul.

The smile faded and she dropped the slip of film back into the hidden compartment, replacing the false bottom. What she'd found on the microfiche had been printed onto sheets of paper, carefully folded and tucked under the rest of the papers in the case. Some were documents and memos that were chilling in their detail, and some were drawings. It was the drawings that she needed help with. The documents were clear enough, and she now fully understood the gravity of the contents and why her father had been so insistent in his letter that she trust no one and take extreme care of the package. Her lips tightened into a grim line as she replaced the contents of the case. She also understood why whoever had possession of the documents was in such danger. The German High Command would stop at nothing to get them back; they were far too important to be lost in the midst of a war.

Evelyn closed the case and turned to leave the room. The documents were one thing, but the drawings were quite another. She didn't trust her rudimentary knowledge of motors and physics enough to think that she was reading them correctly. She needed to have someone else look at them; someone who would be able to interpret what they were looking at. Unfortunately, those kinds of people were not immediately within her sphere of acquaintance.

Running lightly down the stairs to the ground floor, she shook her head. Bill liked to say that she was like her father in that she was able to cultivate contacts easily in any area she chose, but she didn't see that at all. Her father probably knew any number of scientifically inclined people, engineers or professors who would have been able to help him. She knew no one. Yet she had to find *someone*, and just how on earth was she going to do that?

The wireless was playing jazz in the front parlor and the music flowed into the hallway as she rounded the bottom of the stairs and went towards the telephone on the stand. She picked up the receiver and dialed the number for the Northolt exchange from memory, setting aside the problem of the hidden plans in her toiletries case for the moment. She would worry about finding an expert later. Right now, she wanted to reach Sergeant Cunningham before she went off duty. Bill wanted her to go to Lancashire and stay there, and she would go home for a few days. But she also had every intention of going back to her RAF station to have a nice chat with her Sergeant.

When Bill had confessed to her that the woman was really an assistant section officer, and that she was placed at Northolt solely to assist in protecting Evelyn's true role, Evelyn had been intrigued. She'd thought of an idea and had had every intention of putting it to Sergeant Cunningham last week before being sidetracked with the Round Club. Her lips tightened with the thought as she waited for her call to be routed to the correct office on the station.

The Round Club was still out there, and they were still free. Anthony Morrow, her father's friend from the Secret Service, had made it very clear that the woman known as Molly wouldn't be apprehended, despite her attempt to kill Evelyn, in the interest of keeping his mole undetected within the Round Club. After she left him, Evelyn realized that that amnesty would have to extend to the entire inner circle of the traitorous organization. Not one of them would be arrested for treason. They would all continue just as they had before, as if the entire incident in Weymouth had never occurred. The only difference between now and two weeks ago was that both MI6 and MI5 were now aware of the identities of the traitors roaming London's high society.

And they had no intention of doing a thing about it.

Frustration rolled through her and her fingers tightened on the receiver as Evelyn stared at her reflection in the mirror. She was still furious over the gall of these people, who claimed to be the upper crust elite of British society. They cared nothing for the lives of the young men flying so courageously above their properties to protect them. They cared nothing for their country, or the men and women who made up the British Isles. They cared only for their own comfort and the spoils of war they were convinced would be theirs when the Nazi regime marched into Britain. She wondered what they would say if they'd seen the children and animals blown to pieces on the road in France. Would they still be so willing to have it happen here? Or would they consider the lives of the lower classes as unimportant?

"Hallo? Sergeant Cunningham speaking."

"Hello, Sergeant. This is ASO Ainsworth calling."

"Oh hello, ma'am. How are you enjoying your leave?"

"I'm having a whale of a time. How are things there? Is it very hectic?"

"Rather a bit, yes. The station has been very busy, and the squadrons are up more than they're down. Last night was. . .well, I've never seen anything like it. Scrambles all the time. I believe the final count was over twenty-five sorties for the station yesterday alone, all in the afternoon and evening."

Evelyn swallowed and dropped into the chair next to the little table.

"Good heavens," she breathed. "Did they all come back?"

"Unfortunately not. Today hasn't been as frantic, but they're saying that it's due to the lousy weather we've had."

Evelyn felt her gut clench and she took a deep, steadying breath.

"And Flying Officer Durton? Is his squadron intact?"

"The last that I heard, yes." Sergeant Cunningham paused and then cleared her throat. "He was in here this morning harassing the girls. I'm afraid I was rather short with him, ma'am."

Evelyn choked out a laugh as relief went through her.

"As you should be, Sergeant. He knows better than that."

"Yes, ma'am." The sergeant cleared her throat again. "I don't mind saying that I'm very glad for the camouflage on the tops of our buildings. They're saying that Jerry is going for the airfields."

"Yes. Yes, I suppose they would, although at the moment they seem to be concentrating on the coastal areas." Evelyn exhaled. "Well, I'm glad that you're all safe for now, at any rate. I'm not due back until the twenty-fourth, but I rang to tell you that I'll be coming onto the station at the weekend to pick up a few things. I thought I'd let you know so that you can have anything ready for me that might need my signature and can't wait. I was going to come on Saturday."

"Very good, ma'am. Section Officer Madson has been taking care of a lot of it, but there *are* one or two things. I'll have them waiting for you."

"Thank you. While I'm there, I thought perhaps we could have lunch together. Not at that awful excuse for a dining mess, but perhaps at the local pub?"

"Oh!"

The exclamation of surprise was genuine and Evelyn grimaced. The woman had done so much to make her life at Northolt as easy as possible, and yet she'd never once asked her to join her for a meal or even a cup of tea. Had she really been that self-absorbed and, well, snobbish? And had it really taken the experiences of the past five months to make her realize it?

"I understand that it might not be convenient, and we can certainly do it another time if you'd rather."

"No! Not at all. Lunch at the pub would be lovely."

"Wonderful. Oh, and Sergeant? This is strictly confidential." Evelyn cleared her throat and chuckled ruefully. "I'm afraid Sir William wouldn't approve. He's made it clear that he doesn't want me near Northolt until it's time for me to return to work."

To her surprise, Sergeant Cunningham let out a low laugh.

"Don't worry, ma'am. Mum's the word."

"Thanks, awfully."

"I'll see you on Saturday, then."

"Yes. Thank you, Sergeant. I'll see you then."

Evelyn hung up and stared at the telephone for a moment. Over twenty-five sorties? In just a few hours? When they said that 11 Group would get the brunt of the attack, Evelyn knew that Northolt would be in the thick of it. Yet she was still shaken. The real thrust had barely begun, and they were already flying that many sorties? Right now, Göring was concentrating on the radar towers and port cities, but once they were knocked out, he would unleash the bulk of his forces on the airfields. He knew the only way to gain superiority over the skies was to destroy the aircraft on the ground. It's how he'd won Belgium, and how he'd devastated France. When he shifted his focus, how on earth would the squadrons keep up with them all?

She took a deep, unsteady breath and frowned as she realized that her hands were shaking. She was afraid, not just for Fred and the other pilots at Northolt, but for her brother, and for Miles. They, and a mere few hundred like them, were all that stood between Britain and the destruction that she'd witnessed on the road in France. They were outnumbered in both pilots and aircraft, and they were already getting tired. How would they ever hold on?

Standing, she moved towards the front parlor. She didn't even have a photograph of Miles, she realized with a start. She'd never thought to ask for one, and she didn't suppose it ever occurred to him to give her one. If anything happened. . .

Evelyn pushed the thought out of her head resolutely. She would enclose a photograph of herself in her next letter to him and perhaps that would encourage him to do the same.

And then she would have to pray that it would be enough to get her through the nightmare if he didn't make it.

RAF Coltishall
August 15

Miles finished scanning the article he was reading in the morning paper before folding and throwing it down disgustedly beside his plate.

"More good news?" Rob asked, looking up from his plate of eggs and sausages.

"They're saying that 11 Group is defending all of Britain," Miles said, picking up his utensils and returning to his forgotten breakfast. "All they talk about is the southern squadrons and airfields. It's as if we don't even exist. Nothing in there about 12 Group, or the bloody great big formations of bombers we saw yesterday. It's all about the coastal stations. No mention of anyone else at all."

"We're not the ones in the hot seat, old boy. Do they say how many came over yesterday?" Rob asked before raising a forkful of sausage to his lips.

"No. It says we destroyed forty German aircraft to a loss of only five of our own."

Rob raised an eyebrow skeptically as he chewed.

"That seems a bit low on our end. I heard that Gravesend alone lost three Hurricanes yesterday," he said after he'd swallowed.

"Who told you that?"

"Jones. He had it from a rigger somewhere."

"Well, it wouldn't surprise me. You've seen how many of the bastards are flying over. I think they're manufacturing more as we eat." Miles exhaled and pushed his empty plate to the side, reaching for the pot of tea on the table. "Aren't you the least bit frustrated?"

"Me? Not a bit." Rob wiped his mouth with his napkin. "Our turn will come. I think this is one of those occasions when there will be quite enough to go 'round."

"I suppose you're right." Miles was silent for a moment, then he shook his head. "But think of the difference we could be making! Our squadron has over twenty confirmed kills!"

"Yes, but some of those are from Dunkirk, and there are twice as many of the blasted Jerries now," Rob pointed out. "That's twice as many shooting back at us!"

"You seem awfully negative this morning," Miles said, pulling out his cigarette case. "Did you get up on the wrong side of the bed?"

"And you, my dear Lacey, seem awfully bloodthirsty this morning," came the cheerful reply. "I don't know why you're so eager to go up and get shot at, but it will happen soon enough. It's bright and sunny out there at the moment, which means the bastards will be nipping along in all their droves and ugliness."

"And we'll be missing them in all their droves and ugliness," an American voice said from behind Miles. Chris dropped into the chair next to him with his cup of coffee. "What a total waste of time it is!"

"Waste of time?" Rob peered at him over the rim of his teacup. "Why do you say that?"

"All the bombers yesterday had already hit their targets and were heading home by the time our so-called Big Wing got there," Chris said with a shrug. "What's the point of trying to defend your country if the enemy's already dropped their load before we even get there?"

"He's got a point," Miles said, lighting his cigarette.

Rob looked from one to the other and shook his head.

"I can see that I have to remind both of you of the science behind the Big Wing. We attack in large numbers so that we can shoot large numbers of the bastards down. Whether that's before or after they hit their targets, those are still aircraft that won't be making a return trip."

"And that's the point?" Chris demanded.

"That's the point."

"Well, it's a shitty point. Just ask the poor bastards farther south who have no airplane to fly, or runway to land on."

"You know, Miles, every time I think we're making some headway with our American friend here, he comes out with delightfully gauche statements such as that," Rob complained.

"I'm very much afraid that we can't make a silk purse out of a sow's ear," Miles agreed sadly. "However, despite all of that, I think the Yank actually does have a valid point. The Big Wing is a good idea on paper, but not very practical in reality. Not when Jerry is going for the airfields and radar towers."

"Why, thanks awfully, old chap," Chris drawled in a perfect imitation of their public-school accent.

"Well, it doesn't much matter what we think, does it? We didn't come up with the battle strategy," Rob said sensibly. "Our job is to fly it, and that's all there is to it."

"True enough." Miles finished his tea and stood. "I'll see you at the ready. I'm off to try to get through to m'father before we start."

Chris watched him go, then turned his eyes on Rob.

"Do you really think what we're doing will work in the long run?" he asked seriously. "I mean, it sounds like 11 Group will get clobbered, if they're not already. How long can they hold out if we can't stop the bombers from getting to their airfields?"

"I have absolutely no idea, but let's hope that it's long enough." Rob reached for his tea. "If it's not, we're buggered."

Chapter Four

Hyde Park, London

Henry watched as a bird launched from its perch in a tree to disappear into the distance, soaring majestically high above them all as if there wasn't anything amiss in the world. That bird was carrying on its daily existence without any worry or anxiety, as were all the birds and critters who made the park their home. They were going about just the same as if there were no war on at all. Not that he supposed it should be any other way. The dumb creatures of the planet didn't know what their overlords were doing, much less care.

He wished the same were true for himself.

"I think that the situation along the southern coast is becoming quite crucial."

Henry reluctantly brought his attention back to the fashionable woman walking sedately beside him. Her hair was pulled up into the latest style, and a hat that most likely cost more than most women's entire wardrobes was perched cheekily on the fading waves. Lady Rothman had been quite the beauty in her day, or so he was reliably informed. She'd retained her statuesque build, and she certainly believed that she was still the most important female to grace the park with her presence, but Henry had always found her rather annoying. Today was no different.

"The onslaught is impressive," he admitted. "Of course, we knew it would be. Göring commands the largest and most advanced air force in all the world. The RAF doesn't stand a chance."

"No, indeed. I heard that they've all but obliterated the defenses along the coast, along with those radar towers you made such a fuss over." Lady Rothman shot him a look under her lashes. "I suppose we have you to thank for that. Rather than do as I asked you to, you took it upon yourself to take photographs and mark the positions of the installations to send along to Berlin. In retrospect, I must congratulate you."

Henry's lips twisted sardonically, and he inclined his head in acknowledgement. Despite her light tone now, Lady Rothman had been furious when he'd ignored her instructions a few weeks ago, as he well knew. He'd heard from Molly that Mata had actually threatened to expel him from the Round Club. She'd have a job, considering that he wasn't officially *in* her silly amateur hour club, but her anger had been enough to cause the duke to step in. Since then, Henry hadn't had any problems with the woman, thank the good Lord.

"It seemed the more pressing issue at the time," he murmured now, only the barest trace of smugness in his voice. "And, as you say, it's been key to the successful start of the invasion."

"So this is the beginning?"

"Oh yes, I think we can safely say that this is the start of it. Once the Luftwaffe destroys the RAF on the ground, just as they destroyed the Norwegian, Belgian, and French air forces, the invasion across the channel will commence."

He paused in their walk to extract a cigarette case from his inner pocket. Another couple approached on the footpath, and he fell silent, taking his time selecting a cigarette from the case and offering it to Lady Rothman. When she shook her head, he snapped it closed and tucked it back into his pocket.

"Things are going very well considering the appalling weather and cloud cover that we've been experiencing," he continued once the other couple were well out of earshot. Bending his head, he lit his cigarette. "Several stations have been hit in the south, and I fully expect that the remainder of the fighter squadrons will be destroyed within the week. I'm rather surprised that they haven't had a go at London; I haven't heard any air raid sirens yet."

"Thank heaven for that!" Lady Rothman grimaced comically and shuddered. "The thought of having to take cover in that awful Anderson shelter Thomas insisted on installing in the garden is beyond bearable. It's a horrible, squalid thing, and I really don't see how it will protect us from a direct hit in any case! It's completely absurd to think it, and I told Thomas so, but he never listens to a word I say."

Henry felt a sudden kinship with Mata's husband and suppressed a smile.

"I daresay there will be no need to attack London at all," he said comfortingly. "Once the RAF is destroyed, they will send their ground troops, and that will be that. After all, they didn't drop one bomb on Paris, did they?"

"Do you really think it will be all over in a week or so?" Lady Rothman asked after a moment of thoughtful silence.

"Yes. They outnumber us five to one, you know. And their aircraft and pilots are superior in every way. They flew in Spain and gained all their experience before our little skirmish was even a thought. Where were our pilots two years ago? Still at school."

"Well, I do hope you're right. I'm very concerned about the whereabouts of the packet Molly was carrying when she was foolish enough to allow it to be stolen from her. The sooner the Germans arrive, the better all around."

"The girl can hardly be blamed for losing it," Henry said stiffly. "She was unconscious when it was taken!"

"Yes, and who allowed that but herself?" Mata made a disgusted sound in her throat. "It's really quite infuriating. The packet has been missing for five days now, and we still have no idea where it is, or even who this secretary is that took it!"

"If it *was* the mysterious secretary who took it. Personally, I find it difficult to believe that a woman could overcome Molly *and* shoot two men in the forehead before the rest of the group arrived."

"Oh? Then what do you think happened?"

"My dear Lady Rothman, I haven't the faintest idea. I don't presume to know what could have happened on that road to Weymouth. All I'm saying is that I would be very surprised to find that the woman pretending to be a secretary did all of that, especially given Sir Ronald's description of her. You heard it yourself. The woman was over forty-five years old if she was a day. Now, do you really believe that an older woman could have got the better, not only of Molly but also of two fairly dangerous men in their own right?"

"When you phrase it like that, no, I suppose not," she admitted. "But then, who took it? Who even knew that it was there? And where is it *now*?"

"All questions that we are endeavoring to answer as quickly as possible, but as you say, it *has* only been five days."

"Which is three days too many," she retorted pertly. "It must be found! Why, it implicates all of us! Should it fall into the wrong hands. . ."

Henry looked at her sharply and she glowered at him.

"Oh, you needn't look at me like that," she muttered. "You, of course, were not named at all, although Lord knows that you should have been on that cursed list. How they ever convinced me to send them a list of all our inner circle and founding members I'm still trying to understand."

"To be completely fair, there was no reason to suspect that the list would fall into the wrong hands," Henry said after a moment.

"There was no reason to suspect that Sir Oswald's secretary was anything other than what she said either, but you sniffed it out right enough." Lady Rothman looked at him curiously. "How *did* you know?"

"I contacted Berlin and asked them to confirm that they had a person in that position. I don't trust anyone, Lady Rothman."

"Not even the incompetent Molly?"

Henry didn't take the bait, and instead, paused to drop his cigarette onto the ground and put it out with his shoe.

"Are you certain that my name didn't appear anywhere in those pages?" he asked, shooting her a sharp glance.

"Quite certain. Berlin was very clear about keeping you out of the Round Club's books. As it transpired, it was a very fortuitous precaution on their part."

Henry's shoulders relaxed and he nodded as they continued walking.

"Molly is keeping an ear out in Whitehall," Mata said after another moment of silence. "If the package had been turned over to the Security Service, it would have caused an uproar, and everyone would know about it. However, she hasn't heard a thing, so it doesn't appear to have made its way to them yet."

"The best thing to do is to remain calm and continue to look for any clues as to what happened that night," Henry said reasonably. "If the Security Service does end up in possession of it, there's nothing that can be done. It's of no use getting worked up and losing sleep over it."

"That's very easy for you to say," she snapped. "You won't be the one going to prison for treason, even if it would only be for a few days at most. After all, the Germans will be here by the end of the summer."

"Sooner, more like." Henry looked at her and gave her a thin smile. "So you see, there really isn't anything to be so concerned over. The RAF will be destroyed, and the Nazi's will be here before we know it, probably before we ever find out what happened that night on the road to Weymouth."

RAF Coltishall

Miles peered into the cloudless blue sky and exhaled. He'd got up from his chair in front of the dispersal hut to stretch his legs, standing in the warm, early afternoon sunlight. If it wasn't for what the sun meant for the little island of England, Scotland, and Wales, he would have been enjoying the seasonably fine weather.

"Gorgeous day, isn't it?" Rob asked, putting out his cigarette.

"Mm."

"I s'pose that means bloody hell for 11 Group."

"And us as well, if Jerry has an ounce of sense." Miles looked over to where the rest of the squadron was scattered about, waiting. "This is the first completely clear day we've had since they started coming over here in earnest."

"SCRAMBLE!!!"

The window of the little hut behind them flew open and the dispersal sergeant's head poked out as he yelled, ringing the bell.

"You had to say it, didn't you?" Rob demanded as they turned to run to their airplanes. "You just couldn't keep it to yourself!"

"Wouldn't have made any difference, old man," Miles retorted, his long legs rapidly covering the distance to his Spit. "It's too bloody nice out!"

Rob shook his head and continued past Miles' kite to his own. Miles rounded the nose and leapt onto the wing, waving the young corporal who'd already started the engine out of the cockpit.

"Get a move on, will you?" he demanded as Jones helped him on with his parachute.

The young man jumped out and nodded with a grin.

"She's all ready for you, sir. Good hunting!"

Jones finished helping him with his gear and jumped off the wing, pulling the wheel chocks and running out of the way as Miles climbed into the cockpit. Less than thirty seconds later, he was turning into the wind and accelerating down the landing strip, his heart pounding in time with the increasing speed. When his wheels left the ground, the familiar lurch in his gut was accompanied by something that was becoming just as familiar: fear.

Reaching up to slide the canopy closed, Miles took a deep breath, his lips pressing together in annoyance. He didn't consider himself a coward, but after seeing the swarms of 100 plus bandits the day before, he was very much aware of a healthy dose of apprehension. Well, it was only natural, wasn't it? Knowing that they were going to face hundreds of fighters and bombers with just a handful of machines was enough to make any man blanch. However, knowing that it was completely natural and actually accepting it were two very different things, and Miles was not about to accept the fear that was trying to grip his gut like some kind of parasite.

"Red Leader to Cowslip. Fibus Squadron airborne."

Ashmore's calm voice jerked Miles out of his reverie, and he looked around to find that Chris and Thomas were both off his wings and the rest of the squadron was with them. Swallowing, he took another deep breath and looked at his instruments, checking that everything was normal and functioning. Now was not the time for human emotion. Now was the time for efficiency and accuracy.

Deadly accuracy.

"Cowslip to Red Leader, roger that. Steer Angels 1-2-0 to intercept bandits 100 plus."

"Roger, Cowslip."

Miles rolled his shoulders. 100 plus. Again.

"They're really ambitious with these numbers, aren't they?" Chris asked, breaking the radio silence.

"Just keep your eyes peeled for the fighter cover, Field," Ashmore replied grimly.

Miles looked at his instruments, then frowned and looked out of the windshield.

"They're coming over the North Sea," he said. "Their fighters won't have enough fuel for anything, surely!"

"How's that?" Chris asked.

"This raid must be coming from Denmark. France is too far south."

"Or Norway," Thomas offered.

"That's a good point, Blue Leader, but let's not assume anything until we see what's there," Ashmore said.

"Where are the other squadrons?" Boyd, the flight leader of Yellow section, asked suddenly. "Did I miss the transmission? My radio switch is a bit wonky."

"No, you didn't miss it. We're on our own."

Silence greeted that calm statement from their squadron leader and then Chris could be heard cursing in a low voice.

"'Course we are. What do they think we are? Invincible?"

"I thought this is what you wanted, Yank?" Miles demanded, glancing over to his wingman. "Could swear that's what you were just saying yesterday."

"All right. That's enough chatter!" Ashmore said sternly. "Unless it's important, stay off the radio!"

Miles grinned at the half-hearted admonishment. Ashmore was a stickler for radio silence, as he should be, but there was no bite in his bark this time. He suspected it was due to the relief of realizing that Miles may be right about the fighter cover. Nonetheless, Miles fell silent as they flew to intercept another massive raid. Chris had the right of it. What did Group think they could possibly do against 100 plus? There were only twelve of them! And yet, when the hordes of bombers came into view below them, Miles felt an overwhelming sense of anger at their nerve.

How dare they? How dare they come over here and have the absolute gall to think that they could take over? This wasn't their land, and it never had been!

His anger only intensified at the sight of waves upon waves of Heinkels flying over the sea. Twisting his head, he scanned the skies above them for fighter cover.

"I don't see an escort," Boyd called out. "Blue Leader?"

"Not that I can see, Yellow Leader," Miles replied after a second of searching. "Anyone see an escort?"

No one offered a response, and after searching the skies above one last time, Miles turned his attention to the bombers below.

"Red Leader to Cowslip. Enemy sighted. Attacking now." Ashmore's voice couldn't have been any more calm if he were discussing the fine weather they were having. "Take your pick, lads. Looks like there's no fighter escort."

"Yeehaw!" Chris cried as they dove towards the oncoming formation of Heinkel 111s.

Miles felt Chris' elation as they fell upon the bombers. Not having to worry about the fighter escort was a novel experience, and one that he wasn't about to take for granted. Leveling out, Miles picked out the lead bomber in the formation and flew towards it at over 300 mph. He shifted in his seat as he came up on the formation, fast and deadly, his eyes trained on the ominous black Iron Cross painted on the side. The rear gunner laid out a burst of fire, but the bullets streamed past him as Miles shifted the control stick at the last possible second, missing their tail by only a few feet. He pressed the firing button as he flew over the Heinkel, the .303 Browning guns in his wings coming alive and making his kite shudder as he sent a burst of bullets into the right engine. He was already well away when the bomber lurched and fell out of formation, heavy black smoke pouring from the damaged wing.

Miles' satisfaction was short-lived as he flew through the formation, skillfully avoiding the return fire from the nose and dorsal gunners. Narrowly missing a stream from one of the neighboring ships, he pulled up and looped around to attack from the side.

"Bullseye!" Chris cried as another bomber fell out of the formation and he broke away triumphantly.

"Watch the return fire!" Miles warned, coming around and focusing on the fuselage of another machine.

"That's nothing compared to the usual escorts!"

"You won't think that when you're diving into the drink," Ashmore barked. "Stay focused!"

"Got one!" Rob announced a moment later. "This is bloody marvelous!"

Miles allowed himself to grin at the astonishment in Rob's voice. Well, and why not? It *was* bloody marvelous! No fighter cover, and all they had to worry about was the aim of the gunners?

Perhaps today they could make a dent in the seemingly endless supply of bombers Göring had at his disposal.

"I still can't believe our luck today!" Chris exclaimed, dropping into a chair next to Miles with a full pint in his hand. "Why the hell did they send over so many bombers without escorts?"

Miles finished lighting his cigarette and yawned widely. It was past ten at night and they'd just come down from their fourth sortie half an hour before. After that first scramble, they'd only come down to refuel before going back up, and it had been like that all day and well into the evening.

"Perhaps they didn't expect to run into the Spits of 66 Squadron," Rob drawled from his chair. He'd loosened his tie and his jacket hung open, exposing a creased and sweat-stained shirt beneath.

"It's more likely the fact that they don't have fighters with the range to accompany them from Denmark and Norway," Miles murmured.

"They don't," a new voice said from behind him, and he twisted his head to find Bertie, the intelligence officer, standing there with a glass of amber liquid. "At least, not that we know of. The Messerschmidt could get here, but not back."

"Hallo, Bertie! Where did you spring from?" Miles asked.

"The CO's office. He'd like a word, Lacey."

Miles groaned and got up.

"Of course he would. I'd just settled down for a smoke and a drink."

"I'll take that," Chris said, reaching out and plucking the cigarette from Miles. "Can't let a good smoke go to waste."

Miles set his pint down on a small side table and buttoned his jacket.

"If you touch my pint, we'll have words, Yank," he said, turning away.

Bertie seated himself in his vacated chair and sipped his scotch.

"Quite a day you lads had," he said conversationally.

"You probably know more about it than we do," Rob said with a flash of white teeth. "How many in total did 12 Group get today?"

"Goodness, I don't know for certain. I was on the line with Stevens, the IO over at Wittering, y'know, and they claimed quite a few as well."

"You must have some idea, though. That's your job, isn't it?" Chris demanded, blowing smoke towards the ceiling.

"Well, yes, but the figures aren't instant, you know. We're not the only squadron that got scrambled."

"It had to have been a good day, though," Rob said thoughtfully. "Miles and I both have one confirmed and one probable. Even the Yank there got one!"

"Says the man who's sitting last in the pool," Chris responded instantly.

"Ah yes. The infamous pool for who will shoot down the most Jerries." Bertie smiled in amusement. "Is that still on, then?"

"Until the ground crew decide that it's off. They're the ones who started it."

"I've put a few quid on you," Bertie said thoughtfully. "It looks as if it might pay off nicely."

"On me?" Chris looked surprised. "Really?"

"Yes."

"Whyever would you do a thing like that?" Rob asked, peering at him over the rim of his pint glass.

"Because I have a very healthy respect for our American confederate here," Bertie said calmly. "Anyone who can land a bullseye at darts on his first outing has my full support."

Chris burst out laughing.

"I'd forgotten about that!" he chortled. "Well, being as Miles and I are still the front-runners, I think you'll make your investment back, Bertie."

"War's not over yet," Rob said. "No need to get cocky."

Bertie sobered.

"Indeed," he murmured. "As evidenced today by the loss of over twenty aircraft in the south."

"Twenty?"

"That I heard of, yes. While you were rebuffing the efforts of the northern Luftflotte, 11 Group was dealing with the largest force yet from France."

"Miles said the good weather would bring hell," Rob muttered.

"So it did."

"How many pilots?" Chris asked.

Bertie shook his head and swallowed the rest of his drink.

"I don't know," he said, standing. "And even if I did, I wouldn't tell you."

"At least tell us that what we did today made a difference," Rob said, stopping him as he turned away. After a second of silence, Bertie looked over his shoulder at the two pilots.

"Yes. You make a difference every time you go up there."

"Yes, but how much of a difference today?"

"Enough that Herr Göring will think twice before sending his bombers over the North Sea again, I can promise you that."

Chapter Five

Ainsworth Manor, Lancashire

E velyn crossed the sitting room to open the cigarette box on the table near the
window while her Auntie Agatha fiddled with the wireless in the corner.

"Really, I can't see why you don't simply stay right here," her mother was saying
from her seat on the couch. "We have plenty of room, after all, and it's not as if
you know anyone in Northumberland."

"I'd love nothing more than to stay here with you, ma chère soeur." Tante
Adele moved to sit next to her on the couch. "But Claude promised Robert that
he would help with the lodge."

"I can't imagine why he thinks the lodge needs helping," Mrs. Ainsworth said
crisply. "It's a hunting lodge, for heaven's sake, not a farm."

"Mother, really," Evelyn said in amused exasperation, turning from the box
with a cigarette in her hand. "You know that the property was damaged in the
winter by a storm. Robbie simply wants to make sure the repairs are made in a
timely manner while the weather is good enough to allow them!"

"Yes, but why must Adele and Claude go to see to it? That's why we have
stewards, no?"

"I don't expect that it will be for very long," Uncle Claude said soothingly.
"From what Robert said, I gather it's only one or two of the outlying buildings
that were affected. It shouldn't take long at all to arrange for the necessary repairs,
Madeleine."

"There. You see? They'll be back before you even realize that they're gone,"
Evelyn said gaily, crossing over to a chair near the empty fireplace. "Oh, yes
please!" she added when her uncle held up a decanter of brandy questioningly.

"You won't understand a word of what's said to you," Madeleine warned
Adele confidentially. "I never do. They have a peculiar accent, and it's really quite

impossible to comprehend."

"I wouldn't say it's impossible," Agatha said, turning away from the wireless after successfully tuning it to the BBC at last. "It's thick, to be sure. I've always found it rather pretty."

"I don't think you're helping the cause, Auntie Agatha," Evelyn said in a stage whisper, her eyes dancing as she accepted a glass of brandy from her uncle. "Merci."

"It's very easy for you to laugh at me," her mother said with a sniff. "You're involved with your war work and never come home anymore, and when you do, you're off again in ten minutes. I've enjoyed having company in the house these past few months."

"You'll still have Auntie Agatha."

"And you will have us back, Madeleine," Adele assured her with a smile. "I'm afraid we're here to stay for the time being."

"Any news of Gisele and Nicolas?" Evelyn asked, sighing when her aunt shook her head sadly.

"No. We're unable to contact them at all. The last news that we had was that they were safe at the chateau in Monblanc."

"The Germans have restricted all telephone and radio contact, and it's said that they inspect all mail as well." Uncle Claude sat down with a scowl. "We write letters, of course, but have no way of knowing if they're getting there."

"How awful," Evelyn murmured before sipping her drink.

She knew all about the restrictions in effect in France, of course. She also knew that it was impossible to get any information in or out through any means, let alone the post. She had been trying to get word about her cousins for weeks, but even with her extensive contacts, she'd been unsuccessful. Those agents still on the Continent had gone underground when France fell, and even Bill hadn't been able to get much information out of them since. What radios remained had either been destroyed or hidden. Until she was permitted to resume travel to France, she was as much in the dark as her aunt and uncle.

And Evelyn didn't like being in the dark where her cousins were concerned. She knew them too well and was sure that if she didn't get to them soon, they'd align themselves with a resistance group much more dangerous than what she could offer them.

The jazz playing on the radio ended and an advertisement for tooth powder began. Evelyn looked at the pearl and gold watch on her wrist. It was time for the news broadcast, and while she was anxious to hear what had occurred today, she was also apprehensive. There was too much going on and too many lives were at stake.

"Evelyn, how much longer do you have of your holiday?" Tante Adele asked.

"Oh, just over another week or so, although I do have to run onto the station at the weekend. I thought I'd take the car and drive down on Saturday."

"If you're on holiday, why do you have to go back to the airfield?" Auntie Agatha demanded. "Really, I don't understand the air force at all. They give you time off, presumably to rest, and then expect you to continue gallivanting all over!"

"It's not the WAAFs who expect it, Auntie," Evelyn said with a laugh. "It's my own fault, I'm afraid. I forgot some rather important forms that needed to be signed. I won't be longer than a day."

"Hush, you two," Madeleine said suddenly. "The news is coming on."

Evelyn shared an amused smile with her aunt and fell obediently silent as the sober, even tone of the broadcaster began relaying the news of the day. As expected, southern England was hit quite hard throughout the day, and Evelyn's lips tightened when she heard that several Hurricanes had been shot down. Were any of them from Northolt? Was Fred all right?

"While the RAF was busy repulsing the attacks in the south, several large formations of bombers came over the North Sea, creating a two-pronged attack. This is the first time the Luftwaffe has launched aircraft from their captured airfields in Denmark and Norway. They were met by our fighter squadrons. After hours of intense fighting, our fighters shot down fifty-six German aircraft in the north without any losses. On the day, the RAF accounted for over ninety enemy airplanes destroyed to a loss of only twenty-four of our own."

The broadcast paused for another advertisement and Evelyn restlessly put her cigarette out in the ashtray at her elbow.

"I'm going outside for some air," she said, standing abruptly.

Without another word, she strode from the room, leaving her aunts and uncle to look at Madeleine questioningly.

"What on earth's the matter with the girl?" Agatha demanded. "For pity's sake, I swear that child can't sit still for more than a few minutes at a time!"

"I imagine she's been upset by that news update," Madeleine said, her brows furrowed in concern. "It *was* rather unexpected."

"What was so unexpected about it?" Agatha frowned. "The Jerries are attacking England. This can hardly come as a surprise."

"No, but the formations coming over from the north are disconcerting. Until now, all we've been hearing about is the southern coastal regions," Madeleine replied, taking a steadying breath. "Claude, dear, would you mind pouring me a glass of that sherry?"

"Of course not."

He got up and went over to the decanters on the drinks cart.

"Why?" Adele asked, her brows raised in question. "Why would the airplanes coming from Denmark and Norway upset Evie?"

"They would have been met by Robert's squadron, I expect," Claude said, carrying a glass of sherry over to his sister-in-law.

"Yes." Madeleine nodded. "Both Robbie and Evelyn's young man are in the same squadron. They're located on the eastern coast."

The company was silent for a moment, absorbing that, and then Agatha sighed and shook her head. Getting up, she went over to the drinks cart and reached for a decanter of scotch.

"Well, that's certainly enough to worry her," Adele murmured. "And you, Madeleine? How are you?"

Madeleine sipped her sherry and smiled bravely.

"I knew what could happen when Robbie said he was going to join the air force. We all did."

"It doesn't make it any easier," Claude murmured.

"No."

"Well, as much as I feel for the girl, she'll need to toughen up," Agatha said, turning from the cart with more than two fingers of scotch in her glass. "She can't get upset every time she hears of some skirmish where his squadron may be involved. This is war, and it's what they both signed up for when they joined to do their bit. They're as much a part of it as the soldiers in the army, and by their own choice, I might add! They knew the risk involved."

"Oh Agatha, really!" Adele exclaimed in exasperation. "That's hardly helpful."

Madeleine chuckled despite herself.

"It's quite all right, Adele," she assured her. "Agatha is right. Both of my children chose to defend their country, and I couldn't be more proud of them. I know that Evelyn is well aware of the danger her brother faces every day. She works on a station with fighter squadrons. She sees firsthand what they do."

"Then why the outburst?" Agatha asked, sinking back into her seat.

"I can only assume that it had something to do with the fact that it isn't only her brother that she's worried for. It's also her beau. While I may lose my son, Evelyn may lose both of the men in her life. After losing her father last year. . ."

Madeleine shrugged and sipped her sherry as Adele reached over to pat her knee.

"Of course it's completely understandable," she said with a nod. "And as this was the first large attack over the North Sea, perhaps I can appreciate why it came as a shock."

Agatha was quiet for a moment, then she tilted her head and looked at Madeleine.

"Is this affair with the Lacey boy serious, then? As serious as all that?"

Madeleine shrugged. "It's difficult to say. I've certainly never seen Evie like this before. When he was here last Christmas, she seemed to light from within."

"I remember seeing you like that for the first time," Adele said with a smile. "It was the day after you met Robert."

"Yes, well, I was much different from Evelyn. I wanted nothing more than to marry and set up my house. But Evie. . .she's never shown the least inclination to settle down. I was quite in despair until this young man came along, but is it serious? I really have no idea." Madeleine was thoughtful for a moment. "Her father would have known. He always understood her much better than I did."

"Well, have you talked to her about it?" Agatha asked logically, drawing a laugh from Madeleine.

"Oh, it's no use trying to get involved, Agatha. You know that. She's far too independent to allow any interference in her personal life. She always has been. Heavens, I wouldn't even know how to try!"

"She is," Adele agreed with a nod. "Very headstrong, Evie is, even more so than my Gisele."

"Marc Fournier," Claude chimed in with a laugh. "That's the best example I know of. Robbie made the mistake of trying to advance that affair, and Evie made him regret it."

"Was he the one in Paris?" Agatha asked Madeleine.

"Yes. It was a shame because his family is very old and distinguished, and he's French. Of course, Miles Lacey is also from a very good family. The Yorkshire Lacey's have been around almost as long as the Ainsworths, and I believe they have property in France." Madeleine sighed. "It's no use trying to get involved, though. All we can do is wait and see how it turns out. And don't you dare say it, Agatha!"

Agatha had the grace to laugh and look rueful.

"Very well."

Adele looked from one to the other.

"What isn't she to say?" she finally asked.

"That this is all dependent on whether the boy survives the war," Claude said, finishing his drink and setting down his empty glass. "Now, if you ladies will excuse me, I think I'll join Evie in the garden. I'd like to stretch my legs."

Evelyn threw the stick with all her might and watched as Tom, Dick, and Harry, her father's hunting dogs, tore off after it in the fading evening light. She inhaled and looked up at the darkening skies. The air was warm with a brisk breeze coming across the south lawn. It was a beautiful summer evening, and she wished she could clear her head and enjoy it for what it was, but she could not.

Of course she'd always known that Robbie and Miles would be in the thick of the fighting when Göring finally came for Britain. There had never been any doubt, and she had been mentally preparing herself for this day for the past five months—ever since witnessing the hordes of bombers flying over Norway. When she watched from behind a hedgerow as Stukas dive-bombed the radar tower outside Tangmere, she knew it had begun. Goodness, was it only four days ago? Evelyn shook her head and watched as the dogs ran back towards her. Harry had claimed the prize, but a laugh was pulled from her when she spotted an enormous branch gripped between Dick's jaws.

"Really, Dick, what were you thinking?" she demanded, pulling it from his mouth as he bounded up to her. He dropped to his haunches and gazed up at her, his tongue lolling out of the side of his mouth. "This is much too large for you!"

She gripped the branch on either end and raised her knee, breaking it in half. Harry nudged her and dropped his stick at her feet, barking once in command.

"Goodness! Give us a chance, Harry! I've only got two hands!"

She threw one half of the branch and then the other before reaching for the stick at her feet. Once that had been dispatched and the dogs were tearing across the lawn again, Evelyn's laugh faded.

It *had* only been four days since that awful screeching noise that had brought back all the horror of that day on the road in France. Then, the Stukas had been attacking a road filled with refugees. Now they were attacking England, and the already tiring and beleaguered fighter squadrons of 11 Group were thrust into the fight for their island without further ado. That was the crux of the matter, she decided as Harry ran back to her with his stick. She threw it and waited for Dick and Tom to reach her with theirs. For the past few days, the focus had been on 11 Group and their losses and victories. Today, Miles and Rob had their share. While she knew it was coming, it was rather a shock to hear of it in the sitting room with her aunts, uncle, and mother as if it was somehow unconnected to them all. "Large formations," that's what the announcer had said. She knew from residing on a fighter station, no matter how little she was actually there, that "large formations" was code for 50 or 100 plus. And unfortunately, she knew the real numbers where her family did not. Raids of over one hundred enemy aircraft had flown over the North Sea to be met by a fraction of that from Fighter Command.

That had been enough to shock her out of the self-fabricated calm that she'd been carefully nurturing ever since witnessing those Stukas attack the radar tower. The feeling of panic and despair that had rolled over her in the sitting room had taken her completely by surprise, and the only thing she could think to do was to get out of the house as quickly as possible before her mother saw her upset. The last thing she wanted was for her mother to see her strong daughter crumble. She very nearly had, as she realized all at once that today alone, she could have lost the only two men she truly loved. And, Evelyn realized now with a shock, she really was in love with Miles. Somehow those sparkling green eyes had laughed their way right into her heart.

And that was a huge problem.

Not only was she a liar, pretending to be something she wasn't every day, but once she was sent back to France, the chances of her own survival were just as low as Miles and Rob's were now. And how could she love him, and allow him to fall in love with her, knowing that he had absolutely no idea who she really was?

The dogs bounded back, and Evelyn found three sticks dropped at her feet while they ran in circles around her, their tails wagging. She bent and picked them up, throwing them one at a time as the dogs shot off after them.

She was a spy. Plain and simple. She was a spy who, at this very moment, had German plans concealed upstairs in the back of her wardrobe that her father had smuggled out of Austria. German plans which no one, not even MI6, knew anything about. What on earth would Miles say to that? What would he think if he knew she'd killed German soldiers in the mountains of Norway? Or that she'd traveled alone across Belgium and France with not one but *two* strange men? She shuddered despite the warm evening. Heavens, he'd think she was. . .fast! It was bad enough that he already thought her a terrible flirt, thanks to Robbie's loose tongue. If Miles ever found out even a fraction of what she'd been up to in the past year, he'd run as fast as he could away from her, and she wouldn't blame him one bit.

How, in heaven's name, had her father managed it?

The thought calmed her a bit, and she listened to the dogs barking happily in the distance as they retrieved their sticks. If he felt that serving his country in this capacity was important enough to lie to his family, then she had to believe the same. She had to believe that the means would justify the ends, and that the difference she could make was large enough to justify lying to Miles. She knew that he suspected something, but there was no conceivable way that he could ever dream of the truth. She just had to keep it that way.

"Evie!"

Evelyn swung around in surprise as Claude called to her, waving. The dogs, on their way back with their sticks, dropped them at her feet before veering towards her uncle, barking joyfully. She smiled, watching as Claude greeted each of them, bending to properly rub all of them behind their ears before patting their sides fondly. Uncle Claude had always had a soft spot for dogs. Evelyn had long been of the opinion that if Tante Adele would allow it, he'd have the house filled with them.

"Uncle Claude!" she called as he drew closer, the dogs running excited rings around him. "What are you doing out here?"

"I thought I'd join you for the fresh air," he said, joining her. "Do you mind?"

"No, of course not!" She turned and he fell into step beside her. "I'm sorry if I left abruptly. The news was rather disconcerting. I suppose I wasn't expecting it, though I certainly should have."

"There is no need to apologize, my dear. I understand fully."

They were silent for a moment as the pack of dogs trotted beside them, giving up on their game of fetch.

"How are you finding England?" she asked, glancing up at him. "Have you settled in?"

"It's different, but you know that Adele and I have always enjoyed it here. I do miss my language, though. Would you mind if we spoke in French? Your Auntie Agatha gets sour when we don't speak in English, though I'm told she speaks French fluently."

Evelyn laughed.

"Yes, she does. She really doesn't mind, you know. She's just very English, you understand."

He looked at her in some amusement.

"And you're not?"

"Yes, of course I am, but I also embrace my French heritage." She twinkled up at him. "The French are more fun."

Claude let out a bark of laughter.

"Oh, you do remind me of Gisele! She says that England is nice enough, but not fun at all."

"I'm afraid that's very much the case at the moment," Evie said with a sad smile. "But then, I suppose Paris is not very gay these days, either."

"No." Claude was quiet for a moment, then he sighed. "I wish Zell and Nicolas had chosen to come with us, but I wasn't surprised when they insisted on staying. Neither was Adele."

"Nor I," she admitted. "I think Rob was shocked, but I know them so well."

"Yes. You were always one of them. The Three Musketeers, that's what we called you. You were all so full of mischief growing up!"

"Not just while we were growing up, Uncle. When I was there in the spring, Nicolas put a garden snake in Zell's bed!"

Claude chuckled, then grew sober.

"He told me that they were going to stay and fight for France," he said quietly after a moment. "I would never tell their mother, and I trust that you'll keep it to yourself as well."

"I wouldn't dream of worrying Tante Adele any more than she already is," Evelyn assured him. "As soon as I heard that they'd remained in France, I knew that was why. Robbie did too, which is why he was so upset."

"And yet, you were not so upset," he said, casting her a shrewd glance.

She smiled ruefully.

"I'm very much afraid that if the roles were reversed and it was England that was invaded, I would have done the same thing," she said with a nod. "And it just might come to that yet, if Herr Göring has his way."

"I was surprised when you joined the. . .what is it? I can never get the name right."

"The WAAFs?"

"Yes. What does it stand for?"

"Women's Auxiliary Air Force. Why were you surprised? Surely you didn't think that I would sit at home and knit sweaters for the soldiers?"

Claude laughed and shook his head.

"No. I would never expect that of you, my dear. You have far too much energy and passion. I like to think that you get that from your maman's side. No, I was surprised because I thought that you would be more suited to work in other areas."

Evelyn raised her eyebrows and looked at him with a faint smile.

"Other areas?" she repeated.

"Yes. With your skills with languages and knowledge of the Continent, I think you would do very well in. . .well, other areas. I don't know what you call it here in England, but in France it was known as the Deuxième Bureau. They worked with the army and gathered intelligence."

"Spies!" Evelyn let out a light laugh and shook her head. "Good Lord no! I'm not nearly as brave as all that. Besides, England is not like France. I don't think women are allowed anywhere near classified areas here." She allowed a trace of bitter sarcasm into her voice. "We're too dumb, you see, to keep our mouths shut."

Claude shot her a shrewd look.

"Ah. Well, then your government is missing a very large opportunity. I'm told that the women in France were able to succeed where some men failed. Of course, it was all for nothing in the end."

Evelyn thought of Josephine.

"Perhaps not," she murmured. "That will is still present in France. We must believe that people like Zell and Nicolas will organize and make life difficult for the Germans."

"I just hope they aren't foolish and end up prisoners. . .or worse."

Evelyn reached out and tucked her arm through his, hugging it gently.

"We must have faith," she said. "Just as I have to believe that Robbie and. . .well, we must believe that whatever happens, it will be for something much larger than ourselves."

Claude put his hand over hers on his arm and squeezed.

"Your mother tells us that your young man is in Robert's squadron," he said. "Tell me about him."

"Miles?" Evelyn thought of sparkling green eyes and a faded scar at his temple. "Well, he's a pilot, like Robbie. They're a different breed, fighter pilots. Very reckless and unpredictable."

"And his family?"

"In Yorkshire. Their primary income is in sheep as well, so he's actually been quite a help to Robbie since Daddy passed away. Robbie didn't know where to begin, you know. He says Miles helped him immensely."

"I'm sure that's so, but I'm not asking about him and Rob," he said, amused. "Do you love him?"

Evelyn looked up, shocked at his bluntness, but he simply gazed down at her curiously, waiting for her to answer.

"I. . ." she began, then stopped as her throat tightened. She stopped walking and withdrew her arm from his, biting her lip. "It really is the most rotten time for us to have met," she finally said. "To think of anything like that at the moment is madness."

" 'There is always some madness in love. But there is also always some reason in madness,' " Claude quoted softly.

Her lips twisted. "Nietzche."

"Very good."

"He was quite mad, you know, at the end of his life," she pointed out.

"Maybe so, but it doesn't negate what he wrote when he was still sane. Evie, my dear, I do believe you're trying to avoid the question. It's simple enough. Either you're in love, or you're not."

"Uncle Claude, I do love you, as you well know, but I can hardly answer you when I scarcely know how I feel myself." Evelyn smiled and turned to begin walking back towards the house in the far distance. "I enjoy Miles' company. He makes me laugh, and I find him very intelligent. He doesn't bore me, which is something I've never come across before, so it may very well be that I've simply found myself a kindred spirit. But I assure you, if and when something of importance occurs between us, you will be one of the very first to know!"

Claude chuckled.

"Very well. You're very like your cousins, you know. Gisele won't suffer any interference in her personal affairs either."

"Were you going to interfere, then?"

"Absolutely not. I'm only curious. I haven't seen you and Robert in so long that I feel as if we have no place in your lives anymore. Adele and I both miss you."

Evelyn felt a flash of remorse, and she tucked her hand into his arm again.

"And we miss you. I know I can speak for Robbie when I say that we both miss the time before. . .well, before this blasted war took over everything."

"If Hitler hadn't invaded Poland, and if the war had never begun, what would you have done with yourself, Evelyn?" he asked after a few moments of silence.

Evelyn thought for a moment, then shrugged.

"I suppose I would have become a journalist or some such thing," she decided. "Papa always said that I should. He thought it would make tremendous use of my language abilities. I think he envisioned me traveling the world and reporting on what I found."

"That would have been exciting, and something that I very much see you doing. You have the same streak of recklessness in you that your cousins have, and that your brother and beau have. Tell me, what does young Lacey say about your proficiency in that martial art that you picked up in Hong Kong?"

Evelyn looked at him sharply.

"He knows nothing about that, and I wasn't aware that you did!"

Claude laughed.

"Your father told me when you returned from China. He was very proud."

Evelyn stared at him in amazement.

"Really? I always had the impression that he was rather appalled!"

"Far from it. He was very proud of all your unusual skills. He thought you'd make a wonderful success of your life, once you decided just what you wanted to do with it." Claude glanced down at her. "It's really a shame that you're wasting your skills in this women's air force. I'd have thought that you'd be bored to tears, yet you seem more alive than I've ever seen you."

Evelyn swallowed and forced a light-hearted laugh.

"I know it seems dreadfully mysterious, and therefore it must be exciting, but it really is dull work. If I appear more alive, then it must be due to all the traveling they have me doing. It's very hard to be bored when you never know where you're off to next."

Her uncle nodded complacently and fell silent. Evelyn exhaled silently and bit the inside of her lower lip. She had no idea if Uncle Claude had been taken into her father's confidence and was aware of his clandestine activities when he was alive, but it was beginning to look suspiciously as if he had. And if that were the case, then Uncle Claude would naturally expect that she would have followed the same path. She could only hope that their conversation this evening was enough to convince him otherwise. It was bad enough that Miles was suspicious. She didn't need her uncle smelling a rat as well.

Oh, when did everything get so complicated?!

Chapter Six

E velyn shaded her eyes against the bright sun and watched as Tante Adele and Uncle Claude set off in the direction of the stables. They'd just finished enjoying a cup of tea on the back terrace and Auntie Agatha had gone back inside to arrange the roses she'd cut earlier in the morning when Claude announced their intention of taking two of the horses out for some exercise.

"I suppose Uncle Claude is going to sneak the horses some carrots," Evelyn said with a laugh, lowering her hand and looking across the table at her mother. "I'm surprised Barnes hasn't banned him from the stables yet! You know how fussy he is about the horses."

"Barnes is keeping a close eye on them," Madeleine replied, looking up from the newspaper. "I suspect that he's adjusted their feed accordingly."

"Poor Starlight. She really does love her mealtime." Evelyn stretched and took a deep, contented breath. "What a lovely day!"

"Yes, it is, isn't it?" Madeleine set her newspaper aside. "It's much too nice to depress myself with that nonsense. What are your plans today?"

"I thought I'd go into the village to post a few letters. Is there anything you need?"

"I can't think of anything."

"All right." Evelyn was silent for a moment, loathe to get up. A nice breeze was blowing gently against her face, and she was enjoying the sun on her skin. "Mother," she said suddenly after a quiet moment. "Do you remember the Thompsons? Daddy met him in Naples one year?"

Madeleine thought for a moment, her brows creased.

"Yes, I think so. Tall man? His wife was from. . .oh, where was it? Somewhere in America. It was a silly name."

"Is she American?" Evelyn raised her brows in surprise. "I don't think I ever knew that, but then I've never met her."

"Yes. Oh, what was the name of the place?" Madeleine frowned. "It really was the silliest name. How frustrating that I can't remember!"

"Well, didn't they have two sons?"

"Yes, I think so," Madeleine said absently, then clapped her hands together. "Topeka! That was it. She was from somewhere called Topeka."

"Topeka?" Evelyn repeated, a laugh on her lips. "Are you sure you've got that right?"

"Yes. I remember it because it sounds as if someone's peeking at someone else. Silly name. Do you suppose that's where it came from?"

"From someone peeking at something? Really, Mother, I don't think so. It's probably from some American Indian or some such thing. Chris Field, the American who flies with Robbie, says that a lot of places in America are named after native American Indians."

"Really? How interesting. I didn't know Robert flew with an American."

"Yes. He went into Canada to join the RAF so that he could come over here and fly."

"What a nice young man!"

"Yes." Evelyn cleared her throat and tried to get the conversation back on track. "The Thompsons, Mother. Didn't one of them become an engineer of some sort?"

She nodded. "Yes, I believe one did. They came to your father's funeral, you know. They told me all about themselves. Harold, I believe it was. He graduated from university with some sort of engineering degree. Or was it his brother? One of them went to work in airplane production when the war began, and the other received his degree and was snatched up by the war department. Why, dear?"

"Oh, Maryanne and I were trying to remember. I can't recall what brought the subject up, but she was convinced that one of them was a pilot. I didn't think so."

"How does Maryanne Gilhurst know the Thompsons?" Madeleine asked in surprise. "They're hardly a family she would have dealings with. The only reason we know them is because of your father. He knew so many different people, from so many different walks of life."

"It was her brother, I believe," Evelyn lied blithely. "Anthony meets all kinds of people with his work in the Lords."

"Ah." Madeleine nodded, satisfied with that explanation. "How is Lord Anthony? Didn't you say that Maryanne was worried about him?"

"Yes. I believe he's better now. She thinks he was suffering from the pressure of the war, you know. He's become quite active in the House of Lords, and he and his father are under an enormous amount of strain."

Madeleine shook her head. "I can't begin to imagine what it's like trying to govern the country while also attempting to navigate both a new prime minister and this war."

"Well, to be fair, Churchill has been in for a few months now. But yes, I believe there was somewhat of a rocky start."

"I wonder what your father would have thought of him."

"The prime minister? I think he would have been thrilled. He always did like Churchill, despite his rather colorful history."

Madeleine sighed. "I do so miss him."

"So do I, Maman."

She nodded and smiled tremulously at her before gathering up her newspaper and letters.

"I'm going to write a few letters. I thought I'd write to Marguerite Buckley and invite her to stay for a few days before Adele and Claude disappear into the wilds of Northumberland."

"Oh, I think that's a wonderful idea! Mrs. Buckley would enjoy spending time with fellow Frenchmen."

"Yes." Madeleine turned to go into the house. "Don't sit out here too much longer. You'll go red from the sun."

Evelyn watched her mother go through the doors into the house and turned her gaze back to the lovely prospect of the rolling lawns before her. She sat quietly for a moment, her lips pressed together thoughtfully. So the Thompsons' son *had* finished up his degree at university. Now the only question was which one, Harold or the other boy? Her lips curved suddenly in amusement. At least her mother had remembered one of their names. Evelyn hadn't remembered either, and she very nearly hadn't remembered the Thompsons at all. She probably wouldn't have if it weren't for the article in the newspaper this morning that highlighted young men who were working for the war effort in the factories and research laboratories. It was a chance mention of the air production facilities that had jogged her memory. Lucky break, that. All she had to do now was contact this Harold or his brother, whichever was the engineer, and have him look at the drawings that were stashed at the back of her wardrobe. Even if his particular field was something far removed from machinery, he would at least be able to confirm if her own conclusions were correct.

Evelyn gazed out over the lawns, not seeing the expertly manicured hedges or the carefully maintained footpaths that led to a beautiful marble fountain spouting water. It was quite simple, really. All she had to do was find the man and take him a copy of the drawings to look at. So why was everything inside her giving her pause? Instead of feeling elated at having hit upon a solution to her problem, she was feeling as though this was the absolute worst thing she could be contemplating.

She exhaled and got up restlessly, walking over to the low wall that surrounded the terrace. She needed an expert, and it turns out that her father's connections had provided her with one. Why, then, was she hesitating? Evelyn rested her hands on the cool stone of the wall and stared at the fountain in the distance. Was it because she would be showing a stranger one of the documents her father had beseeched her in his last letter to keep secret from everyone? Was it because she would be going behind the collective backs of MI6, and Bill in particular? Or was it something much more basic than that? Was it simply that she had absolutely no idea how to explain the existence of the drawings?

Her lips tightened and she felt her shoulders relax. That was it. That was the crux of all her tension. How in blazes was she going to explain how she came by the drawings? After all, no self-respecting Englishman would agree to help in something that smacked of treason, and that was exactly what this would look like to a civilian. Why else would she have drawings of something that was quite clearly a weapon, and that had German labels and handwritten notes along the edges? Why, he'd turn her in as a spy!

The thought tickled Evelyn's sense of humor and her lips curved in amusement as a small chuckle escaped. Of course, he wouldn't be wrong. He simply would have the wrong end of the stick. It would be an utter disaster, though, and something that she couldn't risk happening at all. So then, she was back to square one. She had someone she could ask, but no way to approach them without them being convinced that she was working for the other side.

"Bugger," she muttered irritably under her breath before hastily looking around to make sure no one was within earshot.

There was no help for it. She was going to have to take William Buckley into her confidence. She really couldn't see any other way. It was all well and good for Daddy to write a letter telling her that MI6 wasn't to know of the package's contents, and that she would know what to do; he obviously thought that she was much more resourceful than she was turning out to be in this instance, and he definitely never would have dreamed that Britain would be standing alone against the might of Germany and Italy. She didn't have the luxury of hopping over to Switzerland and conferring with the night manager at the Bellevue Palace Hotel, who would undoubtedly have been able to direct her to someone. For the time being, she was stuck in England, helplessly watching as the RAF desperately tried to keep the Luftwaffe off of their landing strips, while trying to find an answer to the riddle her father had left behind for her in Zürich.

For it was a riddle. There was no doubt about that. Yes, all the pieces in the box were intelligence smuggled out of Germany, and in that respect, there was no mystery at all. But the letter that her father had included in the box was a puzzle all on its own.

Upon her first reading in the banker's office in Zürich, Evelyn had taken it at face value. She had been so shocked at the numbered accounts that came along with the safe–deposit box that she hadn't thought to examine the letter more closely. It wasn't until she was back in England, and unable to sleep one night, that she'd taken the letter out and read it again. Rested and no longer fleeing ahead of the Nazi war machine, she had been able to study it with a clear head.

And there was nothing clear about it at all.

The letter had been in her father's hand, of that there was no doubt. And his closing phrase of endearment was certainly one he'd used for her letters for as long as she could remember. But the rest of the letter confused her upon that reading, and every subsequent reading after that.

There could be no doubt that her father didn't want MI6 to know about the contents of the package. Nor could there be any doubt that he was warning her to trust no one, and to keep the package safe. However, the phrases he used and the way he worded the entire letter was. . .well, it just wasn't Daddy. It was as if someone else had written the letter, but that was impossible. She knew her father's handwriting. The letter had most definitely been penned by him.

Evelyn sighed and turned away from the low wall. In the end she'd realized that, while the letter had been giving her instructions, it was also laying out a code for her. A riddle that only she would be able to see and break. Her father had known her fondness for riddles and puzzles, but this last one was taking it a bit too far in her estimation. Why the secrecy? Why the codes? Surely, he knew that the only person who could access the box was she herself? So why encode the last letter he ever wrote to her?

It was all extremely frustrating, and if she were completely honest with herself, she was more than a little annoyed with her dearly departed father. Not only had he dumped this entire thing squarely in her lap, but then he had the temerity to make it all a giant mystery!

Evelyn picked up her small collection of letters from the morning post and turned to go into the house. The letter would wait, just like the rest of the package. Right now, she needed to know if the drawings truly posed the threat that she believed they did. And the only way to do that was to enlist Bill's help.

She was going to have to break at least one of the requirements her father had left behind. She just prayed that she was doing the right thing.

Moscow, USSR

Vladimir Lyakhov stiffened when a shadow moved in the darkness across the street. It was after ten and he was walking back to his flat from the square. His purposeful stride never missed a beat, but his fingers closed over the butt of the service pistol in his coat pocket. Though the likelihood of being accosted in his uniform was slim, the risks were never zero. There were many Soviets who held very strong opinions on the NKVD; Soviets who had been directly affected by their ruthlessness. While any attempt on the life of an NKVD officer resulted instantly in death, or worse, it was still known to happen on occasion.

The shadow separated from the cover of the buildings and Vladimir's shoulders relaxed as it took on the familiar outline of a man whom he knew well. He was dressed unremarkably in dark pants and a serviceable jacket that hung open to reveal a workman's shirt. He paused for a moment before crossing the road to join Vladimir on the pavement.

"Maschov." Vladimir greeted him with a nod. "I didn't know you were in Moscow."

"I arrived this morning," Maschov replied, falling into step beside him. "Comrade Bogdan sends his regards and thanks you for the bottle of Shustov that you sent to him."

"How did you find him?"

"Well. He encountered no problems getting to the rendezvous. As you predicted, the border agents never looked twice at him."

"And why should they? He's an established officer in the Abwehr." Vladimir glanced at the man beside him. "And yourself? How did you fare at the border crossings?"

"The credentials you provided got me out of our country without any question. On my way back in, I used papers that Bogdan gave me."

Vladimir grunted in approval.

"Good. Now give me your report."

"Here?" Maschov looked startled, glancing around. "In the street?"

"There is no one about to hear, and it is infinitely more secure than any establishment."

"Very well." Maschov cleared his throat and lowered his voice, nonetheless. "Comrade Bogdan is of the opinion that the Nazis are up to something big."

"Bigger than invading Great Britain?"

"Yes. He considers that invasion to be successfully completed, even though it has just begun. He says that the Luftwaffe has all but destroyed the RAF's fighters on the ground and that the landing crews will move in soon."

"That is not the intelligence that I have received."

"That is what he is being told in Hamburg."

"Interesting. And this new thing that they're up to?"

"Bogdan isn't sure, but he says that there have been several closed meetings with the High Command over the past month, and Canaris is gathering huge amounts of intelligence into reports for them."

"On what?"

"Weather patterns and historical topographical data."

Vladimir was silent for a moment, then he looked at Maschov sharply.

"In what region?"

"He didn't know. It sounds as if they're planning another attack somewhere, but it could be anywhere. Hitler has said that he will stop with England, but no one believes him, especially now that Italy has joined us in opposing Britain."

"Hm. I wonder. . ." Vladimir was silent for a moment, then he shook his head. "What else?"

"He had more information on Eisenjager. The assassin has been in France for the past week."

"And Voss?"

"The only information on Obersturmbannführer Voss is that he remains in

Paris. He has been assigned the task of rounding up any former Deuxième Bureau members, as well as any citizens who may know of, or be a part of, any kind of resistance." Maschov cleared his throat again. "He did say that Voss has contact with a man in Berlin who, he believes, is a handler for overseas agents."

Vladimir nodded, unsurprised.

"And why is Eisenjager in France?"

"No one knows, but that's hardly surprising. Bogdan's theory is that he was sent to eliminate any threats in the unoccupied zone."

The pair came to a corner and Vladimir stopped, looking at Maschov.

"Is that everything?"

"Everything pressing. I have some technical data and drawings that Bogdan sent to me. I will compile them into a formal report and have it on your desk by morning."

Vladimir nodded and held out his hand.

"Good. Stay in the city for a few days. I will have another job for you once I've examined the documents."

Maschov nodded and shook his hand, then crossed the road to disappear back into the shadows while Vladimir turned to continue down the side street. His stride never changed, nor did the set of his shoulders, but he was deep in thought as he completed the final leg to his flat.

So the Germans were planning another big push? Where? And why wasn't the NKVD aware of the plan? He pressed his lips together unpleasantly. His work in Stalingrad and Leningrad over the past few weeks had strengthened both his and Comrade Grigori's belief that the Nazis could not be trusted, but their warning just yesterday had fallen on deaf ears. No one wanted to hear their suspicions, and rather than risk the reprisals that Stalin was so quick to mete out, Vladimir and Grigori had agreed to keep their thoughts to themselves in future. Neither of them wanted to risk triggering yet another purge. Their experienced agents were already reduced to half of what they used to be, making their job more and more difficult.

Vladimir turned his thoughts from a problem he couldn't solve to one that he could. Voss was in contact with a handler in Berlin who ran overseas agents. Vladimir had known this for months, and he also knew *who* Voss was most interested in locating: Lotus. She had returned to England safely just steps ahead of the German armies in France. He had warned her over a week ago that the Round Club, a group of Nazi sympathizers in London, were looking for a female spy who had been active on the Continent. While he had no real fear of her being apprehended in her own country now, if Göring was successful in paving the way for the Nazis to walk into England, the situation would be very different. Voss would undoubtedly go himself, as would Eisenjager. If England fell, so, too, would Lotus.

And all his carefully laid plans would be destroyed in an instant.

Vladimir frowned. His own intelligence had reported that, far from being destroyed on the ground, the RAF had just yesterday accounted for a loss of seventy-five German aircraft. While Göring certainly had the machines to lose, Vladimir doubted that he would happily sustain losses of that magnitude each day and count it a victory. No. Comrade Bogdan must be listening to Goebbels' propaganda. Vladimir trusted his own man in London over the report of a comrade in Hamburg. He was on the ground, watching the battle in person. As long as the RAF could hold on, Hitler wouldn't risk invading Britain. Not yet, at any rate. And if the Nazis stayed out of England, then Lotus was safe.

For now.

Vladimir stopped at a building and walked up the few shallow steps to the door, extracting his keys from his coat pocket. She was safe, but it wouldn't hurt to send her another warning. Knowing the SD as he did, they were undoubtedly ramping up their search ahead of the invasion they were so hopeful would occur. It would be a great accomplishment to be able to present Voss with his prize as the Nazis marched into England. It would be a fantastic coup, and added insult to MI6, to nab one of their agents in their own backyard. It would broadcast their cunning and superiority, and that was something Vladimir knew the Nazis valued above all else.

It was time to send another message to Lotus, and if at all possible, have his man in London gain information on what she'd been doing with herself for the past few weeks. As Vladimir went into his house and closed the door, he exhaled silently. He hoped to God that MI6 had been subjecting her to rigorous training while she was temporarily in from the cold.

For if they hadn't, his Lotus would never survive the months and years ahead.

Chapter Seven

Ainsworth Manor

E velyn walked down the stairs, her evening dress brushing her ankles as she went. The telephone on the stand in the hall below her rang shrilly and she watched as Thomas made his stately way across the marble floor to answer. She glanced at her watch and raised an eyebrow in surprise. Who was ringing at dinnertime? A shock of alarm went through her with the thought and her stomach clenched involuntarily. God, had something happened to Robbie? Or. . .

She stopped the thought before it could even form and took a deep, calming breath as she descended the last few steps.

"Miss Ainsworth," Thomas said, turning towards her. "A telephone call for you."

He set the receiver down on the stand beside the telephone and turned to go back into the dining room where he was arranging the table. Evelyn smiled and murmured her thanks as she passed him, going over to pick up the heavy, cream and gold edged handset.

"Hello?"

"Evelyn? Evelyn, it's Bill."

"Oh, hello!"

"I'm sorry to disturb you at this time of the evening," he said, his voice even. "You must be sitting down to dinner."

"Oh, that's all right. We haven't gone in yet," she said cheerfully. "All you're keeping me from is a cocktail."

"I've just returned to the office and Fitch relayed your message. You want to see me?"

"Yes." She lowered her voice. "I know you said you didn't want me in London, but I'd like to talk to you about something that really can't wait. I was planning on coming to town Saturday night. Would you be available then, or Sunday?"

"Yes, of course, but I don't want you coming to Broadway. I'll meet you in Brook Street, if you like."

"That would be perfect. Shall I ring you when I arrive?"

"No, God willing, I won't be here. Marguerite and I have a dinner party Saturday night. Why don't we say Sunday? About two?"

"Perfect. Thank you! I'm sorry to intrude on your weekend."

"Is everything all right?"

"Oh yes! Nothing to be worried about. It's just something I've come across that I want to discuss with you."

"You haven't uncovered another group of traitors in our midst, have you?" His voice was wary, drawing a laugh from her.

"No. Nothing like that."

"Good. Then I'll see you on Sunday."

Evelyn hung up the telephone and turned away, the laugh on her lips fading. She would almost rather that it was something to do with the Round Club! She wasn't happy at all with taking Bill into her confidence over the plans, but it really couldn't be helped. She just had to believe that her gut was correct and that he could be trusted, even if her father may not have thought so.

"There you are!" Agatha exclaimed as Evelyn stepped into the parlor. "I was about to come and fetch you! Where have you been, child?"

"I'm sorry I'm late down," Evelyn apologized with a smile. "I'm afraid I had a little nap and slept longer than I intended."

"It's no surprise," her mother said. "You're never in one place long enough to have a rest!"

"At least she isn't half dead as she was in the spring," Agatha pointed out.

"Half dead?" Adele looked up from her cocktail. "Surely you're exaggerating!"

"Well, she might as well have been. She came home for a week looking absolutely terrible. She was all skin and bones, the poor thing!"

"I had a bout of the flu," Evelyn explained to her aunt, accepting a glass from her uncle with a smile of thanks. "I was quite poorly, but nothing a few days of rest didn't cure."

"You should never have been permitted to become that ill to begin with," Agatha said briskly. "If the WAAFs can't take better care of their girls than that, then I don't see how they expect to win the war at all!"

"Auntie, it's hardly their fault I came down with the flu!" Evelyn protested with a laugh. "It could happen to anybody!"

"Yes, dear, but it happened to you," Madeleine said gently. "I can't help but feel that if you didn't travel quite so often, you wouldn't be so exhausted when we do see you."

"Yes, well, about that. . ." Evelyn took a fortifying sip of her drink and cleared her throat. "I'm afraid I must go to London for two days. I've been called in for a training course. I just received a telephone call from Northolt."

"But you're on leave!" Her mother protested. "How can they call you back for training?"

"Very easily. They relay the information to my sergeant, and she hunts me down," Evelyn said with a shrug.

"What if you were unavailable?"

"Mother, I'm in the Women's Auxiliary Air Force. I won't be unavailable until my commission expires."

"Well, I think it's outside of enough for them to expect you to work on your holiday."

"That may be so, but I don't suppose they can control when the training courses come open, and if it is one that I must complete in order to do my job. . ." Evelyn's voice trailed off and she shrugged, sipping her drink. "It's only for two days, after all, and it's in London. It could be worse."

"I worry about you going into London so often," Madeleine fretted. "It's so dangerous, especially with all of these bombers coming over now. What if they bomb London while you're there?"

"Then I expect I'll take cover in one of the air raid shelters. Mother, you really must stop worrying about me. I'll be just fine."

"I must say, London is probably a sight safer than that airfield she works on," Claude said thoughtfully. "The bombers are starting to target them, just as they did in France."

Evelyn stifled a groan and sent her uncle an exasperated look.

"You're not helping, Uncle Claude," she murmured, eliciting a rueful chuckle from him.

"No, I suppose not. My apologies, ma chère."

"Well, I don't know why you can't stay in one place for more than a minute," Agatha said, shaking her head. "When I was your age, we were never so restless and flighty. Why, we wouldn't dream of gallivanting off to London alone at the drop of a hat!"

"Yes, but when you were my age, things were different," Evelyn replied, swallowing the rest of her drink as Thomas opened the door to announce dinner. "Although, to be fair, if there wasn't a war on, I expect that I'd be off to some house party near the seaside with a group of friends. At least this way I'm spending my time much more productively!"

"I think I'd rather you were off to a house party," Madeleine announced, standing. "At least then I'd have the hope of you finding yourself a nice husband!"

Evelyn grimaced and tucked her arm through her mother's. "Perish the thought!"

"Even if it was that nice Miles Lacey?" Adele asked with a wink and a smile.

To her annoyance, Evelyn felt her cheeks grow pink.

"If there was no war, I would probably have never met Miles Lacey," she said tartly. "So yes, perish the thought!"

RAF Coltishall

Miles looked up when a shadow fell over the evening paper he was reading in his favorite armchair in the officer's recreation room. He and Rob had been ensconced in comfortable silence for the better part of an hour, he with his paper and Rob with a book. Now it appeared that their peace was at an end. Chris stood there, his jacket hanging open and his tie loosened, holding a pint of beer in one hand and a cigarette in the other.

"Anything good?" he asked, nodding to the newspaper.

"Not especially." Miles folded the paper and tossed it onto the side table beside his chair. "I thought you were off to write letters."

"I thought I was too, but then I saw Tomcat going up and I changed my mind." Chris dropped into a chair and crossed his legs carelessly. "It's not that I mind bunking with him, but he could talk the hind leg off a mule—and does!"

"Comparing yourself to farm animals again, Yank?" Rob demanded, peering over the edge of his book.

"I guess I walked into that one."

"You did, indeed." Miles pulled a cigarette case from the breast pocket of his jacket and felt for his lighter. "You really should know better at this stage of our acquaintance."

"I'm too tired to know anything right now," Chris retorted, following the statement with a jaw-cracking yawn. "How are you reading, Rob? If I opened a book, it would send me right to sleep."

"I couldn't tell you what I've been reading," Rob admitted, closing the book and dropping it onto the floor. "I believe I've been reading the same page over again for the past ten minutes. Anything in the rag, Miles?"

"Nothing worth discussing."

"Where's old Bertie? He seems to know more than the newspapers these days anyway."

"He was on his way towards the COs office when I came in here," Chris offered. "He didn't look too happy."

"Well, that doesn't bode well, does it?" Rob yawned and pushed himself out of his chair. "I'm for one more pint before I knock off to bed. Anyone else?"

"I'll take one, there's a good chap," Miles said with a nod.

Rob nodded and moved away to the bar on the other side of the large room.

"Does the paper say anything about the day's raids?" Chris asked after a moment.

"Only that there were a lot of them." Miles blew smoke towards the ceiling and reached up to loosen his own tie. "According to them, we're keeping pace, at least."

Chris tilted his head and studied Miles thoughtfully.

"Do you think that's true?"

"Lord knows! It doesn't feel like it when we're up there."

"And we're not getting half the action they're getting down south," Chris said glumly. "It must be pretty bad. I heard Bertie say that Biggin Hill lost four planes today. Complete write-offs."

"That's not the worst of it. Ashmore said that Tangmere was bombed. They lost four Hurries on the ground. They weren't even up yet!"

Chris looked startled.

"You don't say! They weren't even up yet?"

"No. The bastards jumped on them before they could get off the ground."

"They're lucky it was only four, then."

"Bertie thinks they were refueling. The landing strip is a shambles, and the rest of the squadrons had to try to get in at Biggin Hill and Kenley."

"Any casualties?"

"Bertie didn't know. Stands to reason there must have been, though."

"Must have been what?" Rob asked, returning with a pint in either hand. He handed one to Miles.

"Casualties. Tangmere was bombed today. They lost four Hurricanes; the poor bastards didn't even get off the ground!" Chris told him before raising his glass to his lips.

"That never was in the evening newspaper!" Rob exclaimed, looking at Miles.

"No. The omniscient Bertie told me."

"That man is a mine of information. I don't know why we read the papers at all!" Rob said, seating himself once more. "How bad was it?"

"He says the squadrons couldn't land. They had to try to get in at Biggin Hill and Kenley for tonight."

"Good Lord." Rob drank some beer. "That's not good a'tall."

"How long can the guys hold out down there?" Chris asked after a moment, looking from one to the other. "If they can't even land to refuel, what will they do?"

"Make use of the satellite airfields, I imagine," Miles said thoughtfully. "We have them. They were training outposts, flying clubs, and the like. I don't imagine Jerry even knows about them."

"Well, that's something, at least."

"You wouldn't say that if you had to go and land at one," Rob muttered. "Old huts, no showers. Ghastly places."

"Beats the alternative," Chris pointed out.

"It would be better if we could keep them away from the airfields altogether!" Miles said, stubbing his cigarette out in the ashtray at his elbow.

"Why don't they send us down there?" Chris asked after a moment. "We can help."

"Because of what happened yesterday. Jerry wasn't expecting to see so many fighter squadrons in the north. That's why they sent that raid without fighter escort."

"They thought they were going to fly right in unopposed," Rob agreed. "Bertie thinks they thought all the fighter squadrons were in the south. He says we're the RAF's element of surprise."

"Not much of a surprise anymore," Miles said. "They know we're here now. I wonder if we can expect to be bombed as well."

"I say, do you think Northolt got it as well?" Rob asked suddenly. "Not that m'sister is there at the moment, but she will be."

"Bertie didn't say anything about Northolt," Chris said, shooting a glance at Miles' grim face. "I think they're still okay."

"Can't expect that to last, can we? Not if Jerry is going after all the others." Rob exhaled and rubbed his face. "At least Evie's out of it for a few more days."

"When does she report back?" Chris asked.

"She was very vague on that point, actually," Rob said thoughtfully before drinking some of his beer. "Miles? Has she told you?"

"No. She only said she had a few more days, and she was spending them in Lancashire."

"That's what she told me when I spoke to her the other day. I'll tell you what, I'm glad she's at the pile and not at work at the moment. I just wish we could keep her there!"

"I'm sure they have air raid shelters at Northolt, just as we do," Chris said in amusement. "She's a big girl, you know. She'll be fine. It's us that we should be worrying about. We're the ones going up there and fighting the bastards off!"

"Yes, but that's our job, Yank," Miles said dryly.

"And it's her job to do. . .whatever it is that she does," Chris retorted. "Anyway, from what I hear, she's hardly ever there anyway!"

"That's true!" Rob brightened. "They're always sending her off on some training stint somewhere, and more often than not, it's in some remote, out-of-the-way hole."

Chris finished his beer with a final gulp and stood up.

"There you go, then. No need to worry about Evie, and I'm glad. I liked her."

"She liked you, too," Miles said with a faint smile.

"Just shows that she has good taste." Chris touched his fingers to his forehead in a half salute, half wave. "I'm beat. I'll see you in the morning."

"Bright and early," Rob murmured, ruining it with a yawn. "Lord, I'm tired!"

"We'd best get used to it. I don't imagine we're half as tired as the poor bastards at Tangmere," Miles said grimly. "I can't think how exhausted they must be."

"I can't even begin to imagine trying to refuel and take off in the middle of a bombing raid. How the devil did they do it?"

"I've no idea, but they obviously did." Miles rubbed his face tiredly. "What's more, is that we could well face the same thing if we go south."

Rob raised an eyebrow. "Are we? Going south?"

"Eventually. They're talking about rotating the squadrons so the hardest hit can rest and recover."

Rob exhaled and his lips twisted humorously.

"Chris will finally get his wish to abandon the Big Wing, then," he said with a quick grin. "He'll be pleased."

"Until he gets shot at trying to take off."

RAF Northolt
August 17

Evelyn waited for a refueling truck to rumble past on the road before running across ahead of a couple of trucks filled with weary ground crew. Reaching the pavement on the other side, she turned to watch as the trucks passed on their way to the hangars. The men inside looked exhausted, but the snippets of conversation she heard coming from the backs of the trucks sounded positive enough. Someone whistled as they passed and Evelyn turned to continue to the building where her office was located, suppressing a grin firmly. At least the poor blokes tasked with repairing the aircraft seemed to be in good spirits. That was something at least.

Although she would never admit it to a living soul, Evelyn was rather shocked by the atmosphere of the station. It had changed dramatically from just last week when she'd popped in to pick up a few things. Then, there had been an air of expectation hanging over the place. Now, there was chaos. Controlled chaos, admittedly, but chaos just the same. The sounds of metal clanging from the hangars echoed constantly over the main road passing through the station, testament to the continuous flow of airplanes being repaired. Overhead, two squadrons of Hurricanes had been active when she arrived, one coming back and the other taking off. WAAFs and RAFs hurried about with an unfamiliar urgency in their step, and the sound of cheerful conversation that she was used to was conspicuously missing. RAF Northolt was fighting for its life, and it showed in every face and in every sound that reached her ears.

Evelyn went up the steps of the building and through the doors, nodding to the aircraftwoman on duty at the desk.

"Welcome back, ma'am," she said respectfully. "It's good to see you again. Sergeant Cunningham said you'd be stopping by. I'll just ring her now. She's over in the radio building."

"Thank you, ACW."

Evelyn continued down a corridor, her serviceable shoes clicking evenly on the tiled floor. She wondered if Miles' station was in this same state of hurried chaos, or if they were continuing on with business as usual. Surely the squadrons in the north were helping to repel the Luftwaffe as much as the ones down here. They must be!

Reaching her office, Evelyn went in quickly, removing her hat and hanging it on the coatrack in the corner behind the door. She crossed the office to the window, looking outside. From her vantage point, she had an unimpeded view to one of the landing strips in the not very far distance. It had been laid with cement last year, something she knew that the RAF was trying to do with all the fighter stations. However, the rapid escalation of hostilities had slowed the process and Evelyn knew that only some of them had been completed.

While she stood there, gazing out the window and watching the flurry of activity in the distance, three Hurricanes came into view, preparing to land. One had thick, black smoke pouring from under a wing, and as it grew closer, a fire engine started towards the landing strip. She couldn't hear it, but Evelyn knew the bells would be ringing in warning. She squinted to see the markings on the nose as the wounded aircraft landed on the cement. The smoke made identification difficult, but as the fighter slowed to a stop a burst of wind swirled the black clouds away from the side of the plane and she caught a glimpse of the identification letters. Evelyn inhaled silently, her shoulders tightening. It was a Hurricane from Fred's squadron.

The fire engine reached the stricken fighter, and she watched as emergency crew scrambled to put out the flames while two medics climbed up onto the opposite wing. After a moment, she exhaled in relief as the pilot climbed out of the cockpit unassisted. At least the pilot was all right, even if his kite was a mess. From this distance, she had absolutely no way of knowing if it was Fred climbing off the wing or not, but Evelyn was relieved just the same.

She turned away from the window resolutely and went over to her desk, sinking into the wooden chair. It made no difference if it was Fred, or if Fred was still up there somewhere defending them. Wherever he was, Fred was doing his part—fighting with everything he had—just as every other pilot in the RAF was doing. And it was her duty to do the same.

It didn't matter if they were pilots, sailors, soldiers, or spies. They were all fighting together, and some of them, if not most, would die. This was what war was. It wasn't glamorous, and it certainly wasn't pretty. It was brutal and awful.

Evelyn thought of the soldiers she'd shot in the mountains of Norway, and of the bodies strewn across the road in France. All had died, but only half of them had been the enemy. War didn't discriminate. Death could come for any of them, at any time.

A knock on the door interrupted her morbid thoughts and Evelyn called the command to enter. Sergeant Cunningham came in carrying a tea tray with a pot, two cups and saucers, and a stack of folders.

"Good morning, ma'am," she said cheerfully. "Did you have a safe ride in?"

"Yes, thank you." Evelyn got up and cleared a spot on her desk for the tray. "It looks as though things haven't been as uneventful here while I've been gone."

"No, we're in a bit of a crunch." Cunningham set the tray down and lifted the pile of folders, handing them to Evelyn. "We gained a few Spitfires last night. A squadron from Tangmere came here when they couldn't land at their station."

Evelyn looked up in shock, setting the folders down on the desk.

"What?"

"Tangmere was hit pretty badly yesterday. Bombs tore up the landing strips, and they say four Hurricanes were destroyed on the ground. When the poor lads came back, they couldn't land. I understand some of them went to Biggin Hill, and some came here."

"Good heavens!" Evelyn sank into her chair. "What will they do?"

"Oh, I'm sure they've filled in the holes by now. Whether or not the hangars are intact, though, is quite another story. I thought you'd like a spot of tea. Shall I pour?"

Evelyn choked back a laugh and waved her hand vaguely.

"By all means, Cunningham. Thank you."

She cleared her throat and reached for the folder on top of the stack. It wouldn't do to show her sergeant, ASO or not, how flustered she was at the news that Tangmere had been ruthlessly bombed.

"It seems all hell has broken loose since I left."

"Yes, ma'am." The sergeant poured tea into the two cups. "They say that the Jerries are going after all the airfields, trying to do here what they did in France.

Four stations were hit yesterday, though it sounds as if Tangmere was the one that got it the hardest."

"I suppose it was to be expected, but how awful!" Evelyn accepted her tea with a nod of thanks. "We can't withstand many raids like that. If they hit the same stations again and again. . ."

"Well, that's what they're banking on, isn't it?" Cunningham seated herself in a chair and sipped her tea. "Destroy the airfields and our boys won't have anywhere to refuel and rearm. They've hit Manston three times now."

Evelyn sipped her tea and was silent for a moment. Cunningham was right. That was exactly how they'd overrun Belgium. The Luftwaffe had destroyed the entire Belgian air force on the ground, and the army went in behind them. Then they had done the same thing in France. Blitzkrieg. Terrible, and terribly effective.

"Well, we'll just have to pray that our pilots give them a run for their money," she said briskly, setting down her cup and turning her attention to the stack of folders in front of her. "Now, what do you have for me? Let's get this out of the way, shall we?"

Chapter Eight

London

B ill looked up when a shadow filled the open door of his office. His boss stood there, peering in at him with a look of resignation. Jasper Montclair was on the shorter side with a stocky, square frame. Seen in a crowd, one wouldn't look twice at the man. However, what he lacked in stature was more than made up for in personality, as anyone who'd ever exchanged more than two words with him would attest.

"Working through your lunch hour, Buckley?" He moved into the office, eyeing the half-eaten sandwich on a plate beside the pile of reports in front of Bill. "I thought we'd been over this."

"We have, sir." Bill got to his feet with a rueful smile and came around the desk, his hand outstretched. "Come in."

"I see you've taken to keeping the door open." Jasper shook his hand and sat down when Bill waved him into a chair.

"I'm trying to get some airflow through here. It was an absolute oven earlier." Bill went over to close the door. "How was your meeting with Churchill?"

"About what I expected it would be."

"Are things as bad as they say?" Bill asked, going back to his seat.

"Worse. We're losing fighters at an astonishing rate, but even more concerning is the number of pilots going down." Jasper crossed his legs. "Winston's afraid we'll run out of flyers before this battle has been won. Dowding has started poaching bomber pilots and giving them a crash course in fighters."

"It's as bad as that?" Bill asked, startled.

"It is. Between the pilots lost during Dunkirk and the ones lost over the Channel during those blasted convoy raids, they've been picking us off for months. Now it's all ramped up even more. We've lost twenty pilots this week alone."

Jasper exhaled and rubbed his face. "Now they're attacking the airfields and destroying aircraft on the ground. It's grim, Buckley. Very grim."

"Things aren't much better on our front, I'm afraid." Bill sat back in his chair. "One of my agents from France made it into Spain and sent a message last night. He's the only one left from his group. The rest were killed."

"Not captured?" Jasper asked sharply.

"No. Apparently they fought back hard enough to make it more desirable for the soldiers to kill them instead of taking them alive."

"Well, that's something at least. And the radio?"

"Destroyed."

"The agent?"

"Making his way back to England."

Jasper exhaled. "Well, we suspected that many of those who remained wouldn't come back."

"Yes. Unfortunately, the fate of his group leaves me with only two agents possibly still alive and free."

"What about the French network? They went to ground when France fell. Have you heard anything from them?"

"I know one went south with Jian. As far as she's aware, the woman was going to set up near Bordeaux. The other members of her team scattered. Jian believes at least one is in Lyon, and we have one ally in the Vichy government, but we haven't been able to make contact with any of them." Bill shook his head. " 'I have no eyes to see with, and no ears to hear with.' "

"Do you know if the man in Bordeaux was able to make contact with Jian's cousins? The ones who stayed behind?"

"Yes." Bill sat forward and rummaged through the files covering his desk. "He got a message out a few days ago. Sent it from some kind of fishing boat. I've got it here, somewhere."

"You're more than welcome to summarize, my dear chap," Jasper said, amused.

"Yes, well, it's all rather a muddle, I'm afraid. From what I can piece together, he made contact with them and they're onboard with us. He still has his radio, but he isn't using it because he wants to make sure he knows when it's safe. The Germans are actively monitoring all the port cities for radio activity."

"Then how did he send his report?"

"As I said, from a fishing boat. He used an unknown radio that isn't ours. I'm not sure where he got it, but we've added it to our list of friendly contacts."

"Are you sure it's not the Germans?"

"Yes. He followed the protocol and used the correct words to indicate that it *was* him, and that he was not under duress." Bill gave up looking for the file and sat back. "I really must get Fitch in here and get this mess all sorted out. As far as I can remember, Jian's cousins are with us, and they have obtained the proper papers from both Vichy and the Nazis to be able to move between the occupied and unoccupied zones. They can travel to Paris freely, but that's where it gets a bit muddy. It seems they aren't fond of the idea of passing any information to my man in Bordeaux."

"Why on earth not?"

"They think it's too risky to move the intelligence from Paris all the way south to Bordeaux, and they haven't anyone in between. They've come up with something that they think is more secure." Bill cleared his throat. "They're going to have the Germans relay it for them."

Jasper stared at him in astonishment.

"I beg your pardon?"

For the first time since he'd entered the office, a grin cracked Bill's lips. "You heard me."

"How the bloody hell do they think they'll manage that?"

"I have absolutely no idea, but Leon will make contact again once they have it all arranged."

"It's impossible!" Jasper blustered, uncrossing his legs and leaning forward. "They must be insane!"

To his surprise, Bill laughed.

"They're not insane, I assure you," he said, still chuckling. "I'll remind you whose cousins they are. Their father called the three of them the Three Musketeers, and for very good reason. They were always getting into mischief. More importantly, they always got themselves out of it again, and rather brilliantly, I might add."

"This is hardly school day pranks," Jasper retorted. "This is dangerous work!"

"And no one knows that more than they do, I'm sure. However, I'll tell you this, if there is any possible way to manipulate the Germans and use their own technology against them, Gisele and Nicolas will find it. Well, it appears that they already have."

"I don't like this at all," Jasper decided, shaking his head. "Can't you put a stop to it?"

"I don't see how. There's only one person that was ever able to talk sense into those two, and she's not going back to France until things have calmed down and we know what we're dealing with."

"And even then, she can never know her cousins are working for us," Jasper muttered. "It's best to keep them all in the dark. Less likelihood of any of them being betrayed that way."

"Precisely. The only recourse we have at the moment is to wait and see what they're able to contrive."

"And Leon is sure that he hasn't been compromised? He's safe?"

"For now, yes. His pâtisserie is open again, and they're allowing him to retain control of it and his apartment above. As far as the Germans are concerned, he is simply another baker in Bordeaux and no threat to them."

"At least one German knows otherwise," Jasper pointed grimly. "Why hasn't he alerted the authorities?"

"I have no idea, and I'll admit that worries me," Bill said with a frown. "Leon is aware of the danger, and he's taking all the precautions he can. It's one of the reasons he refuses to use his own radio for the time being."

Jasper exhaled and shook his head.

"If our boys don't keep the Jerries out of Britain, it may end up being a moot point," he muttered. "If the RAF fails, we'll be buggered, and there'll be no one left for him to send the messages to."

"Yes, well, let's pray that doesn't happen."

RAF Northolt

Evelyn looked at her watch and reached for the cap of her pen. That was it. She had finished signing everything that Cunningham had left for her. All that was needed now was for her to gather her belongings, hunt down the sergeant, and go to the pub for lunch. That was going to be the most difficult part of this visit, she reflected ruefully, getting up from her desk and stretching. She had no idea how the sergeant who wasn't a sergeant was going to react to her proposition, nor did she have any idea if Bill would even allow what she was going to propose. She hadn't run it by him yet, wanting to get Cunningham's agreement first. Once she was on board, then Evelyn would broach the topic with Bill.

Going around the desk, she retrieved her hat from the stand and went over to the little mirror on the wall to settle it on her blonde hair. Really, she didn't see how Bill could refuse. It wasn't as if Cunningham wasn't already working for them in a way. She was at Northolt to make sure that Evelyn's WAAF work got done when she wasn't there to do it herself. If she was already familiar with MI6 and Evelyn's role therein, it only made sense to bring her properly onboard in a full support role, and that was precisely what Evelyn wanted to do. If Cunningham was game, then she would find a way to work it out with Bill.

Turning away from the mirror, Evelyn hooked her gas mask case over her shoulder and went out the door, closing it behind her. A few minutes later she was going down the steps at the front of the building and lifting her face to the warmth of the sun. Sergeant Cunningham had said that she would meet her here, in front of the building, but a quick glance around revealed that the sergeant was nowhere in sight. Evelyn looked at her watch and hesitated before turning to start up the road towards the hangars. The WAAF enlisted quarters were a few buildings away in that direction. Perhaps she could catch Cunningham on her way.

A couple of RAF officers walked towards her, and they both nodded cheerfully. She nodded back and murmured a thank you when one stepped off the path to allow her to pass. The day was warm, the sun was bright, and she was more than happy to be out of that dingy little office. Her step lightened as a warm summer breeze brushed against her face, bringing the scent of engine oil and the echo of clanking tools from the repair hangars.

"Assistant Section Officer Ainsworth!"

She looked up to find Sergeant Cunningham waving from the door of the enlisted quarters. She waved back and watched as the other woman ran lightly down the steps and came towards her.

"I'm sorry, ma'am. I got caught up with one of the girls and couldn't get away," she said, joining her.

"Oh, that's quite all right. I thought I'd walk to meet you instead." Evelyn smiled. "It's such a lovely day."

"Yes. The bus should be along any moment. If we hurry, we can catch it."

"Oh, I have my car! It's parked behind the supply hut."

Before Cunningham could respond, the air raid sirens started, low at first before gaining momentum into the loud, earsplitting wail that was meant to alert everyone far and wide to imminent danger.

"Wouldn't you know it?" Cunningham demanded, looking around. "Another drill! They've been having them all week."

Evelyn frowned and looked up to the sky, trying to hear over the sound of the sirens if there was an accompanying sound of bombers.

"Come on, ma'am. We'd better make our way to the shelter."

Evelyn gave up trying to hear anything over the siren and nodded, looking around. She spotted the air raid shelter across the street, which was nothing more than a trench protected by a wall of sandbags piled up at the edges, and started towards it. The two RAF officers she'd passed a moment before were ambling back, but Cunningham grabbed her arm and shook her head.

"Not that one, ma'am. That's for the men. Ours is way down there," she added, motioning about a hundred yards away.

Before Evelyn could open her mouth, the ground shook and there was a deafening explosion. She spun around and watched as flames spiked into the air from the area just beyond the hangars.

"Take cover!" she yelled, grabbing Cunningham's arm and yanking her along towards the men's shelter.

"But ma'am. . ." Cunningham started to protest but another bomb exploding behind the enlisted quarters made her start running next to Evelyn. They reached the entrance to the shelter at the same time as the RAF officers who hastened them down the rough steps ahead of them.

"Bloody bastards!"

Evelyn was inclined to agree with whichever officer had muttered that remark and she hurriedly moved along into the trench before crouching down and pulling her hard hat from its hook on her gas mask case. She settled it on her head as the ground shook violently and more people piled into the shelter dug into the ground. RAFs and WAAFs alike dove into the trench as the bombs exploding around them drowned out the sound of the air raid sirens. The smell of smoke and burning earth filled the shelter and Evelyn ducked her head down as a bomb exploded nearby, shaking the sandbags piled up along the edge of the trench for blast protection.

"That one was close!" Cunningham gasped beside her.

Evelyn glanced at her, relieved to find that the other woman wasn't panicking. Her eyes were wide with fright, and her face was pale, but she was nowhere near the hysterics emanating from one of the enlisted girls closer to the entrance. The ground shook again and debris hit the sandbag wall, causing the two pilots who dove in last to stand up and press their weight against them to prevent them from falling inward.

"They're not going anywhere, but you will if you don't get down," one of the officers barked. "Take cover, men! Don't be daft!"

"For heaven's sake, girl!" Evelyn snapped, looking at the wailing aircraft-woman. "Pull yourself together!"

"I'll handle it, ma'am," Cunningham said, moving past Evelyn and the press of bodies to the young woman. She wrapped her arm around her shoulders, and she shuddered, trying valiantly to stem her hysterics.

A moment later, a deafening explosion sent glass and metal raining down into the street, slamming against the sandbags. Shards of wood and glass made their way into the shelter and Evelyn lowered her head again, sucking in her breath as something substantial hit her helmet. The ground was still shaking, and she could smell fire nearby, the smoke wafting into the trench to mingle with the smell of damp earth and stone supports.

Evelyn squeezed her eyes shut, listening for the sound of screaming engines to announce the arrival of the dive bombers. Suddenly she wasn't in the crowded shelter on the station but huddled in a copse of trees in the south of France with Josephine, listening in horror as the road was bombed and strafed by Stukas. Sweat poured down the back of her neck and she bit her bottom lip as fear streaked through her.

My God, it's happening again!

Except there were no Stukas, she realized, taking a slow, deep breath to stop the violent tremors going through her. The only gun fire was that of the anti-aircraft batteries firing away at the light bombers that she could now see flying overhead. The sirens were still wailing, she noticed, then realized that she could hear them because the explosions had stopped. The ground wasn't shaking anymore, and she lifted her head to stare at the sky. The bombers were fading into the distance, their mission accomplished.

"I think it's over," someone said. "Someone go and look."

"You go and look!" someone else exclaimed. "I'm not sticking my head out just to have it blown off."

Evelyn rolled her eyes and, despite her own fright, started to stand up.

"For heaven's Sake, I'll. . ." she began, but then stopped as a tall pilot stood up and climbed over a young man to the steps.

"I go," he announced in a heavily accented voice. "Stay."

He disappeared out of the opening and Evelyn looked at Cunningham questioningly, but she was still trying to comfort the now-sobbing aircraftwoman.

"I'll go as well." One of the RAF officers who had nodded to Evelyn in the road straightened up.

"Wait until we know it's all clear!" His mate protested.

"And let a bloody Pole sacrifice himself alone for us? Not while I'm still alive." With that statement, he made his way to the entrance and went up the steps without another word.

Evelyn watched him go, her lips pursed thoughtfully. That answered that question at any rate. The accent that she hadn't recognized had been Polish. He must be from one of the Polish squadrons that had been posted at Northolt. She hadn't met any of them, but Fred had mentioned them once or twice. He didn't seem to have the same opinion as the officer who had gone out just now, however. Fred liked them, or so it had appeared to her. But then again, Fred seemed to like everyone.

Her heart was slowing now that the immediate threat seemed to have passed and she reached up a hand to feel the top of her helmet. Evelyn let out an involuntary gasp when she felt a dent in the smooth metal.

"What is it, ma'am?" Cunningham asked in alarm. "Are you hit?"

"Well, in a way. Something hit my helmet and there's a bloody great dent in it!"

The stress of the attack had frayed her nerves and Evelyn didn't think to mind her language or tone. Her matter-of-fact statement was very much at odds with her upper-class diction, and after a second of stunned silence, the entire company in the trench burst out laughing. The young RAF sergeant next to her straightened up a bit to peer at her helmet, still chuckling, then he let out a whistle.

"Lord, she's right! Something really clunked her in the head!" he exclaimed, looking around the tight space for the culprit.

Cunningham released the young woman and made her way back to Evelyn, examining the damaged helmet.

"If you hadn't been wearing that, you'd be in a bad way," she announced.

"What could have done it?"

"Here it is!" The RAF sergeant held up what looked to be a chunk of brick. "It had to have been this!"

Evelyn reached out a hand and took it from him, staring at it. The piece of brick looked as if it had been blown from a much larger slab, and it was heavy.

"Good heavens," she breathed. "I'd be more than in a bad way, Cunningham. I'd be dead!"

"And that's why we wear the helmets!" someone exclaimed. "I know I won't fail to wear mine from now on!"

"Is over." The Polish pilot was back, sticking his head through the entrance. "You can disembark."

"I think you mean that we can come out," Evelyn said, forcing a cheerfulness that she didn't feel. "With pleasure!"

She stood up and the pilot moved out of the way so they could all climb out. When she emerged from the shelter, Evelyn looked around in dismay. The building directly across from the shelter had been hit, which explained the violence of the debris that slammed into the protective wall of sandbags. Flames licked from under the rubble, and a fire engine was already trying to make its way towards it. The road, however, was obstructed by both debris and craters, causing the truck to have to weave carefully around them.

All around them was noise. The ringing of fire engines, the shouted orders from officers trying to organize the chaos, the screams of pain from those who had been wounded in the blasts, and over it all, the incessant wailing of the air raid siren.

"Oh, will somebody shut that bloody thing off?!" someone cried. "We know already!"

Almost as if "someone" heard him, the piercing wail suddenly stopped, the abruptness making Evelyn's ears ring for a moment.

"Thank God," Cunningham said beside her. "I don't know what's worse, hearing the bombs or hearing that thing!"

"Bombs." A deep voice said from behind them. "Bombs worse."

Evelyn turned to face the Polish pilot. He was tall, almost six feet, with light brown hair, almost blond, that waved over his forehead. His face was angular, and he had a long, straight nose that reminded her of someone, but she couldn't place who. His brown eyes looked down at her soberly, and she nodded.

"Yes," she agreed. "I suppose you're right. Bombs are most definitely worse."

"You are all right?" he asked in concern, taking in her dented helmet.

"Lord, yes." Evelyn took it off and looked at it ruefully. "Thanks in no small part to this. I'm Assistant Section Officer Ainsworth," she added, holding out her hand.

"I am Flying Officer Tomasz Wyszynski," he replied in thickly accented English, taking her hand and bowing slightly over it.

"And this is Sergeant Cunningham," Evelyn said, motioning to Cunningham. "Pleasure."

Evelyn turned to look at the destruction surrounding them, balking when she caught sight of a prone woman in blue lying at the side of the road. She stared at her for a moment, then sucked in her breath.

"Cunningham, we'd best start looking for. . ." Her voice trailed off and she cleared her throat. "What I mean to say is, we need to find our girls."

"Yes, ma'am." Cunningham motioned to the aircraftwomen who were huddled nearby surveying the damage around them. "Go find a corporal and tell her that she's needed here," she ordered, "and you, see if you can find any stretchers."

"Yes, ma'am."

They went off, the one who had been hysterical in the trench resolutely drying her cheeks as she went, and Cunningham looked across the street at the figure lying motionless.

"Let's move her over there," she suggested, pointing to the expanse of grass that separated the partially destroyed building from the first hangar which, remarkably, was untouched.

Flying Officer Wyszynski followed their gaze to the fallen WAAF and strode forward. Without a word, he bent down and felt for a pulse, looking up and shaking his head when they joined him.

"I didn't think so," Cunningham said quietly.

"Where?" he asked, picking the body up gently.

Evelyn motioned to the grass, and he nodded, walking over to lay her down on the grass, away from the rubble, fire, and commotion. Evelyn watched him for a moment, then turned back to Cunningham.

"I'll search for any more," she told her resolutely. "You go and find some more people to help. Between the fires and the buildings that have been hit, it's no use waiting for medics to come along. And see if you can locate Section Officer Madson."

"Yes, ma'am." Cunningham turned away, then turned back. "Are you sure you're all right? Your head, I mean."

"Yes, yes, I'm fine," Evelyn waved her away. "Don't worry about me. Let's just get organized and try to do what we can."

"Yes, ma'am."

Chapter Nine

Bordeaux, France

E isenjager looked up from his newspaper when the door to Café Rosa opened, lowering his gaze again when two older women entered. They carried cloth shopping bags on their arms containing the results of the morning rounds. Judging by the baguettes sticking out, the baker had been one of them. This was the third such party that had come into the little pâtisserie in the past half hour, none of whom interested Eisenjager in the slightest.

He sipped his coffee and turned the page of the newspaper. The owner of the shop, Leon Petron, was behind the counter, smiling widely as the customers approached. He was a slender man, on the shorter side, who sported a perfectly trimmed mustache and dressed with precision. He moved with a suppressed energy that Eisenjager found bordering on exhausting. The man was a machine, and while Eisenjager could readily appreciate the necessity of waking before dawn to begin the day's work, he had never been much of a morning person himself. Leon was just that: an energetic whirlwind of humor and efficiency before the sun ever crested the horizon. As if that wasn't enough, the man then remained active far into the night, often going to bed only a few hours before rising again. And yet, for all that wakefulness, Eisenjager hadn't witnessed anything to indicate that the man was anything other than what he appeared to be: a very personable baker of select pâtisseries.

Except that Eisenjager knew differently.

Three months before, the Englishwoman and her companion had come into this very bakery to visit Monsieur Petron. He had then taken them to the es- timable Captain Beaulieu, who had whisked them out of France and out of Eisenjager's reach.

Monsieur Petron was most definitely more than he pretended to be, and it was

Eisenjager's duty to report both his and Captain Beaulieu's actions that day to the authorities, as well as his own superiors. Yet he had no intention of doing so. Not yet, anyway, and perhaps never.

He sipped his coffee again, never taking his eyes from his paper. If he reported their involvement with the Englishwoman's escape in May, both men would be taken by the Sicherheitsdienst, never to be seen again, and what a waste that would be. While they remained free and firm in the belief that their activities were unknown, Eisenjager had a chance of tracking down the woman closest to the Englishwoman, the woman who had come south with her. Once he had *her*, then it was only a matter of time before she would lead him to the Englishwoman.

No. Both the baker and the smuggler were of much more use to him alive and free at the moment.

Eisenjager recognized that it was a gamble to spend his time in Bordeaux surveilling the two men and waiting, but it was a gamble that he felt would pay off. Between them, one of them would lead him to her. It was simply a matter of time.

The door to the bakery opened again and he raised his eyes, his shoulders stiffening when a woman with dark hair walked in, a tall gentleman at her side. She was the right height, and the hair was the right color. Was this his quarry at last?

The couple went to a table on the other side of the little dining room. The woman seated herself, speaking in a low voice to her companion. After a brief nod, the man turned and went to the counter while the woman set her handbag on the table, sending a quick glance around the room. Bright blue eyes met his briefly before moving on without a flicker of interest, and Eisenjager suppressed a sigh, his lips tightening in frustration. The eyes were the wrong color, and the face was completely unknown to him. He'd never seen this woman before in his life.

He went back to his paper, shifting in his seat. He was just settling in again when he caught a snippet of the conversation at the counter.

"I'm told that you make the best cannelés in Bordeaux," the man was saying.

"That is true! But to whom do I owe thanks for the acknowledgement?"

"My friend William, from Paris, mentioned it in passing. Of course, we had to come to see for ourselves!"

"Ah! Then prepare to be amazed, monsieur. I will bring them to you. Café?"

"Yes, of course."

The man went to join the woman at the table and Eisenjager watched them for a moment from behind his paper. It was a strange interaction that he'd had with the baker. On the surface it seemed perfectly reasonable, yet every instinct of his was humming. Travel around France was difficult, not to mention inconvenient these days. If the couple were from Paris, why had they traveled all the way to Bordeaux for the sake of a pastry? And why would he tell Leon his friend's name, for all the world as if Leon knew him himself?

He lowered his gaze back to the print before him thoughtfully. If it was a code, then it was a very good one. No one would question it in the natural order of things. Leon's smile and voice hadn't changed a bit during the exchange, and even now, he was whistling cheerfully as he had been all morning while he got the customer's order. Absolutely nothing was out of the ordinary.

And yet Eisenjager was convinced that something was very different about that customer.

When Leon took their coffee and pastries to their table, Eisenjager carefully folded his newspaper again and swallowed the last of his cold coffee. He stood up and nodded to Leon, walking over to pay for his own light breakfast of coffee and croissant.

"Was everything to your taste?" Leon asked, returning to the counter.

"Oui. Merci." Eisenjager spoke in French. "I couldn't help but overhear that gentleman. Perhaps next time I will try your cannelés."

Leon beamed as he passed him his change, his eyes sparkling.

"I make the best in Bordeaux," he boasted. "No! The best in France!"

Eisenjager gave him a thin smile and a nod, turning to leave the café. As he passed the couple, he shot them a quick glance out of the corner of his eye. They were looking down at their pastries, paying no attention to him or anything around them. He continued to the door, opening it and stepping out into the late morning sunshine.

He never saw two pairs of blue eyes look up sharply once he'd passed, nor did he see the look that passed between the brother and sister as he exited the café.

RAF Northolt

"Is that all of them, Assistant Section Officer Ainsworth?"

Evelyn wiped the sweat off her brow and surveyed the row of bodies that had been covered with whatever they could get their hands on.

"Yes, Section Officer Madson. That's the last of them. Everyone else is accounted for."

The woman who was, ostensibly, her superior nodded turned to look at the casualties, her face grim.

"Very well. Thank you for your assistance. I'll wager that you regret coming back from your holiday today."

"I'm thankful that I was here and could be of help," Evelyn told her, dragging her eyes from the gruesome sight.

"Nevertheless, I'm sure you'll be happy to leave again." Section Officer Madson turned to give her a tired smile. "I'll be sure to inform Sir William of your courage today. It takes a special person to step in and organize a response the way you did. I hope he knows what a valuable asset you are."

"Thank you, ma'am, but really, I only did what needed to be done."

"Yes, but you did it with compassion and grace. Not such an easy thing to do, under these circumstances." The woman sighed and turned towards the bodies. "I'll take it from here and handle the rest."

"Ma'am."

Evelyn saluted smartly and turned away, exhaling tiredly. Section Officer Madson knew something of her true position here, it was unavoidable, but Evelyn knew that she'd been told an altered version of the truth. As far as the woman was aware, Evelyn worked for the Foreign Office, and was engaged in analyzing classified material. Her lips twisted briefly. Not entirely inaccurate, in a roundabout way, but also not anywhere near to the truth. When Madson found her gathering enlisted women to help search out bodies and take a headcount of survivors, she hadn't questioned why she was back. She'd simply handed her a clipboard with an updated roster and asked her to go over it again and double-check that everyone was accounted for, alive or otherwise.

Cunningham had been sent to the infirmary after she burned her arm helping to pull what remained of a corporal from the rubble of the building across from the air raid shelter. Once she was finished there, she was relieved of her duties for the remainder of the day. Section Officer Madson had already approved her leaving the station for dinner with Ainsworth, just as long as she was back before the curfew. Evelyn felt something like amusement go through her. She wasn't even sure that Cunningham would want to go to dinner now. She knew that she certainly didn't feel much like it.

"Ma'am! Assistant!"

Evelyn looked around to find Flying Officer Wyszynski waving to her. He was walking with another pilot, and when she paused, they hurried to catch up to her.

"Assistant Section Officer," he enunciated carefully, "this is Pilot Officer Ludwig Jaskowiak. Ludwig, this is Assistant. . ."

"You may call me Evelyn," Evelyn stopped the painful enunciation of her long title with a laugh, holding out her hand. "It's very nice to meet you."

"I sorry for your sorrow," Pilot Officer Ludwig said with a heavy accent, waving his hand to encompass the destruction.

"I think you may mean loss," she said gently with a smile, "but thank you."

"We have been helping others find dead," Tomasz told her. "Is bad. Very bad."

Evelyn shaded her eyes from the sun and peered up at the two men.

"Do you speak anything other than Polish?" she asked. "French, perhaps?"

They both grinned ruefully and shook their heads.

"I speak little Russian," Tomasz said with a shrug. "We learn the English, but is hard. It is bad. We know."

"Oh no, you're doing beautifully," she hastened to assure them. "It's only that I speak other languages and thought, perhaps, you would be more comfortable."

"Polski?" Ludwig asked hopefully.

"I'm sorry." She shook her head with a smile. "Not Polski."

Ludwig said something in Polish to Tomasz before turning to Evelyn again.

"I go. Must meet man." He held out his hand with a smile. "Joy to meet you."

"Goodbye." Evelyn shook his hand and watched as he turned and jogged back the way they'd come. "Is everything all right?"

"He goes to squadron leader. Wants to talk." Tomasz tried to explain, then sighed in frustration. "This sounds bad. Even I know."

Evelyn burst out laughing.

"I speak Russian. Would you be more comfortable using that?" she asked in Russian.

The look of astonishment on his face made her flush ruefully.

"I know quite a few languages, but sadly Polish is not one of them. My father encouraged me to use my gifts, and I have a knack for languages," she explained.

"Your father was a wise man," Tomasz replied in Russian. "I, too, speak other languages. I was learning English when the Nazis invaded. I speak German and Romanian as well. Do you?"

Evelyn shook her head, unwilling to admit that she spoke German.

"I'm afraid not. Your Russian is very good. I thought you said you only speak a little."

"I lie." Tomasz said with a grin. "The pilots, they don't like to think we can speak the communist language, but not their own. I studied in Moscow when I was a boy."

"How did that happen?" Evelyn asked, fascinated. "I thought the Soviet's don't allow students to go there to study."

"They don't. However, I have relatives there."

"Oh! Well, then I suppose that makes a difference," she said easily.

They were walking towards the office building, the smell of smoke heavy in the air, and a truck with tired airmen rattled by on its way to the hangars. Evelyn watched it go, her lips twisting in a humorless smile. While the Germans had undoubtedly wanted to destroy all the hangars, amazingly only one had been hit. The others were fully operational, and damaged fighters that could be repaired were already waiting to be towed into them.

"How do you know Russian? Surely, it's not a popular language in England."

"Not very, no. However, I was getting bored with the Romance languages, to be completely honest. Russian posed a nice challenge for me." Evelyn shrugged. "It's nice to be able to practice with someone!"

They were quiet for a moment, then she glanced at him curiously.

"Why are you not up flying?" she asked. "Were you shot down?"

"What? Oh no." Something resembling a scowl passed over his face but was immediately concealed. "They won't allow us to fly combat sorties yet. They say we're not operational. We only fly training flights."

Evelyn frowned, her brows coming together in consternation.

"How long have you been here?"

"We came here at the beginning of the month. Before that we were at a training school."

"And you're still not operational?" she asked in surprise. "How ridiculous!"

His lips twisted sardonically. "I agree, but that is how it is. I flew in Poland, and I flew in France. Yet England will not let me fly yet."

Evelyn was silent, her lips pressed together. What on earth was the RAF playing at? They needed pilots now! And she knew full well that they were putting English men in the cockpits with less than ten hours of flying time and sending them up. So why not the Poles?

"How did you wind up in France?" she asked, abandoning the topic of flying.

"We escaped through Romania when Poland fell and made our way through Yugoslavia to the Adriatic Sea, where we took a boat to France." He paused for a moment, and she glanced up to find his lips pressed together. "Twenty of us started out together. Only eleven of us made it to England."

"I'm so sorry."

He shook his head and shrugged. "I watched the villages in my country burn, and the livestock slaughtered for no reason. Women, children, all gone. After that, I became numb. I am happy that I survive to repay in kind."

"I suppose I can understand that very well," she murmured, thinking of the fury that had gripped her in France and that never fully went away.

They had reached the office building which, miraculously, was untouched by any of the damage around them. He stopped walking and looked down at her, a faint smile about his mouth.

"And you? How do you come to be on an RAF station? It hardly seems the place for one such as yourself."

She raised an eyebrow and her chin inched up marginally.

"And just what is that supposed to mean?"

The faint smile stretched into a tired grin.

"It's obvious that you are from that class of people who do not have to serve in the military unless they wish it." He held up his hands defensively. "No, don't be angry. In Poland, I was one. My family is an old one, and I chose to learn to fly because it amused me."

Evelyn chuckled ruefully. "As did my brother," she admitted. "You're quite correct. I wanted to do something to help my country, and knitting sweaters and making jam with the Women's Institute didn't interest me. So here I am."

"Your brother is a pilot?"

"Yes. He flies Spitfires."

Tomasz's face lit up. "Spitfires! Now that's an airplane I'd love to get into.

Where is he stationed?"

"In 12 Group."

"Do you worry about him?"

"Of course! Just as I worry about all of the pilots. And now, having had this nice conversation, I'll worry about you as well."

"Well, there's no reason to worry about me at moment," he said disgustedly. "That's what Ludwig is speaking to the squadron leader about right now. This is absurd. We could be up there helping to defend the airfields!"

"I'm sure they'll sort it out soon. We need pilots desperately." Evelyn looked at her watch and held out her hand. "It was wonderful to meet you, and I thank you for all your help today. I must get back now. I still have a few things to attend to before I leave."

"Are you leaving?" He gripped her hand in a warm handshake.

"Yes. I'm actually on leave at the moment. I only came back today to sign some papers and pick up a few things."

He grimaced as he released her hand.

"You chose a terrible day to come back," he told her. "I'm glad you weren't hurt. May I ask you a question?"

"Yes, of course."

"Why are you carrying a brick?"

Evelyn looked down at the chunk of brick in her hand and laughed.

"It hit me in the air raid shelter. Dented my tin hat!"

"Good Lord! You're lucky you were wearing one! What will you do with it?"

"I'm going to save it as a reminder of how quickly life can end," she told him. "It will be my constant reminder to stay alert and take cover."

"And, perhaps, to wear your helmet?" he asked with a grin.

"That as well."

Chapter Ten

E velyn seated herself at the scarred, wooden table and watched as Sergeant Cunningham settled herself across from her.

"I'm glad you felt up to coming out for supper," she said with a smile. "It's been quite a day."

"I wasn't about to pass up the opportunity for a pub meal," Cunningham said with a short laugh. "Especially since the mess was only offering cold sandwiches. A gas line was hit and knocked the kitchens out of operation."

"They'll have that fixed quickly, don't worry."

"I hope so. It also leaves us without hot water."

The barmaid came over then, looking from one to the other, her eyes wide with curiosity.

"Good evening. Pardon my asking, but are you from Northolt?"

"Yes, we are," Evelyn replied with a smile.

"Is it true what they're saying? That it was bombed today?"

"That's right. It was."

"How awful! Was it terrible?"

"It certainly wasn't a picnic," Cunningham said dryly.

"Bloody bastards," the barmaid muttered, then flushed and looked from one to the other guiltily. "Begging your pardon. I shouldn't have said that out loud."

"No, no! You're quite right!" Evelyn said cheerfully. "They are, and we could use a drink."

"Of course, miss! What can I get for you?"

They gave her their drink orders and she nodded, promising to be back with them shortly. Once she left, they looked at each other and shared a grin.

"She's not wrong," Cunningham said. "I wish I could express my thoughts as colorfully."

"Agreed, although I had quite a slip earlier in the air raid shelter." Evelyn pulled out a cigarette case and offered it to Cunningham. "I'm afraid I'm still a bit shaken," she said when Cunningham declined. "How's your arm?"

"Burns like the devil. The salve they slathered it with doesn't seem to be doing anything for the pain, even though they said that it would." Cunningham shrugged and moved the offending arm gingerly. "Nothing to be done about it except to keep it clean and covered until it heals. It was a silly thing to do. I should have known there would be embers under that beam."

"It was a brave thing to do," Evelyn said firmly, "and you were very courageous for doing it."

"What about you and your dented hat?" Cunningham shook her head. "It's lucky you had it on. I wouldn't have thought to put mine on except that I saw you getting yours."

The barmaid returned with their drinks and set them down.

"Here you are," she said cheerfully. "I told Harry that you're from Northolt and he rushed the drinks for you."

"Tell him it's much appreciated," Evelyn said with a laugh. "What do you have in the way of food?"

"We have fish pie tonight, or there's a lovely rabbit stew," she offered. "We also have bangers and mash."

"I'll have the fish pie, please," Evelyn decided.

"So will I. That sounds like a nice change from the enlisted mess staples."

The barmaid nodded and went away again, leaving Evelyn trying to think how to start the conversation she wanted to have with Cunningham. Before she could, however, Cunningham broached it for her.

"What did you want to speak to me about, Assistant Section Officer?" she asked, reaching for her drink.

Evelyn looked at her in surprise. "How on earth did you know?"

"Well, I can't think why else you would come back to the station in the middle of your holiday and ask me to lunch," Cunningham answered with a laugh.

"No. No, I suppose it was rather obvious, wasn't it?" Evelyn asked ruefully. "And, please, call me Evelyn."

"Oh, thank you, but I can't do that, ma'am," she said hastily.

"Of course you can," Evelyn said briskly. "You're the same rank."

Sergeant Cunningham stilled and stared at her like a deer in headlights.

"Ma'am?"

"Cunningham, I know you're really an Assistant Section Officer. Sir William told me a few weeks ago. That's part of why I wanted to meet with you. It can't be easy living as enlisted when you're an officer, and I want to thank you for pretending to be a sergeant in order to help cover for me."

Sergeant Cunningham laughed and shook her head.

"There's no need to thank me, ma'am. I'm having a whale of a time!"

"Are you?"

"Oh yes! I'm getting a look at life from the other side, so to speak," Cunningham said sincerely. "It'll only help me when I return to my job as an ASO. I've already identified several ways that we can make procedures more efficient and keep the lower ranks more content."

Evelyn blinked, somewhat bemused. "Well, I suppose that's wonderful, but are you only with me temporarily, then?"

"Well, I don't know, really. Sir William never gave a timeframe, but I suppose I assumed that you'd leave Northolt at some point, and then there would be no need for me to continue."

Evelyn was quiet for a moment, then she put her cigarette out in the ashtray.

"Sergeant Cunningham," she began, but Cunningham stopped her.

"Call me Sam," she said with a smile. "Everyone does."

"Very well. Sam, what do you think it is that I do, exactly?"

Sam looked at her for a moment, then glanced around before lowering her voice.

"I know that you work with Sir William, who I happen to know is rather high up in MI6. Therefore, I assume that you work with MI6. Beyond that, I haven't a clue."

Her voice was calm and even, and Evelyn smiled faintly. Samantha Cunningham was a sensible woman with a cool head on her shoulders. She didn't show the slightest discomfort or unease discussing something that, until now, had been kept classified from her.

"Why did you join the WAAFs?" Evelyn asked, reaching for her glass of wine. "I understand your family is old and quite well respected. I'd have thought you would prefer to remain in Dorset with your mother."

"Why did you decide to do what you do?" Sam countered, a smile softening the words.

Evelyn chuckled. "Very fair point. My brother is a pilot, and when he joined the RAF, I wanted to do something for my country as well."

"Just doing your bit?"

"That's right."

"Well, it was the same for me. I'm an only child, so I don't have a sibling fighting for Britain, but I wanted to do *something*. I couldn't just sit home with Mother and knit sweaters for the soldiers."

Evelyn was surprised into a laugh.

"That's precisely what my thoughts were on the matter," she exclaimed. "My father understood, while my mother did not."

"Since we're being completely frank with each other, I was looking for a bit of excitement," Sam confided. "Dorset is dreadfully dull, you know. I was terrified of ending up as an old maid in the Women's Institute without ever having had any adventure. So I joined the WAAFs as an officer and went to a station in Devon. That's where Sir William found me."

She hesitated for a moment, then sighed.

"I suppose you've had a few adventures, haven't you?" she asked wistfully. "You seem as if you have."

"Do I?" Evelyn asked in surprise. "In what way?"

"Well, for one, you didn't even blink when bombs started dropping today. I've never seen anyone so calm, almost as if you'd been through it all before. Have you?"

"Have I what?"

"Been bombed before?"

Evelyn thought of the road in France and her lips tightened. She was quiet for a moment, then she nodded.

"I have, and it doesn't get any easier on the second go-around," she said.

"And your adventures? Have you had many?"

Evelyn laughed ruefully, uncomfortably aware of the pair of bright brown eyes studying her curiously.

"Just a few," she murmured dryly. She looked at Sam thoughtfully for a moment and tilted her head. "Where do you think I go? When I'm not at Northolt, I mean?"

"I have an idea, but I've never been told anything specifically," Sam said slowly, her voice low.

"What's your idea?"

"I always supposed that you were on the Continent, in France, or perhaps Belgium."

"Why would you think that?"

The look she encountered from Sam was one of amusement.

"Evelyn, I know full well what MI6's function is, and it's not working here in England," she said calmly. "I'm also aware of your proficiency with languages. My father told me."

"Your father!" Evelyn exclaimed. "How does he know?"

"I believe he and your father were on rather good terms."

"Oh. Of course. I'm afraid Daddy used to brag a bit about me." Evelyn took a fortifying sip of wine. "It seems to me that you've put it all together rather well. You're quite right. I was traveling to different countries on the Continent., and I was forced to flee through France as the Nazis were coming in."

Sam stared at her in shock.

"You were there?" she breathed. "While they were. . .invading?"

"Unfortunately, yes. It wasn't planned, of course. It was just rotten timing."

"What was it like?"

"Terrifying, if I'm to be honest. Seeing the Nazi war machine at work isn't something I would wish on anyone."

"And yet all of Europe has been subjected to it," Sam said in a low voice. "Is it true that their Luftwaffe attack civilians?"

"Yes."

Evelyn answered without hesitation, her voice flat, and Sam looked at her for a moment in silence.

"Why are you telling me all of this?" she asked, dropping the subject of the German armies for the moment. "You could be arrested and imprisoned for telling me anything."

"Well, I'm trusting you to keep the information to yourself. Sir William obviously trusts you, so I assume that I can as well."

"Yes, of course!" Sam hastened to assure her. "I'll never breathe a word. But it still doesn't explain why you're confiding in me."

Evelyn exhaled and pulled out a cigarette. This time Sam nodded and accepted one.

"I'm being held in England until things settle down a bit over in France," she said, holding out her lighter. "But I'll be sent back. There's no question about that. When I do, it will all be completely different."

"Well, yes. You'll be going into enemy occupied territory," Sam said slowly. "It will be terribly dangerous."

"Yes."

Evelyn lit her cigarette and tried to think of a way to word what she wanted to say without alarming her companion. Sam watched her for a moment, then cleared her throat.

"You may not return," she said softly.

"That's certainly a likely outcome." Evelyn blew smoke towards the ceiling and leaned forward. "The thing is, Sam, that the rules have changed. I'll no longer have contacts and safe ways to move about. There won't be anyone I can trust when I go back. Not really. Essentially, I'll be blind over there."

"But surely some of the contacts you made are still there?"

"Yes, but they will have been living under Nazi occupation. How will I know if they've been—"

"Turned?" Sam finished for her. "Oh, it's just like a spy novel! You *are* living an adventure, aren't you?"

Evelyn laughed despite herself.

"I suppose that I am, but it doesn't feel very thrilling, and I'm not confident of a happy ending. In fact, I'm rather expecting a messy end, if I'm honest. But that's where you can help."

"Me?" Sam stared at her in bemusement. "How can I help you?"

"I'll need someone that I can trust, completely and utterly trust, here in England. Someone who I can trust with my life."

"And you think that that someone is me?"

"Am I mistaken?"

"No, of course not! I'm flattered! But I honestly don't understand how I can be of any help to you while you're over there and I'm here."

"It's very difficult to explain, but I'll try. When I go back into France, I'll have to send any information back via radio. That intelligence will then be passed on to Sir William. The problem that I'm having at the moment is that I'm not sure I will trust anyone in MI6 to keep the intelligence, well, to themselves."

"You're afraid you'll have a mole on the other end of the radio." Sam sucked on her cigarette thoughtfully. "I suppose I can understand that. Daddy says that there are fifth columnists everywhere."

"It's not only that," Evelyn said after a moment. "Whoever is on the other end of the radio will be tasked with sending me into dangerous areas and getting me out again. My life will be in their hands, and to be frank, I've had some rather close calls due to some people knowing things that I didn't, and other people knowing things that they shouldn't. I'm not very much a fan of either. I want someone that has the sense and the loyalty not to play games but to do their job efficiently and keep it to themselves."

"You mean, someone who doesn't have any other connections that might compromise their ability to assist you," Sam said.

"Precisely. Now, I must be upfront with you and tell you that I've done some extensive digging into you, your family, and all of your associations and acquaintances. You're beyond reproach in every way."

Sam flushed but nodded in acknowledgement.

"I feel that I could trust you to keep me informed of anything I might need to know while over there, and also to keep any intelligence that I send back safe and secure." Evelyn shrugged. "I'd like you to work with me and be my radio handler."

"Radio handler? What does that mean?"

"It means that I would contact you, and only you. You would give me Sir William's instructions and work with his assistant—who's a lovely man, by the way—to stay on top of Nazi troop movements or intelligence that would affect where I am so that you can get me moving if I'm in immediate danger, and I would send all my intelligence to you. You would then make sure it gets to Sir William immediately. It would involve learning to operate a radio, learning the codes, procedures, and, oh, all kinds of things."

Sam sat back, stunned, and stared across the table at her.

"What about Sir William? What does he say?"

"I'm hoping that he will agree to what I'm proposing. He trusts me to choose my own contacts, so I see no reason why he would balk at this. It's not as if you'd be leaving England. You won't even have to leave Northolt if you don't want to."

"And my duties here? And my commitment to the WAAF?"

"Well, your duties would have to be amended. You would need to be available at strange hours, and perhaps at all times. I don't really know, but Sir William will be able to arrange it all." Evelyn sipped her wine. "You would have to undergo quite a bit of training, of course, and I suppose you would have to come over to MI6 altogether. So, perhaps, you would have to leave Northolt after all," she said thoughtfully. "I'm not really sure how it works. I know that, as far as the WAAF is concerned, I am fulfilling my commitment to them, but I'm in a somewhat different position. I came into the WAAF already working with MI6."

"Well, I don't mind leaving if it's necessary, both Northolt and the WAAF, though I'd like to stay if I could," Sam said slowly. "Have you done this before? Had a radio handler, I mean?"

"Yes, but it was always a different radio operator, and I never knew if they were prompt with the messages, or if they were working with multiple agents. When time is a matter of life or death, I'd like to know that the operator on the other end is committed to my safety, and mine alone."

"Heavens, I suppose so." Sam leaned forward and put out her cigarette. "Well, I said I was looking for some excitement. I can't think of anything more exciting than being your eyes and ears while you're slinking through enemy territory."

Evelyn hadn't realized that she was partially holding her breath until Sam spoke, then she exhaled in relief.

"You'll do it?"

"Yes, of course I will! I can't very well say no after that explanation, can I? I'd be leaving you in the hands of who knows who. A man who doesn't think that women have any business in this war, most likely!"

"That's such a relief!" Evelyn laughed and leaned forward to put out her cigarette as she spied the barmaid approaching with their pies. "Someday I'll explain just why I'm so unwilling to have a stranger on the radio, but for now, thank you. You have no idea how much this means!"

"Nonsense," Sam said briskly. "I can see very well how important it is, and I'm very happy to do whatever is needed to make sure that you are successful. And don't worry about my discretion. No one will ever have an inkling of what it is that I'm doing, I assure you. Now, when will I start training?"

Evelyn smiled slowly. "Just as soon as I speak with Sir William. Whether he likes it or not, I'm going back as soon as possible, and I want you ready!"

Chapter Eleven

"Assistant Section Officer Ainsworth!"

Evelyn turned when a male voice called her name. Her heart gave a little leap of relief and joy at the sight of Fred Durton striding towards her, his tie loosened, and his flying jacket slung over his shoulder. His face was weary and smudged with oil, and his uniform was creased from long hours in the cockpit, but he looked wonderful to her.

"Fred!" she exclaimed. "I'm so glad—"

She broke off abruptly, and his lips twisted sardonically as he joined her.

"That I'm alive?" he finished for her, tossing his flight jacket onto the bonnet of her Lagonda and unceremoniously catching her about the waist and picking her up in a bear hug. "So am I, Assistant Section Officer. So am I."

He smelled of engine oil and smoke, and as he hugged her close, she could feel the trembling in his arms.

"Flying Officer Durton!" she hissed in his ear. "What do you think you're playing at? Put me down before someone sees!"

"I don't give a bloody hoot who sees," he muttered before nevertheless setting her back on her feet. "After the day I've had, let the old bastards say something. I'll give them what for!"

Evelyn stared up into his face in the fading light, noting the grimness about his mouth and the lack of sparkle in his blue eyes that she'd grown so used to seeing. He hadn't released her yet, and she made no move to pull away. He seemed to need the comfort, and she was loathe to deprive him of it.

"Is it very bad?"

"I lost my numbers two and three today, the CO went down over the Channel, and I barely made it back in one piece. My kite's all shot to hell, and Lord knows what I'll be flying in the morning." Fred finally released her and rubbed his face tiredly. "Where have you been? I haven't seen you in months!"

"Don't be dramatic. It hasn't been months. It's only been two weeks," she said briskly. "Have you eaten?"

" After a fashion. I had a sandwich between scrambles a few hours ago." He yawned widely and ran a hand through his hair. "Don't suppose you fancy a trip to the pub?"

"I've just been," she said with a laugh. "Besides, you look as if you'd fall asleep at the table."

"I just might, at that," he admitted, leaning back against her car and looking at her pensively. "But I have to do something, or I'll go out of my mind. I'm too wound up to sleep, though Lord knows I need to. Why don't I take you to the Red Lion? It's a little farther afield, but not too far."

"Wouldn't you rather go with your pilots?"

"What pilots? There aren't many left," he retorted bitterly. "And the ones that are have already buggered off to the pub. The adjutant wanted a word, and when I came out, they were gone."

Evelyn studied him for a moment, noting that he didn't seem disgruntled or upset. Simply resigned.

"All right, then. The Red Lion it is. But why don't *I* take *you*? You've done enough for one day; you look run off your feet."

"You'll get no argument from me there, dear Evelyn," he said, straightening up, grabbing his jacket, and turning towards the passenger door. "I've had enough of being behind the controls for one day."

Evelyn nodded and walked around the driver side door. As she opened it, she looked over the car to find Fred staring at her.

"What?"

"Do you know, I can't think of anyone I'd rather have run into tonight? You're like an angel, somehow, here to lift me up."

"Now I *know* you're exhausted," Evelyn said with a laugh. "Get in before you start spouting Shakespeare at me."

"Would you like that?"

"Absolutely not. I can't abide the man!"

"That's good, then, because I couldn't quote him if my life depended on it."

Evelyn got behind the wheel as he slid into the seat next to her, closing the door and leaning his head back with a sigh before turning to look at her.

"What are you doing here? That sergeant of yours said you were on leave."

"I am." Evelyn started the engine and put it in gear. "I just stopped by to sign a few forms and pick up a few things."

"You picked a hell of a day to do it," he said, looking out the window as they drove towards the entrance of the station. "I had to land at Kenley earlier to refuel and rearm. Couldn't get in here. Luckily, they'd cleared the landing strip by the time I came down."

"Did your CO really go down?" she asked after a moment of silence.

"Yes. His kite exploded before he could get out."

"How awful!"

"At least it was quick." Fred muttered. "Probably didn't know anything about it."

"Who's acting CO, then?"

"Dawson, most likely." He sighed and lifted his head, searching in his pockets for his cigarette case. "He's the senior officer now."

"And when did you become flight leader?" she asked, motioning to the extra stripe on his lower sleeve.

"Last week, when mine bought it over Hawkinge." He lit a cigarette and lowered his window. "War is wonderful for advancement, you know. I'm on par with your pilot now, so he won't have rank as an advantage anymore."

"An advantage for what?"

"Why, for *you*, fair Evelyn!"

"Oh, don't be absurd," she said crossly. "His rank has nothing to do with anything. You make me sound like an opportunist!"

"Never thought it for a minute. If you were, you could have a squadron leader if you wanted, and you certainly wouldn't go about with me, would you? Turn off up here. The lane will cut across to the next village." He glanced at her. "Why *do* you put up with me?"

"Because you don't leave me much choice," she answered promptly. "And now that you're a flight lieutenant, there's really no reason not to."

Fred let out a bark of laughter and she looked at him, a smile pulling at her lips. For the first time since he'd called her name, Evelyn saw the sparkle return to his eyes. She turned her attention back to the road, holding on to the smile. Fred was going through hell, and if she could give him even a glimmer of joy in the short time she had him with her, then perhaps he would be able to better handle his burdens. And they needed him to keep fighting.

They needed all the pilots to keep fighting. Britain was depending on them.

18th August, 1940
Dearest Miles,

It's very early in the morning, the sun isn't quite up yet, and I'm writing this propped up in bed by the light of one lamp. I feel rather lazy, in a way, because you've probably been up and are on your way to dispersal already. I'll pray for you and the others in church this morning. It doesn't seem like much, but I don't know what else I can do for you. I wish I could hug you before you go up every morning and be there to welcome you when you come back.

I saw Fred Durton last night. I had to run to Northolt to sign some forms and pick up a few things. He'd just come down and spotted me as I was getting ready to leave again. I've never seen him look so tired. He lost both his number one and his number two yesterday, as well as his CO. Last week he lost his flight leader and was bumped up, just as you were. To hear him tell it, they're stretched dreadfully thin and are losing someone every day now. We went to a pub so that he could have a proper meal, as the kitchen was only offering cold sandwiches after a gas main leak caused by a group of Jerries and their bombs. (Don't worry, though. I'm fit as a fiddle.)

Did you know we have two squadrons of Polish pilots? I finally met one of them yesterday. He's a very nice man who hails from a very affluent family in his home country. His English is at least under-standable, although sometimes difficult to hear. I was surprised to learn that they aren't operational yet, despite being here since the beginning of the month. He flew in Poland, and in France, and yet he's not allowed up during scrambles. Fred told me last night that they actually had them riding tricycles in formation, equipped with instruments and direction finders, when they first arrived. I can't think of anything more ridiculous. Here we need every pilot that we can get up there, and the RAF won't allow the Poles to help.

Fred's none too happy about it, either. He's got to know them quite well, apparently, and Tomasz, the one that I met, actually shot down a Jerry in France. Fred thinks it's absurd that they're still considered training squadrons. He says that the language barrier won't mean a thing once they're up and in a scrap. Well, anyway, they're all trying to learn English as quickly as possible, so Group can't stick with that reasoning for much longer. I know that Fred and what's left of his squadron are exhausted, and they need the help. Fred almost fell asleep in his stew last night! He says he barely made it back in one piece yesterday, and Lord knows how long it will be before his kite's repaired. He thinks they'll be going up in gliders armed with service pistols soon!

I'm sending along a photograph of myself. I hope you don't mind. I heard on the wireless the other night that large formations had come over the North Sea from Denmark and Norway, and I thought that I hadn't even a snap of you. So here's one for you, and I fully expect you to send one back of yourself, Flight Lieutenant Lacey. After all, who knows when we'll have a chance to see each other in person again.

The sun's up now, and I must bestir myself to get ready for church. I'll pray for all of you, but most especially for you.

Take care of your Spit.

Yours,
Evelyn

London

Evelyn laid down her pen when the bell sounded from the front door. Glancing at her watch, she moved a sheet of paper to cover the account of the bombing that she'd been writing for her journal and got up, leaving the parlor. Bill was right on time. Hardly surprising. She'd never known him to be late.

"Sir William!" she greeted him, opening the door wide. "How lovely to see you again!" she added for the benefit of the two women walking up the steps of the house next door.

"Your mother told me you were in town for the weekend," Bill replied easily. "I thought I'd stop by and see how you're getting on."

"Do come in!" She held the door wider, nodding and smiling to the curious women. "Good afternoon, Lady Standish! Lovely weather today, isn't it?"

"Yes, very pleasant," that august woman responded promptly with a smile.

Evelyn kept the wide smile on her face as she closed the door behind Bill, then it was replaced with a comical grimace.

"Of all the rotten timing," she said. "They *would* be coming home just as you arrived!"

"Do you know, I never thought to question what your neighbors think of you coming to London alone so often," Bill said, dropping his gloves into his hat and placing it in her outstretched hands. "Do they bother you very much?"

"Not at all. I rarely see them, to be honest. I'm sure they know when I come and go, but they also see Robbie come and go occasionally. Regardless, they're always terribly nice and polite when we do see each other. Would you like some tea?"

"Actually, that would be very nice. I haven't stopped since breakfast."

"Goodness! Even on a Sunday?" Evelyn led the way to the kitchen.

"Because it's Sunday," he said dryly, following. "After the morning service, Marguerite wanted to visit the hospital. A new group of pilots were admitted yesterday."

Evelyn waved him into a seat at the table and turned to lift the kettle off of the hob.

"You've lost me somewhere, Bill," she said with a laugh. "Hospital?"

"Yes. Marguerite's been going regularly. She learned that pilots are getting. . .well, she goes to talk to them, or read to them, until they're transferred to a different hospital that can tend to them."

Evelyn swallowed and turned to fill the kettle.

"You mean the burn patients?" she asked, forcing her voice to remain even.

"Yes. I didn't want to say anything because, well, it doesn't do to cause you even more worry."

"I'm well aware of the dangers, Bill." Evelyn set the kettle on the hob and lit it. Turning, she leaned against the counter and smiled at him. "If Robbie gets burned, then we'll handle it. No sense in worrying about it when it might never happen."

"Quite right."

"It's wonderful that she goes to sit with them. I'm sure they appreciate it."

"Yes, though it's rather a lot sometimes." He sat back and crossed his legs. "Speaking of a lot, I received a telegram from Section Officer Madson late last night."

Evelyn swallowed and turned to open a cabinet for cups and saucers.

"Oh?" she asked airily. "What did she have to say?"

"You know very well what she had to say, Evie." There was a trace of amusement in his voice. "I thought we agreed you would stay away from Northolt for the time being."

"It was only a quick stop. I wouldn't have been there more than a few hours if—"

"Jerry hadn't decided to unload hundreds of pounds of bombs?"

"Oh really, Bill, you make it sound as if it were all aimed at me!" She spun around with a laugh. "I was perfectly safe hunkered down in an air raid shelter with a lot of other people. I was never in any real danger."

"I think the WAAFs that were killed would beg to differ on that point," he said, the amusement in his voice gone. "Evie, it's because of things like that I wanted you to stay in Lancashire for the remainder of your leave!"

"I'll have to return, you know, and this war isn't likely to be over in a week, is it?" she pointed calmly. "Do stop fussing, Bill. I'll be in much more danger when I go back to France, after all."

Bill frowned but dropped the topic for the moment.

"Why did you go back? And don't give me any nonsense about picking something up or signing forms."

"I went to have a chat with Sergeant Cunningham, actually. I had a proposition for her."

"What kind of proposition?" he asked suspiciously. "Really, Evie, I don't care for it when you get that look in your eye. What have you done?"

"I've asked Sam to come work for us and be my radio handler," Evelyn said bluntly.

"You've what?!"

She exhaled and sank into the chair opposite him. "I suppose I should have run it by you first."

"Yes, you damn well should have!" he snapped. "We have radio handlers."

"Yes, but I don't know them." Her voice was even and firm. "Bill, we have traitors all over London, and one spy is so well hidden that we haven't been able to find even a clue of his identity. Henry is out there, and for all we know, he could have people everywhere. Forgive me if I want to know and trust the person who will be holding my life in their hands while I'm in enemy territory."

Bill was silent, his eyes boring into hers for a long moment, before he exhaled.

"Yes, I suppose I can see that," he said grudgingly. "What made you choose Cunningham?"

"She already knows some of what I do and has been keeping the secret for over a year now. I looked into her family and her background, and you yourself vouched for her father when you told me about who she really was. I wanted to talk to her and get a feel for whether or not we would suit." Evelyn smiled sheepishly. "That's why I went to Northolt, but I got a little more than I bargained for, admittedly. However, it did show me how calm and collected she is in a crisis. She really kept her head in an awful situation."

The kettle began whistling and she got up to make the tea.

"I'm told that you did as well."

"Yes, well, that wasn't my first time, was it?" she asked wryly. "At least this time I had somewhere to take cover."

"Thank God that you did. Manston took a direct hit on the barracks this morning. Lord knows how many casualties there are."

"My God," she breathed, pausing in warming the teapot. "They're really going for all the airfields."

"Oh yes, and they won't stop until they've destroyed the air force." Bill shook his head. "I'm afraid we're in for a long haul."

Evelyn felt a wave of frustration go through her. Bill was right. The Luftwaffe wouldn't stop until they'd achieved air superiority, and that meant annihilating the RAF and all their pilots. They were sending over massive formations, but she knew that it wasn't even half of Göring's forces. And, while Fred, Robbie, Miles, and all the others were shooting them down as fast as they could, Göring could afford the losses; they could not.

"I went to the pub last night with Fred Durton, a pilot from Northolt," she said slowly, setting the teapot down and scooping tea into the opening. "He's losing pilots in his squadron at an alarming rate. He's exhausted, and who can blame him? Yesterday alone he lost both his wingmen and his CO. If his squadron keeps losing pilots at that rate, there won't be anyone left."

"Yes. The pilots are under a tremendous strain. Dowding will have to do something, but what can be done? I'm told that he's already cutting corners off the pilot training program to try to get them up as quickly as possible, and they're pulling pilots from the bombers to help replace the ones we're losing." Bill sighed and shook his head. "I don't envy Dowding, Parks, or any of the brass in the RAF their positions. How they're to win this battle with not enough men or aircraft is the stuff of nightmares!"

Evelyn set the teapot and cups on a tray and picked it up.

"Let's move into the front parlor, shall we?" she asked. "It's more comfortable there."

Bill stood and took the tray from her. "Allow me, my dear."

"Thank you."

She led the way to the front parlor and motioned for him to set the tray on the table before the couch.

"I'm sorry that I don't have any biscuits," she said, seating herself and reaching for the milk jug. "Will you take milk?"

"Yes, thank you." Bill sat down in a chair. "What did you want to see me about?"

"I have something to tell you, and I'm afraid it might upset you."

"More than the fact that you approached Samantha Cunningham without consulting me first?"

"Unfortunately, yes." She handed him his tea and began to prepare her own. "Although, I didn't think you would be quite that upset about Cunningham. Was I very out of line?"

"I suppose not, not when you put it the way you did." He stirred his tea and sighed. "You have every right to be uneasy and mistrustful of anyone connected with MI6 at the moment. After all, Henry is responsible for almost getting you killed a number of times. I understand, and you're right to want to choose your own handler here. The system we've been using was far from ideal, and when you go back, we'll need a solid and reliable person on our end to ferry information and help you navigate out of France again. In the normal course of things, that would be done by your direct superior. However, as that honor is mine, it puts us in rather an unusual position. In fact, your entire role is unusual. There's not another agent like you. We created your position as a unique one, and it only follows that your radio handler would also have to be something a bit out of the ordinary. I suppose I should be thankful that you addressed it before I had to."

He sipped his tea appreciatively, then looked at her, sitting back in his chair and setting the cup and saucer on the table at his elbow.

"Very well, then. Spit it out. You're not quitting on me, are you?"

"Good heavens, no!" She looked up in surprise. "Whatever gave you that idea?"

"I've learned that when agents say that they have something to tell me and that I won't be happy, it usually follows that they're quitting or want to be transferred."

"No, it's nothing like that. Although," she said with a grimace, "you may wish me to quit or be transferred in a few minutes."

Bill's lips curved in amusement. "I very much doubt that."

Evelyn was quiet for a moment, trying to decide how to approach the subject, stirring her tea thoughtfully. Bill watched, waiting, and finally, she set her cup down resolutely.

"There's really no easy way to say this, so I'll simply be blunt. I've lied to you," she said briskly. "When I told you that the trip to Switzerland was a wild goose chase, I lied."

Bill stared at her, his face impassive, but she caught a flash of shock in his eyes. Swallowing, she got up restlessly and went to the cigarette box on the mantel.

"I didn't like doing it," she said over her shoulder. "In fact, I hated it, but once I've explained, I hope that you'll understand why."

"I hope so as well," he murmured, reaching for his tea.

"Cigarette?" she offered. When he shook his head, she took one out for herself and picked up the lighter from next to the box. "When I arrived in Bern, I learned that the address wasn't too far from the hotel. I arranged to hire a bicycle, and off I went the next day. It was an abandoned stone cottage. A local man that I met on the way said that it belonged to a farmer who died last summer. He had a heart attack, just like Daddy."

"And that was the address your father left you?"

"Yes."

"Where was it?"

"In Blasenflue."

Bill stilled, his eyes studying her from over the rim of his teacup. "Go on."

"Well, I arrived, and the house was completely empty and abandoned." Evelyn lit the cigarette and set the lighter down, turning to pace restlessly in front of the cold hearth. "I went through it but didn't expect to find anything."

"But you did," he stated rather than asked, setting his teacup down.

"Yes. One of Daddy's cigarette cases."

Bill sucked in his breath, his face suddenly arrested.

"That's impossible!" he exclaimed. "I searched that house myself after Robert died. We all went through it, and more than once!"

Evelyn stared at him.

"You knew about the house?" she demanded.

"Yes. The farmer was an associate of your father's who helped us on several occasions. When Robert died so close to the old man's cottage, we searched it thoroughly on the chance that your father had left something behind." Bill shook his head and rubbed his eyes. "Apparently, we didn't search well enough."

Evelyn's lips twisted wryly. "Don't be too hard on yourself. You would never have found it. The only reason I did was because I saw the engraving on the chimney. The same image was on the puzzle box where Daddy concealed the address, you see. He must have had the box made specially."

"The engraving on the chimney was the same as the box?" Bill smiled slowly. "The sneaky devil."

"Once I saw that, I knew something was in the chimney. It was fixed onto the inside, towards the flue." She crossed over to tap her cigarette into the ashtray on the table and sank down onto the couch. "The case had a key inside, and a business card for a bank in Zürich. On the back of the card, Daddy had written an account number."

"Good Lord."

"So I went to Zürich, and to the bank. The manager knew me, or at least, of me. It turns out that Daddy had left a bank account and a safe-deposit box, with instructions that I was the only one able to access the box."

Evelyn paused and sipped her tea before continuing. Although she had decided to come clean with Bill, she wasn't about to tell him about the multiple cash accounts, or the absolute fortune that her father had stashed away in Switzerland.

She didn't know where the money had come from, but she knew that she wasn't about to let it all end up in the hands of MI6.

"And inside the box?"

Evelyn set the cup down and lifted her eyes to his.

"I believe it's the missing package that everyone has been in such a tizzy over."

Chapter Twelve

RAF Northolt

F red climbed out of the cockpit and examined the fresh holes in the side of his Hurricane.

"Hit again, sir?" Manny, one of the ground crew sergeants, ran up to him.

"Damn bullets were pinging off the armor plating like bloody ping-pong balls," Fred said, turning away. "I'll tell you what, I'm getting bloody tired of it. Nothing much is damaged, though, thank God. Instruments are all good."

"And you, sir?"

"Oh, I'm just dandy, Manny. Tickety-boo."

Manny grinned at his sarcasm and nodded to the rest of the flight coming in. "Looks like everyone's back, though. That's something!"

"Yes. A very big something."

Fred jumped off the wing and began walking towards the dispersal hut, stripping off his gloves as he went. They'd been going up since just after dawn; that was his fourth scramble, and it wasn't even one in the afternoon.

"Any joy, Durton?" The intelligence officer called from the hut as he approached.

"Not a damn thing!" Fred kicked the grass as he made that statement. "It's a bloody joke. I managed to get some new holes in my kite, but never saw who did it. They disappeared into the clouds before I could get a look in."

"Low on fuel, most like." The older man clapped him on his shoulder as he went by. "Never mind, lad. At least you all came back."

Fred nodded and went into the hut, his eyes automatically going to the chalkboard with the squadron flights chalked up.

"Bloody hell," he muttered, seeing that his flight was still at readiness. "Are we even going to get lunch?"

"Doubtful," the duty sergeant said with a shrug. "Jerry's sending everything today. The radars are picking up raids everywhere."

"Of course they are." Fred threw himself into a chair and pulled out a cigarette. "Doesn't bother them if we're starving!"

"I'll ring round for some sandwiches to be sent out," the sergeant offered, reaching for the telephone.

"Thanks."

Fred lit a cigarette, leaning his head back and propping his boots onto a table. He yawned and scratched his jaw as his new number two came into the hut.

"Oh, it's you, is it?" Fred asked, peering up at him. "You didn't happen to see the bastards who jumped us coming in, did you?"

"Not one." The young pilot dropped into a seat next to him and shrugged out of his jacket. "First I knew they were there was when you cursed and said you'd been shot again. When I looked around, they were gone."

"Hell of a first day for you. Here. Have a cigarette." Fred held out his case. "You're doing fine. Just stay close to me and keep your eyes open."

"Thanks." The young man reached out and took a cigarette. "It all happens very fast, doesn't it?"

"Yes. Fast to go up, and even faster to go down." Fred leaned his head back again and stared at the wooden beams above their heads. "How many hours did you say you had on Hurries?"

"Six, sir. But now I have thirteen."

"Good God." Fred turned his head to stare at him. "You don't even know which end your arse is yet!"

"I'm a fast learner," the young man said quickly. "You'll see."

"You'll have to be to survive the day," a new voice said as a tall pilot stepped through the door. "Did I hear him say he only had six hours coming in?"

The newcomer looked at Fred, cursing when Fred nodded.

"For God's sake, what the bloody hell is Group thinking?"

"Don't mind him, George," Fred said, glancing at his number two. "Allan hasn't had his daily pint of blood yet. He's not himself."

"Flight Lieutenant Allan Boyd," the newcomer said, holding out his hand to George. "Flight leader of Green Section."

"Pilot Officer Timothy George," the young pilot said, getting up and shaking his hand.

"Well, young George, keep your eyes peeled and stick to Durton like glue. And don't ever fly in a straight line for more than a second, or you'll be Swiss cheese on Jerry's plate." Allan dropped into a chair tiredly. "Bloody ridiculous sending babies to square off against the bastards."

"Anything else you can tell me, sir?"

Allan glanced at Fred, amusement lighting his eyes. "Keen, isn't he?"

"Lord knows why."

"That's all the advice I've got for you, George. You won't remember anything else, anyway."

The telephone rang and they all stiffened, three pairs of eyes watching intently as the sergeant picked up the receiver. He listened for a moment, then said 'right' and hung up.

"Tea's on its way," he told them.

Fred relaxed and sucked on his cigarette, leaning his head back once more and closing his eyes. After a moment, he heard Timothy get up and stumble to the back door of the hut. A second later, they heard him retching outside.

"Poor sod," Allan muttered. "I remember that feeling."

"Do you?" Fred cracked open his eyes and peered at him. "I don't. It's been weeks since I remember feeling much of anything."

"It's probably for the best. Can't have the veteran pilots going soft. Then where would we be?"

"Up the creek, though it seems like we're there anyway."

"Dawson clipped a Heinkel this morning," Allan said as Timothy came back into the hut. "It fell out of formation, but no one saw it go down."

"Doesn't count then, does it?"

"At least we're hitting them as much as they're hitting us."

Fred grunted and opened his mouth to respond just as the telephone rang again. This time, the sergeant stuck his head out the window and yelled.

"One Squadron, SCRAMBLE!!!"

"Bloody hell!" Fred jumped up and ran for the door, Timothy close behind.

"Are we refueled already?" he panted beside him as they joined the rest of their flight outside.

"I'd worry more about being rearmed!" Fred shot back. "Move it! And remember, stick to me like glue!"

London

The statement hung between them, and Bill was silent for a long moment before he leaned forward and set his empty cup on the table.

"So it's surfaced at last. I must say that I'm relieved it landed in your hands and not Henry's." He stood up. "I think I'll take that cigarette now. No, don't get up. I'll help myself."

"Do you know what's in it?" she asked, watching as he took a cigarette and then felt in his pocket for his own lighter. "The missing packet, I mean?"

"I haven't the foggiest, and neither does Jasper. Robert refused to tell me what it was, or even how he came by it. He said it was for my own protection. Utter nonsense, of course."

"I'm not so sure it was nonsense," she said slowly. "Several people who were involved with this packet are dead. All of them, in fact, except me."

Bill lit his cigarette and considered her in silence for a moment, his face unreadable.

"Is that why you lied about finding it?"

"No." Evelyn leaned forward to put out her own. "No, I lied because Daddy told me to."

He sucked in his breath and stared hard at her.

"Say that again?"

"Daddy left a letter in the box, addressed to me. He was very clear. He told me, on no account could the contents end up with MI6." Evelyn lifted her eyes to his calmly. "He said no one could be trusted."

"Why the hell would he. . ." Bill's voice trailed off as understanding dawned. "He knew we had a mole."

"I think so, yes. He instructed me to keep the information safe and secret, and said that I would know what to do."

Bill exhaled and paced back and forth a few times before turning to look at her.

"What was in the packet?"

"There were some drawings, some blueprints, and a few strips of microfiche. The drawings appear to be some kind of motor, though it's nothing like any motor I've ever seen. I've been trying to find a way to read the microfiche since I returned from France. It wasn't until earlier this week that I remembered Uncle Lenny." Evelyn finished her tea, setting the empty cup down with a clink. "He's not my uncle at all, of course, but I've called him that since I was a girl. He was great friends with Daddy, and he's a newspaper editor. I suddenly thought that they must have a microfiche reader."

"But we have one at—" Bill broke off with a shake of his head and waved his hand for her to continue.

"I went to see him and was able to read the documents on the microfiche."

"And?"

"The Germans are building some sort of a contraption that, if I'm reading the documents and blueprints correctly, would be devastating." Evelyn sat back and crossed her legs. "I'd like to have someone more familiar with engineering to take a look and confirm that I'm reading them correctly, though."

"That's out of the question," Bill said firmly. "These are classified documents! You can't simply show them around to any Tom, Dick, or Harry."

"Montague, actually. Harry is his brother."

"Pardon?"

"Montague Thompson. He's an engineer with the air ministry. He's working in Coventry at the moment."

"Yes, I know who he is." Bill said impatiently, waving his hand. "We've used him before, actually, but never for anything like this. I don't care if he's working in the Antarctic, you're not showing him classified documents stolen from Germany!"

"It's the only way to know what the Germans are building!"

"No, it's not. You can give them to me, and I can have one of our specialists look at them; a specialist that's bound by the Official Secrets Act!"

"Daddy warned against that." A thread of steel entered her voice. "I'm sorry, Sir William, but I won't betray my father's last wishes. MI6 will not see these documents. Period."

Bill swore under his breath and took an impatient turn about the room, pausing after a lap to ash his cigarette. He shot her a sharp glance as he did so.

"Why come to me at all, then? Why tell me any of this?"

"Montague is a civilian engineer. He and my father were friendly, so I'm not unknown to him. Even so, if I go to him now, he'll be convinced that I'm a

German spy. He'll turn me in, just as any self-respecting Englishman would."

"You want me to contact him first."

"It would certainly go over better if it were coming from the government."

He exhaled loudly and resumed pacing about the room. Evelyn watched him, wondering what was going through his head. She couldn't read his expression at all. His face was impassive, and if not for the pacing, she wouldn't know that he was disturbed out of his usual calm at all.

"If I refuse, you'll only go anyway, won't you?"

"Most likely."

He grunted and continued his laps around the parlor. After a few more minutes went by in silence, Evelyn sighed and poured herself another fortifying cup of tea.

"Even if you do find out that your hunch is correct, what do you think you can do about it without turning it over to us?" he asked, stopping to put his cigarette out in the ash tray. "If it's a weapon, which is the most likely scenario, our people will have to know so that we can work on defensive measures."

"I know. I'm rather hoping that we will find Henry before it comes to that."

"And if we do, and he's removed from the equation, will you entrust this package to me then?"

"I don't know, Bill, and please don't ask me to promise something that I cannot." Evelyn shook her head and looked at him beseechingly. "Daddy said that I would know what to do, and I have to trust that he was right. When the time comes, I'll know what to do. In the meantime, let's find out exactly what we're dealing with, and then go from there."

Bill sighed heavily and sat down.

"You're right about one thing," he said. "We must know what we're dealing with. Not only did Robert risk his life to get this information here, but we know that the Germans are desperate to get it back. That alone is proof of its value."

He was quiet for another moment, then he shook his head.

"Very well," he said, throwing up his hands. "I see no other way. I'll set up a meeting with Thompson and we'll go together."

"I think it would be best for me go alone," Evelyn said slowly. "There's no sense in making it seem like a larger affair than it is. If you go with me, he'll know it's something dreadfully important. Don't you think it would better for him to believe that it's nothing?"

"My dear girl, he'll know better when he sees the plans. If it's indeed a new weapon, he'll know. And he'll know it's no small thing."

"Perhaps."

"Definitely!"

"You really do underestimate my ability to make people believe something that isn't at all true," she said humorously. "Let me do what you trained me to do, if you please. When I'm finished with him, he'll believe the entire thing was simply an exercise in experimental brainstorming, or some such thing."

Bill stared at her for a moment, then a reluctant laugh sprang to his lips.

"Experimental exercise?" he repeated. "What codswallop!"

"Yes, but he won't know that," she said calmly. "I'm going back to Ainsworth this evening. You can reach me there when you've set the meeting."

"You do know that I am your superior? That I'm the one who gives the orders?" Bill demanded, drawing an impish grin from her.

"Of course I do! That's why we're having this conversation at all!" She finished her tea and looked at him, the laugh fading from her lips. "Bill, I really am sorry for keeping this from you. It was never that I didn't trust you."

He waved a hand impatiently. "That's a problem for another day, Evie. If we can't trust each other, then we both might as well pack it in now. We'll never get through this war."

"I know. I give you my word, Bill, that I will never lie to you again. I promise."

He studied her soberly for a long moment, then nodded and got to his feet.

"I'll make the arrangements, both for Thompson and for Cunningham. She'll have to undergo extensive training, of course."

"Yes, I did warn her." Evelyn got to her feet and followed him from the parlor. "I believe she's looking forward to it."

She picked up his hat and gloves from the hallstand and turned to hand them to him.

"Where are the plans now?" he asked, taking them.

"Somewhere safe."

"Good. Let's keep them that way. For God's sake, don't take the original to Coventry."

"I've already made copies."

"Good girl." He went to the front door and opened it, settling his hat on his head. "God help us both if this ever gets out."

"It won't." She smiled and watched as he stepped out onto the stoop, pulling on his gloves. "No one will ever be the wiser. At least, not until they have to be."

"You really have an aversion to taking a holiday, don't you?" Bill asked, turning to look at her. "First the business with the Round Club, now this. If you keep on at this pace, you'll need another holiday to recover from this one!"

"This is nothing like the affair with the Round Club. That was dodgy from the beginning. This is a simple task of having an engineer look at a few drawings." She smiled at him brightly. "What could possibly go wrong?"

Chapter Thirteen

RAF Coltishall

M iles reached up and pushed open his canopy, unclipping his oxygen mask and taking a deep breath as fresh air rushed into the cockpit, cooling the sweat on his face. As he taxied along the landing strip, a flare went out from the control tower, and he twisted his head around to see Chris coming into view behind him. Thick, black smoke was pouring from his engine, and as Miles parked and shut down his engine, he could hear Chris' Spit coughing and sputtering as he approached to land. He climbed out and stood on the wing, watching as Chris struggled to keep the fighter level and at speed as he lowered his wheels.

"Come on, you silly bastard," Miles murmured, his gut clenching as he watched the left wing dip suddenly. "Stop mucking about."

The wing came up again and the sound of the failing engine was blocked out by the screech of sirens from the fire truck that came barreling alongside the landing strip. Miles held his breath, his eyes glued to the unsteady Spitfire as Chris struggled to control the machine as he descended. He was going much too fast, and Miles unconsciously clamped his jaw shut.

"Cut the engine, you fool!"

The fire sirens stopped just in time for Miles to hear the engine give one last sputter before becoming quiet. Either the engine had finally had enough, or Chris had somehow heard him. The fighter coasted down, the wings dipping and bobbing unsteadily. Miles wanted to close his eyes and not watch, but he couldn't tear his gaze away. Chris was the best pilot he'd ever flown with, but coming in with a damaged rudder, no radio, and an engine that had been shot to hell was near to impossible. Miles wasn't sure he would have attempted it himself, but Chris was a crazy, stubborn American. Everyone knew they were a bit touched.

The ground crew stood in a cluster near the landing strip, watching grimly as Chris dropped down the last fifty feet. His wheels touched the ground, but before they could breathe a collective sigh of relief, the left wing dipped again suddenly. Miles sucked in his breath as the tip brushed the ground. The contact was enough to spin the fighter to the left, sending it careening off the landing strip towards a long row of hedges.

Miles didn't stop to think. He jumped off his wing and started running towards the Spitfire that was out of control and barreling towards the edge of the station property. He joined the ground crew as they raced behind the fire truck. Only one thought kept repeating itself in his head as his flying boots pounded the ground:

"Don't you dare end up like Slippy, you bloody fool!"

The corporal running close to him looked at him, startled, and Miles realized he'd yelled the thought out loud. He didn't care, and ignored the young mechanic as he passed him, his heart pounding as he willed himself to run faster. A tremendous crash ripped through the air as the airplane hit the hedgerow, but the sturdy hawthorn that had been growing for decades acted in their favor, slowing its speed significantly. The fighter went through the hedge, and after a few feet, the wheels rolled into a ditch, abruptly halting its progress. The Spitfire lurched forward, the nose and propellers hitting the ground and burrowing into the field.

The fire brigade plowed through the opening made by the plane, pulling alongside the stricken fighter but stopping just clear of the trench. Miles saw the men swarm to pull the hoses from the truck as he crossed the grass, heading for the break in the hedgerow. There was no movement from the cockpit, and he could see flames licking around the nose of the Spitfire.

"Bloody hell," a voice gasped near to him, and Miles turned his head to find Jones panting right behind him.

Miles couldn't answer, but he mentally echoed the sentiment as they pushed through the hedge opening and the acrid smell of smoke engulfed them. The scent brought back the horror of waking up in his own cockpit with smoke and flames surrounding it, and Miles stumbled to a stop behind the wreckage, gasping for breath. As he watched the rescue crew swarm onto the mangled wing, he vividly remembered struggling to get the canopy open on a beach in Belgium, praying that he would get out in time. Despite the wave of terror gripping him all over again at the memories, he forced his legs to move, sprinting to the other side of the wreckage. He was running to jump onto the wing and help from the other side when strong hands grabbed him from behind.

"No, sir!" Jones yelled breathlessly. "The fire's already in it!"

Miles tried to pull away, but Jones held fast.

"Look, sir!"

The words made it through the haze in his brain and Miles finally saw what Jones had spotted already. Hidden within the smoke, orange flames were licking around the underside of the wing.

Just as they had on that damned beach in Belgium.

"They have to get him out!" he cried, turning to cross behind the airplane and go around the other side. "He only has a few seconds!"

Miles rounded the shredded tail of the Spitfire to find the rescue crew prying at the canopy with crowbars while the fire brigade was charging the hose with water from the tank on the truck. He clambered up onto the wing behind the two men pulling at the hood and looked inside, almost fearfully. Chris was slumped forward and motionless, thrown forward over the instrument panel.

"I've got it!" one of the men cried triumphantly. "Give us a hand!"

Miles watched as the two men gripped the hood and heaved. After a moment, the canopy gave way and began to slide back. As soon as they had pulled it far enough back to where he could reach it, Miles grabbed it, straining with everything he had to get it the rest of the way open. One of the other men dove headfirst into the cockpit, ignoring the flames that were now on top of the wing on the other side, and pushed Chris back in the seat so that he could reach the harness clasps. The canopy reached the end of its track and stopped moving, but Miles could feel the pressure on his hands. It was going to close again the moment he let go. Gritting his teeth, he braced his feet, leaned backward, and held on for dear life.

The second man glanced at him, his face grim.

"'Urry up, mate. He can't hold it for long!" he urged his companion.

"Almost there," the other man gasped, shifting and pulling off Chris' headset and disconnecting his oxygen mask.

Miles started as a blast of water hit the flames climbing the opposite side of the cockpit, then exhaled in relief. As long as the fuel tanks didn't go, that water was buying them precious seconds to get Chris out.

"All right, here we go." He grabbed Chris under his arms and began to heave him out of the seat.

"'Ere, let me in," the first man said, angling between him and the side of the cockpit. He reached inside and released the half door, giving them more room to drag Chris' unconscious form out of the cockpit.

Miles watched, the edge of the canopy digging into his hands through his flying gloves, as they pulled Chris out. He was almost completely clear of the cockpit when he came to with a start, sucking in a sharp, ragged gulp of air as his eyes flew open.

"Easy, lad. We've got you."

In stark contrast to the anxious panic that had been in his voice just seconds before, the man's tone was even and calming. It had the desired effect and Miles could almost see Chris relax. Once he was completely free of the cockpit, one of the men grabbed his ankles.

"I can walk, you idiot!" Chris protested, shaking his head and starting to struggle. "I'm not dead yet. Let go of me!"

"Don't be a damn fool, Yank!" Miles snapped. "The kite's about to go up!"

He released the canopy, and it sprang forward, slamming into the front groove with a sickening crunch. The sound jolted Chris and he stopped struggling, staring at the canopy, then at Miles as the two men struggled to get him off the wing.

"Then what the hell are you doing up here?" he cried. "Get the hell out of here, you stupid prick!"

Miles choked back a laugh and leapt off the wing, turning to help them lift Chris down just as there was an ominously loud creak from the other wing. Someone yelled, and the Spitfire shuddered violently, falling sideways. The motion pulled the wing upwards, throwing all three men against the cockpit.

"And leave you to blow into pieces? Not bloody likely!"

The two airmen recovered quickly and grabbed Chris, shoving him towards the edge of the wing.

As soon as Chris' boots cleared the wing, the men let go and he dropped onto his feet.

"Take cover!"

The shout came from the other side of the wreckage and Miles grabbed Chris' arm, breaking into a sprint.

"Move!"

Chris needed no prodding; he lurched forward unsteadily, churning his legs to propel himself forward. The other rescue workers leapt off the wing and the four men dashed away from the wreckage. A second later, there was a deafening roar and heat smacked them in the back as an explosion ripped through the fighter plane. The fire had finally reached the fuel tanks. Miles felt himself thrown forward with the blast and he held on to Chris with a death grip as they lost their footing and pitched forward.

Miles hit the ground, letting go of Chris and turning to look for the two men who had pried him loose. Relief coursed through him when he spotted them a few feet away. They had also been thrown to the ground by the blast, but they were crawling away from the burning Spitfire, none the worse for it. He exhaled and struggled to his feet, reaching down to pull Chris up. They stumbled out of range of the heat and the smoke, then doubled over, coughing and gasping for breath.

With his hands braced on his knees, Miles looked at Chris. His face was smudged with dirt and oil, his head wet with sweat, and blood trickled from a gash above his left eye where he'd slammed into the instrument panel.

"You look like hell," he gasped.

Chris' blue eyes met his and he started to laugh but ended up coughing. Miles straightened up and clapped him on the back between his shoulders.

"That was, without a doubt, the worst landing I've ever seen," he told him, still catching his breath.

"I thought I was a goner," Chris rasped out, spitting before straightening up. "When the wing hit the dirt, I thought I was done."

"You were!"

"I thought she'd cartwheel. I'll take the trip through the hedge over that any day."

Miles took a few deep gulps of air, and they stood watching as flames engulfed the hapless airplane. The fire brigade turned the hose on the wreckage, and after a moment, Chris turned away.

"I hit that hedge, and it was lights out," he said, wiping the blood from his eye. "Bloody Kraut. I really thought I could make it back."

"Well, you did."

"Barely. I should've jumped out, but I thought I could save the plane. God knows we need them."

"That'll teach you to be so bloody-minded."

"You saved my ass," Chris said, looking at him. "That 109 was following me in. Did you get him?"

"No. Ran out of ammunition."

Chris' mouth dropped open. "What?!"

Miles shrugged and grinned. "I went head-to-head with him, pressed the button, and nothing happened. I buggered off out of there right quick."

"Holy shit. Well, it stopped him from finishing me off, at any rate. So thanks."

"Any time, old chap." Miles nodded to him. "Anyway, can't lose you, can I? I'd

be left with only young Thomas then, and he doesn't play darts nearly as well as
you."

Henry looked up as a squadron of Hurricanes roared overhead, climbing rapidly
into the clouds. They must have just taken off from a nearby airfield, but he didn't
have the faintest idea where. He wasn't aware of any stations nearby. He lowered
his gaze again to the pint before him and flicked a wasp off the rim of the glass.
Unless, of course, it was an auxiliary airfield, he mused, lifting his beer. If that were
the case, their home station must have been badly bombed, leaving it impossible
for them to take off or land. A small smile twisted his lips, and he swatted away the
wasp again as he lowered the glass. It wouldn't be long now. The RAF couldn't
take much more of the abuse.

He had to admire the pilots' determination. Despite the onslaught of a far
superior force, and staggering losses, they kept going up there to meet them. Brave
fellows, but it would all be for naught in the end.

Henry pulled out his cigarette case, nodding to the landlord pleasantly as he
wiped down a table next to his. There were only a few patrons at the pub, despite
it being summer and situated only a few miles from the coast, but Henry was
grateful for the quiet. He'd driven out of London that morning, intent on getting
away and clearing his head. If the truth were told, he'd had a few nights with little
sleep, and the strain was making him short-tempered. Why, he'd even been short
with Molly last evening, and that was something he rarely allowed to happen.
After all, there was no reason to take out his bad mood on her. She hadn't done
anything to deserve it, if you discounted her losing that damn packet.

Henry lit his cigarette, his mood souring. It was that damn packet that was
costing him sleep and peace of mind. It still hadn't surfaced, and neither Mata
nor Molly had been able to discover even a whisper of where it might have gone.
As far as Henry was concerned, the lack of clues could only mean one thing: the
Secret Service had it.

Despite what he'd told Lady Rothman, he now firmly believed that the woman
posing as Sir Oswald's secretary must have taken the packet from Molly. He had

no idea how it could be so, but he was convinced of it. There was no other explanation for its complete disappearance. Lord Gilhurst hadn't seen anyone fleeing the scene when he arrived, and he swore that the packet was missing when he got there. The only person who could have it was the secretary, and she would have undoubtedly passed it on to MI5. And yet no arrests had been made, and he hadn't heard any whispers of traitors in London. Why?

Henry tucked his case back into his pocket and stared pensively across the little garden of the pub. Birds chirped from the trees nearby, the sun was shining brightly, and if it weren't for the group of fighters a few moments ago, he might had been able to forget that there was a mighty battle raging overhead. He smoked for a moment, then reached for his beer.

He'd been expecting the packet to be turned over to MI5. That wasn't the problem, really. What was keeping him up at night was why they hadn't acted on it yet! He'd been hoping that they would round up Lady Rothman and her ridiculous group of amateurs. They were more dangerous than helpful. Why, just look at what had happened! Molly's involvement notwithstanding, the blasted Round Club didn't have the faintest idea how to navigate the world that he'd lived in for the past four years. It was only by the merest chance that his name hadn't been on that list. If Berlin hadn't. . .well, there was no point in thinking of it. It hadn't been included, and that was that. But he wanted Lady Rothman and her Round Club picked up and removed from the field of action before they got him caught. He'd worked too hard to ensure that he remained well hidden to have it all blow up now because Lady Rothman had grown bored with her London life. The very fact that they hadn't been arrested yet suggested that MI5 didn't have the packet after all. But if they didn't have it, then who did? Where in blazes was it?

And where the hell was Ainsworth's packet?

He drained his beer and set the empty pint down. That was another package that he needed to find, and it made two that had disappeared in England alone. Berlin was never going to believe the two incidents weren't connected, but the only thing that connected them both was him. Henry's lips thinned. It was only a matter of time before Berlin questioned his loyalty, and he really couldn't blame them. Of all the bloody luck, he had to be involved with both of them! That, more than anything, was what had been keeping him lying awake, staring at the ceiling, night after night. He had to find at least one of the missing packets before the Nazis landed, or he might as well go to the Secret Service and turn himself in. Either way, he was facing the same penalty for treason, whether against the crown or against the Führer.

Henry stubbed out his cigarette and stood up, reaching for his discarded hat. He was getting nowhere sitting at a pub, drinking and lamenting his situation. He had to do something about it, and there was only one thing he could do.

He would find Ratsel. If he could present his superior in Berlin with the spy they so desperately wanted, his fate would be much more assured. And as he already had a description, such as it was, of the spy, that's where he would focus his energy.

Bordeaux, France

Captain Jacques Beaulieu stood perfectly still, blending with the deep shadows that engulfed him, his back pressed against the wall of a building. His breathing was even and silent as he listened intently to the two soldiers patrolling the street just feet away around the corner.

"I don't know why you're complaining. You were rewarded with a weekend pass to Paris," one was saying as they paused near the corner of the building. "I haven't even been there yet. All I did was wave as we passed by!"

"Yes, and I was called back early this morning," the other replied disgustedly. "And for what? To walk the streets and enforce curfew!"

Jacques heard the sound of a match flaring.

"What are you doing?" the first man demanded. "You know it is forbidden while on patrol!"

"Who is there to see?" the other retorted. "Everyone is at the general's party."

"Don't be ridiculous. Only the officers went, and it isn't a party."

"What then?"

"I heard that they are planning for the invasion of Britain. They say it will launch in a week. The RAF is all but destroyed."

The other man snorted in disbelief. "We can't be so lucky."

Jacques inhaled the smell of cigarette smoke, then listened as two pairs of boots crossed the empty street to the opposite side.

"Why not? You got to go to Paris. . ."

Their voices faded off as they continued down the street. After a moment, Jacques peered around the corner of the building and spotted them walking away from him. He moved silently out from behind the building and went up to the front corner, glancing up and down the street. Aside from the two soldiers, the road was empty, and he ran across the street, keeping one eye on the departing pair. They never once looked around, and gaining the other side, Jacques ducked into an alley and out of sight. Exhaling, he straightened his jacket and adjusted his open-collar shirt before continuing at a more leisurely pace down the narrow alley.

Moving about Bordeaux after curfew was like navigating a minefield these days. Anyone caught out and about after ten o'clock was first arrested by the occupying forces, then passed on to the French police for questioning. If you were lucky, the French police were the ones who caught you. In those cases, a few well-placed coins earned you a reprieve and a stern warning. However, if the occupying forces were the first ones to spot you, things were much worse. Most were released by morning, but some had disappeared into the Gestapo's hands, never to be heard of or seen again, while others were sent to the work camps. Jacques wasn't sure which fate was worse, but he was sure that the whole thing was a damned nuisance.

Coming to the end of the alley, he paused and looked both ways before slipping around the corner and walking a few hundred feet only to cross the road and disappear into another pitch-black alley. The streetlamps were shut off when curfew began, but he had no need of light to guide his way. He'd grown up in the back alleys of Bordeaux as a boy and used them still as shortcuts around the increasingly crowded streets. As a smuggler, he utilized the lanes and alleys to easily move contraband. He was as much at home in the dark, narrow passages that crisscrossed the seaport town as he was on his own boat. This was his world, and no German was going to keep him out of it.

A few minutes later, he rounded a corner and stepped into yet another alley. This one stank of cabbage and urine, but he ignored the smell.

"What kept you?" a low voice demanded as a shadow separated from the darkness, taking the form of a slight man on the shorter side. "You're late."

"I was avoiding the patrols," Jacques replied with a shrug. "I couldn't leave at my usual time to avoid them."

"Trouble?"

"Nothing serious, but it delayed my leaving." Jacques motioned for the other man to follow him. "Come. Let's get inside and away from this stench."

The two men swiftly moved deeper into the alley until they passed a metal staircase leading up to the backdoor of an apartment. Directly past the stairs, was another door. Jacques pulled out a key, and a second later, they slipped inside, closing the door silently behind them. He flipped a switch on the wall and a single electric bulb lit up, casting its glow over a large room filled with crates, boxes, metal drums, and casks. He turned to face the smaller man.

"Well, Leon? You got me here," he said cheerfully. "What do you want?"

"A favor," Leon said with a flash of teeth. "Only a favor."

"Only?" Jacques was betrayed into a short laugh. "The last time you said that I almost lost my best lieutenant, *and* my boat!"

"Come now, Captain, that was only a skirmish," Leon said, spreading out his hands. "And you were laughing the entire time! Admit it. You enjoy the danger."

"I will never deny it, Leon. What I object to is your continued belief that the events you pull me into are of little importance." Jacques went over to perch on the edge of a large crate, swinging one leg carelessly. "What is it this time?"

"A short trip."

Jacques raised an eyebrow suspiciously. "To where?"

"Paris."

He threw back his head and laughed in genuine amusement.

"Paris! That is no short trip, my friend, nor is it a fun one anymore. There are no less than four checkpoints to go through, and that's taking a God-forsaken roundabout way to avoid the other three!"

"Yes, I know, Jacques, but it must be done, and I cannot go. I have no one to watch the café."

"You have several people who can watch the café," he retorted.

"Yes, but none for that amount of time. I don't trust that I would have a café to return to!"

Jacques studied the other man for a long moment. He'd known Leon for half their lives and felt as if he had known him in a past life as well. They met when they were both still in school and had become fast friends immediately. He believed that there were never two more unlikely people to forge such a friendship, yet here they were. Years later and they were still dragging each other into scrapes.

"What is it this time?" he finally asked reluctantly. "What's so important that you would have me leave my restaurant, my boat, and my men?"

"This." Leon pulled open his jacket and felt along the seam until his hand disappeared into the lining. He extracted a thin packet and handed it to him. "It must get to a man named Nicolas in Paris. It's urgent."

"A man named Nicolas? In Paris? Mon Dieu, there must be hundreds of them!" Jacques muttered, taking the packet and looking at it curiously. "What is it?"

"Nothing that you would want to know about," Leon answered with a grin.

"What's to stop me from getting curious?"

"I know you too well, my friend. You have smuggled enough goods to know when ignorance is the better path."

Jacques grunted and got up, going over to a nearby strongbox and pulling out a set of keys.

"What are you doing?" Leon asked.

"I presume it is too valuable to stuff in my pocket while I'm out after curfew," he said dryly. "I'm putting it in here for safekeeping. It will be safe tonight. I'll get it in the morning when I leave and can secure it in the Citroën."

"You'll do it, then?"

"Yes, but only because I am bored out of my mind. I miss the open sea." Jacques set the packet in the strongbox and locked it again. "And the Spanish sherry. Andalusia is perfect this time of year."

"I'm more partial to rum, myself. My uncle brought a case back from the Caribbean Islands a few years ago. Wonderful!" Leon tilted his head and studied Jacques. "How can you be bored when your restaurant is filled with the enemy every night?"

"It grows tiresome, babysitting the Nazis."

Leon chuckled. "You will join me eventually, you know. It's only a matter of time. You cannot stay on the fence forever, and I'll never see you land on the German side."

Jacques snorted. "I think not. I'll leave the cloak and dagger nonsense to you. Me, I'll wait until I can sail beyond the bloody German perimeter once again."

"I'll wager you wouldn't refuse if it were Mademoiselle Dufour here in my place," he said with a wicked grin.

Jacques threw his head back and laughed. "That little mademoiselle was fascinating, and I've never met a woman who handled being shot at so calmly."

"As I say."

A gold tooth flashed and sparkled under the bare light of the bulb and Jacques winked.

"If Mademoiselle Dufour were here, she could talk me into walking into hell and I would willingly go," he admitted. "But she is not here. I have only you, Leon, and you are a poor substitute."

"I know it." Leon grinned and shrugged. "Such is our life, my friend. We are destined to fall in love with the women we cannot touch."

The two men went to leave, and Jacques flipped the light off before opening the door. They stepped into the alley, and he locked up the storehouse before turning to face his old friend.

"I will see you in a few days."

"Godspeed," Leon said, holding out his hand. "And please don't drink the city dry. Leave some for my comrades."

Jacques gripped his hand firmly and turned to leave. He went a few steps, then stopped and turned back.

"This Nicolas," he said in a low voice. "What is his surname? How do I find him?"

"Go to Maxim's, rue Royale. Speak with the porter Francois."

"And his surname?"

Leon shrugged. "He doesn't have one, and if he does, I do not know it. Just as he does not know mine."

Jacques rolled his eyes. "Of course not. I look for a man with no name. Fantastic."

Leon chuckled and turned to walk in the opposite direction.

"When has that ever stopped you before?" he said over his shoulder. "Good night, my friend, and have a safe journey."

Chapter Fourteen

London

E velyn set her case on the floor near the front door and went into the parlor. Crossing to the desk, she began gathering up papers and notepads. All she had to do was clear off the writing desk and empty the ashtrays, and she would be ready to leave. She had wanted to be on the road already, on her way back to Ainsworth, but the meeting with Bill had taken longer than she'd expected.

He really wasn't happy with her, and in all honesty, she couldn't blame him. She'd lied to him, allowed him to believe that the package everyone and their dog was looking for was still missing, and then she'd gone and invited Cunningham to work for them without consulting him first. Really, she had treated him very shabbily. He was right to be upset with her, and that acknowledgement didn't sit well with her at all. She wouldn't have dreamed of deceiving him a few months ago, but the final letter from her father had led her down a path where she felt that she had no choice.

Evelyn took one last look at the desk and turned to carry her notes and half-written letters to her travel cases in the hallway. She was just tucking them away when the sudden ring of the front doorbell made her start. She straightened up with an involuntary gasp, glancing at her watch with a frown. She wasn't expecting anyone, and she really did want to leave and get out of London before the sun went down and the blackout was enforced.

Stepping over her bag, she went to the door and opened it. One of the messenger boys from Broadway stood on the stoop, and when she opened the door, he touched his cap respectfully.

"Message for you, miss," he said, holding out a sealed white envelope.

"Thank you."

Evelyn took it and watched as he jumped off the top step and took off again, darting down the road. She shook her head and closed the door, turning to go back into the parlor. Ripping open the envelope, she pulled out a single, thin sheet of paper.

There are clear skies over the Red Square.

The words were neatly typed in a single line, and she sucked in her breath. Again? This was the second time in a month that Shustov had sent word that he had a message for her. The last time had been to warn her that the Round Club was in contact with Voss, and that Voss was still hunting for her. A frown settled on her face as she went to the mantel and picked up the lighter next to the cigarette box. What was it now? Was Voss on his way to London himself? As she held a corner of the message to the flame, her lips twisted wryly. She supposed, really, that the entire German army was on its way to London. They just had to get through the RAF first.

The paper caught fire and she set the lighter down, watching as the flames began to lick across the sheet. Somehow, she wouldn't be surprised to learn that Voss had found a way to get into England to look for her himself. She knew that he was furious at his failure to catch her in France, just as she knew that Eisenjager must be just as furious. It really was ridiculous. Why were both German agents so desperate to apprehend her? She was hardly anyone of any importance.

The heat from the flames reached her fingers and Evelyn tossed the burning paper into the empty hearth, watching pensively as what remained curled under the flames, disintegrating until only charred embers were left. It was something that had bothered her all along, this obsession the two German agents had with her. Yes, she had thoroughly tricked one of them in Strasbourg before the war even began, but was that really a reason to still be hunting her two years later?

You cost him a traitor when you distracted them long enough to allow Karl to escape.

She exhaled at the thought, watching as the last of the embers in the hearth flickered out. She supposed that was the crux of the matter. Voss had lost a man who was handing information over to the British because of her. The Nazis didn't take kindly to anyone interfering in their affairs, but most especially young women who bamboozled their higher-ranking officers.

She turned away from the fireplace and looked at her watch again. Letting out a decidedly unladylike curse, she went over to the telephone on the writing desk.

Sitting down, she picked up the receiver and dialed the extension for Lancashire. She would have to tell her mother that she would be staying another night in London, though Lord knew what excuse she would give her this time. But if Shustov had a message for her, she had to retrieve it as soon as possible, and that meant staying in London. She would have to send a telegram to the night manager at the Bellevue Palace Hotel in Bern, and then she had to wait for instructions.

As she waited for the operator to connect her, Evelyn shook her head. It was lucky that she hadn't left when she wanted to after all. She would only have had to turn around and come straight back. At least this way she was already in London.

She pursed her lips thoughtfully, staring at the curtains drawn across the window overlooking Brook Street. Did Vladimir have men in other parts of England? Would she always have to come to London to retrieve messages? Or were there other locations? Despite the warm afternoon, a shiver went through her at the thought. It was bad enough that the Soviet NKVD had agents in London; if they had them all over the country, that was even worse. And, according to Bill, they didn't even have the satisfaction of returning the favor in Moscow!

The call connected and Evelyn gave Ainsworth Manor's number to the operator. A laugh sprang to her lips as she considered the fact that she very well might be considered one of Shustov's assets in England herself. After all, he gave her information to pass on to MI6, and in the process, he was able to glean information from her, she was sure. The only reason she went along with it was because her father had done the same, and Bill and Jasper had both requested that she continue in her father's stead. Although, if she were honest with herself, she was surprisingly comfortable with her association with a senior NKVD officer. He put her at ease each time they met, and in Belgium he had given her valuable pointers on how to conduct herself in the field. They were sensible recommendations that she would never have known otherwise, and for that alone she felt she owed him something.

As she waited for Thomas, their butler, to answer the ringing line, Evelyn's lips tightened. She supposed there was always the possibility that her feeling of obligation, no matter how minor it was, had been Shustov's intention. She was well aware of the psychology behind gaining someone's loyalty through a sense of indebtedness, and she had no doubt that the Soviets utilized that very thing at every opportunity. But whether or not that had been Vladimir's intention, the fact remained that without his gentle guidance that day, she may not have made it as far as she had in this war. And that wasn't very far at all, really, so in her mind, the tips he'd imparted were all the more crucial.

And so she would collect his message and see what was so important that he'd initiated contact once again. The rest would have to be dealt with as it came along.

RAF Coltishall

Miles walked into the recreation room and looked around. Most of the pilots had gone off to the pub, but the few that had remained were scattered about the large room. A steward looked up from where he was drying a pint glass behind the bar and nodded to him cheerfully.

"Evening, sir," he said as Miles walked up. "Pint?"

"Yes, thank you, Charles." Miles looked over to where Chris was slouched in an armchair, reading a newspaper, an empty glass at his elbow. "And another for Flying Officer Field, please."

"Very good, sir."

Miles reached into his jacket breast pocket and pulled out his cigarette case, flipping it open to extract a cigarette. He was tired, but too restless to call it a night and take himself off to his quarters. After completing all the reports for B Flight, he'd stopped by the CO's office for a quick word only to find that he'd gone off to HQ an hour before. He'd hunted Bertie down, but for once that estimable man was at a loss. All he knew was that a call had come in while they were still up requesting Squadron Leader Ashmore's presence at HQ that evening. Miles hoped to God that didn't mean Ashmore was getting reassigned. Aside from being a good and fair CO, Ashmore was one hell of a good flyer. And, Lord knew, they needed to keep all the good pilots they could!

"'Ere you go, sir."

The steward set two full pints in front of him, and Miles nodded, reaching into his pocket and extracting a coin. He set it on the bar and picked up the two glasses, his unlit cigarette dangling from his lips, and turned to make his way over to the corner where Chris was sprawled.

"Still awake, Yank?" he asked, stopping next to him.

Chris started and peered up at him from behind his newspaper.

"Barely," he said, his eyes going to the two pints. "Is one of those mine?"

"I'm certainly not going to drink both of them." Miles handed him one and moved to seat himself in the armchair opposite. "How's your noggin?"

"Oh, fine. I come from a long line of hardheads. It takes more than a bump to do any real damage to us." Chris sipped his beer and set it next to the empty glass. "Tried to tell that to the doc, but he wasn't having any of it. Told me to stay down for the rest of the day."

Miles raised his eyebrow. "Then why were you up with us for that last scramble?"

"Ashmore said we were short a set of wings." Chris shrugged and grinned. "I moseyed over to the hangar, and lo and behold, they were just finishing patching up a Spit, just for me."

Miles bent to light his cigarette, then shook his head, a reluctant grin pulling at his lips.

"And Ashmore cleared you?"

"I didn't ask him. Figured if he wanted me to stay down, he'd tell me to go home."

"I should reprimand you for disregarding the order to stay on the ground. What if you have a concussion?"

"I don't. I'm just dandy. It was ridiculous for me to be sitting it out when there's nothing wrong with me except a scraped forehead."

"Didn't he put a stitch in that?"

"Yeah, so?"

"That's rather more than a scrape, then."

"Not in my book." Chris folded his paper and tossed it onto the table between them. "Will you end up in a jam because I tagged along?"

"No, I don't expect so," Miles admitted. "I doubt anyone noticed, and if the doctor doesn't hear about it, who's to complain? I certainly shan't."

"Not that it did any good, in the end. I didn't hit a damn thing."

"Nor I." Miles exhaled and leaned his head back tiredly. "Seems like we spend most of our time looking for the bastards, then run out of fuel when we find them."

"It all seems like a damned merry-go-round to me."

Miles lifted his head and looked at him. "How so?"

"Well, we get called up, and then by the time we've found them, the Krauts have already hit their targets and are on their way home. We maybe get one or two, then we come down again. Then the whole thing repeats itself. We don't seem to get any further ahead, and they seem to be hitting whatever they like!"

"It would help if the raiding parties were where HQ said they were," Miles murmured, interrupting himself with a wide yawn. "Nine times out of ten they're nowhere near where Cowslip sends us."

"Yeah, why is that?" Chris demanded, pulling out a cigarette case. "You'd think they'd know where the bastards are."

"If I had to guess, I'd say that the radar isn't catching all of them, and the observer corps are miscalculating." Miles shrugged, watching as Chris hunted in his pockets for his lighter. "It's a bloody nuisance, whatever the problem."

"How come 11 Group doesn't seem to have any problems intercepting them?" Chris gave up looking. "Can I get a light?"

Miles reached into his pocket and tossed him his lighter.

"We don't know that they don't."

"Well, they're certainly engaging them enough." Chris paused to light his cigarette before tossing the lighter back. "They're shooting them down every day!"

"And getting shot down," Miles said grimly. "I heard that Kenley lost twelve planes today, along with eight of their pilots! At that rate, I don't see how we can keep pace at all."

Chris was silent for a minute, then he exhaled and shook his head.

"At least they're getting after the bastards."

"You know, for someone who had a close shave today of his own, I'd think you'd be more conscious of the gravity of the situation."

"It's because of my close shave that I'm pissed off! If you think I don't have a huge grudge against the Luftwaffe, think again. I want their asses, all of them."

Miles couldn't stop a chuckle. "Well, I know that feeling well enough. That's how I felt after Dunkirk."

"I just think we could be doing more than what we are."

"No doubt we'll get our chance, Yank."

Chris grunted and reached for his pint. "Not soon enough."

"Are all Americans as eager to get shot at?" Miles asked, tilting his head and studying him.

"I'm not eager to get shot at, just eager to do the shooting."

"Unfortunately, one comes along with the other."

"There you are!" A new voice exclaimed. "I've been looking for both of you!"

"Well, you weren't looking very hard," Miles drawled as Rob dropped into the third chair. "We've been here for the better part of half an hour."

"Ashmore just got back from HQ," Rob told them, leaning forward and bracing his elbows on his knees. "Tangmere lost an entire squadron today. A whole squadron!"

Miles stared at him, his mouth tightening. "How many planes?"

"Eight. And they lost four more on the ground a couple of days ago." Rob shook his head and ran a hand through his hair. "Can you imagine? Everyone, even the squadron leader, just. . .gone!"

"Do you still want to go south and get in the middle of that?" Miles asked Chris.

"It's our job, ain't it?"

Miles shook his head and drained his pint in a few swallows.

"Yes, and we'll do it." He pushed himself to his feet. "As we've been doing it. God help us, though, if we lose any more full squadrons. I'm off. Goodnight!"

"Already? It's only just past nine!" Rob protested, but Miles waved his hand as he turned away.

"I have a letter to write before lights out, and I'm knackered," he said over his shoulder.

Rob grinned.

"Tell m'sister I said hello," he called, bursting out laughing when Miles held up two fingers in a rude gesture on his way to the door.

Evelyn watched as the number fourteen bus slowed to a halt at the curb. She was standing with a group of about seven sailors and three other women. As the bus doors opened, one of the young sailors in front of her turned and smiled, motioning her ahead of him.

"After you, luv," he said cheerfully.

"Oh, thank you," she smiled at him and stepped forward to climb onto the double decker bus.

She'd never ridden a bus in London before, and Evelyn was feeling rather out of her depth. The driver nodded to her cheerfully and, as if sensing her discomfort, asked her where to.

"Piccadilly, please," she said, pulling out her change purse.

He gave her the amount and she handed him the coins, rather shocked at how inexpensive it was. Why, the fare was next to nothing! Why on earth didn't she ride the bus instead of taking cabs everywhere?!

"Is it all right to go upstairs?" she asked, taking the change he handed to her.

"Of course, luv. Just mind your head as you go."

Evelyn nodded and turned to the narrow stairwell that led to the upper level. Gripping the railing, she went up the steps to emerge onto the second deck of the bus. There were only one or two passengers up there at this time of night, and she made her way down the aisle to the seventh row. Reaching it, she slid into the seat on the left near the window and settled her purse on her lap. Her gloved hands gripped the handles and Evelyn was conscious of her heart beating faster than usual.

Her instructions from Philip Moreau, the night manager of the hotel in Bern, had been surprisingly detailed. She was to catch the 8:05 p.m. bus at Covent Garden and take it to Piccadilly. She was to go to the upper deck and sit in this very seat, next to the window. There would be an envelope between the seat and the side of the bus. Retrieve the envelope and get off at Piccadilly.

It had seemed simple enough, but now that she was actually sitting in the seat, Evelyn was struck with how completely surreal the whole thing was. How on earth did Shustov arrange these things? And why? And was his agent still on the bus? Were they watching her even now?

Evelyn's spine stiffened and her chin inched up in reaction to the unsettling thought. While she didn't like the idea of being watched, she supposed that Vladimir would want confirmation that she'd received his message. One of the other three up here must be his agent, but she had no idea which. One was an elderly lady carrying a tote filled with children's toys, one was an army lieutenant who looked as if he'd had one too many pints, and the last was a girl, who looked to be no more than fifteen, dressed in a factory uniform. None were what she'd think of as a Soviet spy, although she realized that any of them could be.

The bus lurched into motion and pulled into traffic, swaying as it picked up speed. Evelyn turned her face to look out of the window over the darkened streets. London at night depressed her these days. While the sun wasn't quite gone yet, the blackout was already in effect. Streetlights were off, and thick curtains were drawn over windows. The streets that once were full of gaiety and lights were now cloaked in blackness, and navigating them was an exercise in self-preservation. It just wasn't the same anymore, and she wondered if it ever would be again. Certainly not until the war was over.

She moved her hand and slid it between the seat and the bus wall, feeling for the envelope. After a moment, something crinkled beneath her fingers, and she felt her heart skip. There! It was right where the instructions had said it would be. Evelyn eased it up and pulled it free, sliding it into her purse in a swift, smooth motion. Snapping her purse closed, she never turned her gaze from the contemplation of the streets passing by beneath the window.

That had been much less exciting than she'd expected, Evelyn decided with a flash of disappointment. It had been almost too easy. She supposed that was a good thing, but somehow, she'd grown used to nothing going as planned. She almost expected complications now.

Of course, she still had to get to Piccadilly and get off the bus, then make her way back to Brook Street. There was plenty of time for something to go wrong, she reminded herself grimly. It was best not to relax just yet.

But the bus arrived at Piccadilly without incident, and Evelyn made her way down the narrow stairwell to get off, nodding to the driver as she passed him. As she stepped onto the pavement, she turned to look up at the second level. The elderly lady was still in her seat, but she didn't even glance at Evelyn as the bus lurched into motion once more. Whoever Shustov's agent was, they hadn't even looked twice at her. Evelyn didn't know which was more unnerving: the fact that he had people in London, or the fact that she couldn't recognize them even when it was obvious they were right in front of her. She had turned and begun walking away from the stop, lost in contemplation, when she bumped into someone in the darkness. Murmuring an apology, she stepped aside and tried to go around them.

"It's quite all—Evie?" A male voice asked in astonishment. "Is that you?"

Evelyn peered up into the face in surprise.

"Is that Stephen? Stephen Mansbridge?"

A grin stretched across the tall man's face, and he laughed.

"I was the last time I checked in the mirror. Has it been so long that you've forgotten what I look like?"

"Goodness, no! It's this blasted blackout. I can't see a thing!" Evelyn laughed and held her hat on her head as a sharp gust of wind swirled down the street. "Although, it's been ages since I've seen you."

"Far too long." Stephen looked around and took her arm, leading her to stand in a darkened shop entryway and out of the flow of pedestrians. "But what are you doing in London? I thought you were stationed on an airfield somewhere!"

"I am, but I was given a few days leave. I came to town for some shopping. How are you? Are you still with the Foreign Office?"

"Oh yes. I'm as busy as ever." He smiled down at her. "If you're in town for a few days, we must go to dinner. I'd suggest it now, but I'm in the devil of a rush, more's the pity."

"Oh, I would love that, really, but I'm leaving to go back to Ainsworth in the morning. I want to spend some more time with Mother before I go back."

"How is she? And Robbie? How is he faring?"

"Oh, everyone's just fine. Mother is worried, of course, but she has Tante Adele and Uncle Claude with her now. Did you know that they escaped France when the Nazis invaded?"

"No! I must try to get out there to visit. Are Gisele and Nicolas here as well?"

"No." Evelyn's smile faded as she shook her head. "No, they remained in France."

Stephen stared at her in astonishment. "They did what?"

"I know, but you know how they are. They didn't want to leave."

"Bloody fools," he muttered. "Still, I suppose that's their choice. If they stay in the unoccupied zone, I'm sure they'll be safe enough," he added with a rueful smile. "I'm sorry, Evie. You must be worried sick about them."

"Yes, but as you say, it was their choice."

Stephen held up his watch and strained to see it, cursing when he made out the time.

"God, is that the time? I really must go. I'll be late for a dinner with the American ambassador."

"My, that sounds terribly important!" Evelyn teased him. "Are you sure you're the Stephen Mansbridge I punched in the nose in Hong Kong?"

Stephen let out a bark of laughter and then grimaced comically.

"I can assure you, my nose is still the same, at any rate. I really must fly. Please give your mother and Robbie my regards!"

"Yes, of course!"

"And the next time you're in London, send a message round to my office and we'll go to dinner."

Evelyn smiled. "I will."

He nodded, kissed her on her cheek, and then disappeared back into the throng of pedestrians. Evelyn watched him go, then turned to walk in the opposite direction, a smile pulling at her lips. Fancy running into Stephen, of all people, in Piccadilly! Her brows came together as she tried to remember the last time she'd seen her childhood playmate. It must have been before she went to Norway. Heavens, was it really that long? That was a lifetime away!

The smile faded with the thought, and she tightened her grip on her purse, thinking of the message inside. So much had changed! The last time she saw Stephen, the war hadn't exploded yet, and she wasn't receiving messages from a Soviet agent on a semiregular basis. Goodness, Norway was only five months ago, yet look at everything that had happened in those five months! It didn't seem possible, really, for so many countries to have fallen to the Nazis in that time.

And now England, Scotland, and Wales were fighting not to join them.

Reaching the corner, Evelyn walked to the edge of the curb and looked about for a taxi. Spotting an unoccupied one coming towards her, she flagged it down, sighing in relief when it pulled to a stop in front of her.

"Brook Street, please," she said, getting in. "Number twenty-four."

"Very good, miss."

The cab pulled away from the curb and Evelyn settled back in the seat, relaxing.

"Did you hear the guns, miss?" the driver asked, glancing over his shoulder at her.

"What? No! What guns?"

"The battery guns. Antiaircraft they call 'em. They were pounding away this afternoon," he told her. "Don't know how you could've missed them. They're loud enough. I reckoned all of London 'eard."

"No, I didn't." Evelyn was shaken. "How awful! The bombers must have come very close!"

"Aye," the cabbie nodded. "But our lads are doing a job up there, right enough. None got through, leastways none that I know of."

"Yes, our pilots are dreadfully brave, doing what they do," she said.

"That they are, miss. The evenin' paper says today saw the most raids yet."

"Did they say anything about losses?" she asked, her heart pounding a little faster.

"Not for today. We got quite a few yesterday, though. I reckon today's figures will be in the mornin' paper." The driver slowed to turn a corner. "Do you have someone in the RAF?"

"Yes. My brother is a fighter pilot." Evelyn felt her throat tighten and she cleared it briskly. "He's stationed up north at the moment."

"Well, God bless 'im and keep 'im safe, miss," he said fervently. "Wot they do is nothing short of a miracle. I saw one of them airplanes fly at a fair before the war. The Spitfire, they called it. It was fair magic, that was."

Evelyn couldn't stop the surge of pride that filled her, or the smile that sprang to her lips.

"Yes, they are. That's what he flies. The Spitfire. He loves it. Says it's an amazing machine."

"Better 'im than me! I come over all unsteady if I 'ave to go up a ladder. Can't imagine flying up in the clouds like that! And then to be shot at while doin' it? Not on your Nelly!"

Evelyn laughed.

"Oh, I don't know. It seems rather exciting. Well, without the shooting part, of course." The laugh faded from her lips. "I suppose they've all got used to getting shot at."

"Just as long as they're doing their fair share of shootin' back," he said with a nod. "That's wot matters now."

"Yes."

Evelyn looked out of the window, falling silent. He was more right than he knew. Their young men had to shoot down Göring's young men at a rate of four-to-one if they were to have any hope of keeping the Nazis out of England.

"Well, here we are, miss," the driver said presently, slowing to a stop outside the house. "You tell your brother that we're all behind him."

Evelyn passed him the fare and opened the door.

"Thank you. I will."

She climbed out and went up the steps as the taxi pulled away. Turning her head, she watched him go before unlocking the door and going inside. The cab driver was a good representation of the people of London, and it comforted her to know that they were so supportive of the RAF. She'd been in France as it fell and had heard what the French people had to say about their air force. They had felt betrayed, and it had showed. God willing, the people of London would never feel betrayed by the RAF.

For if they did, it would be because the Nazis were marching up Whitehall.

Chapter Fifteen

August 19

Evelyn sat down at the kitchen table with a fresh, steaming cup of tea and took a sip before reaching for the envelope. She would love to know how Shustov got the messages into England. It wasn't as if he could simply send a telegram. So how did he do it? And while she was thinking of it, how did he get messages to Moreau in Bern? Those were just two of the many questions she had regarding the mysterious Soviet agent who had been on such close terms with her father.

She turned the envelope over in her hands thoughtfully. She supposed he could have a radio that he used to send coded messages, but how would he send them without them being intercepted by his government? Admittedly, she was far from an expert on the situation within the Soviet borders, but she was fairly certain that government agents were not allowed to send radio messages all willy-nilly. She sucked in her breath. Unless, of course, they were communicating with spies in other countries. That must be how Shustov managed it! Under the guise of receiving information from his assets. She shook her head after a moment. That was if it was even a radio that he used, although she couldn't think of any other way to do this.

She ripped open the envelope and pulled out a folded piece of paper. Opening it, she stared down at the single line neatly typed on a typewriter.

Homer's The Iliad. *English edition gifted to your father.*

Beneath it, two neat columns ran the length of the paper, each containing numbers. Evelyn turned the paper over to find nothing else typed or written on the sheet. She set it down and her lips curved into a smile. It was a code, and she needed a copy of *The Iliad* to figure it out.

Folding the paper, she slid it back into the envelope and picked up her tea. She knew there wasn't a copy there, but her father wouldn't have kept a gift like that here in London. It must be in the library at Ainsworth.. She would look for it when she returned home tomorrow.

Suddenly, Evelyn was exhausted, and she stifled a yawn as she drank her tea. The house was as silent as a home in the heart of London could be, and she was suddenly glad that she hadn't left for Ainsworth Manor this afternoon as she had planned. She would still be driving now, most likely, and that would have been challenging with the sudden fatigue overtaking her. She would finish her tea, go to bed, and get an early start in the morning.

She thought of the cab driver and his claim that the antiaircraft guns had been firing today. How had she missed it? Was it when Bill was here? Or was it later, when she was packing to return home? Either way, she should have heard them. They were massive guns, after all. She shook her head tiredly. As far as she knew, they hadn't been fired before today. The German bombers must have been very close indeed.

A shiver went through her as she thought of the Luftwaffe bombardment she'd endured in the protected trench at Northolt. London had prepared for it. All over the city, sandbags protected government buildings and air raid shelters were clearly marked. Anderson shelters had been erected in every garden where the owners could afford it, and those unfortunates who couldn't were instructed to go to their nearest public shelter in the event of an attack. But even though the preparations had been made, Evelyn could only imagine the chaos and panic if bombs began to fall on London.

Getting up, she carried her empty cup to the sink and rinsed it out, setting it on the draining rack. She supposed it was inevitable that bombs *would* fall on London. The Germans had no qualms about attacking civilians and were, in fact, ordered to do so by their superior officers. Yes, London would be bombed. The only question was when?

Evelyn turned from the sink and picked up the envelope, carrying it with her as she went to switch off the light and head upstairs to bed. For once, she was very glad to be leaving London in the morning, although she was well aware of the selfishness of that thought. But she wasn't sure she could calmly face another round of bombs so close to the last.

And she was certain that her tin hat couldn't.

France

Jacques slowed as he approached his second checkpoint of the day. The first had gone relatively smoothly, although the soldier manning it had been reluctant to believe that he had been allowed to keep his vehicle by the occupying forces. Even after carefully examining his papers, which allowed for his Citroën, the soldier had been dubious. However, unable to find anything amiss with his paperwork, he'd allowed him to continue his journey. Now he had every expectation of facing the same thing. He just hoped that it would go more quickly than the last time.

Following the policeman's hand motions, Jacques pulled to the side of the road and shut the engine off. He watched as the barrier was raised by a German soldier and a military truck rumbled through, coming towards him on the narrow lane. The barrier was lowered once more, and when the truck had passed, another soldier approached the car.

"Papers," he said in heavily accented French.

Jacques nodded and passed them through the window, but the soldier motioned for him to get out of the car. He rattled something off in German and the French policeman stepped forward.

"Step out, please," he translated. "He wants to know where you are going and why."

"Is this really necessary?" Jacques asked, climbing out of the Citroën and speaking in French.

While he spoke German and could understand it very well, he had no intention of making it easy on the occupiers. If they wanted to come into his country and take over, then they could damn well use interpreters.

"Yes. My apologies." The policeman was apologetic. "Where are you going?"

"To Paris."

"And what is your business there?"

"I'm going to deliver pastries to my cousin." Jacques motioned to the box tied with twine on the passenger seat. "They are her favorite, and she is ill."

The policeman repeated this to the soldier in German, and the soldier looked up from his papers, speaking sharply.

"Where does your cousin live?"

"In the 15th arrondissement."

The Frenchman translated and the soldier lowered his gaze to the papers again. After a moment, he folded them and handed them back to Jacques, speaking again.

"What kind of pastries?"

"Cannelés. A café in Bordeaux makes particularly good ones."

The policeman repeated this and the soldiers countenance lighted immediately. He spoke quickly and the policeman looked surprised, then turned to Jacques.

"He has heard of these from his friend who was sent to Bordeaux."

Jacques allowed a wide smile to stretch across his face.

"I will give him one!" he exclaimed. "They are very good, and everyone should have one at least once."

"They must be very good for you to drive them all the way to Paris for your cousin," the policeman said with a cough. "I haven't had the opportunity myself to try them. . ."

"Say no more! You shall try one now," Jacques announced cheerfully.

The man translated for the soldier and the German grinned and nodded. Jacques turned to duck back into his car, pulling the box off the passenger's seat and undoing the twine. The German said something sharply and he felt the policeman put a hand on his shoulder.

"You must let me," he said. "You cannot open it for safety reasons," he added apologetically.

Jacques peered at him over his shoulder incredulously, then straightened, making a face.

"Does he think I will shoot him with a cannelés?" he demanded, then he sighed dramatically and stepped aside. "Very well."

The policeman quickly finished untying the twine, the soldier never taking his eyes from the box, his rifle ready to hand should it be needed. The box was opened and presented to the soldier, revealing that it was, indeed, filled with the little cakes. The German smiled widely and took one, nodding to the policeman. The Frenchman helped himself to one, then handed the box back to Jacques. As Jacques bent over to tie the box closed on the driver seat, he heard murmurs of appreciation behind him. When he'd finished and turned around again, the soldier was just licking his fingers, the cannelés gone.

"He says that it did not disappoint. They are delicious." The policeman told him, his mouth filled with the cake. "They are very good. Thank you!"

"Of course, officer. My cousin will not miss them, I assure you."

The soldier spoke again, and the policeman laughed.

"He says that you have made his day. His breakfast left much to be desired, and this has made up for it nicely."

"I'm glad he enjoyed it. If he goes to Bordeaux, Café Rosa is where he will find them."

The policeman repeated this, and the soldier nodded and rattled something off before nodding to Jacques.

"Danke."

He turned on his heel and called something to the soldier manning the barrier.

"He says he will remember. You may go through. Enjoy Paris."

Jacques nodded and climbed behind the wheel again, starting the engine as the barrier was raised. He pulled back onto the road and drove through the checkpoint, exhaling silently as he did so. Once he was through, he looked in his rearview mirror, watching as the barrier was lowered again. A sudden grin pulled at his lips. He didn't come from generations of successful smugglers for nothing. He now knew how to get through that particular checkpoint without any unpleasantness: it was through that soldier's sweet tooth.

And he had every intention of using it to his advantage.

London

Evelyn finished washing her breakfast dishes and reached for the tea towel to dry them. After a thoroughly restful night's sleep, she felt much more refreshed than she had the evening before. She'd had a spring in her step since she got up, and even the dull, overcast day outside the window couldn't dampen her spirit. It was amazing what a good night's rest could do, she reflected as she dried her plate and put it away. She felt much more equipped to face whatever was in that message from Shustov now, and she was eager to get home to Ainsworth to decode it.

She finished drying, wiped the counter down and hung the towel over the side of the sink to dry. Then, with a final look around the kitchen, she went into the hallway where her cases were, once again, sitting near the front door, ready for her departure.

As she passed the hallstand, the phone rang shrilly, making her start. She frowned, glancing at her watch as she picked up the receiver.

"Hello? Ainsworth residence?"

"Hello? Is that Assistant Section Officer Ainsworth speaking?" A female voice asked over the line.

"Yes, this is Assistant Section Officer Ainsworth."

"This is Sergeant Cunningham ringing."

"Sam!" Evelyn exclaimed in surprise. "I can barely recognize you. It's an appalling connection."

"Yes, it is, rather. I hope I'm not disturbing you? Sir William said that I might reach you there."

"Not at all. You're lucky to have caught me, actually. I was on my way out to return to Lancashire. Is everything all right? You haven't changed your mind, have you?"

"Heavens no!" Sam laughed. "In fact, I'm just about to leave for the station. I'm coming to London to meet with Sir William. We're to go over my training."

"Jolly good!" Evelyn smiled in relief. "I'm sure you'll find it all rather strange at first, but I think you'll do very well."

"I certainly hope so. I don't want to let you down."

"I don't think there's any likelihood of that." Evelyn looked at her watch again. "If you aren't calling to say you've changed your mind, what can I do for you?"

Sam cleared her throat. "It's probably not my place at all, but I wanted to ring and tell you. . ."

She hesitated, then cleared her throat again, and Evelyn felt a wave of foreboding crash over her.

"What is it?" she asked, her voice sharper than she intended.

"It's about Flight Lieutenant Durton." There was another, shorter pause, then Sam spoke again. "He went down over Kent yesterday. One of his squadron thought he saw a chute, but there's been no word from him, and they can't find him. He was posted missing this morning."

Evelyn's gut clenched fiercely as it had so many times when she'd been hit in the stomach by her sensei in Hong Kong. Only this time, it wasn't a physical blow that caused her to want to double over. The breath left her in a whoosh and her legs went weak, causing her to drop heavily into the chair next to the telephone.

"Fred?" she repeated, dazed, her heart pounding.

"I'm so sorry to tell you over the telephone, but I thought you'd want to know," Sam told her. "I know you're close."

"But someone thinks they saw a chute?" Evelyn asked, staring at the wall opposite her while her brain scrambled to cling to some hope.

"Yes, but he wasn't sure that it was Lieutenant Durton's. It was rather a bad scrap, apparently. A lot of aircraft milling about, and several going down." Sam coughed. "He's been posted missing, you know, not killed. He may still turn up."

But Evelyn could hear the doubt in Sam's voice even over the awful telephone line.

"But it's not very likely, is it?" she asked, trying to regain her composure. She took a deep, calming breath. "If he landed safely in Kent, the CO would have received word, either from a hospital or from Fred himself."

"Yes, I suppose so."

Evelyn sucked in another deep breath, forcing hot tears back.

"Thank you for letting me know, Sam," she said, her voice unsteady. "I do appreciate it."

"I'm very sorry, Evelyn. If there's anything I can do. . ."

"No, thank you." Evelyn cleared her throat, trying to loosen the muscles that were insistent on closing up. "I'll be all right."

"I'll ring off, then. Try to enjoy the rest of your holiday."

"Thank you."

Evelyn placed the receiver in the cradle and stared at the telephone for a long moment before she realized it was blurred from the tears that refused to be denied. She felt them overflow her lashes and start to slide down her face. Poor Fred! He'd been so tired when she saw him the other night, absolutely exhausted, but he'd hugged her as if he would never let her go.

A sob escaped and Evelyn leapt to her feet, striding into the parlor and brushing the tears off her cheeks as she went. She knew this could, and most likely would, happen. They were losing pilots in huge numbers every day. Why should Fred be exempt? Or Robbie? Or Miles?

With that thought, more tears came, and she sobbed again. It wasn't fair! This war, this battle, all the lives lost so far; none of it was fair! What did the young men flying against the Luftwaffe ever do wrong to be required to sacrifice themselves like this? What had *any* of them done to be forced into this war?

She opened the cigarette box on the mantel and pulled one out with shaking hands, reaching for the lighter. It took several tries before she could light it, and that only made her more frustrated with the tears streaming down her face and the anguish rolling through her in waves. All at once, she remembered the smell of engine oil and smoke from Fred's jacket the other night as he picked her up. He'd been so. . .alive! Exhausted and decidedly despondent, but very much alive. And now, just like that, he hadn't come back—just like the others in his squadron before him.

Evelyn sank down into a chair and lifted her cigarette to her lips, staring blindly across the sitting room. He'd bailed out, and someone thought they had seen a chute, but they'd all heard rumors of the Germans shooting pilots in the air as they came down with their parachutes. After what she'd seen in France, she could readily believe that they would be so evil as to shoot defenseless pilots. After all, they showed no qualms shooting defenseless refugees on the road. But if that had been what happened to Fred, surely someone would have recovered his body.

She stilled suddenly as an awful thought occurred to her. Was he burned? She sucked in her breath, her stomach clenching again. Had he been so badly burned that his body wasn't immediately recognizable?

Evelyn dismissed that thought almost as soon as it hatched. The pilots flew with identification discs, one waterproof and one fireproof. She'd seen the chain around Fred's neck the other night. While she didn't know if they all wore them about their necks, they all had them. Robbie showed her his at the start of the war when she'd been issued a set herself as a WAAF. No. Even if Fred had been terribly burned, they would know whose body they'd found.

If they found it.

She shook her head, fresh tears springing to her eyes. Poor Fred! Where was he? Had he fallen to earth somewhere remote and just hadn't been found yet? It must be something like that. The RAF simply didn't lose pilots in England. Over the Channel or the sea, of course, but not over England. He had to be somewhere, but if his body had fallen into a remote corner of the countryside, then who knew how long it would be before it was discovered. She couldn't think of anything more horrible.

Evelyn finished her cigarette numbly and stubbed it out into the ashtray. The thought flitted through her mind that she had to clean that ashtray again before leaving for Ainsworth. Somehow, the idea of the mundane task helped to calm her, and after a moment, she got up, picking up the crystal ashtray. As miserable as she was at the moment, life had to continue. It was over for Fred, but not for her.

She had to carry on.

Chapter Sixteen

Broadway

B ill knocked, then opened the door, stepping into Jasper's office with a sense of foreboding. Montclair had sounded none too happy on the telephone a few moments earlier when he rang and asked Bill to come up. In fact, he'd sounded downright irritable.

"Ah, Buckley. Good. Come in, will you?"

Jasper stood near the window with a cup and saucer in his hand, and as Bill closed the door behind him, he saw that two other men were seated in the chairs before the large desk.

"You know Morrow, from the Secret Service, don't you?"

"Yes, indeed. How are you?" Bill crossed the room to grasp Anthony Morrow's hand.

"Hello, Bill. I'm well. How's Marguerite?"

"She's doing well. She's working with downed pilots at the moment, reading to them and keeping their spirits up."

"Jolly good!"

"And this is Frederick Nelson, from the Home Office," Jasper introduced the second man. "He sits on a committee investigating fifth columnists."

"Pleased to meet you, Sir William!" Frederick had a booming voice to go with his ruddy complexion. "Montclair tells me very good things."

"Thank you." Bill shook his hand and Jasper waved to the tea cart.

"Tea?"

"No, thanks. I've had mine downstairs."

"Then pull over that chair from the corner, will you?" Jasper went to sit down behind the desk. "Sorry to call you up here so suddenly. I hope I didn't pull you away from anything urgent."

"Nothing that won't wait, I daresay," Bill murmured, moving a chair over and seating himself.

"Morrow's just been telling me about a situation he's stumbled across," Jasper said once he was settled. "Rather unsettling, actually."

"Oh?"

"He thinks he's found a group of Nazi sympathizers right here in London."

Bill hoped that his face betrayed the correct amount of surprise as he looked from one man to the other.

"Nazi sympathizers?" he repeated in disbelief. "Here in London?"

Both men nodded solemnly, and Bill blew his cheeks out, sitting back heavily in his chair.

"That *is* rather unsettling."

"It was brought to our attention a few months ago, and we've had a man trying to infiltrate their ranks ever since," Morrow told him. "Last week, we got something. A list. However, my man thinks that it's incomplete."

"Good Lord, there's a list?" Bill raised his eyebrows. "How many are there?"

"Over twenty, and that's only the upper levels. We believe they have an entire network of couriers and. . .whatnot." Morrow cleared his throat. "In the normal course of things, we wouldn't be sharing this information with MI6, of course. Montclair has assured us of your discretion."

Bill allowed himself to look amused.

"I should hope so. I'm in charge of all the intelligence coming in from France, Belgium, Holland, and Norway," he said dryly. "It would be a rum thing indeed if I couldn't keep my mouth shut."

Frederick, who had been quietly watching him the whole time, guffawed.

"Quite right," he said with a grin. "Don't take offense, Buckley. It's just that it's devilish tricky. Some of the names, you see, are quite well known to all of us in our social circles. It would cause one hell of a scandal if they were to get out."

"Well, as I haven't been privileged to see the list, I don't think that's much of a concern, gentlemen."

"I think we're getting off track," Jasper said. "Morrow thinks that he's got a lead on Henry, Bill. That's why I called you in."

This time Bill's surprise wasn't feigned.

"What?" he said sharply. "How? And how does he even know of Henry?"

"Well, we aren't getting anywhere, so I read Morrow in on Operation Fawkes last week." Jasper shrugged calmly. "I thought perhaps something might turn up on their side, and I was right."

Bill sternly repressed the trembling of his lips and nodded instead, not trusting himself to say anything just yet. The old fox! He *knew* Morrow had something because Jian had been the one to give it to him. To call Morrow into their hunt for Henry was a stroke of brilliance, and one that Bill wished he'd thought of first.

"I can't tell you much, of course, but my man inside the Round Club says—"

"I'm sorry to interrupt," Bill said, cutting him off. "The Round Club?"

"Yes. That's what the bastards call themselves," Frederick told him. "Bloody ridiculous. It sounds like a boys' club."

"I've never heard of it."

"No, well, neither had we until we came across a message that was supposed to have been burned and wasn't," Morrow said. "As I was saying, my man inside believes that there's a name that wasn't on the list. Someone who is working with the Round Club, and quite high up, as well."

"Then the list is incomplete," Bill stated. "It must be."

"That's just it. My man confirms that the names on it are all the names of the inner circle."

"How does he know?"

"Because he's just become part of it. And before you ask, his name *does* appear on the list."

Bill frowned. "Then why does he think a name is missing?"

"He overheard one of the leaders discussing it. He says that their handlers in Berlin demanded that one name be excluded from their books, and not appear anywhere."

Bill sucked in his breath and met Jasper's gaze.

"Precisely," Jasper said with a nod. "If it is indeed Henry, then he's being protected by the Nazis even now."

"Which means that he has proved himself invaluable to them," Bill said grimly. "It may be worse than we thought. Is there any way to find out more?"

"That's why I'm here," Morrow said with a smile. "Now, my man is more than willing to dig around and see what he can discover, but he will only report to me. His safety is my primary concern."

"Yes, of course. So where does that leave us?"

"If you're agreeable, Bill, we've come up with a plan. It's a bit risky, but if Morrow's mole is as good as he says he is, it could prove to be the answer we've been looking for."

"Well, what is it?"

"We're going to lure him out with something big enough for him to do something reckless," Jasper said.

Bill snorted inelegantly. "He's too careful to be tricked. If he's as well entrenched in Whitehall as we think, it's because he's been doing this for years. He won't fall for any bait unless it's something he knows the Nazis would do anything to have."

Jasper smiled and sat back.

"Exactly. And that's what we're going to use."

Bill felt unease steal through him, and he looked at each man, his eyes narrowed. "What? What are you going to use?"

"The package that Robert Ainsworth smuggled out of Austria just before he died."

Ainsworth Manor

Evelyn sat back in the chair and closed the book, pushing it aside. She had arrived back in Lancashire just in time for tea and had sat down to enjoy it with not only her mother, aunts, and uncle but also Bill's wife, Marguerite. She'd arrived the day before and, from what Evelyn saw at tea, had settled right in to enjoy herself. However, when she began speaking of her work with the burned pilots in the hospital, Evelyn had quickly excused herself. While she'd managed to compose herself on the drive from London, hearing about pilots who had survived their battle only to end up in a hospital in excruciating pain was more than she could handle so soon after Fred going down. Instead, she'd retired to the library to hunt for the leather-bound copy of *The Iliad* that Shustov had given to her father.

Now she stared down at the message from Shustov, her sadness forgotten for the moment as it was replaced by an uneasy feeling of trepidation. Vladimir hadn't minced words in his communication, and she could almost hear him saying it in his even, serious tone.

Eisenjager in Bordeaux. Voss in Paris. Both determined to find you. Using Round

Club to that end. Concerned for your safety should Nazis succeed in invasion. If Britain falls, go to hotel in Bern and make contact. Be prepared to use any means necessary to preserve your identity. Shustov.

Evelyn exhaled and rubbed the back of her neck, feeling the tension there. If England fell, she had loosely planned to flee north to Scotland with her mother and aunts and uncle. While it was unlikely that it would prove to be a refuge for very long, she hadn't thought much beyond that. After all, if Britain fell, there was nowhere else to run. It hadn't occurred to her to leave altogether. Strangely enough, Bill's plan for an invasion was very similar. He'd told her to go to Scotland, to the Highlands. They would meet there. She wondered if he'd given it any thought beyond that. She was sure that he must have. Sir William wasn't the kind of man to simply roll over and allow himself to be executed by the Nazis.

But why was Shustov so concerned with her safety if Britain were to fall?

She pressed her lips together and stared at the paper on the desk pensively. This seemed to be more personal than an informant relationship should be. After all, if Britain fell, their association with their Soviet contact ended. Why would he be so anxious that she get to safety? It couldn't be because of his friendship with her father, could it? Surely that was merely a professional association.

A frown crossed her brow as an idea took hold. Was Vladimir worried that his activities passing information out of the Soviet Union would be uncovered if Britain fell to the Nazis? The Nazis and the Soviet Union held a non-aggression pact and had joined forces to invade Poland. She supposed it was possible that Shustov was worried that his activities would be uncovered by the Nazis if they *were* to invade. But did he really think that she would be the one to talk if that happened? Was that why he wanted her out of England if it came down to it?

Evelyn got up and went over to the window that overlooked the wide gravel driveway where it curved back towards the garage and stables. That really didn't make much sense, she admitted to herself. If Britain fell, the Nazis were more likely to learn of Shustov's association with MI6 from captured documents than from her. And Vladimir had to know that if Britain were truly invaded, many of those documents would be destroyed before they could fall into German hands. All of which led her back to square one. Why was he so adamant that she escape to Switzerland if the worst scenario came to pass? Did he know something that she didn't?

Her lips twisted wryly. Of course he did. Vladimir Lyakhov knew heaps more than she did, and in just about every area imaginable. He'd been at this much,

much longer than she had, and his agency had probably written the book on espionage and spying. They were certainly more adept at it than MI6, as the presence of Soviet agents in London made clear.

Evelyn turned away from the window and went back to the desk, picking up the message and reading it through once more before reaching for a box of matches. Regardless of the reasons behind it, it appeared that her safety was a priority for her Soviet friend, and she wasn't about to argue with getting herself to safety if the Nazis came marching into England. If the RAF failed, and they ended up facing the Nazis as the people in France had, Evelyn would find a way to get herself to Switzerland. She had no choice. That was where her father had multiple bank accounts with enough money to get her, her mother, and their extended family to America. It would be their only recourse, as much as she knew her mother and aunts would hate it. The United States would be the last remaining place of freedom from the Nazi scourge. She would do whatever was necessary to make sure her family got there.

And then she would return to fight back.

London

"Are those going to Sir William, Fitch?"

Wesley Fitch started and spun around, a stack of afternoon correspondence in his hands.

"Oh! Hello, sir. I didn't hear you come up behind me," he told Jasper with a rueful laugh. "Some of them are, yes."

"I'll take them if you'd like. I'm heading that way now."

If Wesley was taken aback, he was too well trained to show it. Instead, he smiled and pulled out a selection from the top of the stack.

"If you're sure, sir," he said, handing them to him. "Thank you."

"Yes, of course."

Jasper watched as the young man continued down the corridor with his usual air of frenzied calm. Every time Jasper saw him, Fitch was hurrying, yet without the appearance of being in a rush. It was the damndest thing; Bill's assistant never slowed to take a breath, but he did it with such calmness that one forgot to notice that he was rushing about like a chicken without a head. He wished his own assistants were that unflappable.

"Your Wesley Fitch is an absolute gem, Bill," he announced, opening Bill's door without warning and going in. "I really don't know where you find your people, but I wish you'd find a few for me."

Bill looked up from the paperwork spread across his desk with a grin.

"Fitch found me, I'm afraid," he said, throwing his pen down and getting up to come around the corner of the desk. "Or rather, his father did, on his behalf. He wanted to join the navy when he came down from Cambridge, but his father thought it would be a waste of his brain. Are those mine?"

"Yes. I told Fitch I'd deliver them." Jasper handed him the stack and seated himself in a chair before the desk. "And was his father right?"

"Undoubtedly. Wesley's been a Godsend, as well you know."

Bill flipped through the envelopes, then dropped them onto his desk and turned to look at Jasper.

"What the hell were you thinking, Jasper?" he demanded, crossing his arms over his chest. "Telling Morrow that we'd use Ainsworth's package to lure Henry out into the open? We don't have the bloody thing!"

Jasper chuckled. "You know that, Buckley, and I know that. But Morrow doesn't."

Bill shook his head and pinched the bridge of his nose.

"And when he finds out that we don't?"

"He won't," Jasper said simply. "I'm sure you can come up with some documents that might pass muster for something that Ainsworth might very well have smuggled out of Austria. Or would you prefer that we use Jian as bait instead? Because that was the other option open to me. I was fairly sure that you would prefer the package."

Bill grunted and dropped his arms, going around his desk to settle into his chair.

"Infinitely," he agreed reluctantly.

"Can you manufacture a few plausible documents, do you think?" Jasper asked after a moment of silence.

"What? Oh, yes, of course. I'll come up with something. Will Henry have to see them?"

"Hopefully not, but we'd best be prepared for the possibility."

"In that case, nothing that is in active files. Very well. I'll put something together that we can use." Bill sat back in his chair and studied Jasper. "But how will we draw Henry out when we don't even know how to get to him?"

"We won't have to." Jasper crossed his legs comfortably. "Morrow's taking care of it. Gilhurst will make sure that the existence of the package is leaked into the Round Club. Once he's done that, all we have to do is sit back and wait. Henry will take the bait. He can't afford not to."

"We know for certain Lord Anthony is Morrow's mole inside? He told you?" Jasper scoffed and shook his head.

"No, of course not. He's as closed as a clam about his agents, as well he should be. But Jian's report stated that Gilhurst was working with Morrow. Who else would be able to infiltrate the inner circle so convincingly? It must be Gilhurst."

"Does Morrow have a plan to get him out if everything goes sideways? They won't take kindly to him setting up one of their own."

"It's my understanding that they won't know it was Gilhurst who released the information." Jasper tilted his head and frowned. "This isn't the Secret Service's first time on the roundabout. It's not like you to be so reticent in an operation, Bill. What's on your mind?"

"Oh, I don't know." Bill sighed and rubbed his eyes tiredly. "I suppose this invasion nonsense has me a bit rattled. I've been working on the contingency plan should the RAF fail to keep the Luftwaffe out."

"Well, that's enough to make anyone see the dreary side of anything," Jasper said sympathetically. "It must be done, though. If the Nazis make it as far as London, we can't leave anything behind for them to find."

"I know."

Jasper watched him for a moment, a keen look in his eyes.

"You're worried," he stated. "Is it Jian? Or the Czech lad, Oscar?"

"Both, and many others. They're all here, and the Nazis would love nothing more than to get their hands on all of them." Bill got up restlessly and came around the desk to open the cigarette box. "And don't forget General de Gaulle. The French want to execute him for treason. Cigarette?"

"No thanks."

He nodded and took one, extracting his lighter from his pocket.

"Well, de Gaulle and the other foreign ministers will have to make their own arrangements, and I'm sure that they already have. For ourselves, we have the shelters built and prepared in Scotland," Jasper reminded him as he lit his cigarette. "They're there for just such an event. Our people and operations will move north and the battle hubs along the Scottish border will be the ace up our sleeve. The Germans won't be able to see them, and they certainly have no idea they're there. The local populations don't even realize they exist."

"Yes, I know." Bill leaned against his desk. "I know all the underground bunkers are in place. However, it won't be very much of a consolation if we're overrun with Nazis."

"We must have faith that our lads in the RAF will prevail, Bill." Jasper cleared his throat. "We can't control what happens above our heads, but we can damn well control what happens down here. Catching Henry will go a long way to ensuring Jian's safety, at least, as well as removing what's become a rather irritating thorn in our sides."

Bill couldn't help but laugh at the calm, dry statement.

"That's quite the understatement," he murmured. "Henry's been nothing short of a bloody nuisance."

"And we have a chance to finally catch the bastard, so let's not bugger it all up, hm?"

Bill nodded. "No. I'll get the package put together and let you know once it's ready. It will take a few days. I'll have to find some authentic scraps to use, perhaps from the archives."

"Good man." Jasper stood and buttoned his jacket. "Why don't you knock off and get away from this place. Go out to dinner. Take Marguerite. Get some air."

"I'm fine, Jasper. Really."

Jasper glared at him.

"No, you're not, Bill. You're showing signs of stress. I won't have you over-working yourself so early in this war. We've a long way to go yet."

"If the Nazis succeed in their invasion scheme, it won't be such a long way," Bill retorted, stubbing out his half-smoked cigarette.

"Yes, well, if the Nazis succeed, that's another problem for another day. Today, you're my problem, and I want you to take a break. I mean it, Bill. Leave and take your wife out."

"She's in Lancashire at present, and I'm driving up myself tomorrow to spend a few days with her," Bill said, going back to his seat behind his desk. "I did tell you about it last week. I'll rest then."

"Lancashire?"

"Yes. She's gone to visit Madeleine Ainsworth and her sister, from France, you know."

"Ah yes! Of course. The family refugees from Paris are staying there, aren't they?"

Bill choked down a laugh. "Good God, I wouldn't dare call them that to their faces."

"Well, that's what they are, isn't it? No shame in it. London's full of Europe's elite at the moment. King Haakon and the Crown Prince are hunkered down in Buckingham Palace, and Queen Wilhemina has taken up residence in Eaton Square."

"Yes, but I shudder to think what Adele Bouchard would say if I pointed out that she was here in exile." The grin pulled at his lips again. "I daresay I wouldn't come out on the winning side of that encounter."

"Then you'd best not mention it. I need you," Jasper said cheerfully, going to the door. "Do give Madeleine my regards, won't you? And your wife, of course."

"Yes, I will."

"And Bill?"

"Yes?"

"Don't come back until you're rested and in a better frame of mind."

Chapter Seventeen

August 20

Henry ducked into the crowded pub and looked around, scanning faces until he found the one he was looking for. He made his way to the end of the bar where a dark-haired woman in a conservative suit was chatting with two other girls, also in office attire. She looked up as he approached, and her eyes widened in surprise as her lips parted on an involuntary smile. She murmured something to her companions and moved to meet him halfway.

"Darling! What are you doing here?" she asked, her eyes meeting his in question. "I thought we were meeting later this evening."

"We need to talk, Molly," he told her briskly. "Preferably not in the middle of this rabble."

The smile never left her lips, but her eyes narrowed a bit and she nodded.

"Very well. Give me just a moment."

She went back to her friends, gathering her purse and making her excuses, and a moment later was back at his side.

"Shall we go to the park across the road?" she asked as they moved to the door of the pub. "It should be quiet this time of day."

"Yes, all right."

They exited the pub and Henry settled his hat on his head again before lightly grasping her elbow and guiding her across the busy London street to the little park.

"I apologize for pulling you away so abruptly," he said once they'd gained the other side. "Mata did insist that I find you immediately."

"Mata!" Molly exclaimed in surprise. "What is it? Has something happened?"

"In a way." They walked into the park, and he let his hand fall away from her arm. "She's become convinced that we have another spy in our midst."

Molly gaped at him for a silent moment, then shook her head disgustedly.

"After what happened in Weymouth, she's seeing them everywhere," she muttered. "Who is it this time? A scullery maid? The footman?"

"Actually, I think she believes that it's one of us," Henry said calmly.

"What?!"

His teeth flashed white in the dusk. "I know. Utterly absurd, of course."

"Why would she think such a thing?"

"She's convinced herself that the Secret Service has that damned package you lost, but they haven't made any moves to apprehend any of you."

"So?"

"So in her ridiculous mind, that must mean that one of us is holding them off while we set her up to be captured."

Molly stopped walking and turned to face him.

"You're joking!"

"I wish I were. I had it from Martin last night. He stopped round my club to have a bit of a chat and warn me. Said that Sir Ronald was also suspicious. I thought it was all a load of bosh until Mata called me round this afternoon."

"What did she say?"

"A lot of damned nonsense," he said frankly. "I managed to smooth her feathers and calm her down, but she wants to have a go at you now."

"Oh, for the love of. . ." Molly cursed and started walking again. "She still blames me for the package going missing in the first place. Though what she thought I could do about it when I was lying unconscious, I really don't know."

"I know."

"Do you think she'll expose us?" she asked, glancing up at him.

"Hardly that. To expose us is to expose herself, and she has a very healthy sense of self-preservation, our Mata." Henry took her hand and placed it in the crook of his arm, patting it comfortingly. "She's just fishing, and there's nothing for her to find. Neither of us are betraying the Round Club. Though, I am curious as to where she got the idea that the authorities would hold off arresting anyone at the request of one of us. Seems barmy to me."

"I don't care where she got the idea, only that she believes it!"

"Oh, I wouldn't worry too much about it. Answer her summons, act outraged, and demand her proof. That's what I did, and it stopped her in her tracks."

"Yes, but you're much higher up on the food chain than I am," she muttered. "She can make life very difficult for me."

"Not for much longer, my dear."

"What do you mean?"

Henry stopped walking and took her hands in his. He stared down at her in the fading light and smiled faintly.

"Do you trust me?"

"Of course I do."

He looked around and spotted a bench not far away. Turning, he led her to it.

"You know that I've been working independently for a handler in Berlin for over four years?"

"Yes."

"Well, they've asked me to find someone here in England. When I do, I will be assured of standing much higher in their esteem than the Round Club, or Mata."

"I think that you already do," she said with a smile. "Why else would they demand that your name not appear on the books?"

He looked at her sharply. "How do you know that?" he demanded.

"Oh, Mata has been very vocal with her thoughts on the matter." Molly laughed and fished in her purse for a packet of cigarettes. "I think she's jealous. You obviously command a higher opinion in Berlin than she does, and she can't tolerate that. Do you have a light?"

Henry pulled out his lighter and held it to her cigarette.

"I wish she hadn't told anyone," he murmured, snapping the lid closed when she lifted her head.

"Why? No one thinks twice about it. If anything, she's making herself look a fool, and everyone can see that. Except, perhaps, Sir Ronald," she added thoughtfully. "And why doesn't he have a silly codename?"

"Because he refused it. Told her he wasn't a schoolboy, and he wasn't about to play silly schoolyard games." A smile cracked his countenance. "I wish I'd been there to hear it."

"So do I!" Molly smoked for a moment, then looked at him curiously. "Why did you tell me about your operation for Berlin?"

"Because, my dear, anyone who helps me will be mentioned in my report when I succeed," he said, smiling at her. "So you see, you have nothing to fear from Mata. You will be protected by your association with me."

"Do you need help, then?"

"If you're willing."

She laughed and blew smoke into the air.

"Of course, darling! Who are we looking for?"

"A spy. One of ours."

Molly raised her eyebrows and stared at him. "And by one of ours, you mean. . ."

"England's. MI6, to be precise."

Her mouth dropped open and the laugh left her face.

"A British spy?" she repeated, lowering her voice into a whisper. "Are you insane?"

"Are you frightened?"

"Are you suicidal?" she countered swiftly. "Think about this!"

"Oh, I have, extensively, and I think I've hit upon the way to find them."

"And when you find them? Then what?"

"The Nazis will be here in a few weeks," he told her. "The RAF can't hold out much longer. They have hardly any fighters left, and they're losing pilots at an unsustainable rate. When the air force fails, the Germans will land and take over."

"And you'll turn over their spy," Molly finished. She was silent for a long moment, then she shook her head. "And if the RAF does hold out?"

"Unlikely, but if that were to happen, then I forward the spy's identity and location to Berlin, and they'll handle it in their own fashion."

She stared at him. "How? It's not as if they can come here and arrest them!"

Henry stared silently back at her, waiting patiently. He didn't have to wait long. Molly suddenly sucked in her breath.

"They'll kill them!" she exclaimed. "They'll have *you* kill them."

"Perhaps not. Perhaps someone else." Henry shrugged. "It doesn't matter. My part would be finished, a success, and we will be protected from any of Mata's nonsense."

Molly was silent, smoking her cigarette and staring out over the path that wound through the park. He watched her for a moment, then sighed.

"What is it?"

"I don't know. I'm not sure that I'm comfortable with being responsible for someone's death," she said slowly. "It's one thing to desire a regime change and work for that, but it's quite another to condemn another human being to their death."

"You were prepared to kill on the road to Weymouth," he pointed out logically.

"Yes, and it's been eating at me ever since," she confessed, turning to look at him. "In a way, I'm glad I was knocked unconscious. It prevented me from doing something that I think I would have regretted for the rest of my life."

"They're a spy, Molly." Henry tried a different tact. "They've been responsible for countless other deaths, German deaths. It's what they do. It's only fair for the

Nazis to want revenge. And besides, we don't know that they want the spy dead. What's more than likely is that they want them for questioning, to learn what they know and who their contacts are in France."

"And once they have their information?"

"Probably the work camp," he lied with a shrug.

Molly's eyes met his searchingly for a moment, looking for any sign that what he said might not be true. His shoulders relaxed imperceptibly when she finally lowered her gaze and nodded.

"Very well. How are we going to find this spy?"

"Identification cards," he said promptly.

"Identification cards?"

"Yes. Every government department has them, and they all include a photograph. In the case of MI6, two photographs are created, one for the identification card and one for the agent's file."

"You want to find them from a photograph in MI6's classified and secure files?" Molly dropped her cigarette butt on the ground and put it out under her shoe. "That's impossible!"

"For me, yes. But not for you."

"I can't get into MI6's files!" she exclaimed. "I don't have anywhere near the clearance needed for that."

"No, but your boss does."

"Lord Halifax? Don't be ridiculous."

"Molly, trust me. I've worked out just how you can do it."

She exhaled loudly and shook her head.

"I don't care what you think you've worked out. I'm telling you that it's not possible. Why, I don't even know what the person looks like! So the photograph will be of no help."

Henry smiled.

"Oh, but it will, my dear. You see, I happen to have a description, along with their operational codename."

RAF Coltishall

Miles' pen moved across the paper, then stopped. He was tired and should, by rights, be in bed, but he was too restless to sleep. He hadn't had much energy or inclination to answer the letters that had begun to mound on his desk of late, so this seemed as good a time as any to try to tackle them. He'd picked out his mother's last letter to start, thinking that it would be quick and easy. After all, his missives to her were usually only a page or so long. However, once he'd pulled a fresh piece of stationery towards him, he'd been stumped. What on earth should he write? That they'd lost three Spitfires and one pilot in the past two days? That would only serve to worry her, but what else did he have to say? That they were unfairly outnumbered up there? That the German pilots' skill was ripping their new, young pilots to shreds? That half of their replacement pilots had less than six hours in a Spit?

Miles read the few lines he'd managed and made a disgusted noise, balling the paper up and tossing it into the bin. That was no good. He'd have to start again. There wasn't any possibility of his mother finding what he'd eaten for dinner interesting. Nor did she care that the tea this morning had been quite cold. He'd have to do better than that. But what? What would he say? That his American friend had almost burned to death when he was shot up and his engine failed whilst trying to land?

A soft knock fell on his door and Miles turned in his chair, calling the invitation to enter. Rob poked his head in, looking around, then stepped into the room when he saw Miles sitting at the desk.

"Oh good, you're still up," he said, closing the door.

"Couldn't sleep."

"Neither can I." Rob crossed the room and dropped onto the foot of the bed. "Can't stop my mind from churning. Writing letters again?"

"Trying to." Miles capped his pen and dropped it onto the desk. "I can't seem to think of anything to write to my mother. Everything is either far too mundane, or far too honest."

"I know what you mean. I have the same trouble with mine. It'd never do to worry the old girl, but what else is there to say?"

"Precisely." Miles sat back in the chair and stretched. "I tried to write to your sister the other night. Gave up halfway through."

"At least you don't have to worry about sugarcoating anything to her. She's on a fighter station in 11 Group. Not much you can say that she doesn't already know, I'll wager."

"I suppose not." Miles frowned. "I had a letter from her today. Northolt was bombed. Sounds as if she was there when it happened."

Rob sat up, his face grim.

"What? I thought she was at Ainsworth!"

"So did I. She said she had to go sign some forms or some such nonsense." Miles picked up his cigarette case from the desk and began to feel in his dressing gown pockets for his lighter. "She mentioned it in passing. Said not to worry, she's as fit as a fiddle."

"Easy for her to say not to worry," Rob muttered, getting up and offering his own lighter. "Did she say how the pilots are getting on?"

"Not well, I'm afraid." Miles lit a cigarette and offered the case to Rob. "It sounds like they're losing quite a few. Her friend Durton lost both of his wingmen and his CO in the same day. He's a flight leader now, bumped up when his went down last week. So his squadron is getting pummeled right enough, at any rate."

Rob lit a cigarette, then shook his head.

"Damn. His CO as well?"

"Sobering, isn't it? We may be losing a Spit here and there, and the odd pilot, but at least we still have Ashmore."

"Have you heard about Barker?" Rob asked, sitting on the edge of the bed again.

"The lad that was shot down over the sea yesterday?"

"Yes. I spoke to Bertie before I came up. He was picked up by a fishing trawler and taken to a hospital. Poor bastard never regained consciousness. Died this morning. I only had chance to speak to him once, and that was only to offer him a light."

"That leaves Green section down one," Miles exhaled. "He was only here a day or two!"

"What can the RAF expect when they're sending us replacements with fuzz on their cheeks and only a few hours of flying time? No wonder 11 Group is losing so many."

"Did you see that London was bombed Sunday?" Miles asked suddenly.

"Yes. Chris showed me the newspaper yesterday. Or was it the day before?" Rob shook his head tiredly. "Can't remember a damn thing anymore. It said the antiaircraft guns were going all afternoon. It wasn't very bad, though, was it?"

"No. One bomb, and no one was killed. Made a hell of a mess, though."

"I suppose more of that will happen if they can get through." Rob scratched his jaw thoughtfully. "Strange, though. I thought Jerry was going for all the airfields, not London."

"They are, but I suppose one went astray. Horrible thought, though, bombs falling on London." Miles tapped ash into the ashtray on his desk. "Ashmore said that Sunday was the largest day for raids yet. Over seven hundred bombers and their fighter escort came over just in the afternoon. He thinks we'll start getting called in to help out over London."

"I thought we already were," Rob said with a short laugh. "We certainly seem to go south quite a bit, but we never see anything."

Miles' lips twisted humorously. "You've been speaking to our American friend. He's just about beside himself with the order of battle."

Rob chuckled. "I know. I keep telling him that we'll get sent into it soon enough. You'd think after his brush with death the other day, he'd be feeling a bit more mortal than he is."

"You would, wouldn't you?" Miles grinned. "I'll tell you what, I wouldn't want to pick a fight with America. Not if they're all like Chris."

Rob nodded, then sobered and looked at Miles.

"In all seriousness, Miles, do you think we're winning this thing? Or is the press just blowing smoke?"

"What do you mean?"

"Well, the papers all say that we're shooting down more than they are, but it certainly doesn't look that way to me." Rob frowned. "For example, they said we shot down seventy-five bombers the other day, for a loss of only twenty. But if Northolt lost three pilots from the same squadron in one day, and Tangmere lost an entire squadron in one day, and Kenley lost eight in one day. . .well, you can see where I'm going. It seems to me that we're losing a lot more than the press is letting on."

Miles was silent for a long moment. Rob was right, of course. What they were hearing and seeing every day certainly did seem to be at odds with what the newspapers were reporting.

"Yes, it does seem to be going worse than the newspapers are admitting," he finally said. "But would you really have the general public know what we know? Hell, we don't even want our mothers to know."

"That's true," Rob admitted. "Do you think the press might be getting it right, though? Do you think we might be winning?"

"I think it's too early to think anything. We're shooting the bastards down, but they've got a lot more to send over, while we don't have any reserves."

"Well, to hear the RAF tell it, we do. We're it. We're the reserves," Rob muttered. "Then you think the rags are generally right?"

"I think if they're right, the Nazis won't invade. If they're wrong, we'll know soon enough."

Chapter Eighteen

Paris

C aptain Beaulieu stood behind a trio of high-ranking German officers, watching as the maître d' smiled and nodded to them. It was odd how quickly he'd grown used to the gray Nazi uniforms and the sound of German being spoken almost everywhere in France. Odd and unpleasant. Though Jacques would never admit it to Leon, he hated the German occupiers as much as his old friend did. The difference was that he'd spend his life working around the authorities and making a profit from them, and the Nazis were just another authority that was able, in his mind, to be profitable. He didn't need to like them, however, and he didn't. Not at all. As far as he was concerned, they were every bit as bad as the idiot Pétain who'd declared that dancing was of the devil and outlawed all public dancing. Absolutely absurd, and if the puppets in Vichy thought for one moment that anyone was complying with that particular order, well, then he had some property in the Americas that he'd let them have cheap. Between the puppet government's stupid laws and the Nazi's curfews and identity papers, he had no love for any of the authority set over the common man. But that didn't mean he was going to cut off his nose to spite his face. No. He would befriend them, use them, and help kick them out at the very first opportunity.

Despite his harsh thoughts, a pleasant smile graced his lips when one of the officers glanced back at him. The man's haughty look slid to the stunning woman on Jacques' arm, and the coldness disappeared instantly, eliciting a silent, internal laugh. Colette had that effect on every man who clapped eyes on her, himself included, which was precisely why Jacques had brough her along to the restaurant.

Upon arriving in Paris, it hadn't taken him long to discover which establishments had been requisitioned by the occupying forces and which had remained open to all. And, after a thoroughly enjoyable evening spent in the company of

Colette and a few other cabaret dancers, he'd discovered just about everything he needed to know about Paris life under the Occupation. It wasn't good, but it was also not as bad as he'd been expecting. Yes, several of the better hotels had been requisitioned for German officers, and yes, there were posters up all over the city listing the laws being imposed on the people, but he'd been expecting much worse. At least some of the restaurants were still open to the public, and some of the theatres. He glanced down at the woman on his arm. And, of course, the cabarets were still open.

"Will you excuse me, my sweet?" he asked, releasing her hold on his arm. "I'll only be a minute. I must check my hat."

She murmured her assent and he turned towards the men's cloakroom, reflecting that he wouldn't be surprised if the German officers tried to commandeer her company for the evening. If they tried, they were doomed to disappointment. Colette also had no love for the occupiers, and while she was paid to tolerate them in her professional capacity, she would not welcome their society outside of that. He almost wished he could watch from around the corner, but he had business to attend to. As much as he was enjoying himself in Paris, he wasn't here solely for pleasure.

"Good evening," he murmured to the boy behind the counter, handing him his hat. "Tell me, could you point out Francois to me? He's a porter. I'd like to thank him for a service that he performed for my brother."

"Yes, monsieur. He is over there."

The boy pointed him out to Jacques, and he smiled, slipping him a coin as he took the ticket for his hat. The boy's eyes widened, and he swiftly pocketed the coin.

"Merci!"

Jacques nodded and turned to leave, moving towards the porter who was standing just outside the cloakroom.

"Pardon," he said to the man apologetically. "I'm looking for Francois?"

"And you've found him, monsieur," Francois said pleasantly. "In what way may I be of service?"

"I'm looking for an old acquaintance of mine. From my school days, you understand. I ran into some of the old crew last night and asked after Nicolas, but it seems no one has seen him for ages. Pierre, he always knows everything, thought that he dines here quite a bit, but no one seems to have seen him recently." Jacques smiled engagingly and spread his hands helplessly. "I realize that this is quite out of the ordinary, but I owe him a debt, you see. Have since we were children. I didn't have the means to repay him then, but now, well, life has been good to me."

Francois smiled politely and nodded.

"I understand, monsieur. Your friend, he would be about your height? Dark hair?"

Jacques grinned widely. "That sounds like him, unless he's going gray from all the excitement around Paris recently."

Francois was betrayed into a small laugh.

"Not he. Nicolas is the same as he always was," he said. "Indeed, he comes here often. Maxim's has the honor of being a favorite of the monsieur."

"When might I be able to catch him, do you think?"

"If you return in two nights, you should catch your friend. He usually arrives around seven."

"Merci!"

Jacques turned to leave, and his hand brushed the porter's, depositing a coin into a ready palm. It seemed as though he would be back in two nights' time. What a nuisance! He'd been hoping to resolve this business of Leon's tonight and be on his way back to Bordeaux by then. Still, he reflected, there were any number of ways to amuse himself in the meantime. He caught sight of Colette, waiting near the maître d', and smiled as he joined her.

"Oh, you're back! Thank goodness. I'm starving, darling," she exclaimed, tucking her hand into his arm.

Jacques smiled down at her and nodded to the maître d'.

"Then, by all means, we shall eat!"

Eisenjager watched as the man walked into the restaurant with the woman on his arm, for all the world as if he owned Paris. Once the door had closed behind the couple, he waited a moment, then moved from behind the lamppost where he had been watching from across the street. Looking around, he crossed the road and continued walking down the pavement, passing the restaurant. As he did so, he glanced through the doors. The thick, ornate glass in the heavy doors made it difficult, but he could just make out the captain and his companion standing behind a group of German officers, presumably waiting for the maître d' to show them to their table. His stride never faltered and within seconds, he was past the restaurant and moving steadily along the street.

He'd followed Jacques Beaulieu from Bordeaux when, quite by accident, he spotted him stowing a case in the back of his car very early in the morning. It was a piece of luck, really. He'd been on his way to the Café Rosa for what he fully anticipated would be another uneventful morning spent watching for the mysterious Jeannine. Upon seeing his other person of interest preparing for some kind of trip, he'd made the decision to temporarily abandon the pâtisserie for the much more interesting task of staying with the enigmatic captain.

It hadn't been easy to avoid being seen once they'd left the city behind, but Eisenjager wasn't considered one of the best assassins in all of Europe for nothing. The farther they got from Bordeaux, the more curious Eisenjager became. His suspicions that the man was going to Paris were soon confirmed, and by evening, he'd been able to close the gap between them as the urban traffic increased on the roadways.

Crossing the road again, Eisenjager turned to retrace his steps on the other side, his eyes going back to the signature red awning of Maxim's. If he'd been hoping for the captain to engage in openly questionable activities in the capital city, he was doomed to disappointment. So far, Beaulieu had been nothing but predictable, given what Eisenjager knew of the man.

Upon arriving, he'd checked into a modest hotel in the 9th arrondissement and had immediately gone out in search of entertainment. Within hours, he was ensconced at a table in Les Folies Bergères, one of the more intimate cabarets in the city. And there he had remained until curfew, at which time he left with two dancers, one on each arm. It appeared, at least for now, that Beaulieu was simply intent on enjoying himself during this unexpected and random trip to Paris.

Eisenjager seated himself on a bench that afforded him a clear view of the front of Maxim's and pulled out a packet of cigarettes, reflecting on the turn of events that had led him here. He hadn't been sent to Bordeaux to watch the captain, but rather to eliminate an influential French official who had been spying for Hamburg and, in the process, had become aware of some information that the Abwehr would rather remained secret. The man had been an unpleasant but useful tool up until that incident, when he became a much larger liability than the Nazis were willing to have running free. Eisenjager had completed his mission three days after arriving in the south of France and had remained in the city to resume his own, private, hunt for the woman associate of the English spy.

Now lighting a cigarette, Eisenjager admitted to himself that he was fascinated by the reckless captain from Bordeaux. They said he was a smuggler, and he could fully believe it, though the German army had found no evidence of it. He certainly was in the happy possession of more disposable income than any other restaurant owner in the coastal city, and it appeared that the German officers who regularly skipped out on their tabs in his establishment weren't making a dent in his reserves. Not only that, but they were welcomed back with ready smiles. The captain was up to something, there was no doubt in his mind about that, but what? He'd thought perhaps this trip would shed some light on it, but alas, it didn't appear as if it would amount to much.

Still, he would continue to watch the man and follow him back when he was finished here, provided that his handler didn't send him elsewhere beforehand. Eisenjager hadn't earned his reputation over the years by taking anything for granted, or by being impatient. Eventually, either the captain or the baker would lead him to the woman he was looking for.

He simply had to wait.

"Really, Nicki, you're wearing a path in the rug," the lovely, dark-haired beauty complained, looking up from her book. "What is the matter with you tonight?"

"I don't know." Her brother sighed and crossed the room to throw himself into a chair. "I'm restless. This curfew is ridiculous."

"I don't really see that it's very bad," she said thoughtfully, closing her book. "After all, it isn't as if we pay much attention to it. We just can't go to the nightclubs and dance until dawn anymore. But it's easy enough to sneak around to our friends."

"That's just it, Zell," he said with a frown. "I'm tired of it all. Being told that we cannot dance, we cannot listen to jazz, we cannot read certain materials. Do you know, I even heard that they are going to begin to ban books? As they did in Berlin?"

His sister looked at the book in her hand in alarm and set it aside.

"I'd like to see them try to take my books," she muttered, getting up and going over to the sideboard where a bottle of cognac sat with two glasses. "Perfectly horrid idea!"

"Yet it will happen, Zell. You know that it will." He exhaled and felt in his jacket for his cigarette case. "If you're pouring a drink, I'll take one."

"When is this man going to come? The one that Leon told you about?"

"In another hour," Nicolas said, glancing at his watch. "He will come to the kitchen door."

Gisele turned with the bottle in one hand and a glass in the other.

"What about Eloise?" she asked in alarm. "What will we tell her?"

"Oh, that's all right. She's gone out to her sister's. Won't be back until morning." Nicolas lit a cigarette. "And Marcel won't hear a thing from his rooms upstairs."

Gisele Bouchard met her twin's eyes and nodded, turning to finish pouring the drinks. When they made the decision to remain behind in France rather than go to England with their parents, she had thought it would be an adventure. And so it was, right up until they finally returned to Paris and to the reality of the Occupation.

"Do you think perhaps we should have gone to England with Maman and Papa?" she asked, carrying the glasses over to hand him one.

"And not raise a finger to defend France?" he raised an eyebrow as he took the drink from her. "What's got into you? This was all your idea!"

"Yes, I know." She returned to her seat on the settee and sipped her drink. "It's only that. . .well, I didn't think I would dislike it so much."

"Dislike what? Living under the German boot?"

"No, I knew I would hate that. I suppose I didn't expect to dislike the Germans themselves so much." She set her glass down on the little table next to her elbow and crossed her legs carelessly, looking across to her brother. "I suppose I thought they would be like us, but they aren't. They're arrogant and condescending, and most of the time I just want to punch them."

"That's what you get for being so damned attractive," her brother said ruthlessly. "They look at you as their rightful spoils, my dear sister, just as we knew that they would. Anyway, it isn't any easier for me. I have to pretend to be impressed by their military conquests and let them win at cards. Do you have any idea how difficult it is to lose so much at cards?"

That brought a laugh to Gisele's lips.

"Is it very terrible?" she asked sympathetically.

"Yes!"

She sighed and swung her foot, studying her heeled slipper thoughtfully.

"I don't suppose it's any worse than trying to keep that American's hands off me. What was his name? The one who was going about with Marc Fournier for a while last year."

"Lord, I don't remember. I remember him, but not his name." Nicolas studied her for a moment. "Just say the word, Zell, and we'll go back to the chateau. We don't have to do this here, you know. We can help gather information in Monblanc just as well as we can here."

"No, we can't, and you know it as well as I do. The High Command is here, in Paris. If we're going to pass on anything worth dying for, we have to stay here. At least for now."

"Not at the risk of you being assaulted at every turn."

Gisele laughed, reaching for her drink.

"I'm hardly being assaulted. Annoyed is more apt, I think, and it will be worth it if we can undermine their silly regime."

Nicolas tapped ash into the ashtray at his elbow and finished his drink in one swallow before getting up for a refill.

"Do you really think this scheme of yours will work?" he asked over his shoulder as he went to the sideboard. "Do you really think that we can get them to transmit the messages themselves for MI6 to hear?"

"Of course I do. I wouldn't have suggested it otherwise."

"How will you get the messages into the transmissions?"

"Oh, that's the easy part," she said cheerfully. "I've already arranged it. The difficult part will be getting them to the right operator."

Nicolas turned from the sideboard, a look of astonishment on his face.

"You mean that you've already managed to convince a German radio operator to send messages with the daily supply and requisition reports?" he demanded incredulously. "How on earth did you do it?"

His sister smiled a decidedly feline smile. "I convinced him that he was in love with me, of course."

"Don't be absurd, Zell! This is serious."

"So am I!" she exclaimed. "I was prepared to pay him, bribe him, promise him whatever he wanted, but as it turned out, I didn't have to do any of that. He's very young, poor thing."

"Young? God, he didn't stand a chance, did he?" Nicolas shook his head and finished pouring his drink. "All the same, we need to have a backup plan."

"I know. I'm open to suggestions. Leon won't transmit from his radio until things have calmed down. He says they're already confiscating shortwave radios in Bordeaux, so he's unwilling to use his right now."

"Then how did he get the message to MI6?"

"He said he knew someone else who would let him use theirs."

"Who is the someone else?"

"He wouldn't say." Gisele sipped her drink. "We'll use my new admirer for now, but you're right. We do need a backup plan. We'll have to think of something."

"Perhaps this Luc will be able to help," Nicolas said, going back to his chair.

"Is that his name? Luc?"

"Yes."

Gisele was quiet for a moment, then she looked up.

"How long will you be gone?"

"I don't know. I wouldn't wait up. He's going to introduce me to some others here in Paris."

"Please be careful, Nicki," she said suddenly, leaning forward. "I've heard that the Sicherheitsdienst is hunting out people who they think are risks for forming a resistance. They have a list of names, and they're looking for them. What if this Luc is on it?"

"Then I don't imagine he would be running around Paris after curfew," Nicolas said easily, sipping his drink. "Do stop your fretting, Zell. We need to know who we can trust, and who we can't. Leon says Luc is a friend and worked with the Deuxième Bureau. If anyone will know who we can trust, he will."

"And if anyone will be on the SD's list, he will!"

"We don't even know that there *is* a list!"

Gisele made a face and exhaled loudly, finishing her drink.

"Well, if I were going to this meeting, I would find out what they know about it, and also what they know about the man in charge of it here. We need to know exactly who our enemy is."

"I agree," Nicolas said, surprising her. He put out his cigarette in the ashtray. "I'll see what I can find out, but you really must stop worrying. Right now, no one would ever suspect us. We're too well established here, and we're far too well connected. As long as we're careful, no one will ever know anything."

Chapter Nineteen

Ainsworth Manor
August 21

"Those boots had best be clean of mud, Miss Evelyn," a voice said warningly from in front of the stove in the large, sunny kitchen. "I've just cleaned the floors."

"I cleaned them on the boot scraper outside, Millie," Evelyn replied with a laugh. "I wouldn't dare come through here otherwise!"

The housekeeper, who had been with the Ainsworth's since before Evelyn was born, turned from where she and the cook were inspecting soup on the hob and nodded, wiping her hands on her apron, a twinkle in her eyes.

"And that's just as it should be. How was your ride, miss?"

"Delightful. How long do I have before dinner?" she asked, pausing next to the large kitchen island to snatch a handful of chopped up carrots off the wood surface.

"The same as you have every night," Millie said, smacking her hand and shooing her towards the door. "Dinner is at the usual time. Now, you go and get yourself washed and dressed. No one wants to see you in all your riding dirt!"

Evelyn laughed and blew her a kiss on her way out the door, popping a piece of carrot into her mouth as she went. Millie was a saint to have put up with her and Rob all these years. In addition to being the housekeeper, she'd stepped into the role of nanny when both Evelyn and Rob had outgrown theirs, claiming that if they would act like wild children, then she would treat them as such. She still did to this day, and Evelyn wouldn't have it any other way.

She went down the hallway, munching on her stolen carrots, until she reached the large, square entry hall at the front of the house. Evelyn was just crossing the marble floor when the door to the study opened and Bill and Uncle Claude emerged, chuckling over something.

"Oh, Evelyn!" Uncle Claude exclaimed when he spotted her. "I was just telling Sir William about the time when you, Gisele, and Nicolas were locked in that library overnight in Paris."

Evelyn raised her eyebrows and let out a short laugh.

"Heavens! I'd forgotten all about that! We were very young."

"You must have been about eight, I should think," he said thoughtfully. "Adele was beside herself when you didn't arrive home. She had the police out looking for you all night. No one imagined that they were still at the library," he added to Bill. "It was the one place we didn't look."

"And you were there all night?" Bill asked incredulously.

"Oh yes! It was quite an adventure. We discovered all the best hiding places, and all the secret corridors. It's quite old, that library. It was built during the reign of Louis XIV. Over the years, several hidden passages were added, all leading out of the library. Alas, they were all locked to the outside." Evelyn shrugged. "In the end, we were exhausted and went to sleep on the circulation desk."

"The three of you were always into mischief," Claude said fondly. "I don't know how any of us had a moment of rest. Thankfully, that was the worst of the escapades."

"That you know of, Uncle," Evelyn said with a grin and wink.

"I think I'd prefer to keep it that way," he said decidedly, moving to the stairs. "If you see Adele, tell her that I've gone to change for dinner, will you?"

"Yes, of course."

Evelyn and Bill watched him start up the wide, grand staircase, and Bill looked at her with a laugh in his eyes.

"How did you manage to get yourselves locked in?"

"Oh, we'd found an old book that interested us. It was about dragons, I think. We were hidden in a corner, reading it, when they locked up for the night. We had no idea of the time. It wasn't until the lights went out that we had any inkling that something was amiss."

"And you didn't panic?"

"Heavens, no. We were much too adventurous for that." Evelyn laughed. "Or perhaps fearless is a better word. We certainly managed to get into our fair share of scrapes."

Bill smiled and glanced up the staircase. Seeing that Claude had disappeared upstairs, he turned his attention back to Evelyn, lowering his voice.

"I've arranged the meeting with Thompson," he told her. "He's expecting you

Friday. He'll be in his office after dinner."

"And the address?"

Bill reached into his inside jacket pocket and pulled out a folded piece of paper, handing it to her.

"He couldn't make it any earlier, I'm afraid. I did try. It will have you driving back after dark."

"That's hardly anything unusual," she said, amused. "I've driven back from London after dark, and that's much farther than Coventry. Who does he think he's meeting with?"

"No one of any importance. He doesn't need to know anything other than he already does."

"And that is?"

"That we want him to examine some technical drawings and give his opinion of what the device may be."

Evelyn stared at him in astonishment.

"That's it? I'm going to show up with these plans and he won't ask any questions? He won't ask where I got them? Or who I am? He'll just take my word that I was sent by MI6?"

"This is England, Jian," he said with a wry smile. "Your average Englishman is not accustomed to looking for spies behind every door. He knows we're sending someone to him Friday, and that is all that he needs to know."

She made a face. "Perhaps the average Englishman *should* begin to look for spies behind every door," she muttered. "Then it wouldn't be quite so easy for the Round Club to hide."

"Yes, well, that's another issue altogether. You just go meet with Thompson and let's see what your father brought back, shall we?"

"And Henry?"

Bill sobered.

"We've come up with a plan, actually," he said reluctantly, turning and starting up the stairs. "If it works, we'll have him."

Evelyn fell into step beside him, shooting him a sharp look.

"A plan? What kind of plan?"

"Well, your old friend Morrow came up with an idea," he admitted in a low voice.

"Morrow! You mean the Security Service is helping?"

"Shh. Yes. They came to us when Gilhurst overheard something." Bill raised his hand when she opened her mouth to speak. "I'm not saying any more. If it works,

Henry will be apprehended, and your safety will be back in our hands without any fear of more leaks."

"And if it doesn't?"

Bill was silent as they mounted the stairs to the second level. When they reached the top, he turned to face her, his face grim.

"It must; it's our best chance at drawing him out."

"That sounds suspiciously as if you're not very confident in this plan."

"Oh, I think it will work. My concern is what we'll stir up when it does," he said cryptically. "However, I want you to do something for me."

"Of course. What is it?"

"Be very careful on Friday, make sure that you're not followed, and no matter what happens or what you're told, come straight back."

Evelyn stood near the window and peered out from behind the curtains into the darkness. She was restless, and the conversation in progress behind her was doing nothing to settle her nerves. Dinner was over and they had retired into the sitting room for after-dinner drinks and to listen to the wireless. Unfortunately, the BBC Home Service was filled with the news of the day's raids from the Luftwaffe. She'd risen suddenly from her seat on the report of three Dornier's being shot down in the northeast in a single battle, crossing the room to refill her glass from the drinks cart in the corner. While she was desperate for news of the battle overhead, when she heard it, she became filled with an all-consuming restlessness, as if she should be doing something to help the pilots rather than simply listening to the reports on the wireless.

"At least we're shooting them down as well," Agatha said as the news broke for an advertisement. "It sounds as if we're holding our own."

"Evelyn, is it true that the airfields are being bombed?" Marguerite asked suddenly.

Evelyn released the curtain and turned from the window, but before she could answer, Agatha spoke up.

"I think that must be very unlikely," she announced. "The newspapers and the

BBC haven't said a word about it."

"Actually, it *is* true." Evelyn walked over to the empty, cold hearth and set her drink on the mantel as she went into the box for a cigarette. "The Germans are trying to destroy the air force on the ground, just as they did in Norway, Belgium, and France."

Silence greeted that as everyone with the exception of Bill stared at her in astonishment.

"What? But we haven't heard anything about that on the wireless," her mother protested. "How can that be?"

"I don't imagine they want to alarm everyone," Claude said, finishing his drink and getting up to pour another. "The government did the same in France, though on a much larger scale. The invasion came as a complete shock, as a result."

"How did you hear about it, Lady Buckley?" Evelyn asked, lighting a cigarette.

"I overheard two men talking in the village today," she said, shaking her head. "But that's too horrible! Are you sure that it's really happening?"

"Oh yes. I don't suppose they will be able to keep it a secret much longer." Evelyn looked up with a tight smile. "Northolt was bombed on Saturday while I was there."

Her mother gasped and Adele let out a little shriek while Claude swung around with a muttered, French expletive.

"What? You never said a word!" Madeleine exclaimed. "What happened?"

"How awful!" Marguerite cried at the same moment.

Evelyn smiled sheepishly and shrugged.

"I didn't want to worry you, Mother," she said. "I was never in any real danger, and as you can see, I wasn't hurt in the slightest. They were aiming for the landing strips and the hangars."

"Why aren't we being told?" Agatha demanded. "It's really the outside of enough. They should tell us what's really happening."

"They are. They're telling you that our boys are shooting down their boys at an even rate," Bill said quietly. "That's all you really need to know. Anything more is just upsetting. And remember, the Germans listen to our broadcasts to hear how they're doing. No sense in confirming their successes to them. Though, Evelyn is right. They won't be able to get away with not reporting it for much longer. Too many people know what's happening."

"Was anyone killed at your station?" Adele asked Evelyn.

Evelyn met her gaze and then glanced at the others. After a split second, she silently exhaled and nodded.

"Yes, I'm afraid some were."

"Bastards," Claude muttered. "Refill, my dearest?" he asked Adele.

She nodded and held out her glass to him.

"That's just terrible. First, they overrun France, now they bomb England," she said. "I feel as if we're in a nightmare."

"We are," Madeleine said firmly. "Evelyn, you can't go back to that station. I won't allow it."

"You can't stop me. I have my orders. I belong to the WAAFs now. I must go back."

"But what if they bomb again?"

"Then I shall have another story to tell," she replied with a reassuring smile. "Really, Mother, this is why I didn't tell you. All you'll do is worry, and there really isn't any need."

"Isn't any—" her mother began, then broke off, muttering something under her breath.

"Maddie!" Agatha gasped beside her, shocked. "Really!"

"What did she say?" Claude asked from the cart where he was refilling Adele's glass.

"Nothing that I'll repeat," Agatha said stiffly, drawing a laugh from both Evelyn and Claude.

"Well, at least you're not there now," Marguerite said calmly, trying to smooth over the upset.

"Yes, indeed. We're very glad that you're away from there now," Agatha agreed.

"Yes, but I do have to go back," Evelyn said. "I'm due back at the weekend."

"Oh no! Can't you stay away longer?" Madeleine asked.

"No, Mother, I can't. You know that."

"Well, I must say that this is all unsettling," she said, shaking her head. "I had a letter from Robbie today and he isn't seeing any of what we're hearing about. He wrote that it was all rather anticlimactic!"

Evelyn bit her lip and turned to reach for her glass again. Of course he wrote that. Her brother didn't want to worry their mother any more than she did. Yet she knew that what he and Miles were facing was anything but anticlimactic.

"Perhaps it isn't as bad where he is," Adele suggested.

"It isn't." Evelyn smiled at her mother reassuringly. "Because of where they are 12 Group isn't getting hit nearly as hard as 11 Group."

Her mother seemed to relax at that, and Bill cleared his throat.

"Why don't we change the subject?" he suggested.

"Fantastic idea," Claude agreed, handing his wife her drink. "I'm sure there must be other news that we can discuss."

"Leon Trotsky was killed today in Mexico City," Marguerite said after a moment. "It was on the wireless before dinner."

Evelyn looked up in astonishment, her drink in one hand and her cigarette in the other.

"What?" she exclaimed.

Her mother looked at her in surprise.

"Do you know who he was?" she asked. "I don't have the faintest idea."

"He was a Bolshevist," Agatha said dismissively.

"A Bolshevist who opposed Stalin, as I understood it," Claude said thoughtfully.

"Quite so." Bill nodded. "He was thrown out of the party after Lenin's death, when Stalin seized power. He held a very high position in the Soviet government until then, but he was vocal about his opposition to Stalin."

"So he was exiled?" Madeleine asked. "For speaking out against Stalin?"

"Yes."

"But you said that he was killed?" Evelyn asked, her voice tight. "He didn't simply die?"

"No. The press are saying that he was stabbed to death."

Evelyn met Bill's glance and quickly turned to put out her cigarette in a nearby ashtray.

"Why would someone stab the man in Mexico?" Adele wondered. "Do you think he owed someone money?"

"I think it was much more sinister than a gambling debt." Claude shook his head. "I remember reading that gunmen broke into his villa a few months ago. Riddled his bedroom with gunfire."

Evelyn's lips tightened and she drained her glass for the second time that evening.

"I think it more likely that his old Soviet cohorts arranged it," Claude continued behind her. "We all know how Stalin rules his so-called Soviet Union."

"But to go all the way to Mexico simply to assassinate someone for speaking out against him?" Agatha looked dubious. "That seems a bit much."

"I'm told that the Soviet intelligence arm is ruthless," Claude said, oblivious to the suddenly rigid figure at the fireplace. "When I was in Paris, I worked quite closely with members of the government, you know. They were very concerned with some of the incidents that they heard of. I won't repeat them, of course, but they are violent people."

"Well, what can you expect from communists, after all?" Adele asked. "I never understood their revolution."

"Some would say that it was much like our own," Madeleine murmured. "They wanted a new government, one that wasn't a monarchy."

"And now they want to do the same thing here," Agatha muttered. "Do you know, I heard that the fifth columnists are gaining traction in London? Even now?"

Evelyn turned from the mantel, her breathing even and her face composed. She met Bill's questioning look with a small smile. While she had been shocked out of her calm on hearing of what was obviously an assassination by the NKVD, she had managed to control her involuntary reaction by remembering a simple fact: Vladimir Lyakhov was betraying the regime that he worked for to pass them information. That simple act may not absolve him of the stain of what his agency did, but it went a long way to reassure her that he was not the monster that his comrades were. He couldn't be. He was too intent on keeping her safe.

"Well, I certainly wouldn't want to have anything to do with any of them," Madeleine was saying. "They can't be trusted. They've shown that, even without this Trotsky's death."

Evelyn swallowed and crossed to the bar cart. A moment later, Bill joined her.

"I'm sure he had no part of it," he said under his breath.

"But you think his agency did?"

Bill was silent and Evelyn poured herself a drink.

"So do I," she whispered. "Everyone knows Stalin will hear no criticism of himself or his ministers, and Trotsky wrote some very inflammatory pieces."

"Yes, he did."

She finished pouring and set the decanter down, picking up her glass and looking at Bill.

"Well, I'll just have to be sure to keep my thoughts and opinions to myself," she said with a wry smile.

"As, I'm sure, does he."

21st August, 1940
My Dear Evelyn,

It's late and I'm tired, but I can't seem to settle to sleep. We had an awfully busy day today, but it seems as if that's becoming the norm. After several sorties in the morning, we kept at readiness all through lunch! It wasn't until teatime that I got my hands on some cold sandwiches, which we ate in the sun next to our Spits. We missed dinner completely, so went round to the pub when we were finally stood down for the night. The Yank says the Germans have spies in the RAF and that they're trying to starve us out of action.

I saw in the evening paper that the Jerries have taken to attacking civilians in the streets in the coastal towns. The article I read said that one flew right down and strafed a street where women were shopping. No one was hurt, thank God. I can't imagine what kind of person would do that. Well, I suppose I can. It's the same kind of person who can fire on pilots coming down in their parachutes: a monster. Except, they can't all be monsters. There must be some like me, just doing their duty and waiting for the day that it's over.

Chris had a bit of a dodgy landing the other day. He was hit and should have bailed out, but he thought he could bring the kite home. He did, as well. The problem was that the engine was on fire and cut out as he was trying to land. He'd lost his rudder and couldn't control it very well. Watching him coming in, I thought there was no way he'd make it. He did it, the lucky bugger, but then lost control. The airplane spun off the landing strip and went through a hedgerow.

When we got to it, he'd hit his head and was unconscious with a fire coming over the wing. It took three of us to get him out, but we did, and just in time. The kite exploded seconds after we cleared the crash. I think he must be part cat because he certainly seems to have a few extra lives stored up. Not that I'm complaining. If I lose my best pilot, I'll be jolly upset.

How's Fred Durton? I thought of him yesterday when I heard that Northolt lost some Hurricanes. I hope he wasn't one of them. He seems like a good chap, and I know he's a good friend of yours.

We've heard about the Polish squadrons, but I didn't realize that they were at your station. I also didn't know that they weren't operational. Why the hell not? We need all the pilots we can get, and at least they've had experience. Green section lost a pilot earlier this week. I don't think he even reached fifteen hours flying time before he bought it. If we have experienced pilots available, they should be up and fighting. Rather ridiculous that they aren't.

My eyes are closing now, so I'll sign off. I'm including a photograph, as you requested. For God's sake, don't tell Rob. I'll never hear the end of it.

Always yours,
Flight Lieutenant Miles Lacey

Chapter Twenty

M iles stared at the group of bombers in the distance. It was a large formation of at least 40 plus, perhaps even 60 plus. He glanced to his left, then to his right. Call it at least fifty bombers, plus their fighter cover, to their two squadrons of a combined seventeen aircraft.

"Tallyho, one o'clock," Ashmore said, his voice even over the radio. "Fibus Leader to Cowslip. Bandits sighted. Engaging now. Red and Blue sections will take the bombers."

"Green and Yellow have the escort," Billy responded.

Miles glanced at the leader of Green section and watched as they peeled off to ascend to the higher clouds where the German fighter escort were known to conceal themselves.

"Right. Let's have at it," Ashmore said, leading them towards the large formation of Heinkels. "Watch for return fire, and their escort."

With a final look at the disappearing Spits of Green and Yellow sections, Miles turned his attention to the targets that were now dead ahead of them.

"Um, Blue Two to Blue Leader, you do realize you're heading straight for them, right?" Chris drawled over the headset.

"I'll split them up, Blue Two. You go after them when they scatter," Miles replied, his voice even.

"Don't be a bloody fool, Blue Leader," Ashmore snapped, suddenly shaken out of his perpetual calm. "You'll run right into the bastards!"

"Not a'tall, Red Leader. I'll just shake them up a bit."

"This is either completely insane or brilliant, and I don't know which," Chris announced cheerfully, "but I'm right with you, Blue Leader. I'll go right."

"You're both barmy!" Thomas exclaimed, only the faintest tremor in his voice.

Miles picked out the lead bomber in the formation and flew straight towards it at over 300 mph. He shifted in his seat as he came upon the bombers, fast and deadly, his eyes trained on the lead aircraft dead ahead of him. He'd learned over Dunkirk that the bomber pilots didn't enjoy having the much smaller and faster fighters attack from the front, and more often than not, inexperienced pilots would drop out of formation when fighters went head-to-head with them. Keeping one eye on the glass bubble that contained the cockpit and the other eye on his instruments, he took a deep, even breath. He had to keep his speed up and time it perfectly. One second too late and he ran the risk of either being hit by the front gunner or crashing into the wing as he banked over. The risk was high, and he was probably crazy for trying it, but if it worked, the formation would break up and his squadron's terrible odds would be instantly improved. As the formation stood now, their gunners were perfectly positioned to defend the entire lot of them, and he knew from experience that they were damn good at it. Break them up, however, and the Spitfire could outmaneuver them all day.

He swallowed a sudden lump in his throat as he rushed towards the nose of the bomber. He held his course, wondering if he truly had gone insane. He could see the pilots of the Heinkel staring at him as he streaked towards them, and for a split second, he felt almost as if they were the only aircraft in the sky. Time seemed to suspend itself as he stared into the cockpit, seeing the men clearly in their flight gear and helmets. Then, as instantly as it had come upon him, the spell was broken. They weren't the only aircraft in the sky, and if he didn't break off, he'd be target practice for the bastards in the gun turrets.

At the last possible second, Miles pressed the firing button on his round control stick and broke up and to the left. His bullets tore into the body of the Heinkel as he streaked over the wing and between his target and the plane next to it. The hits didn't do anything, but then, they weren't meant to. As he climbed above the formation, he glanced down, and a wave of satisfaction went through him as he saw his bomber start to drop down out of the formation. It wasn't hurt, but it was spooked.

"It's like playing chicken!" Chris crowed. "Look at them scatter!"

Miles turned to dive down to attack the formation again and grinned. Chris was right. The heavy, cumbersome bombers were falling away from their formation and scattering, trying to avoid the much smaller and faster fighter planes swarming around them.

"Bloody hell," Thomas said in awe, going after one of the bombers closest to him. "It actually worked! Look!"

Miles felt like laughing and gasping with relief at the same time. He did neither but refocused his sights on the lead bomber that he'd already targeted with his harmless burst. Now that the enemy was out of formation, he was able to skillfully evade the rear gunner's fire as he streaked towards it, his eyes on his firing sight, waiting for the starboard engine to center in the circle.

"Fighters, twelve o'clock high!" Chris cried.

Miles cursed but held his course. He was so close! Another second and he'd have a perfect shot!

"On your tail, Red Leader!" Rob exclaimed.

The engine slid into the circle and Miles pressed his button, the Spitfire shuddering as the Browning guns responded with a stream of bullets. He banked right, twisting his head to search for Ashmore as a burst of black smoke came from the injured engine of the bomber. After a moment of frantic searching, he spotted his squadron leader just as he twisted out of range of a 109, avoiding what would have been a direct stream of bullets from the enemy. He exhaled in relief, then turned to dive back into the Heinkel formation. Ashmore was all right. He'd take care of himself.

"Got one!" Thomas cried excitedly as flames burst from one of the bombers. "Look at that!"

"Look behind you instead!" Chris snapped. "You've got company!"

Miles unloaded a stream of bullets into the wing of a Heinkel before peeling off and looking round for Thomas. He cursed when he saw two 109s engaging the younger pilot.

"You've got two on you, Blue Three," he said, twisting up and to the left. "Keep moving. I'm going for the second in line."

Miles maneuvered through the formation, heading for the writhing silhouettes at his nine o'clock. He locked his focus onto the second enemy fighter who was angling for a shot on Thomas. Glancing at his instruments, he was just pressing his firing button when he heard bullets tear into his left wing and the Spitfire jerked suddenly. Miles watched his bullets soar under the belly of the ME109 and cursed again, banking up. Another scan of his instrument panel and a sharp turn later, he determined that the damage wasn't crucial and dove back after the German fighter. This time his shot was true, and he clipped the enemy's tail, causing him to give up his pursuit of young Thomas. He dropped down and leveled off, turning away from the scrap.

"He's heading home, Blue Three."

Thomas didn't answer, engaged in a fierce fight with the remaining 109. Miles turned around to lend a hand just as he saw another Messerschmidt flash in behind him. He pulled back on the control stick and spiraled up, leading the enemy into a tight, fast spiral that he knew full well the other fighter would be unable to maintain. The blood pounded in his ears and his vision began to get fuzzy, the force of the turns pulling all the blood to his head. Miles forced himself to breath the oxygen from his mask steadily with deep, even breaths. After a few seconds, he pulled out of the maneuver, taking a single deep gulp before twisting around and diving down onto the hapless 109.

His vision cleared in time for him to get a clear view of the enemy fighter. He pressed his firing button, sending a burst towards it. The pilot dodged his bullets, banking at the last second, and Miles' lips tightened. But before his could fire again, he felt bullets tear into his kite again and he broke off, twisting his head around, searching for the bastard. Only there wasn't one. No enemy fighter was near him, but a squadron of Hurricanes was joining the melee.

"For Christ's sake!" he exploded. "Someone tell these shits what the enemy looks like!"

"You okay there, Blue Leader?" Chris asked, sounding breathless as he came out of the clouds above.

"No, I'm bloody not! I just got hit by one of those Hurries!" Miles cursed again. "I'm losing altitude and fuel."

"Get on out of it, Blue Leader," Ashmore commanded. "Save us some tea."

"Roger, Red Leader. Disengaging."

Miles pulled out of the fight and turned his nose for home, keeping a wary eye on the gauges. Sweat broke out on his brow as he remembered flying over the channel at Dunkirk, losing altitude and pressure just as he was now. But this time it wasn't even a damn Jerry responsible! Another jolt of anger went through him, but before he could reflect on the immaturity and ignorance of kids climbing into cockpits with only a handful of hours flying time, and obviously no real aircraft recognition training, he saw a shadow flash to his right out of the corner of his eye. The anger was instantly replaced with a streak of fear as an ME110 shot into range behind him.

Miles managed to evade the first burst of fire from the enemy, but when he tried to twist into an evasive turn, the Spitfire didn't respond. A feeling of horror washed over him as he realized that his controls had also been damaged. There was no way to outmaneuver the bastard. His only hope was to outrun him, and at the rate that he was losing fuel and pressure, Miles didn't hold out much hope for that either.

Clamping his jaw shut, he sent up a frantic prayer as he opened the throttle. The wounded aircraft missed a rotation, but increased speed, putting some distance between him and the 110. Miles took a deep breath. He just might make it!

Then the whole airplane shuddered violently as bullets tore into his right wing and the front of the nose. An all-too-familiar smell filled the cockpit and Miles knew he wasn't making it back. Flames streaked out of the front of his Spit, and he stopped thinking. He reached up and ripped off his oxygen mask and radio, gasping as searing heat smacked him in his face. The flames weren't in the cockpit yet, but the heat was almost unbearable as he reached above his head and began pulling on the canopy.

It didn't budge.

He cursed as panic rolled through him and he remembered Chris' canopy and how it took two of them with a crowbar to get it open. Miles swallowed and forced himself to calm down. Chris' canopy had been damaged. His wasn't. It was just stuck.

Miles moved the control stick and the Spit flipped over. Ignoring the ground that was now visible far below him, he tried again. This time, the canopy slid open and smoke from the fire poured into the cockpit, dissipating almost as quickly as a burst of fresh air followed. Righting the airplane, Miles undid his restraints, checking to ensure that his parachute was there and still attached. More smoke flowed in around him, and then flames broke through the underside of the floor. It was time to go.

Coughing, Miles jerked his legs away from the fire, tamping down sheer terror as he stared at the flames licking towards him. Trying to see through the smoke, he fumbled with the latch to the half door, climbing onto the seat to get away from the flames before finally getting it open. With a last ragged cough and a push, he threw himself out of the burning fighter.

Evelyn closed the trunk and sat back on her heels, a frown creasing her brows. This was a waste of time. There was nothing here that would work. Pushing herself up, she brushed dust off her hands and turned to look around the room. She was in one of the empty bedrooms in the wing that was only used for storage now. Several of the trunks contained old clothes that had been packed away years ago, while others were filled with old books, photographs, and toys from when she and Robbie were small. And none of it would be an ounce of good for what she needed.

She left the room, closing the door firmly behind her. There was absolute silence in this part of the house, and she exhaled, looking down the long corridor. She remembered when she was young, and this wing was still used for entertaining. Her parents used to hold weekend parties regularly, inviting their friends up from London. There was always something going on. Sun would stream in from the windows along this corridor, and inevitably there would be a spaniel or two trotting nicely along behind their owners.

Evelyn smiled with the memories, absently running a finger along the molding on the wall. She and Robbie had loved it when they had visitors. More often than not, there were other children, like Stephen Mansbridge, who accompanied their parents. They would race down this very corridor, she and Stephen, trying to see who could reach the stairs at the end first. She could almost hear their laughter, and the grown-ups' admonishments not to run in the house.

Evelyn pulled her finger away and grimaced at the dust, rubbing her forefinger and thumb together to dispel it. This wing had been closed since the war began and her father died. Her mother had ordered it out of practicality. The sprawling, centuries-old manor was difficult enough to maintain as it was, but war brought with it more challenges. The parties had naturally stopped with the death of her father, and it only made sense to close this wing. Still, it was sad to see it so dusty. She knew that Thomas, their butler, made regular rounds in the closed wings to ensure that the roof and the windows were intact and that no critters had moved in, but other than that, no one ever came here anymore. A feeling of melancholy went through her, and Evelyn shook her head impatiently. It served no purpose to stand here getting maudlin over something that was out of her control. There was enough within her control to worry about at the moment.

Such as how to contrive a disguise for her meeting with the engineer.

She turned to make her way towards the door at the far end that led to the main house. It was kept locked now, but Thomas had given her the key readily enough when she said that she wanted to look for something in the trunks they'd moved there last year. She'd thought perhaps there would be something she could use as a disguise for her meeting with Montague Thompson, but everything was far too out of date, or just plain inappropriate. She chewed her bottom lip thoughtfully. That she was going to that meeting in some sort of disguise was without question. There was no way she was going to let Montague be in a position to give an accurate description of her, or worse yet, recognize her.

Shustov's warning was still very fresh in her mind, and if she were completely honest with herself, it had rattled her enough to question the wisdom of pursuing this entire operation. Both Hans Voss, the obersturmbannführer in the Sicherheitsdienst, and Eisenjager, the assassin-spy, were using the Round Club to try to locate her here in England. As if that weren't alarming enough, they knew that Henry had a description of her from Sam, the pilot. Granted, the description applied to half the women in England, but if Montague were to give the same one? That would give Henry a starting point, something he didn't yet have.

No. A disguise was mandatory, but how? She couldn't find anything here to use, and the village shops were out of the question. Everyone there knew her, and even if she could come up with a ruse to convince them that she wasn't completely out of her mind, there was only one shop in the village that carried any kind of clothing, and she knew they wouldn't have anything that she could use either.

Evelyn went through the door and locked it again, stepping down the three, shallow steps that led to it. She had to think of something. She was running out of time, and she had to be in Coventry the following evening.

Think, Evie!

She was striding past Robbie's bedroom a few moments later, on her way to her own, when she suddenly stopped and sucked in her breath. Spinning around, she went back to his door and opened it, stepping inside the silent bedroom. It smelled faintly of her brother's cologne and furniture polish. Even though he wasn't here, Thomas and Millie made sure that it was kept dusted and cleaned, ready in case he dropped by unexpectedly. They did the same thing with her own room, something she always appreciated when she did return home.

Evelyn closed the door in case someone came along the corridor and wondered what she was doing in there, then crossed swiftly to the wardrobe. Flinging it open, she surveyed the clothing hanging neatly inside. Her eye fell on a uniform and her lips curved involuntarily as she remembered dressing in one and being smuggled into the officers' recreation hall and mess by Fred. He had dared her to do it months ago, and Evelyn was never one to back down from a dare, no matter how outrageous.

The smile faded as a sharp, almost physical, stab of loss went straight through her. Fred was missing, presumed dead, and she'd never laugh with him again.

Never witness the pranks he got up to on a regular basis. She let out a muffled cross between a sob and a laugh. She'd never ride in that awful jalopy with a door tied on with string again.

Evelyn wiped away the sudden, hot tears that sprang to her eyes and turned her attention back to the clothes in the wardrobe. She would go dressed as a man. It was so obvious that she didn't know why she hadn't thought of it sooner. Montague would be expecting a man anyway. Bill had made it clear that he hadn't told him anything about her, and no Englishman would be expecting a woman to come see him with such complicated drawings. It was perfect. She would go as a man, and no description would ever point back to Evelyn Ainsworth, society belle and wealthy heiress.

Miles hurtled through the air, gasping lungfuls of cool, fresh air as he probed his chest gingerly. He hadn't been prepared to be slammed back from his Spitfire with quite so much force when he jumped out, though he supposed he should have been. After all, his kite was nipping along at close to 200 mph when he bailed out. The abrupt shift in speed was enough to throw anyone back, and the angle from which he jumped had centered the force directly onto his chest. There had been one terrifying moment when he thought he would hit his tail wing, but somehow the wind had whipped him away from it just in time.

Satisfied that his chest wasn't crushed, Miles felt for his ripcord, a strange feeling of calm taking over. After seeing the flames erupt at his feet, he didn't remember much of anything except blind panic until he was slammed back and away from the airplane. Now the panic was gone, and he was actually quite enjoying the colder air on his hot face after the inferno that his cockpit had become. He pulled the cord and his parachute opened above him, yanking him up abruptly as it slowed his descent. Miles grunted as the jerk added to the soreness in his chest, but the discomfort was gone almost immediately. Turning his head, he scanned the skies above him for the enemy aircraft, but the bastard was gone, undoubtedly going home to claim one Spitfire destroyed. And he would be correct, Miles reflected bitterly as he watched his kite hit the ground far below him, bursting into a fireball.

It was a strange feeling to see his airplane crash while he was soaring on the wind high above, holding on to the guiding cords of his parachute, waiting for gravity to bring him safely back to earth. Yet he was also bloody grateful to not have still been in it.

Or to be burned.

Miles looked down at his legs and flying boots. His boots weren't even singed, which was a miracle in itself. He had felt the heat from the flames well enough as he'd tumbled out of the cockpit. A glimmer of amusement went through him as he reflected that he was glad his boots weren't ruined. It had taken him a bloody long time to break them in. He didn't want to have to start the process all over again.

Green fields spotted with cows and separated by hedgerows stretched out below him and Miles wondered where he was. Somewhere near Norwich, he should think, based on that last glance at his instrument panel before all hell broke loose. As he drew closer to earth, cow pastures gave way to freshly plowed fields. Miles soared over a row of hedges and into another field with long, evenly spaced grooves in the dirt. The farmers were preparing to plant the autumn crops, he thought absently as he floated over the tidy rows. Was it really that time already? It didn't seem possible, but of course it was.

Miles descended the last few feet and braced himself, consciously relaxing his knees as they'd been taught in training. His boots hit soft, recently plowed earth and stuck, sending a jarring shock up his spine and throwing him off balance. He pitched forward, reaching out his arms to break his fall as his knees sank into the soft dirt. The parachute fell behind him as his elbows hit the ground, preventing him from face planting in freshly tilled and composted earth.

He exhaled in relief and struggled to his feet, resisting a sudden urge to kiss the fertile ground that they were fighting so hard to defend. He was undoing the clasps for the chute when he heard shouting from behind him. Throwing off the restraints from the parachute, he turned around to find five burly farmers tramping towards him, four with pitchforks and one with a hunting rifle.

"Just you hold it right there, laddie!" The one with the rifle called, brandishing it threateningly. "Don't ye move!"

Miles stared at them, dumbfounded, and didn't know whether to laugh or put his hands up in surrender. After a stunned moment, he did neither as the astonishment was replaced swiftly by irritation.

"Don't be bloody stupid, man!" he snapped angrily. "I've had enough friendly fire for one day!"

The farmer to the right of the one toting the rifle grinned and looked over at the others.

"It's all right, men. 'E's one of us!"

"Who the bloody hell did you think it was?" Miles demanded, stepping away from the parachute strings before he got tangled up again. "Who else would be wearing an RAF uniform?"

"Can't see the uniform under that jacket and them boots," the man with the rifle said cheerfully, holding out his hand to Miles. "Had a bloody Jerry land three fields over last week. Now we come prepared. The name's Landon."

Miles gripped his hand. "Flight Lieutenant Miles Lacey. What happened to Jerry?"

"Dunno. Local Defense Volunteers came and took 'im." The farmer shrugged. "Very polite in the end, he was, after we disarmed 'im."

"You're not hurt?" One of the other men asked.

"No, thanks. I'll be all right. I bailed out just in time."

Miles turned to start gathering up his parachute, but one of them stopped him.

"Leave it be, laddie," he said. "I'll do that. Here. 'Ave a snort of this. That'll get your feet back under ye."

Miles had a flask shoved into his hand as the man passed him on his way to gather the parachute.

"Cheers." Miles took a gulp and felt whiskey burn a welcome path as it went down. "Would you mind pointing me in the direction of the nearest village?"

"I can do better 'n that if you don't mind riding in the back of me hay cart," the man with the rifle told him.

Miles screwed the cap back on the flask and handed it to him.

"I'll ride in the back of a manure cart if it means getting back to my squadron and going back up to shoot those bastards."

"Anxious to do it all again, are ya?" Landon clapped him on his shoulder. "Admire your spirt, son. Come on, then. Let's get you on your way."

Chapter Twenty-One

Paris

J acques finished giving their dinner order to the waiter and smiled across the table at the pretty redhead. Her name was Marie, she was friends with Colette, and that was the extent of what he knew about her. Colette had asked him to bring her to dinner instead as she was recovering from an unspecified heartbreak and could use cheering up. Never one to refuse a damsel in need, he'd agreed. When he suggested Maxim's, Marie's eyes had almost popped out of her head. She'd protested that she had nothing to wear, and so Jacques had bought her the gown she was wearing. If the dinner wasn't enough, the gown had certainly had her smiling nonstop.

"Have you lived in Paris all your life?" he asked, pouring her a glass of wine.

"No. I came here from Orléans a few years ago."

"And do you miss Orléans?"

"Perhaps a bit, but Paris was so exciting and fun that I didn't want to leave."

Jacques smiled, not missing the past tense. Paris was no longer fun and exciting, not since the Occupation, and especially not for the working girls like Marie and Colette. They faced the Germans every day and had to entertain them as if they were Frenchmen. He couldn't imagine how they did it.

He was sipping his wine a moment later when Francois passed their table. Jacques met his eyes briefly over the rim of his glass, and as the man passed, a linen napkin fluttered to the floor next to his chair. Jacques set down his glass and smoothly bent to retrieve the napkin, setting it on his lap atop his own. He glanced down as he adjusted it and saw the note written on the fabric.

Suis-moi.

Jacques lifted the napkin and dabbed his mouth.

"Pardon," he said apologetically. "I've just seen someone that I'd like to have a quick word with. I'll return in an instant."

Marie smiled and nodded, reaching for her wine as he pushed his chair back and set his own napkin on the table while slipping Francois' swiftly into his pocket. He smiled at Marie and made his way to the front of the restaurant, where Francois was standing just inside the door.

"In the cloakroom, monsieur," he said in a low voice as Jacques passed him.

Jacques acknowledged the instructions with a very slight nod and continued out the door, turning to go to the gentlemen's cloakroom where he'd checked his hat earlier. Stepping inside, the same boy from the other night was behind the counter. When he saw him, the boy smiled widely and nodded to a gentleman standing in the corner. He was on the taller side, with dark hair, and dressed impeccably in a suit that had been tailored for him.

"Bonjour," he said, approaching the man. "Nicolas?"

The man nodded. "You are the captain?"

"At your service," Jacques said, bowing with a flourish. As he did so, the envelope that Leon had handed him in Bordeaux appeared in his hand. "A pleasure to meet you."

Nicolas didn't miss a beat, taking the envelope from his fingers swiftly. The entire transaction was over before it had really begun, and Nicolas was smiling at him.

"And you. Thank you."

The envelope disappeared into the inside pocket of his jacket and Jacques glanced at the desk to find the boy engrossed in a serial comic, not paying either of them the least amount of attention.

"Leon sends his regards."

"Please return them when you see him again. How is Bordeaux?"

"Tedious these days, but certainly not dull."

A genuine smile lit the man's eyes, and he was betrayed into a grin.

"It sounds suspiciously like Paris," he said cheerfully. "Such is our reality now."

"So it is." Jacques smiled. "Now I must return to my companion. She has had her heart broken, and I am on a mission to make her smile again."

"Then, by all means, rejoin her. Thank you again."

"The pleasure was mine."

Jacques turned to leave the cloakroom. Stepping into the entry hall, he looked up in surprise when a woman dressed in shimmering silver bumped into him.

"Oh! I'm terribly sorry!" she exclaimed with a gasp, looking up from her open purse. "I wasn't looking where I was going!"

"It is quite all right, mademoiselle," he assured her with a smile and flash of a gold tooth. "You are not hurt?"

"No, not at all. I was looking for my lipstick." She snapped her purse closed and smiled ruefully at him. "My brother is always telling me I should be more careful."

"No, no, mademoiselle! Never that! For if you were, I would not have had the pleasure of your smile!"

"Ah, Gisele!" Nicolas came up behind them. "There you are. Have you met the captain, then?"

"I'm afraid I just ran him down."

"Good Lord, you didn't! Let me guess: your mirror?"

"Lipstick, darling, but it's quite all right. He's assured me that my smile has quite made up for it!"

"And so it has!" Jacques bowed low over her hand, then nodded to Nicolas. "Au revoir!"

He turned to go back into the dining room and Nicolas held his arm out to his sister.

"Come. The major and his wife are waiting for us. We mustn't keep them."

When Captain Beaulieu left the table to go out of the dining room, Eisenjager lifted his head from his drink at the bar and watched him go curiously. From his position, he could see the cloakroom door and he watched from the corner of his eye as the captain disappeared inside. Now what was the man up to?

Eisenjager sipped his cognac thoughtfully. The captain had been getting up to all kinds of shenanigans since he'd been in Paris, but none of them could be considered suspicious. The smuggler had an affinity for the ladies, the prettier the better, and also seemed to enjoy the finer things that Paris had to offer. However, that was hardly a crime, and if it were, most of his fellow Germans would be in trouble.

Getting up and going to the cloakroom not five minutes after being seated for dinner at Maxim's, however, was decidedly odd. He set down his glass and waited patiently for his mark to reappear. If he didn't show himself in a moment or two, he would have to go to investigate. As it was, though, he didn't have very long to wait. Less than a few minutes later, Captain Beaulieu strode out of the cloakroom again. Perhaps he'd forgotten something in his coat pocket. A lighter, perhaps

Eisenjager watched as a woman dressed in a silver evening gown, her nose buried in her purse, walked into the captain, almost pushing the man over. His attention caught by the collision, he was watching curiously when another man appeared in the cloakroom entrance behind the captain. He was a tall, dark-haired gentleman, and Eisenjager shifted in his seat to get a better look. Suddenly the captain's visit to the cloakroom made much more sense and was decidedly suspicious. Who was the man? And why was the captain meeting him in a cloakroom in what could only be regarded as a clandestine manner?

The three stood talking for a moment, then Jacques bowed low over the lady's hand and turned to go back into the dining room. As he did, Eisenjager turned his head quickly forward, avoiding any possibility of the captain seeing his face. He passed the bar on his way back to his table, never once glancing in Eisenjager's direction. Good. He had no idea he was being followed or watched.

The couple followed a moment later and he glanced up as they passed him. Eisenjager sucked in his breath silently, recognizing the woman instantly. The dark hair, the stunning blue eyes, they were the same as the woman in Café Rosa. He had thought for a moment that she was Jeannine, until he'd seen her eyes. Once seen, those eyes were unforgettable.

He watched them cross the dining room and approach a table on the far side. A major rose to his feet politely while his companion smiled up at the man, holding out her hand in greeting. Whoever they were, they were dining with a major in the Wehrmacht and appeared to be on quite good terms with his companion. Who were they? And why were they at the café in Bordeaux just days before?

Eisenjager turned back to his drink, his eyes narrowed thoughtfully. He didn't believe in coincidence, and never had. The couple had been in Leon's pâtisserie, and now they were in Paris, meeting with Captain Beaulieu. He could think of only one reason for that, and it was something that he should definitely report to both his superiors and the SD. Yet, as he sipped his drink, Eisenjager realized that he had absolutely no intention of doing that.

It appeared that his weeks of patience were beginning to pay off. He didn't know who these new players were, or how they factored into Leon's network of spies, but his gut was telling him that they would lead him to Jeannine.

And Jeannine would get him to the Englishwoman.

August 23

Evelyn looked up in surprise when she heard an all-too-familiar sound high above. She was seated on a bench in the rose garden, enjoying a pleasant, if cloudy, afternoon respite. Until now, the only sounds to reach her were those of the birds and wildlife from the meadow located on the other side of the boxwood hedge that surrounded the garden. Squinting, she searched the sky, looking for the squadron of airplanes that she could hear.

"You hear them as well?"

She started and turned on the bench to see Bill gazing upwards behind her.

"Yes. It's strange. I've just realized that I haven't heard any airplanes since I've been here."

"Nor have I, but they're certainly up there somewhere. Above the cloud cover, no doubt. Do you mind if I join you?"

"Of course not." Evelyn motioned to the seat beside her. "Have you had enough of Auntie Agatha's conspiracy theories?"

"She's certainly convinced herself that there are German spies in every village, hasn't she?" he asked, sitting beside her.

"Yes. She read an article last year about the fifth column, and now she's convinced that the communists and the Nazis are everywhere. She even accused one of the deacons of the church of having fascist sympathies after he remarked that the interrogations of Italians in London were uncalled for." Evelyn grinned. "It then transpired that he has Italian ancestry, and one of those questioned was a great uncle of his."

"What happened to him? The uncle?"

"As far as I know, nothing. He was questioned and released. He was labeled a Category C alien after they determined that he was too old to be a threat. Well, supposedly he's lived in London for over forty years, so they really couldn't decide anything else, could they?"

"And the deacon?"

"Oh, he's still opposed to the internment of the Italians, though he supports it for the Germans."

They were quiet for a moment, the sound of the aircraft fading into the distance.

"You know, I'm due back at Northolt tomorrow," she said, breaking the silence.

"I'll arrange for your leave to be extended."

"I'd rather you didn't."

Bill looked at her in surprise. "You can't be serious?"

"Yes, of course I am."

"You went back for one day and the airfield was bombed! I can't afford to lose my agents to a bombing raid right here in England. We'll extend your leave and send you back when the threat isn't so severe."

"That could be months," she pointed out calmly. "It's not as if the Luftwaffe is going to simply go away. The Germans are right on the other side of the Channel, twenty-one miles from Dover. They're hardly going to stop sending over their bombers. It will never be completely safe."

"No, but they can't keep this sort of intensity up for long. They're losing too many aircraft. Even Göring will have to concede eventually."

"With his arrogance? I wouldn't hold your breath." Evelyn was quiet for a moment, then she shook her head. "I want to go back. My place is there, for the time that I'm in England, and the longer I stay away, the more questions will be raised."

"Section Officer Madson is fully aware—"

"Yes, but the other officers are not," she cut him off. "I'm already something of a pariah among them. I'd rather not make it worse."

"Well, we can always transfer you to another station," he said thoughtfully.

"Good heavens, no. That would be worse. At least at Northolt they're used to me! No one blinks when I go away anymore."

"I'm simply trying to keep you safe. Lord knows you'll be in enough danger when you go back to France. At least here in England you should be able to relax without fear of being killed in a raid."

"Or fear of being discovered by Henry or the Round Club?" Evelyn looked at him humorously. "Bill, I'm already in just as much danger here as I was in France. Moving stations won't change anything."

He was silent for a long time, then he exhaled.

"Very well," he reluctantly agreed. "So be it."

"Thank you."

"Though I don't see why you're so anxious to get back to the war when you've got the choice of staying here, in this peaceful haven."

"Oh, the longer you stay, the less peaceful it becomes," she said with a laugh. "It's becoming more and more difficult to come up with excuses to leave. If Mother and Auntie Agatha had their way, I'd remain here and help them knit sweaters for the soldiers for the rest of the war."

"Sometimes I wonder if that's not just what you should be doing," Bill said tiredly, rubbing his face. "I often think what your father would say if he knew what I'd got you into."

"He knew."

Bill's head shot up and he looked at her sharply. "What?!"

She nodded and smiled sadly. "It was in the letter that he left in the box in Switzerland. He knew I was working for MI6, though how I have no idea. I certainly never slipped around him."

"How the bloody hell—pardon. How on earth did he discover it? We did everything to keep it from him, just as we did to keep his activities from you."

"I'm beginning to think that there was much more to Daddy than any of us realized," Evelyn said. "In any event, I wouldn't let what he would have thought worry you too much, as he apparently already knew and wasn't very surprised by it. Quite the contrary. The last thing he did was to ensure that I was drawn into his last operation."

"Mm. That's true." Bill glanced at her. "What will you do if Thompson confirms that these plans *are* what you think they are? Which is what, by the way? You've yet to tell me."

"I'll tell you when I know for certain that I'm right. There's absolutely no point in giving you more to worry about until there's need."

"And when there is?"

"Well, then I'll tell you and we'll think of a way to handle it."

Bill looked at her shrewdly. "You've no intention of letting those plans come to MI6, do you?"

"I wouldn't say that."

"Then what would you say?"

"That perhaps it will be better to gather more intelligence before releasing them."

Bill snorted. "I can demand them, you know, and throw you into a cell if you don't give them to me."

Evelyn grinned mischievously and stood up.

"You could, but I know that you won't."

"What makes you so sure?"

"Because you're going to need me, and my contacts in France. As you said yourself, you can't afford to lose me to a bomb, or to prison."

Chapter Twenty-Two

M olly went into the drab and unremarkable building on Broadway with an extreme sense of uncertainty. When she reached the address that Henry had given her, she had stared up at the building with misgiving. Surely this wasn't the headquarters of the British Secret Intelligence Service! A small, unadorned brass plaque next to the door declared it to be the location of the Minimax Fire Extinguisher Company, further confusing her until she remembered that this was MI6. They would hardly broadcast their identity to all and sundry.

Stepping into a small reception hall, she looked around curiously. A bench ran along one wall, while the other held various framed photographs and drawings of fire extinguishers. The floor was clean but basic tile, and the walls had wood paneling that, though outdated, was kept spotless and polished. A reception desk faced her, and she smiled at the man seated behind it, walking forward.

"Good afternoon," she said cheerfully. "I'm from Lord Halifax's office. He sent me to collect some files."

The man was just as unremarkable as the building itself, dressed in a plain and rather dull suit that stretched rather tightly across his shoulders. He looked as if he would be more comfortable in workmen's coveralls if it weren't for the neat haircut and tidy mustache.

"May I see your identification? And your pass, please."

Molly nodded and handed him both.

"It's not at all like what I expected," she said with a smile.

"And what did you expect?"

"Well, I don't really know," she confessed.

The man glanced up from her credentials, unimpressed.

"Then I'm not surprised. It can hardly live up to nonexistent expectations, can it?" he murmured, dropping his gaze back to her paperwork. "This pass says you're here for a personnel file."

"That's right."

He finally raised his eyes to her face and passed her credentials back.

"Have a seat over there, please," he said, standing. "I'll return in a moment."

Molly nodded and went over to the bench, sinking down and settling her purse on her lap. The man went through a door, and a second later, another one emerged to replace him at the desk carrying a newspaper. The new arrival paid her no attention, and Molly soon lost interest in him, shifting her gaze across the entry hall to the framed drawings. The only sound was the occasional rustle of a newspaper page, and the continued silence caused her to shift uncomfortably on the bench.

The man had seemed suspicious of her. He had taken an awfully long time looking over her credentials, and he hadn't even smiled at her once. Was something wrong? Had she done something to give herself away? Henry had assured her that her pass was valid, issued just that morning. And her credentials were certainly legitimate. She was one of Lord Halifax's personal secretaries. So why did she have the distinct impression that the man didn't believe any of it?

It was only because she'd never done anything like this before, using her government credentials to access somewhere that she had no business being, she decided. She was nervous, that was all, and there was no reason to be. She had a valid pass, and Henry had even assured her that a phone call to Lord Halifax's office would elicit the information that he had sent one of his secretaries over for him. She had absolutely nothing to worry about.

Even so, as the minutes ticked by, her unease grew. If she was found out. . .but she mustn't think that. There was no reason that she would be found out. Henry had made sure of that. Hadn't he?

When Molly looked at her watch and saw that she'd been waiting for over ten minutes, her unease turned to alarm. It shouldn't take this long to verify her, should it? Something *had* to have gone wrong. It was all well and good for Henry to say that she was perfectly safe and protected; he wasn't the one sitting in the headquarters of MI6, waiting to be escorted to the archives where she was going to steal the file of one of their agents! Good God, she must be out of her mind!

Molly got to her feet, her heart pounding. She couldn't do it. She must have been insane to agree to it in the first place. No amount of recognition with the handlers in Berlin was worth landing herself in jail. Henry would have to find another way to get what he wanted.

The door opened just as she was turning towards the outer door to leave, her purse clutched in a white-knuckled grasp.

"Miss Pollack?"

The man was back, and she turned around quickly, pasting a bright smile on her face.

"Yes?"

"Would you follow me?"

She swallowed and nodded, crossing the entry hall to follow him through the door and down a long, narrow corridor, her heart sinking. It was too late. Her opportunity to back out had passed, and now she was well and truly committed.

"I apologize for the delay. I had difficulty locating the keys. The archival room is locked, you see."

"I understand."

Molly was pleased when her voice came out steady and calm, belying her pounding heart. She followed him to the end of the corridor where he opened a door and motioned for her to precede him. She stepped into a stairwell and glanced over her shoulder, laying a gloved hand on the iron railing.

"Just follow me, miss."

He moved around her and went swiftly down the steps. Molly grasped the railing and followed, watching her footing on the narrow stairs as they descended four levels before he finally opened another door.

"Right this way."

She nodded and followed him down yet another narrow corridor until, at last, he stopped outside a door. Unlocking it, he went inside and flipped a switch on the wall.

"Here you are. When you've found what you're looking for, just press that button over there and I'll come to collect you. I'll be right down the hall."

"Thank you."

He left, closing the door behind him, and Molly looked around. She was standing in a massive area that looked more like a library than a government office. Rows of shelving held an assortment of thick ledgers, binders, folders, and boxes. Each row was neatly labeled with numbers and letters, just like a library, and she opened her purse to pull out the slip of paper Henry had given her. All she had to do was find the right row and search for a name: Jian.

She was in.

RAF Coltishall

Miles lit a cigarette and stood in the doorway of the dispersal hut, looking out over the row of Spitfires, fueled and rearmed, waiting and gleaming in the sun. The clouds that had been hanging over them at dawn had dissipated by midmorning, giving way to a bright, perfect summer's day. A day that was ideal weather for raids, and that was just what Jerry was doing. They'd been up three times already and it wasn't even lunchtime. Good weather brought German bombers, unfortunately, making Miles almost wish for storms just so that they would get a break.

"Busy morning," Thomas said from behind him. "I suppose we can thank this weather for that."

"I was just thinking the same thing."

"At least we had time to refuel and rearm this time. I went up with only half my fuel on that last one."

Miles shook his head and stepped out into the sunlight, squinting from the glare of the sun.

"I wish they'd stay home for a day."

"What are you complaining about?" Rob demanded from his chair outside the hut. "You had a lovely walkabout yesterday. You had half a day off!"

"I would hardly call it half a day," Miles said dryly. "I was back before supper."

"I heard that you got a ride back in a beer truck," Chris asked, tilting his head back and shading his eyes so that he could peer up at Miles. "Doesn't sound much like work to me."

"It wasn't a beer truck, Yank. It was a truck that happened to belong to a pub."

"Jones said there was a keg in the back. Sounds like a beer truck to me."

"It was empty."

"You drank it dry?" Rob demanded. "Lucky bastard!"

Miles chuckled. "I bloody well wish."

"We all thought you'd gone for a Burton," Thomas told him.

"Rob here was already fixing to write your girl," Chris added. "I told him we should at least wait a few hours in case you turned up."

"Much obliged." Miles threw his cigarette away and stretched. "Although, there were a few hairy moments when I thought I *was* going to meet my Maker."

"Was the cockpit really on fire?" Thomas asked after a moment.

"Unfortunately."

"At least when I went in the drink, there were no flames involved. None that I could see, anyway."

"Then why the bloody hell did you bail out?" Rob demanded.

"Engine stopped." Thomas shrugged. "It wouldn't restart, so I thought it best to nip out."

"Can't argue with that reasoning," Chris said.

"At least I didn't try to bring home a dead duck," Miles said blithely. "I did what any rational man would do."

"Waited until you were on fire?"

"I wasn't on fire. The floor was. Really, Yank, do keep up."

The telephone in the hut behind rang shrilly, causing all of them to tense and turn as one to stare at the window. After a moment, the corporal opened it and stuck his out.

"Anyone seen the CO about? HQ on the line for 'im," he called.

Thomas visibly relaxed as Miles exhaled, forcing his heart to slow again.

"Boyd!" Rob yelled, clasping his hands about his mouth. "Look lively! Where's Ashmore?"

Green section, who were lounging in the grass near the fighters, pointed to the far Spitfire just as a head popped round the nose and Ashmore moved away from his kite.

"Call for you!" Rob yelled.

"Call for you!" Boyd echoed, yelling the message along.

"Am I the only one who's starting to jump every time that damn phone rings?" Chris asked after a second. "Christ!"

"No." Thomas yawned and wandered over to perch on an overturned metal barrel. "I don't think I'll ever hear a phone ring the same again."

"I'll tell you what, I'm getting hungry," Rob said as Ashmore strode by on his way to the hut behind them. "Can't they stand us down for lunch? It isn't as if we're making any kind of dent in the bastards."

"The newspapers this morning said that we shot down over fifty yesterday," Thomas pointed out, making a face when the other three men snorted. "Well, it did."

"Tomcat, if we were shooting down fifty a day, the Krauts would be rethinking their strategy. Yet they're not. So either our numbers are wrong, or they're suicidal."

"Or they simply have the planes to lose," Miles said, dropping his cigarette butt into the ground and putting his boot over it. "Every time we go up, it's the same thing: 20 plus, 40 plus, and there are always more than that once we get to them."

"At least you know you got one yesterday," Chris said after a second. "That engine went up like a bonfire. There's no way they made it home."

"Speaking of yesterday," Rob said, straightening up and turning in his chair to face Miles. "What the bloody hell were you thinking, flying head-to-head with them like that?!"

"I was thinking it would break up the formation, and it did." Miles raised his eyebrows and looked down at Rob curiously. "I'd have thought that was obvious."

"It was suicide!"

"Clearly not," Miles murmured, amused. "I'm still here."

"It's not as bad it looks," Chris interjected. "You just have to make sure you break in time to clear the wing. I thought it was fantastic! I'll do it again, and I'll bet Miles will too."

"You'd win that wager," Miles agreed. "It works. Admittedly, it isn't for everyone. I wouldn't advise young Thomas here to try it, for instance. Oh, nothing personal, old boy. You simply don't have the experience yet."

"No offense taken," Thomas said cheerfully. "I think you're bloody mad, both of you!"

"What am I supposed to tell m'sister if you crash into a Heinkel at 280 miles per hour?" Rob demanded.

"Just tell her he was playing chicken with a bomber."

"Not helpful, Yank," Rob snapped. "I'm serious. I'm the one who'll have to tell her that you were being a bleeding idiot."

"I don't see why you'll have to tell her anything," Miles said with a shrug. "I'm sure a simple 'killed in action' would suffice. Lord knows that's all my parents will get."

"Oh, you clearly don't understand how Evie operates," Rob muttered. "She'll want to know every detail."

"Well, not for nothing, but I think a little white lie wouldn't be out of the question," Chris said, drawing a look of amusement from Miles and astonishment from Rob.

"Lie to m'sister?" Rob repeated incredulously. "I haven't been able to lie to her since we were in the nursery. Catches me every time."

"Then you *are* in a jam."

"No, he isn't. I have no intention of crashing into the nose of a bomber, or anything else, for that matter."

"Good to hear," a voice said dryly behind them. "Of course, we won't mention the kite you wrote off yesterday."

Miles turned to look at Ashmore with a grin.

"To be fair, I was no longer in it when it crashed, so that hardly counts."

"And I'm very happy that you weren't. Someone heard your prayer, Ainsworth. We've been told to stand down for an hour. Lunch isn't up yet, but I'm told there are sandwiches in the mess."

Rob stood up and stretched.

"Thank God for that. I'm hungry enough to eat a horse."

Ashmore stuck his fingers in his mouth and whistled shrilly to get the attention of the other pilots in the squadron. He waved to them, motioning to the buildings in the distance, before turning and falling into step beside Miles as he started to walk across the grass towards the officers' mess in the distance.

"I understand there were flames in the cockpit when you bailed out," he said, glancing at him. "The doctor says you weren't burned. Is that true?"

"Yes. Not even my boots were singed, which I'm very grateful for. There was a bit of black on them, but Matthews is a wizard. I didn't recognize them this morning."

"There's much to be said for a good batman."

"Yes, sir."

"I don't suppose you got the squadron of the Hurricane who hit you?"

"No. There were two of them, but I couldn't see the markings."

"No, I thought not. I wish I could say this was an isolated incident, but the fact is that this kind of thing happens a lot, you know. They're sending us green pilots who don't know which end their arse is half the time." Ashmore shrugged. "It's bad enough keeping track of the enemy, but we also have to keep track of our own."

"In all fairness, he wasn't the one who did the real damage. Well, not entirely, anyway. He must have hit the controls because I couldn't outmaneuver the 110 that followed me in. That bastard is the one who put the cork in it."

Before Ashmore could respond, they heard the bell ringing at the dispersal hut behind them. Turning, they stared in astonishment as a corporal ran out, waving his hands.

"SCRAMBLE!!!"

"I thought we were stood down?" Miles exclaimed.

"We were."

"Then what the hell is he going on about?"

When the pilots simply stared back at him, the man cupped his hands around his mouth and yelled again.

"66 SQUADRON SCRAMBLE!!!"

"Could it be a mistake?" Miles asked.

"If it is, we'll sort it out later," Ashmore said, breaking into a run and waving the rest of the pilots behind them back to their airplanes. "Well, don't just stand there!" he yelled. "Get a move on!!"

Miles ran with Ashmore, catching up to the rest of the squadron as they all belted back to the row of Spitfires. So much for lunch, and so much for their hour break. As he rounded his new-to-him Spit, Jones was already on the wing waiting with his parachute.

"At least you're all fueled and rearmed this time, sir," he said cheerfully, helping him with the chute.

"The kite is, but I'm not," Miles muttered, doing up the straps and climbing into the cockpit.

"Good hunting, sir!"

Jones jumped off the wing and ran clear as Miles settled his helmet over his head. A minute later, he was pulling out and increasing speed for takeoff, right behind Ashmore. His stomach growled, adding its own protest to the turn of events, and Miles shook his head as he hurtled down the landing strip. His wings caught air and a second later, his wheels left the ground, sending him back to war.

Evelyn sipped her coffee and lifted her face to the warm breeze blowing across the lawn onto the terrace.

"It's such a lovely morning," her mother said. "I'm so glad you suggested moving breakfast outside, Evelyn."

"I'm not sure that Thomas and Millie were as pleased," Evelyn said wryly, setting her cup down and reaching for a piece of toast.

"Oh, we don't mind, miss," Millie said behind her, bustling up with another platter filled with pots of jam and honey, and dishes of fresh berries. "It is a lovely morning, to be sure."

"Oh Millie, you're a saint," Evelyn said with a laugh. "What would we do without you?"

"I dread to think, miss." She set the tray down and looked at Mrs. Ainsworth. "Thomas will be along with the hot food, ma'am. I'll just go get some more tea, shall I?"

"Yes, thank you, Millie."

The woman nodded and turned to leave the terrace again.

"Wherever did they find this table?" Agatha asked, reaching for a pot of honey. "I've never seen it before."

"Oh, we have it for entertaining," Evelyn said cheerfully. "Lord knows where they keep it. It always seems to appear when its needed."

"Oh, isn't this lovely?!" Marguerite exclaimed, coming out onto the terrace with Bill behind her. "Are we breakfasting al fresco?"

"Yes. It was Evelyn's idea when she saw how lovely it is this morning," Madeleine said with a smile. "I hope you don't mind."

"Not at all!" Bill held out a chair for his wife, then seated himself across from Evelyn. "Is that coffee?"

"Yes. Would you like some?"

"Please."

Madeleine poured him a cup and handed it to him, then waited while Thomas came to the table with a large serving platter of covered dishes.

"Thank you, Thomas."

"Ma'am."

He bowed and turned to leave them again.

"There are eggs and sausage and, I think, sardines," Madeleine said. "Please, help yourself to whatever you'd like."

Evelyn finished spreading jam on her toast, smiling at the array of choices on the table before them. When it was only her mother, Auntie Agatha, and herself, they tended to keep to the lighter, French version of breakfast, preferring bread, fruit, and occasionally some cheese. However, as soon as a man graced the premises, her mother insisted on offering both the French and the standard English fare. It was entirely unnecessary, of course, but somehow it always got eaten. Nothing ever went to waste, which was quite a testament to Millie's housekeeping skills.

"Evelyn, what are your plans for today?" Agatha asked her.

"Oh! That reminds me," Evelyn said, setting her toast down and wiping her mouth with her napkin. "I'd completely forgotten that I arranged to meet Maryanne Gilhurst this evening near Coventry. I won't be home for dinner, Maman."

"Coventry!" Agatha gaped at her. "But that's three hours away!"

"Well, it's closer to two hours than three, Auntie," Evelyn said thoughtfully. "Regardless, I'll be perfectly fine."

"But why?" Madeleine asked with a frown. "I thought she was in the. . .oh, what was it? The Land Army?"

"The ATS." Evelyn reached for her coffee. "It stands for Auxiliary Territorial Service, you know," she explained to Adele and Claude. "You're partially right, Mother. They *are* part of the army."

"Well, but why are you going to Coventry if she's in this ATS?"

"She's completed her training and wanted to celebrate before she goes to her first posting. Coventry is the middle mark between us," Evelyn explained. "We arranged it last week, but I completely forgot to tell you. I'm sorry."

"What does this ATS do?" Adele asked.

"Oh, they do all sorts of support duties. Maryanne will be driving. Her brother arranged it."

"Driving what?" Claude asked curiously.

"Oh, I don't know. It could be anything. She could be driving trucks with supplies, or an ambulance, or who knows what. I suppose she'll tell me all about it over dinner."

"Well, if you're going back to your station tomorrow, I'd think at least you would be here for dinner on your last night," Agatha announced sternly. "Why, you've barely been home for two days in a row since you've been on leave!"

Evelyn swallowed and looked at her mother, guilt rolling over her.

"I honestly didn't think of that," she admitted. "I'm sorry, Mother. I'll tell you what, I'll call and speak to Section Officer Madson and see if I can return on Sunday instead. I can't promise that I'll be able to, but I will try."

"I wouldn't think one day would make much of a difference," Agatha muttered.

"Agatha!" Madeleine exclaimed in exasperation. "There *is* a war on, and she has a commission in the air force. As much as I would like her to stay longer, we must understand that it isn't up to her."

"I'll see what I can work out." Evelyn laid her napkin on the table and pushed back her chair. "I'll go and ring Section Officer Madson now."

Getting up, she went into the house, hearing Agatha and her mother arguing as she went. She stepped into the drawing room and exhaled, pausing just out of sight of the terrace to take a deep breath. She hated lying to her mother, and she seemed to be doing it more and more these days. And as the war went on, it would only get worse. This was what she'd agreed to when she'd agreed to join MI6. Her lips twisted wryly, and she made her way to the door to go and pretend to make a phone call.

At least now Bill had seen with his own eyes how challenging it was being here rather than Northolt. Perhaps he would be a bit more understanding of her desire to return to her station now!

Chapter
Twenty-Three

M olly closed the thick ledger and slid it back onto the shelf with a frown. She pulled Henry's note out again and reread the numerical code, then went to the end of the row and looked at the sign on the stack. She was definitely in the correct row, yet all she'd been able to find so far were ledgers filled with billing invoices. Could Henry have made a mistake?

She went back into the row and looked around helplessly. She'd been down here for ten minutes already. While she didn't know how long it generally took people to find files, she was sure it wasn't more than half an hour; a third of her time was gone.

Turning to look at the opposite shelves, Molly pulled out another thick binder and opened it. A muffled curse escaped her lips as she found more invoices. These ones were from a uniform company. Closing it, she slid it back onto the shelf and shook her head. Henry had got it wrong, obviously. Her only choice was to start at one end and go through all the rows until she found the one with the agent files. And she would have to do it quickly.

Molly quickly walked to the end of the massive room and began pulling random books and boxes from along the row and checking inside. She was in the fourth row when she heard the door open. Glancing at her watch, she grimaced. She'd been down here for twenty minutes now. Obviously, someone was coming to check on her.

"Miss Pollack?" A male voice called sharply.

"Yes!" Molly went to the end of the row and looked around the corner. "Here I am."

As she spoke, her mouth went dry, and her heart rate quickened. The man who had shown her down here was nowhere in sight. Instead, she was facing an older gentleman with a stern face. While that was unnerving, it wasn't what had turned her palms suddenly damp. The two uniformed guards standing on either side of the door were responsible for that.

"Miss Pollack, I'm afraid I'll need you to come with us," the man said, walking towards her.

Molly swallowed and opened her eyes very wide.

"Why? Is there something the matter?" she asked innocently.

"Yes, I'm afraid there is." The man stopped in front of her and looked down at her, his face impassive. "You're under arrest."

She stared at him in astonishment. "I beg your pardon?"

"I've been authorized to place you under arrest."

"What on earth for?" she blustered bravely. "I haven't done anything wrong!"

"I'm afraid you're not authorized to be down here," he told her, his tone even. "This building is protected by the Secret Intelligence Service, and trespassing is punishable by arrest and charges under the Official Secrets Act of 1939."

"Trespassing? But I have a pass! Signed by Lord Halifax himself!" Molly protested. "I'm not trespassing!"

"I still need you to come with me. You can come willingly, or we can restrain you."

She stared up at the hard jaw and the stern eyes and gulped.

"I'll come willingly."

Evelyn looked up when the door to the library opened and Bill came in, a book in his hand. Seeing her reading in a chair, he paused.

"Oh, I'm sorry. I didn't know anyone was in here. I'm not disturbing, am I?"

"Not at all! I brought this down to return it, then ended up reading some more," Evelyn assured him, closing the book.

Bill held up the book in his hand. "I'm doing the same. Returning a book on the Waterloo campaign."

"You haven't had enough of war?"

"I could say the same," he murmured, nodding to the copy of *The Iliad* in her lap.

Evelyn glanced down and was betrayed into a laugh.

"So you can!" She stood up and carried it over to a shelf, sliding it back into its place. "I suppose people like us can't get away from it, even when we should."

"Evie, I'm glad I found you alone," Bill said, setting his book down on a small table next to an armchair. "I think I can appreciate your desire to return to Northolt more after breakfast. I didn't realize quite how inquisitive your Auntie Agatha is."

"Nosy, you mean," she said cheerfully, turning away from the shelf and smiling at him. "Oh, that was nothing. Robbie and I called her the Bulldog when we were growing up. She's always been like it, but it never seemed to matter so much."

"Yes, well, I can see how it would be easier for you to continue your work away from here."

Evelyn motioned for him to take a seat and walked over to sink into a chair across from him.

"The more that I have to lie to my family, the more likely it is that I'll be discovered by them," she said softly. "It's simple maths, really. The more I fabricate, the more opportunities there are for me to trip up, or for them to realize that something isn't quite right. Mother and Auntie Agatha don't know very much about the workings of the air force, or of military protocol in general, but Uncle Claude does. He's very astute."

"Yes. Well, of course, he worked with them in France, didn't he? While there will be some differences, far and wide, all military services operate the same way." Bill nodded and crossed his legs comfortably. "Claude is an intelligent man. We've had quite a few conversations while I've been here, and I've thoroughly enjoyed his company. But I can see your concern, and I agree. You should return to Northolt without delay. I'll arrange for you to return on Sunday, all right?"

"Thank you."

He held up a finger warningly. "However, if it's bombed again, I'm moving you to Scotland. No questions. Agreed?"

Evelyn sighed. "Very well."

He nodded, satisfied. "Good. As I've said before, we need you. I can't afford to lose you in a bombing raid."

"Not for nothing, I'm not exactly anxious to get myself blown up, either."

"Quite." Bill chuckled. "Then we're in agreement. Now, are you ready for this evening?"

"Oh yes. You really do need to stop worrying. The plans and I will be perfectly fine."

"And you're taking copies? Not the originals?"

"Yes, of course."

"Good. I might as well tell you that I'm not comfortable with those papers, copies or otherwise, being driven three hours across England. Anything could happen, and then there's classified documents out there in the wind!" He shook his head. "And don't even get me started on Monty looking at them."

"I thought you've used him before," she said with a frown.

"We have, but never with something this important. It's mainly been experimental designs where we wanted to know the feasibility and practicality of production." Bill shrugged. "All top secret, of course, but never quite this sensitive."

"Well, driving it across England is the easy part. After all, it's not as if those papers aren't well traveled! They've made it from Austria to England, by way of Switzerland and France, *and* in the midst of an invasion," Evelyn pointed out in amusement. "If I can carry them safely through France with the Nazis on my tail, I believe I can carry them to Coventry and back."

"It's always when your guard is down that the stunning blow occurs," he told her soberly. "Don't think you're perfectly safe just because you're in England."

"I don't," she said, the smile fading. "Far from it. Until the Round Club and Henry are put out of action, I won't be at ease, regardless of how remote the possibility of my being discovered. And, as far as showing these drawings to someone outside of my circle, I'm certainly not happy about it either. However, I'm realistic enough to know that we need an expert eye on them. I'm sure Daddy would have had someone lined up, so I have to accept that I have to do the same."

"Well, you're right about that. Your father would have had someone lined up." Bill frowned thoughtfully. "I wonder who he would have trusted enough to do it."

"Knowing Daddy, it was probably someone abroad," Evelyn said dryly.

"Well, it certainly wasn't anyone in MI6, at any rate." Bill stood up. "I wish I knew why he was so insistent that you not bring it to me."

"I don't know." Evelyn stood and watched as he picked up the book on Waterloo and carried it to the shelves on the other side of the room to put it away. "I prefer to think that it had nothing to do you, and more to do with Henry."

Bill turned from the bookshelf, his lips pressed together.

"And then there's that," he muttered. "If he knew we had a spy in our ranks, why didn't he tell someone?"

"Perhaps he wasn't positive." Evelyn shrugged. "Daddy wouldn't make an accusation like that without knowing for certain that there was a mole."

Bill smiled faintly.

"No. No, he wouldn't, would he? Very thorough, Robert was. It's one of the things I admired about him." He walked over and looked down at her. "Be very careful tonight. If anything seems off, or if you think something might be wrong, forget the whole thing and come home. We'll find another way to verify the information."

"All right." She smiled at him. "Though I really can't imagine what could possibly go wrong."

Molly shifted on her wooden chair and stared at the worn table in front of her. She was seated in a dank, cold room with no windows and only a single bulb hanging from the ceiling above the table. She had been shown in here over two hours before and left alone. When she'd tried the door and found it unlocked, she opened it only to discover two guards posted outside. They had ordered her back into the room, and there she had remained.

Why, oh why, had she agreed to do this for Henry? She'd known the risk was great, yet she'd somehow allowed him to convince her that there was none at all; that there was no possibility of her being caught. Now here she sat after being humiliatingly searched by a female officer while Henry was finishing up his day, free and clear.

Molly rubbed her arms and shifted again on her chair. She was cold, hungry, miserable, and thoroughly terrified. What were they going to do to her? She hadn't been told anything beyond what the horrid man had said when he arrested her. He'd said that she was trespassing and had no business being there. That was nonsense, of course. She had a pass that allowed her to be there. Henry had given it to her, and she'd seen enough of them to know that it was legitimate. But something had obviously tipped them off that she wasn't supposed to be there. Just before that woman had come in to search her, she'd heard the man talking outside the door. She couldn't hear everything being said, but the word spy had been clear enough. They must know. She didn't know how they could know, but they obviously did.

You've really gone and done it now, haven't you? Molly thought disgustedly. *You could have told Henry no, and should have, too. Now look at the mess you're in.*

They're not going to just let you walk out with a slap on the wrist. Not with a war on.

The Germans would be there soon to take over, but Molly couldn't seem to derive any comfort from that thought. Yes, she would be released when they arrived—Henry would see to it—but in the meantime, she would be sent to a horrible women's prison. She shuddered. She couldn't imagine what horrors were in store for her.

The door to the small room opened suddenly, startling her, and the man strode in, followed by one of the guards from outside the door.

"Miss Pollack," he said with a brisk nod. He reached into his inner pocket to pull out his identification. "I'm Barton. I'm with MI6. I have some questions for you."

He held out the identification for her and she glanced at it, taking in the photograph and official stamp.

"I don't know what you think I can tell you," she said, lifting her gaze from the identification. "I don't even know why I'm here."

Barton sat down on the other side of the table and folded his hands on the surface.

"Oh, I think that's unlikely, Miss Pollack," he said pleasantly. "What were you doing in Broadway today?"

"I was sent by my boss, Lord Halifax, to retrieve a file."

"An agent file?"

"Yes."

"Why?"

"It was my understanding that he wanted to show the file to the prime minister in the War Rooms," she said steadily, pleased when her voice sounded even and calm. She gripped her hands together in her lap, keeping her eyes on Barton's face. "Though, he never really said."

"And why would Lord Halifax want to show an agent's file to Churchill?"

"I have no idea. I'm not privy to Lord Halifax's thoughts," she said tartly. "I only know that I was asked to go get the file and bring it back to him."

"When did he ask this?"

"Late yesterday afternoon, before I left for the day. When I came to work this morning, the pass was signed and waiting for me. It was signed this morning. You can see for yourself. I assume that you have it?"

Barton smiled faintly.

"Yes, we have it. It was indeed signed this morning."

"Then why am I being held like this?" Molly demanded. "You *know* that I wasn't trespassing!"

"The thing is, Miss Pollack," he said, releasing his hands and sitting back in his chair, "I spoke to Lord Halifax personally just half an hour ago."

Molly felt the blood drain out of her face as she swallowed a sudden lump that formed in her throat. Barton was watching her closely, and she knew the game was up. Lord Halifax had told him that he knew nothing about the pass or his secretary going to Broadway in search of a personnel file. She was well and truly caught, and there was absolutely nothing she could do to get out of it. Blast Henry and his bloody ambition to become the SD's most prized mole in England!

"I'm sure you realize that what you did today could be, and most certainly will be, considered a violation to the Official Secrets Act? An act that binds all government officials, as well as their staff. You *are* aware of it?"

"Yes."

"Then you know that you can be charged with treason against the Crown, and that if convicted, it is punishable by death?"

"Yes."

"Then why did you do it?"

Molly remained silent, her heart racing. She didn't know what to do, but she knew enough to keep her mouth shut from now on. If she didn't say anything, she couldn't make the situation worse. And she certainly wasn't about to welch on Henry. She may be a lot of things, but she wasn't going to implicate him just to save her own skin.

Barton waited, watching her, and her jaw tightened stubbornly. Seeing it, he sighed and pushed his chair back, standing up.

"If you won't say anything, then the matter is out of my hands," he told her. "I have no choice but to officially present the case to the Secret Service and have them proceed with charges. Unless you want to cooperate. . ."

Silence followed that suggestion, and Barton let it stretch for a few seconds before he shook his head and turned to the door.

"Very well. But if you happen to change your mind, I'm ready to hear your side." He paused at the door and looked back. "Is he really worth protecting at the cost of your own neck?"

Molly watched as he left on that question, the guard following him out. The door closed behind them, and this time, she heard the lock on the door slide into place. She didn't seem to care that she was locked in now. Her mind was still spinning over that parting shot.

How the hell did they know about Henry?

Chapter Twenty-Four

E velyn sat on a bench in the reception area of the building where Montague Thompson worked, watching the bustle around her. She'd arrived fifteen minutes earlier, expecting the place to be quiet. It was, after all, past the dinner hour. Instead, she found the place as busy as ever inside. Men and women in coveralls and work boots crossed through the reception area frequently, and it didn't take her any time at all to realize that one half of the building was some kind of factory. A woman sat behind the reception desk, eating a supper consisting of a sandwich and an apple while she fielded a telephone that seemed to ring incessantly. After taking her name, she'd motioned Evelyn to the bench to wait, promising to ring Mr. Thompson and let him know that she was here.

And there Evelyn waited, trying not to itch her head under her wig, and doing her best to sit like a man in her brother's suit, his hat sitting next to her on the bench. She was rather shocked at all the activity at this time of night, but of course, there *was* a war on, and obviously whatever the factory manufactured was vital to the war effort. She'd never given much thought to the industrial workers and their timetables, but if she had, she supposed she would have realized that they would work at all hours. Production couldn't stop simply because the dinner hour had come. Things were far too desperate for that.

"Mr. Ankerbottom?"

Evelyn looked up to see a man coming towards her. He was an older version of the Montague Thompson that she vaguely remembered from years past. His brown hair was tussled, as if he'd been running his hands through it, and his lab coat was creased, thrown carelessly over his button-down shirt and brown slacks. She stood up and held her hand out to him.

"Yes. Mr. Thompson?" she asked, pleased when her voice came out several octaves lower than her normal speaking voice. The practice in the car on the way had paid off.

"Call me Monty," he said, gripping her hand firmly. "Everyone does. And you are?"

"Terry." Evelyn smiled and withdrew her hand. "Well, Terrance, but no one's called me that in years."

Monty smiled, his brown eyes friendly.

"Well, Terry, sorry to keep you waiting. I'm afraid you arrived in the middle of a dustup. One of the machines in the factory caught on fire earlier, and we've all been trying to help get it up and running again."

"Good Lord! Was anyone hurt?"

"No, no. It was just a little mishap, thank God." Monty motioned for her to walk with him. "And completely repairable, but it's taken a few of us to get it going again."

Evelyn fell into step beside him, walking with a very distinct limp.

"Have you hurt yourself?" he asked in concern.

"No, no. It's the result of a bout—with polio when I was a boy," she told him cheerfully.

"Ah. I'm sorry."

"Don't be. Aside from preventing me from joining up, it doesn't affect me that much. I'm quite used to it." Evelyn smiled inwardly as Monty slowed his stride to accommodate her limp. The polio excuse not only explained her shorter, female stride, but it also accounted for the ill-fitting suit. After all, if one's hips and spine were out of whack, it would be very difficult to make a suit sit properly. "This fire, is that why it's so busy around here?"

"Lord no. It's always like this. There are three shifts of workers now, so there's always someone milling about."

"What do you do here?" Evelyn asked as they went through a door and started down a long corridor.

"We manufacture electromagnetic components," he answered readily. "Dynamos and magnetos, mainly. Right now, we're the largest supplier of ignition magnetos, for piston engines, you know."

Evelyn didn't know, but she wasn't about to let him know that.

"Oh! For the Spitfires," she said, nodding wisely.

"Among others, yes. Do you know anything about magnetos?"

"'Fraid not. I haven't a clue."

Monty laughed. "Not many do. Here we are."

He opened a door and motioned for her to precede him. Evelyn walked into a small office that had no windows and very little to recommend it aside from a massive technical drawing of some kind of engine hanging on the wall.

"Have a seat." Monty closed the door behind her and motioned to the single chair placed in front of his desk. "I understand that you've brought me some drawings that Sir William wants me to look at."

"That's right." Evelyn sat down and balanced the slim case that she carried on her lap, pulling a key from her pocket. "Thank you for taking the time."

"Oh, it's no problem," he said cheerfully, leaning against his desk. "Usually I come to London, but he's caught me in the middle of a large project this time, and I couldn't get away."

Evelyn unlocked the case and pulled out a portfolio containing the drawings, snapping the case closed again. She handed them over to Monty, tamping down the natural feeling of misgiving at showing a stranger the papers that her father had worked so hard to protect.

"He understands. He was unable to get away from London himself. That's why I'm here," she said with a small smile.

Monty nodded, taking the folder and walking around to sit behind his desk, opening it as he did so. Silence fell over the office as he scanned the documents, examining the drawings carefully. At one point, he sucked in his breath and angled his desk lamp closer, holding the drawing up so that he could study something on the diagram closely.

"Where did he come by these?" he asked, glancing up. "I've never seen a design like this before."

"It's experimental," she told him. "As far as I can tell, they're trying to concoct some kind of false plan to bamboozle the Germans with, though what it might be, I haven't the foggiest. It's above my paygrade," she added with a shrug.

"Of course." He flashed a wry smile and went back to studying the drawings, spreading the pages out on the desk before him. "This is really quite extraordinary. Do you have any experience with motors?"

"A bit, but it really only extends to automobiles, I'm afraid."

"Well, this is far removed from a Vauxhall, though some of the core principles are the same."

"Do you know what it is, then?"

"It appears to be some kind of self-propelled machine. This here, that's clearly the motor, but this over here is a casing of some sort." Monty frowned and looked at the pages in turn, his brows drawn together in concentration. "It's almost as if. . ."

His voice trailed off as if he were speaking to himself, then he made a disgusted sound and reached out and turned one of the pages upside down.

"I'm a bleeding idiot," he muttered. "I had it the wrong way round! *Now* it makes sense."

He sat back in his chair, a look of astonishment on his face. "Extraordinary!"

"What is it, do you think?" Evelyn asked, trying to keep her voice even as her heart rate reacted to the look on his face. She had a horrible feeling that her suspicions were about to be confirmed.

"I think it's a new kind of bomb," he said bluntly, running a hand through his hair. "It's fantastic. It appears to be a self-propelled bomb. I would have said that it's impossible, but these plans show that it isn't."

Evelyn's gut clenched and she sucked in her breath. She had been right. The Germans were working on a new bomb.

"Self-propelled?" she repeated, reaching into the inside pocket of the suit and pulling out a slender notebook and pencil. "You don't mind if I take notes? Sir William did ask me to note your thoughts particularly."

He waved his hand dismissively, not taking his eyes from the papers before him.

"Yes, yes, of course. By self-propelled, I mean that this weapon here would be able to fly on its own, over long distances, guided by a timer of some sort. After traveling a specified distance, it descends. Quite remarkable, really. I've never seen the like!"

"Do you mean it would simply fly through the air, all by itself? Without anything carrying it?"

"That's right."

"But. . .how would it know where to go?"

"Well, that's the crux, isn't it?" Monty rubbed his face and leaned forward. "It would have to be pointed in the right direction. It could really only fly in a straight line."

Evelyn stared at him, her mind spinning. A bomb that would fly over long distances? It seemed so unreal and far-fetched that it could only be true.

"How does it take off?"

"That isn't here, but I expect it would need to be launched from some kind of platform with a very strong propellant. Once airborne, the onboard motor would kick in and. . .well, it would propel itself."

Evelyn was silent for a long moment while she made her notes. When she looked up, Montague was staring at her, the implications of such a weapon sinking in.

"You said it could cover long distances?" she asked, her voice low. "How long of a distance?"

Monty shook his head, looking back down at the drawings with a frown.

"Hard to say. It would depend on so many factors, the materials available, the force of the initial launch. . .And, of course, these plans are incomplete. They're very basic and rudimentary. I'd venture to say that these are the initial drawings. The final product will go through numerous changes and alterations."

"If it were you working on this, what would be your best guess?" Evelyn pressed him. "What do you think would be achievable if you were working with that as a base?"

Monty thought for a long moment, then exhaled and shrugged.

"Based on these drawings, and what I know of this kind of technology, perhaps as far as a hundred miles, or more."

"A hundred miles!" Evelyne exclaimed in astonishment. "Why, that would mean that it could be fired from—"

She broke off and Monty nodded.

"Anywhere in the British Isles," he finished for her. "We could target France, perhaps even Belgium. Which makes it a very good thing that this experimental weapon is only meant to be a ploy to fool the Germans. Why, could you imagine if *they* had something like this? They could target London from the coast of northern France and not send a bomber at all!"

"It would be terrible, wouldn't it?" Evelyn closed her notebook and slipped it back into her pocket. "Thankfully, this is nothing more than an exercise."

"And Bill wanted to know if it would pass muster." Montague gathered the papers together again and tucked them back into the folder. "Well, you can tell him that it certainly does, and tell him that I'm jolly glad this brainchild of his is in England and nowhere else!"

Henry lit a cigarette and looked at his watch. Shaking his head, he crossed the hotel room to the window and moved the blackout curtain a bit, peering down into the darkened street below. He didn't know why he was bothering. He couldn't see a damn thing in the gloom down there. Sighing, he let the curtain fall back into place and turned to pace back across the room.

Molly was late. This was their regular meeting place, and their usual time. Generally, she was there before him, waiting, but that wasn't the case this evening. It had been over an hour since he arrived, and there was still no sign of her. Where on earth had she got to?

A streak of uneasiness went through him. Had something gone wrong today? She had gone to Broadway to look for Jian's file, armed with the pass that he'd obtained for her and the location of the file. It was a very simple operation: get the folder and leave. Could something have gone wrong? Henry shook his head. No. His plan was foolproof, and Molly was certainly no fool. Nothing could have gone wrong. She would have been in and out within half an hour, just as they'd discussed.

But then, where was she?

Henry shook his head and went over to the open bottle of wine on the table next to the bed. Pouring himself a glass, he couldn't stop his mind from going back to the nagging thought that something was very wrong. What if she *had* been caught? It was highly unlikely, but nothing was impossible. He supposed that she could have done or said something that would have given herself away, but what? She had a pass that assured her access to the section, and she had a story that was entirely believable, not least because she really *did* work for Lord Halifax.

Henry sipped his wine, then set the glass down and resumed pacing. There was no reason at all for anyone at Broadway to question her errand. At least, none of the people that she would have come into contact with. Everything was probably fine, and she had simply been held up somewhere. At work, perhaps.

But what if everything wasn't fine? What if something had gone wrong this afternoon? His lips thinned into an ugly line. If MI6 had caught Molly, then the game was up. They would know full well just what she was doing there. They weren't stupid, regardless of what some of the older, stuffier members of the House of Lords thought. They knew someone was leaking information to the Germans about their precious Jian. They knew they had a spy, a traitor. If Molly had been caught, they would find the location of the file on her, and they would know she was looking for the identity of Jian.

They would get her to talk.

A chill went down Henry's spine despite the warmth of the summer night. If Molly talked, there was quite a bit that she could say, and all of it damning, not only to him but to the Round Club as well. Even if that blasted list of names wasn't in the hands of the Secret Service, it soon would be with Molly in custody. Though not part of the inner circle herself, she was certainly well acquainted with who was in it.

He took a deep drag from his cigarette then crushed it out in an ashtray. He was getting ahead of himself. There was absolutely no reason to think that Molly had been detained by the Secret Intelligence Service. She was over an hour late to their regular tryst, yes, but that didn't mean that she had been arrested. She could simply be held up somewhere.

Henry turned to drop onto the bed, propping his back against the headboard and crossing his feet at the ankles. He stared across the room broodingly for a long moment. If she wasn't here in another half an hour, he would leave and go home. There was no point in his hanging around all night waiting for her. An hour and a half was more than a generous amount of time for him to wait.

If Molly gave up his name, what then?

Henry stifled a curse. It was no use. The seed of doubt had taken root, and there was no getting it out of his head now. Until Molly showed up and gave him the file, he would keep thinking that something had gone wrong. He might as well examine the possibility and prepare accordingly.

If she had been arrested, and that was a big if, Molly wouldn't give up his name. She had too much invested in their relationship, and she loved him. Women were silly, sentimental creatures. They didn't turn on the men they loved. And, even if she did, there was absolutely no proof that he was behind any of it. He'd made sure of that. He'd approached this operation just as he approached everything: with extreme caution. There was nothing that could lead back to him, no real proof, aside from Molly herself. If it came down to it, it would be the word of a common secretary against his, and Henry had every confidence that his social standing would win out.

The sticky part would be that it would invite attention, and attention was something that he didn't want from the likes of MI6. But it wouldn't be MI6, would it? Henry cheered slightly at that thought. It was the Secret Service who investigated domestic threats of espionage, and he had several of *them* in his back pocket already. It would be a very simple matter to ensure that the whole thing was dismissed or swept away all together.

The brief feeling of relief faded, and he frowned again. MI6 wouldn't let it go that easily. In fact, it was entirely possible that MI6 wouldn't hand the matter over to the Secret Service at all. They would likely consider it an internal problem, and they would handle it as such. And that landed him right back in the spotlight with MI6. They would focus on him, digging until they found something, anything. Unless, of course, he gave them someone else to focus their attention on; someone else to take the blame for the entire operation. Henry smiled slowly, his cold eyes staring at the dresser across the room.

He knew just who to use.

Chapter Twenty-Five

August 24

The morning sun shone brightly over the rose garden, warming the blooms, while a faint breeze rustled the leaves of the bushes that had been there as long as Evelyn could remember. Some of them had been planted when her father was a boy, and others long before that. The climbing roses that framed the arched entry into the garden had been established well over seventy years before, or so the gardener claimed. Meticulous care had kept all but a few of the bushes healthy throughout the years, and those that had succumbed to the elements had been replaced, ensuring that the garden would still be filled and beautiful when Robbie and his family were settled in at the family home.

If he survived the war and had the opportunity to marry and start a family.

Evelyn walked along the gravel path next to Bill in silence, reflecting that if both she and Robbie were killed, Ainsworth Manor would pass to a distant relative who lived in Spain when her mother died. She couldn't imagine a worse outcome for the lovely old rose garden that had enjoyed generations of Ainsworth care.

"Are you quite sure?" Bill broke the silence, his voice curt.

"Yes, but more importantly, so is Monty."

Evelyn dragged her thoughts back to the matter at hand. She had just finished telling Bill exactly what the drawings her father had smuggled out of Austria were. His silence and grim face told her plainly that he hadn't been expecting anything of this magnitude, and who could blame him? It was like something out of a nightmare. That any country should have a weapon like that was frightening enough, but that it was Hitler's regime developing it was downright terrifying.

"It's unbelievable," Bill said, shaking his head. "And this thing can be fired from a hundred miles away? He's sure?"

"He wouldn't commit himself, but he said that with the right materials, it was certainly possible."

"Then we have to assume that it can."

"Just as we have to assume that the production is well underway," Evelyn said. "Daddy took these plans a year ago. We know the Nazis have poured all their resources into war production. We have to assume that this weapon is being developed as we speak."

"Yes, but it will have to go through extensive testing, and who knows how long that will take. It may not be as imminent a threat as we fear," Bill said thoughtfully. "However, it's a threat just the same. No wonder your father was so careful about keeping the intelligence secret. If anything like this got out, it would cause chaos and panic."

They were silent, walking along the path while the sun warmed their faces. Evelyn inhaled deeply. The rose garden was always a place of peace and tranquility for her, but today that was in stark contrast to the realization that a new form of warfare could target Britain from miles away without even a bomber to carry it.

"I'll have to hand this over, Evelyn," Bill finally said, stopping and looking at her gravely. "This isn't something we can keep to ourselves. Our engineers will have to look at this thing and try to develop a countermeasure against it."

"I agree, but will they?" she asked. "The report from Oslo was buried, and no one did anything about that. You said that it had vital evidence in it, but it was ignored."

"Yes, well, that's true," he muttered, rubbing his neck. "The general feeling is that no one person would have access to all of that information, and so it must be fake, sent by the Germans as misinformation."

"To what purpose?" she scoffed. "That's ridiculous. They have nothing to gain by that, do they?"

He shrugged. "Who's to know what they're thinking? But I know this is too big to be ignored. Even if they do bury it, we would have done our duty by passing the intelligence on. That *is* your duty, remember."

Evelyn pressed her lips together and turned to continue walking. He was right, of course. It *was* her job to turn in the intelligence that she gathered, even if it was intelligence that came from her father. And in any other circumstance, she would do so gladly. But this wasn't any other circumstance.

"Daddy didn't want MI6 anywhere near it," she finally said, her voice even and calm.

Under no circumstance could she allow Bill to hear the uncertainty and frustration that was swirling through her. He had to believe that she was thinking with a clear head, though how on earth she was supposed to do that when faced with the possibility of self-propelled bombs capable of destroying cities from countries away was beyond her.

"We don't know why, and your father had no way of knowing just how serious the war was going to get," Bill replied. "He would never have dreamed that Britain would be standing alone after all of Europe had fallen to Hitler. This isn't the world he was living in when he made that demand, and we need to follow the chain of command."

"I beg to differ," Evelyn said, stopping and facing him. "This *is* the world Daddy was living in. We all knew what could happen should war erupt again, and I think he would have known more than most. After all, he saw this weapon a year ago, before Hitler had even forced us into war. Daddy knew full well what was coming, and he still didn't trust MI6 with this intelligence."

She held up a hand when Bill opened his mouth to speak.

"You're right in that we don't know why he felt that way, but I think we both have a pretty good idea. I believe that he knew we had a spy in London, and he wanted to make sure that the Germans never knew that we had the intelligence at all. It's why he hid it in a safe deposit box in Zürich, and left instructions that only I could access it. He believed I was the only one who he could trust to keep it secret. You're asking me to break that trust."

Bill stared at her for a long moment, then exhaled in frustration and shook his head, turning to walk again,

"This is a right old mess," he muttered. "I don't have any doubt that he knew about Henry, though he obviously didn't know who or where he was. That's the only explanation for him hiding the information and not passing it to me. Lord, I've known your father since we were boys. It stings that he chose to hide it from me, but that's the only reason that I can think of that he would."

"I don't, for one instant, believe that he didn't trust you," she said firmly. "But until he discovered who the spy was, I'm sure he felt the safest place for the package was hidden away out of reach from anyone. Unfortunately, he died before he could do anything else. But the situation still exists. We still don't know who Henry is, or where he is. If we pass this intelligence on now, we may be alerting the Abwehr to the fact that we know about their secret weapon."

"And that's the last thing we want," Bill finished. He cursed under his breath. "This invisible Judas has become much more than just a thorn in my side. I'd like to find him and wring his bloody neck!"

Evelyn was surprised into a laugh.

"Well, you won't hear any disagreement from me on that score."

Silence fell between them again as Bill mulled over the predicament and Evelyn watched a fat bumblebee hover over a rose before settling briefly into the center of the bloom.

"Until we apprehend Henry, we'll have to keep this to ourselves." Bill broke the silence several minutes later, sounding disgruntled. "I can't risk this getting out. Not yet. Not before we've come up with some kind of counterintelligence to convince the enemy that we don't have the package."

"And the fact that Henry is actively looking for it here in England makes it clear that they think we have it. They must know Daddy took it."

"Precisely. We'll have to convince them that they're wrong. The hell of it is that I'm going to be releasing a dummy packet to lure Henry out. If I'd known just what it was that Ainsworth had smuggled out, I'd never have agreed."

"Do you think he knows what's in the real package?" Evelyn asked.

"I have absolutely no idea, but we have to work on the assumption that he does. And once it's leaked that we have it. . ."

"I'm not sure it will be a foregone conclusion," Evelyn said slowly. "His handlers will want to confirm the contents, and Henry will do that. Once he sees the fake documents, he'll alert them of what's inside. Even if they know the plans for this weapon were stolen and moved out of Germany, Henry will confirm that these aren't them. They'll assume the plans are still out there somewhere. In fact, that would play to our advantage. They might be convinced that Daddy never had the plans at all."

Bill was quiet for a moment.

"That would mean actually allowing Henry to gain possession of the package," he murmured. "That wasn't the plan, but you're right. If we allow him to examine the package, then contact his handler, our real package will be safe."

"And we'll have Henry," she agreed. "We'll also discover how he contacts his handler."

Bill was already nodding when she spoke. "Yes, and with any luck, we'll discover anyone else who might be involved."

"In the meantime, could you contact Leon in France?"

"Leon? Whatever for?"

"Well, if the Nazis *are* developing this weapon, they'll need somewhere to fire it from. They would have to build a site in France or Belgium," she pointed out. "Leon could put the word out for his contacts to keep an eye open."

"All right, but I wouldn't get my hopes up, if I were you. If they're building installations to fire that thing, I very much doubt that anyone will be allowed within miles of the place."

"No, but they can't hide the construction of something that large. If we learn of new construction, we can send a reconnaissance flight to take a look." She shrugged. "At any rate, it's better than standing by and doing nothing."

"I'm going back to London today. Leon isn't risking using his radio at the moment, but I'll make sure to let him know when he does make contact. Now the question is what to put in the dummy intelligence packet. If I don't put anything about any weapons at all, will Henry be lured out? We don't know how much he knows about the package that Ainsworth was carrying."

"I think it's best to stick as close to the truth as we can, without including the truth, of course. He may know nothing about it at all, but there's always the possibility that he knows exactly what was in the package."

"Yes, but to be honest, I don't see how he could."

"We don't know where he was a year ago," Evelyn said with a shrug. "We don't know who he is. For all we know, he could have been in Austria at the same time as Daddy, and if he was, then he might very well know what was taken."

Bill sighed and nodded reluctantly.

"True. Very well. I'll include references to some kind of weapon, but nothing similar to what it really is."

"When will Anthony leak it to the Round Club?"

"As soon as it's ready, I imagine." He glanced at her. "Before you ask, no."

Evelyn looked up at him innocently, a grin pulling at her lips.

"What on earth are you talking about? No, what?"

"No, you're not having any part of it," he said firmly. "It's bad enough that you've had one run in with the Secret Service. Let's not press our luck with a second."

"But surely—"

"No! Don't even say a word. It's not happening, Jian, and that's that."

Evelyn laughed.

"Well, you can't blame a girl for trying," she said, drawing a reluctant chuckle from him, "but I suppose you're right. Anthony accepted my accidental involvement the last time. He would never believe I'd stumbled into another operation."

"Precisely. In any event, you'll be back at Northolt tomorrow. There won't be much time for gallivanting around London in search of adventure and excitement."

"Is that what you think I was doing?" she demanded. "Looking for something to do?"

"Isn't it?" Bill stopped and looked down at her. "It's not surprising in the least. You spent a few hair-raising weeks fleeing across Europe ahead of the German army, being chased by an assassin *and* an SD agent. You were never one to sit still, even as a girl, and after getting a taste of that kind of excitement? No, I wasn't surprised at all when you hunted out intrigue right here in England. Hell, we trained you to do it!"

"Yes, but I wasn't quite expecting to find it at the Ramsay's summer bash," she said dryly.

"Well, God willing, you won't find anything to embroil yourself in at Northolt. This is supposed to be time for you to relax and train before going back to France."

"Relax? In the middle of a battle for Britain? Bill, really."

"Remain quiet, then, although I'm beginning to think that's impossible as well!"

Evelyn burst out laughing and tucked her hand in his arm, grinning up at him.

"Am I as bad as all that? I'm terribly sorry. Daddy always said to speak what was on my mind and pay no heed to the dull, dim-witted inanities that other women mutter."

"Good God, no. I'd rather you were exactly what you are." He glanced down at her, a twinkle in his eyes. "And I imagine so does your pilot. Any news from him?"

"I had a letter from him yesterday," she said, annoyed when she felt her cheeks flushing. "He seems in good enough spirits. He almost lost his best pilot on a hairy landing, but the Yank seems to have got out in time."

"An American?" Bill asked, surprised.

"Oh yes. I met him in London when they all got a day off. He's very nice, and Miles and Rob both say he's one of the best pilots they've ever seen. He went to Canada to volunteer to fly for us."

"Then perhaps there's hope that the rest of his countrymen will join us yet. I know Churchill is desperate for America to come into the war, but people say it will never happen."

"Chris says the public opinion in America will change," Evelyn said after a moment. "He says that there *are* people who want to help. We only hear about those who are opposed because they have the loudest voices."

"Don't all Americans?"

Evelyn grinned. "So I've heard, but I must say that Chris seemed quite the gentleman, and he didn't yell across the table during dinner." Her smile faded.

"I suppose they'll come south soon."

"I imagine they will. Dowding wants to rotate squadrons for rest and replenishment." Bill stopped walking. "And Fred Durton? How are you, Evie?"

Evelyn felt her face flush and then the blood drain out of it.

"How did you know?"

"I found out when Sergeant Cunningham came to London. She was worried that you would take it hard." Bill covered her hand on his arm with his. "Are you holding up all right?"

"Yes, I think so." She swallowed and shrugged. "They're fighting for their lives, and ours, up there every day. We're losing so many pilots, it was only a matter of time until it was someone I cared about. It'll be hard going back and him not being there."

"Is that why you're so determined to return now? To get it over with?"

"Perhaps." Evelyn shook her head and took a deep breath. "I'll be all right. Honestly. I just. . .well, Fred was one of those people who are so full of life that you can't imagine that death would win."

Bill nodded, sadness crossing his face. "I know just what you mean. That's how I felt when your father passed on. I like to think that he bounded into the hereafter with more energy than the Almighty was prepared to deal with."

Evelyn chuckled despite her melancholy.

"I do think that he must have. And Fred, bless him, probably barreled in on a bicycle. That's how we met, you know. He was racing another pilot on a bicycle, swerved to miss hitting me, and landed himself in a hedge. I don't think I'll ever forget that."

"Don't try," he advised. "Remember all the good things. That's how they stay alive, in our memories."

They were silent for a few moments, then Evelyn stopped and pulled her hand from his arm.

"I'm rather looking forward to getting back to some kind of routine," she told him with a smile. "I think going back to Northolt will be the best thing for me."

"Just remember our agreement. If one bomb falls on the station again, I'm moving you. No arguments."

"Agreed."

Broadway

Jasper looked up in surprise when a knock fell on the door.

"Come in," he called, sliding a folder over the paper he was reading.

The door opened and a man came in, carrying his coat over his arm and his hat in his hand.

"Barton!" Jasper exclaimed, standing. "What are you doing here on a Saturday?"

"I could ask you the same, sir," Barton replied with a grin. "I'm not interrupting, am I?"

"No. I'm just going over some things that I didn't get to yesterday. Have a seat."

Barton laid his coat over the back of one of the chairs, then sat in the other.

"I heard you were in this morning, so I thought I'd come up and give you my report myself," he said, crossing his legs comfortably.

"And?"

"The girl won't talk. I was at it all night, and again this morning. Even had one of the females try over breakfast. Nothing doing. She's as tight as a clam."

"She hasn't said anything at all?"

"Not since she realized that we knew the truth about that pass. She knows she's in hot water, and she's not about to give anything away." Barton scratched the back of his ear. "She's surprisingly stubborn."

"She doesn't want to incriminate herself." Jasper sat back with a scowl. "I don't imagine she's all that keen in ratting out her friends, either."

"She's protecting someone, right enough. We found directions in her purse, written in a male hand. I took it to the handwriting specialists, but without anything to compare it to, it's purely academic at this point." Barton shook his head. "We should transfer her to the Secret Service and let them handle it. It's more in their wheelhouse, anyway."

"Yes." Jasper was thoughtful for a long moment. "That's what we should do."

Barton nodded and started to push himself up. "I'll put the call through."

But Jasper stopped him when he waved him back into his seat.

"No. I said that's what we *should* do, not that we were going to," he told him. "The rat is in our ship, not theirs. We'll take care of it ourselves."

"I don't see how when the girl's as mum as can be," Barton muttered. "She hasn't uttered a word, sir. Not a word!"

"That won't last forever. Stands to reason that, with the appropriate encouragement, eventually she'll talk."

"That may be, but I can't hold her downstairs indefinitely."

"No, I know. Move her to one of the holding facilities outside of London, but do it at night in case anyone is watching."

"Do you think the person who sent her knows she's been detained?"

"I think it's likely, don't you? She must have been due to report back to someone with the file."

"That's true enough," Barton admitted ruefully. "I'm sorry. I didn't get much sleep last night. I'm not at the top of my game just now."

Jasper waved that away.

"Move her under cover of the blackout, get her settled, and then send one of the others to oversee the interrogation," he said. "Perhaps a move and a less amenable person will help to loosen her tongue."

Barton grinned. "Less amenable? Are you saying I'm soft?"

"I'm saying that someone else will not be familiar. That might shake her up a bit."

"I can send Ned," Barton said after a moment of thought. "He's an intimidating son of a bitch."

"Perfect."

"How long shall I say to keep her there?"

"As long as it takes."

"And what about this person that she's working for?"

"I don't want to run any risk of them knowing that she's been apprehended. Make it look like she's gone on an unexpected trip. A sick relative, perhaps?"

Barton nodded and got up, reaching for his coat.

"You leave it to me, sir. I'll take care of it, and no one will be the wiser."

"Thank you, Barton. I knew I could count on you."

Chapter Twenty-Six

RAF Coltishall

"Are you all right, sir?" Jones called in concern, running up to the fighter plane as Miles climbed out of the cockpit.

"Yes, of course," he said shortly. "Why wouldn't I be?"

"Well, because the side of your kite's all shot up," Jones replied, nodding to the side of the Spitfire riddled with bullet holes.

Miles didn't even glance at the battered airplane as he jumped off the wing.

"So that's what that was," he said dryly, winking at his ground crew sergeant. "Thought I felt something tickle me up there. They'll have to be a better shot than that, Jones," he added, slapping him on the shoulder.

"That looks like a damn good shot from where I'm standing, but never you mind. We'll have you patched up in no time."

"Rearm and refuel first, Jones. That's more important."

Miles turned away and scanned the horizon with a frown. Rob had come in just after him and was shutting down his engine a few yards away, but there was no sign of Ashmore yet.

"Where's the CO?" Chris called from the other side of his Spit.

"Not the foggiest," Miles called back as Rob pushed his canopy back and prepared to climb out.

"I followed him in, but then lost him a couple miles out." Chris joined Miles next to his airplane. "Green section landed already, and so has Yellow. Ashmore's the last one still up."

"Where's the CO?" Rob yelled from his wing. "Anyone seen him?"

"He hasn't come in yet," Miles called back.

Rob leapt off his wing and jogged towards them.

"He was right behind me," he said, joining them. "We got jumped by a couple of 109s, but I thought we got rid of them."

"Are you sure?" Miles asked sharply.

"Yes! They jumped us, gave us a squirt, then buggered off. Running out of juice, most likely." Rob frowned and turned to look up at the horizon. "Where the hell is he?"

"If I could answer that, Ainsworth, then I wouldn't be wasting my time hanging around here with you lot."

"This must be him now," Chris said suddenly as an airplane appeared on the horizon. "Thank God!"

Miles looked up from the cigarette he was lighting and squinted, just able to make out the shape of a Spitfire approaching the landing strip. They watched as the outline grew bigger, descending as the landing gear came down.

"Hold on," Rob said, sucking in his breath. "What's wrong with him? He's all over the bloody place. Look at the wings!"

Miles was looking, and his mouth tightened grimly. He'd seen wings dipping like that before, when Chris came in with a damaged rudder and engine.

"His rudder's gone, and probably his engine too," he said flatly, throwing his cigarette away as their squadron leader descended, the Spitfire eerily silent.

As the airplane grew closer, they saw smoke pouring from the nose and they all sucked in their breath at the same moment. A wail from the fire engine went up from behind the dispersal hut and the truck began making its way towards the landing strip as Ashmore grew closer, his wings dipping left and right as he struggled to maintain enough speed to land.

"God's teeth, he's not going to make it," Rob breathed, staring transfixed.

"He'll make it," Chris said confidently. "I did, didn't I?"

"Just barely," Miles muttered, not taking his eyes off the unsteady, bobbing fighter coming down to land.

The rest of the squadron had piled out of the dispersal hut, standing in a large group, watching their leader trying to land a lame duck. Miles glanced at them, and then turned his attention back to Ashmore. Aside from the wailing of the fire siren, a chilling silence had descended over the group as they watched. And waited.

Beads of sweat broke out over Miles' forehead, and he felt as if he was living through Chris' accident all over again. The wheels were hovering over the ground, the right wingtip dangerously close to the grass. The entire company on the ground held their breath together, watching as the Spitfire bobbed to the left a bit before the right wing dropped again. At the last minute, Ashmore managed to bring it up as the wheels bounced on the ground and the fighter settled into a controlled taxi.

"Now, there's a landing for the books," Rob exclaimed, wiping his forehead with a shaking hand.

"Told you he'd make it," Chris said, slapping Miles on his shoulder in his enthusiasm.

"Much better than that mess of a landing you managed," he replied, relief rolling through him.

Their relief was short-lived. As Ashmore rolled towards them, the smoke from the engine parted briefly, giving them a clear shot of the cockpit. Red smeared the inside of the canopy, and Miles' stomach dropped through his feet.

"Bloody hell," he muttered. "He's been shot!"

The Spitfire came to a shaking stop and the fire truck roared up alongside it. Before it had stopped, firemen were already jumping off and grabbing the hose. Miles ran towards his CO, Chris and Rob on either side, his eyes on the cockpit. He could see Ashmore inside, but he wasn't moving.

"Oh no you don't, lads," a firm voice yelled as the trio ran up to the Spitfire. "Yeh stand back. We'll get 'im out."

Miles turned to see three burly ground crew running towards the airplane, followed by two medics with a stretcher.

"Oh God," Rob gasped, spotting the stretcher. "Do you think he's dead?"

"Don't be a clot! He's just landed the bloody plane," Miles snapped.

"He could have bought it after he landed," Rob argued, his face pale. "It happened at Kenley. Poor sod landed, shut down his engine, and died. Half his chest was blown open."

"And he landed the plane?" Chris stared at him. "You're shitting me."

"No, my dear colonial, I am not shitting you. Ask Uncle Bertie."

"He's not dead," Miles said firmly. "He can't be!"

They watched as one of the ground crew pried open the cockpit and another pulled it back. Once it was open, one of them leaned into the cockpit. After some consultation, one of the others turned to call down to them.

"'E's alive!"

"Oh, thank God," Rob said, his relief palpable.

"I told you he wasn't dead," Miles said, grinning and clapping him on the back in his relief.

"You also called me a clot, and you were wrong about that," Rob retorted.

"Yeah, what's wrong with you, anyway?" Chris demanded, turning to look at

Miles. "You've been like a bear with a sore head all morning. Thomas went to hide in the ready before you landed. He said you bit his head off earlier."

Miles felt a flash of remorse go through him. He knew he'd been snapping at people all morning, he just didn't know why. It seemed everything was rubbing him the wrong way today, including the Luftwaffe.

"I know," he said. "Sorry. I'm out of sorts today. Don't mind anything I say."

"We never do, old man," Rob said with a grin.

"What's happening?" Thomas appeared behind them, looking around them to where they were pulling Ashmore out of the cockpit. "How is he?"

"We don't know yet, Tomcat," Chris said, glancing at him. "They haven't got him out yet, have they?"

"Ainsworth? Did you see him get hit?" Thomas turned his attention to Rob. "You came in with him."

"We were jumped on our way in, but I didn't see him get hit. He didn't say a dicky-bird on the radio. If I'd known, I would have followed him in."

"Radial wire is gone," Chris said after a moment. "Look. It must have been hit as well."

Miles turned to look where the radio cable ran from the tail to the aerial mast just behind the cockpit. Sure enough. The cable was broken.

"Blimey," Thomas breathed. "And look at the tail! It looks like it's been shredded!"

"We'll fix that," a new voice said behind them, and they turned as one to look at Jones. He was standing there, his hands on his hips, nodding. "We'll have the CO's kite back up in the air before you know it."

"What about the CO?" Chris asked.

"I don't fix people, just machines," Jones answered readily. "I leave people to the sawbones."

"I'm sure the CO will be relieved to hear that," Miles said dryly.

"Speaking of the devil, here comes the old boy now," Rob said. "He looks none too happy."

"How happy would you be if you were shot?" Chris demanded. "It's bad enough having your plane torn up."

Ashmore was out of the cockpit now, and the ground crew were trying to help him off the wing. Blood covered his torso, and he had oil streaks on his face, but he kept pushing the men away as he clambered down off the wing.

"Get that bloody thing away from me!" he bellowed at the hapless medics toting the stretcher. "I can damned well walk. I'm not done for just yet!"

Miles felt a laugh well up inside him and he grinned, watching as the medics calmly tried to reason with the squadron leader. They didn't seem offended in the least, and Miles suspected that they'd been subjected to their fair share of abuse from wounded pilots who were in pain.

"Ainsworth!" Ashmore called, looking around while one of the medics was trying to get his flight jacket open to look at the damage done to his torso.

"Right here, sir!" Rob called, striding forward.

"Oh, thank God! I lost you when the bloody bastard jumped me," Ashmore exclaimed, slapping the medics hands away. "Stop fussing! I can tell you what's there. A bullet went through my shoulder, and another one grazed my ribs. I'm perfectly fine to walk back. Where's Lacey? Oh, there you are. Come over here, Miles. I'm not shouting across the bloody field."

Miles grinned and jogged over to the small group moving away from the Spitfire.

"Sir?"

Ashmore looked at him and Miles swallowed. Despite all his blustering, his superior's jaw was clamped closed with pain, and the strain of standing was evident on his face.

"You know what this means," Ashmore said briskly, and Miles sucked in his breath in sudden understanding.

"Oh. Right," he said, his mouth suddenly dry.

"You're acting CO until they clear me to get back in it." Ashmore grimaced suddenly as a spasm went through him and the medic quickly put an arm around him, bracing his weight against him. This time, Ashmore didn't protest. "You'll find everything you need in my office, and Bertie will help guide you through it all."

"Yes, sir."

"And for God's sake, don't lose me my squadron while I'm gone!"

"I'll try my best not to, sir."

"Good." Ashmore stopped walking and breathed heavily for a moment, then looked around for the ambulance. "How much farther is the damned blood wagon? The next town over?"

"It's right over here, sir," the medic said calmly. "You're almost there."

"Let me help, sir," Miles said.

Ashmore made an impatient sound and nodded gruffly. Miles moved to his other side and put an arm around him, taking more of the weight off the smaller medic.

"Did they get your leg as well, sir?" he asked after a moment, noticing that Ashmore was favoring one leg.

"No, I don't think so, but it hurts like the devil."

Miles glanced down at the limb in question, but it was impossible to tell if the blood on the pant leg was from the wounds they knew about or another one on his leg.

"You should have taken the stretcher, sir," he said.

"And have the lads see me carted off like I'm on my way out?" Ashmore shook his head. "Not on my life."

They covered the last few yards to the ambulance and the medic looked at Miles.

"Can you handle him, sir, while I get the door open?"

"Yes, I've got him."

Miles braced himself and Ashmore sagged against him while the other man ran to open the door.

"Lacey? Make sure you take care of yourself," Ashmore said suddenly, sounding very tired. "I didn't even see the bastards until it was too late. The men can't lose you as well."

"Yes, sir. I will. Don't you worry about us. You just get yourself healthy again and come back to relieve me. I've no desire to jump in your shoes just yet."

Ashmore started to laugh and ended up coughing, choking until he spit out some blood. Wiping his mouth with the back of his hand, he shook his head.

"You're in 'em, whether you want to be or not," he rasped. "You're ready, Lacey. I have no qualms leaving them in your hands."

"Thank you, sir."

"You can thank me by keeping yourself alive, and getting as many of those bastards as you can."

Broadway

Bill hung his coat on the hangar in his office and removed his hat. It was past eight o'clock at night and the building was quiet. The security detail hadn't seemed at all surprised to see him, which he supposed spoke volumes for his work habits.

"Hallo! What are you doing here on a Saturday night?"

Bill swung around to find Jasper standing in the doorway, his coat over his arm and his hat in his hand.

"I suppose I could say the same to you, sir," he said humorously.

"I'm just on my way out. I came in this morning to. . .well, you know how it is."

"I do indeed, sir."

Jasper came into the office and looked around.

"Have you just arrived, then?"

"Yes. I drove down from Lancashire today and stopped long enough for a bite to eat before coming in. I thought I'd make a start on that package for Morrow."

"Well, I'm glad I caught you. I have something to run by you, as it happens." He hung his coat on the rack and hooked his hat above it. After setting his briefcase on the floor, he turned to look at Bill. "Any chance of a glass of that scotch you keep locked away?"

"Of course. Have a seat."

Bill went over to unlock the standing cabinet where he kept brandy and scotch.

"How was Lancashire?"

"Very nice. Quiet."

"And Marguerite? Is she enjoying her visit with her fellow countrymen?"

"Very much so. She's staying another few days. She enjoys the countryside."

Bill poured scotch into two glasses and carried one over to Jasper.

"What have I missed?" he asked, seating himself in the other armchair.

"We had a breach in our security here," Jasper said after taking a sip of the amber liquid.

Bill stared at him, astonished. "I beg your pardon?"

"Well, it wasn't a true breach," Jasper allowed, "but it was meant to be. Henry made a play for our agent files."

"What?!"

"Oh, he didn't come himself, of course. He sent a woman. The same woman Jian had her little run-in with, as a matter of fact."

"Molly? Molly Pollack?"

"That's the one. She presented herself here yesterday with a pass signed by Lord Halifax, on the pretext of retrieving a file for him. Said that he wanted to show it to the prime minister."

"Bollocks."

"Precisely." Jasper crossed his legs. "So far, she refuses to say any more. She knows she'll be charged with treason, but she doesn't seem inclined to bargain for her freedom."

"Has the offer been made?" Bill asked in surprise.

"No, but she hasn't suggested it, either."

"Who provided the pass?"

"That's what we're trying to determine. Lord Halifax has no knowledge of it, and nor do any of his assistants or clerks. It was obviously stolen or forged, but whoever did it was very good. It would have passed muster at any of the government buildings."

Jasper sipped his drink and eyed Bill shrewdly.

"I must say, Buckley, that you're taking this all rather well. It's almost as if you expected something like this."

"Not expected, sir, but not surprised, either. I've been waiting for him to step up his attempts to find Jian."

"Oh? Why?"

"If the Luftwaffe succeeds in destroying our airfields and gains control over the skies, as they are trying to do, then Henry will want to have Jian to present to his handler as a prize when Hitler invades," Bill said calmly. "I'd stake my life on it."

"Would you stake Jian's?" Jasper exhaled and shook his head. "No. Don't say it. That was uncalled for. I'm afraid this entire situation has me a bit rattled."

"Why? Because he tried to get to her file?"

"Because he had the effrontery and absolute gall to send someone into my house!"

Bill chuckled. "Well, at least we know that he isn't spineless. Shows rather a good sense of initiative, as a matter of fact."

"Do you know, I think you're enjoying this!"

"I am."

"For God's sake, why?"

"Because this incident has just narrowed the field of possibilities for his identity," Bill said, leaning forward. "Only a limited number of people knew that we kept the agent files in the basement here, and even fewer of them know that they were moved out of London months ago. Henry just handed us the means to find him!"

Jasper nodded, a reluctant answering smile creasing his face.

"Yes. I know. I already have one of my men compiling a list for us. He's cross-referencing everyone who knew the files were downstairs with the handful of people who know we moved them."

"Good!" Bill sat back. "Then why aren't you as pleased as I am? This is the break we've been waiting for!"

"I suppose I will be once we have that list in our hands. Until then, shall we say that I'm cautiously optimistic?"

"I think you can be more than that, sir. Between this and the lure of Ainsworth's missing package, we'll have Henry in custody in no time."

Chapter
Twenty–Seven

RAF Northolt
August 25

Evelyn signed her name on what seemed like the hundredth form and turned it over, face down, on the stack at the side of the blotter. She was almost through the first pile of forms that the young aircraftwoman had carried into her this morning. *I don't know why I bothered to come in last week*, she thought irritably, reaching for the next one. Then she smiled ruefully to herself. Here she sat, doing Cunningham's job for a couple of hours, and she was already getting irritable. How Bill would smirk if he knew! She was the one who insisted on coming back, after all. She could still be at Ainsworth, riding her mare through the meadows before lunch, instead of sitting behind a desk signing her name over and over again.

After reading through the requisition form for additional blankets to replace those lost in the bombing, Evelyn signed again and added the paper to the completed pile. How she missed Cunningham! The sergeant was due to return at the end of the week from her training. Until then, Evelyn was on her own.

A very brief knock fell on her office door and Evelyn was just opening her mouth to call for them to enter when the door swung open unceremoniously, and without warning. She looked up in surprise, but the rebuke died on her lips as she stared at the man striding into her office.

"It's about time you got back, Assistant Section Officer," Fred exclaimed, tossing his hat towards the coat rack in the corner. "It's been bloody dull around here, y'know."

Evelyn staggered to her feet and started to take a step, her eyes locked on his tired face. She tried to take a breath, then felt a wave of heat go through her. Her legs went out from under her, and Evelyn fell back into her chair heavily as Fred's face swam and the office blurred around her. From a long way away, almost as if it were in a tunnel, she heard him curse, and suddenly he was kneeling beside her.

"Good Lord, Evie, don't go and faint on me, you goose!"

His voice still sounded very far away, and Evelyn was vaguely aware of something patting her face. Then, quite suddenly, a ringing slap sounded in her ears and her cheek burned with pain. She sucked in her breath and her eyes widened, the fog clearing as she gasped again with the realization that she'd just been smacked with some force.

"Bloody hell!" she cried, slapping a hand to her cheek and staring at Fred in shock. "That hurt!"

Fred grinned and sat back on his heels, relief all over his face.

"Sorry 'bout that. I didn't know what else to do. I'm not very good with fainting females," he told her. "What on earth's wrong with you, anyway? Are you ill?"

"What's wrong. . .am I. . ." Evelyn stuttered, staring at him in astonishment.

Fred clucked his tongue and got to his feet, looking around.

"Don't you have any water or tea around here?" he demanded, reaching for the telephone on her desk. "You really should, you know, if you're going to make a habit of this sort of thing."

He picked up the receiver and called down for some tea to be sent round immediately to Assistant Section Officer Ainsworth, telling the aircraftwoman on the other end that she'd had a fainting spell. He hung up and turned to look down at Evelyn, still staring up at him in bemusement.

"That'll put a fire under 'em," he said cheerfully. "Jolly good, too. I could use a cup myself after that. Not quite the reception I was expecting."

"Not the. . ." Evelyn tried to speak again, then gave up, settling for shaking her head.

"I say, you're not making much sense," he said with a frown. "Perhaps you should put your head between your knees. Get the blood to your brain, y'know."

He reached out to try and push her head down, but Evelyn slapped his hand away with surprising force.

"I don't need to get blood to my head," she snapped, "and if you try, Fred Durton, so help me, I'll give you a swollen lip!"

Fred threw his head back and laughed.

"That's better!" he approved. "No, no. You sit still like a good girl until the tea comes. I don't want you going lights-out on me again. You know, you're lucky I was here. You might have hurt yourself!"

He perched on the corner of the desk, swinging his leg carelessly, and stared down at her. Evelyn swallowed and stared back, a myriad of emotions swirling through her, not least of which was pure joy to see him sitting on the edge of her desk again.

"I don't understand," she murmured, rubbing her temples as if it would make it all clear to her.

"Well, that makes two of us. What's the matter with you?"

"What's the matter with me?" She dropped her hands and gaped up at him. "You're dead!"

"What?" Fred asked in astonishment. "Who said I went for a Burton?!"

"Sergeant Cunningham! Well, she said you posted missing, which is just about the same thing."

The astonishment on his face cleared and he slapped a hand to his forehead, grimacing comically.

"Good God, that was *yonks* ago!" he exclaimed. "And I was only missing for twenty-four hours. Lord, did you really think I'd gone toes up?"

"Yes!"

"Well, I didn't," he said cheerfully, smiling down at her. "Did you cry for me?"

"You're really asking for a fat lip, Flight Lieutenant," she hissed at him, "and it's only fair to warn you that I hit hard!"

He laughed, getting up as a knock fell on the door. Evelyn gritted her teeth when the man had the audacity to whistle as he crossed the office to admit a woman in uniform pushing a tea tray, followed by a nurse.

"Oh, hallo!" he said, smiling at the nurse. "Jolly glad to see you."

"Oh, for heaven's sake!" Evelyn exclaimed. "I'm all right now."

"I'll be the judge of that, ma'am," the nurse said briskly, going around the tea tray and heading for Evelyn. "I'm Nurse Kensington."

"I'm very pleased to make your acquaintance, but I can assure you that I'm fine," Evelyn said as the nurse picked up her wrist and felt for her pulse. "I had rather a shock, you see."

"What kind of shock?"

Evelyn pointed to Fred who was inspecting the tea tray.

"A flight lieutenant who came back from the dead kind of shock," she said pointedly. "I thought he was dead!"

Nurse Kensington glanced over at Fred, then looked down at Evelyn's flushed face.

"Dead? Are you sure you're feeling the thing, ma'am?"

Fred chuckled and Evelyn looked at him in exasperation.

"You could help me out, you know," she told him.

"Not on your life. I'm having too much fun!"

"Oh!"

Nurse Kensington continued to monitor her pulse, then turned Evelyn's head so that she could examine her eyes while she felt her glands on either side of her neck.

"Your pulse is a bit fast, but that's to be expected," she told her. "There's no sign of cloudiness in your eyes. Has this happened before?"

"No. I don't believe I've ever seen a ghost before."

The other woman was betrayed into a laugh, and she glanced at Fred, who was pouring tea into two cups.

"Why did you think he was dead?"

"Because the last that I heard, he'd posted missing over a week ago!"

"Ah. That would do it." She lowered her hands and motioned for Evelyn to stand up. "Let's just make sure you're all right now. Can you stand on one foot for me?"

Evelyn stifled an exclamation as she heard a muffled guffaw from the direction of the tea cart. She lifted one foot and stood for a moment until the nurse asked her to extend her arms out to the side. She did so, then obediently switched legs, all the while staring daggers at Fred. He'd grabbed a sandwich and was munching on it, grinning back unrepentantly.

"Just you wait, Lieutenant Durton," she said with deceptive calm. "I'll get back at you for this."

"I don't know why you're so bent out of shape," he said after swallowing a mouthful of sandwich. "We can't have you fainting again. I didn't much like slapping you like that."

"Well, that makes two of us!"

"Was she out, then?" Nurse Kensington asked Fred, motioning for Evelyn to put her leg down.

"Just about. Her eyes had rolled up into her head."

She looked at Evelyn and shook her head.

"You're all right now, but if you feel lightheaded at all, come to the infirmary. Right now, I want you to sit down, drink some tea, and have a little nibble of something."

Evelyn sat down and nodded, resigned.

"Promise me that you'll come straight to us if you feel unsteady at all."

"I promise."

Nurse Kensington nodded and turned to leave the office.

"You may feel that it's nothing, but we've had quite a few women coming down with a bad case of nerves after that bombing last week," she said, moving towards the door. "And before you look like that, Lieutenant, we've also had several men with the same complaint!"

Evelyn chuckled at the look on Fred's face as Nurse Kensington sailed out of the office, closing the door behind her.

"What did I do?" he demanded, carrying over a cup and saucer to Evelyn and setting it before her on the desk. "These nurses are the stuff of nightmares. The one this morning shoved a thermometer so far down my throat I thought it would come out. . .sorry. Forgot who I was with for a tick."

Evelyn couldn't help but laugh and reached for her tea.

"Why were you having your temperature taken?" she asked. Then her hand paused as she raised the cup to her lips and she looked up sharply. "Why aren't you flying with your squadron?"

"I've been grounded for the day." He went back to his perch on her desk and sipped his tea. "I blacked out on our first sortie at dawn. Didn't come to until it was almost too late. When I landed, the CO sent me to get checked out. Doc says it's exhaustion and grounded me for the day."

"Good heavens. Why aren't you resting?"

"Because I heard that a certain Assistant Section Officer had decided to grace us with her presence at last." He winked at her. "But I'll be going back and sleeping the rest of the day, don't have any doubts about that. I'm bloody tired."

"You look it," Evelyn said ruthlessly. "What happened when you posted missing?"

"Oh that. I had to bail out when my kite took a belly full of cannon fire. One of the rounds went right through the cockpit floor and just missed me! Swear I heard it whistle as it went by my ear. Anyway, the kite was a shambles and I had no choice but to nip out. I went down over Devon and landed in a copse. Hit my head on a tree going down and was knocked out cold. Didn't come to 'til the next morning!"

"You were lying in a copse the whole time?"

"Yes. Best sleep of my life! When I woke up, I had a ruddy big head, but I was able to flag down a passing lorry and toddled off back here." He got up and went over to the cart. "Cucumber sandwich?"

"Thank you."

"I never dreamed anyone thought I'd bought it. If I'd known that's what you thought, I wouldn't have come barging in here like that." He returned with a plate of sandwiches. "Sorry about that."

Evelyn waved the apology away.

"I'm simply glad you're still alive! I don't think I've ever been so glad to see you sitting on my desk!"

"Is that why you haven't told me off?" He grinned at her. "I'll have to get posted missing more often."

"Don't you dare say things like that! You'll tempt fate."

"How many lives do you think we pilots get?" he asked after a moment.

"The good Lord gives us all one, so make good use of it." Evelyn sipped her tea and considered him thoughtfully. "Why do you ask?"

"I'm starting to feel a bit like a cat," he admitted ruefully. "I go up, I bail out, I come down, and then I do it all again."

"That's because you're a good pilot."

"So was the CO, but he bought it." Fred shook his head. "I reckon if I have nine lives like a cat, I've got about four left."

"Then you're in good shape, aren't you?" Evelyn set down her cup and reached for a sandwich. "Get some rest today and you'll be unstoppable."

"I just hope the others don't think I've gone soft," he muttered, plucking another sandwich from the plate.

"Why would they think that?"

"It happens, y'know. Blokes turn yellow and suddenly it's, "I can't fly today. I'm seeing double," or "I can't go up. I've got the fever." All kinds of excuses to try to get out of going back up."

Evelyn stared at him. "You're serious, aren't you?"

"Oh yes. Just yesterday one of the new pilots tried to get out of operations saying that he couldn't turn his head."

"What happened?"

"CO made him go up anyway. You can't have that kind of thing going on. Not now. We're losing too many as it is."

"But why? Why are they doing it?"

"I suppose they can't handle what we're up against. Well, stands to reason, don't it? When you get scrambled to a vector and come upon 100 plus enemy aircraft, and there's only five or ten of you, well, it's not very pleasant."

Evelyn swallowed and stared at him.

"I never thought of it that way. What do you think when you see it?"

"Nothing. I just pick one out and go after it. That's all you *can* do."

"Well, I don't see how anyone could think that you've lost your nerve," she said after a long moment of silence. "Not after how many sorties you've flown and how many Jerrys you've shot down. And anyway, the doctor's the one who grounded you. You didn't ask for it."

"No, I didn't, and I argued with him, but he wouldn't budge." Fred finished his sandwich and brushed crumbs off his jacket. "Did you see the newspapers this morning? The bastards bombed London yesterday!"

"Yes, I saw. Awful. The docks were all but destroyed, and all those people. . ."

"Strange, really, that they hadn't gone for London yet," he added thoughtfully. "You'd think they'd have made a go at the capital sooner."

"They're employing a different strategy," Evelyn murmured.

"Yes. They're trying to destroy our airfields," he said bitterly. "Manston's been hit so many times I don't know how they're still functioning. They must be working out of tents. And now Kenley's been walloped twice. If it keeps on like this, we won't be able to land anywhere."

Fred felt in his pockets for his cigarettes, pulling out a case a moment later.

"I had to refuel at Hawkinge yesterday. They'd just had a raid go over and there were bloody great fires raging all over the place," he told her, shoving a cigarette in his mouth and offering her one. She shook her head, and he snapped the case closed. "I stayed in my kite while they filled me up and fed in new ammunition. I've never been so glad to get the hell out of anywhere in all my life. I was convinced one of those fires was going to spread to the fuel truck and blow me to kingdom come. It was awfully close."

"I'm very glad it didn't."

"So am I." He lit his cigarette and went over to open the window. "They hit the airfields while we're up fighting somewhere else. It's a shambles. They say that 12 Group's Big Wing is supposed to be protecting our airfields while we're intercepting the blighters, but I don't see that they're doing much of anything. Might as well be the Big Dud."

"That's hardly fair," she said, turning to frown at him. "I'm sure they're up there. Well, I know they are. Miles says they're up all the time."

"I'd like to know where," he muttered, turning from the window. He caught sight of her face and shook his head, waving one hand impatiently. "I'm not saying the pilots aren't doing their job. I'm just saying the Big Wing is a Big Flop."

"Actually, I think they probably would agree with you," Evelyn said with a rueful smile. "I know Robbie said in one of his letters that the American they have flying with them thinks it's a waste of time."

"See? The pilots know. It's the bloody brass that hasn't a clue. Well, of course they don't. They're not the ones up there trying to fight the bastards off. But I'll tell you this much, if they don't figure it out soon, we won't have any airfields left!" He paused and tilted his head to look at her curiously. "They have an American flying with them?"

"Yes. Miles says he's one of the best pilots he's ever seen."

"Can he recruit some more?" he asked with a grimace. "We could use some good help. The new lads coming in from training school haven't got more than four or five hours in the air. I feel sorry for them. They follow us into a scrap and have no idea what they're in for. It's a miracle any of them make it back alive. Well, a lot of them don't."

"Trial by fire?"

"Sometimes literally." He exhaled and shook his head. "I must be more tired than I thought. I shouldn't be unloading like this to you, especially when you've just had a fainting spell."

"I've told you, I'm fine!" she said in exasperation. "You gave me a turn, that's all."

He put out his cigarette on the windowsill and tossed it outside before turning to look at her. The twinkle was back in his eyes.

"Were you very upset when you thought that I was dead?"

"Of course I was! Who else would take me to the pub?"

Fred threw back his head and laughed, walking over to her. He bent down and kissed her cheek.

"You'd have your choice of the lot, m'dear," he said, straightening up. "No doubt about it."

"Well, that's a relief, at any rate."

"But, of course, you know that," he said, turning and going around the desk, heading for the door. "I'm off to sleep. I'll pick you up at six?"

"What for?"

"I can't not take you to the pub when you thought I was dead, can I?" He opened the door and turned to wink at her. "Besides, I think you owe me."

"I owe you? For what?"

"For staying away for so long that you didn't even know that I wasn't missing any longer!"

25th August, 1940
My Dearest Evelyn,

I'm writing this at dispersal while my kite's being refueled and rearmed. We had a busy morning, but now we seem to be in a lull. I don't expect that it will last very long; it never does anymore.

Did you see that London was bombed last night? That's the first time they've gone for London, and I was rather surprised when I read the newspapers this morning. Chris doesn't understand why they haven't done it sooner. I think they're trying to destroy us first, then they'll start on London when there are no more fighters left to oppose them. If that is their game, then they're in for a rude awakening. The RAF isn't going anywhere. Despite their bombing runs on our airfields, we're still here, and we're still fending them off. As our resident Yank says, I'll bet on us any day.

Our CO was shot up rather badly yesterday. As a result, I'm the acting CO at the moment. He took cannon fire through his shoulder and one grazed his ribs. He was coughing up blood, so they thought something had hit a lung, but it turns out he'd only bit a chunk out of his cheek when the round went through his shoulder. He also got some shrapnel from his kite stuck in his leg, so he's laid up for at least a few weeks. As the senior Flight Lieutenant, I'm the next man up. Between just the two of us, I don't think I'm anywhere near fit to step into his shoes, nor do I want to, but it isn't as if I have much of a choice. As our adjutant so blithely said, war is good for promotion. Always has been. Unfortunately, this promotion I'm not in the least pleased to have.

We all went to see him in the hospital yesterday after we came down for the night. As we were leaving, he asked me to stay back. He told me that Chris and I have been recommended for DFCs. Darling, I didn't know what to say or where to look. He says it's on account of all the Jerries we've shot down, but I don't know that it warrants a medal. We're just doing our job, and frankly, I feel that I could be doing much more than I am. Ashmore says there's no doubt that we'll get it. They're looking for heroes to buck up the civilians, and I suppose they're trying to buck up the pilots as well. I know that I should be pleased about the recommendation. I know Chris would be crowing it all over the station if he knew. It's an honor, and I'm fully sensible to that fact. But I can't help but feel that someone else would deserve it more. Like the blokes in 11 Group, or the poor sods who are in the burn wards. But I suppose they may have been put up for one as well.

I know you're back on your station now. I pray every night that it isn't bombed again, and that you're kept safe. I know you can't tell me what you do, but I also know that it must be more dangerous than you'd like me to believe. I hope you stay put until these bombing raids ease up. I don't like the thought of you traveling around in the midst of all of this.

I must sign off now.

Always yours,
Acting CO, Flight Lieutenant Miles Lacey

London

Henry stepped outside, settling his hat on his head before starting down the wide, shallow steps. The pavement was bustling with people hurrying home from work or on their way to an evening out, and if one ignored the walls of sandbags piled up all around them, it was quite a pleasant summer's evening. The air was warm, and a slight breeze swirled through the streets, carrying with it a promise of relief from the heat of the day. Yet there was no way one could pretend that there wasn't a war on. The East End had been hit the night before, bombs falling on the docks and surrounding area. Henry had read in the newspaper that one audience had been trapped in a cinema when a thousand pounder landed nearby. Ghastly thought, that, being trapped in the cinema.

He reached the pavement and turned to walk up the street. Perhaps now the people would begin to see how hopeless it all was. The Nazis were coming. The best thing for them was to accept it and give up this silly idea of resistance. All it was achieving was to get hundreds of pilots needlessly killed.

The newspapers also said that Spitfires and Hurricanes had intercepted three waves of raids before the one that got through to London last night, downing forty-five of the Luftwaffe. Henry didn't believe a word of it. The Luftwaffe pilots were superior in every way. If the RAF had shot down forty-five airplanes the day before, Henry would eat his hat.

Of course, he knew the number of airplanes the Luftwaffe was losing was greater than they'd expected, but he also knew the number of airplanes the RAF was losing. More importantly, he knew the number of pilots going down. Dozens of them were being lost each day, either killed or injured, and the air force didn't have enough replacements to go around. He'd read in a briefing just that morning that several squadrons in 11 Group were down to six or seven airplanes out of sixteen. Why, Tangmere had lost an entire squadron over the course of two days! Fighter Command was on its last legs. There was no possible way that they could have accounted for forty-five downed aircraft.

But the War Cabinet had made it clear that public morale was to be kept up at all costs. Churchill knew full well that if the people gave up, Britain would be lost. And so the numbers were manipulated, the successes inflated, and the fighter pilots hailed as heroes at every turn. It was all a farce, of course. They were failing, and in the end, the Nazis would be in London, just as they were in Paris.

He'd reached the corner and paused, waiting for the light to change so that he could cross, when someone bumped into him from behind. He started, then felt something pressed into his palm. Henry turned his head sharply to watch as a man walked away quickly without a backward glance. His eyes narrowed and he looked down at the rolled-up piece of paper in his gloved hand.

Henry closed his fingers over the note as the light changed. He crossed the street with a group of other pedestrians, then continued a few yards before stepping into the alcove of a building. He unrolled the note, peering down at the message scrawled in pencil.

Meet me at the usual place. Half an hour. —MT

Chapter
Twenty-Eight

Broadway
August 26

"There's this one, sir. I think it came from Poland in the spring. It's a tube of some sort."

Wesley handed Bill a rough drawing of what, indeed, looked like a tube of some sort. The German notations on the drawing had been translated to English and indicated that it was some form of compressor the Germans were using in their U-boats.

"Hm. I'd forgotten about that one. Put it in the possible pile, Fitch."

Wesley nodded and set the paper on a growing stack on the corner of Bill's desk.

"What, exactly, are we trying to do with this packet, if you don't mind my asking?" he asked, picking up another folder and flipping it open.

"We're trying to lure out a very intelligent and conniving spy, Fitch. That's why only the best will do," Bill said distractedly, examining a document closely. "He's too smart to be fooled with run-of-the-mill electrical switches or ignition timers."

"But won't we be letting the enemy know what we know?"

"Yes, but I'll be choosing lesser intelligence that came from very questionable sources to begin with, so the damage will, God willing, be minimal." Bill dropped the document he was examining into the folder before him and snapped it closed. "And this does not qualify. Put that one in the reject pile, Fitch."

"Righto."

The offending file was moved to a pile on one of the chairs. Bill was just reaching for a new folder when a knock fell on the door. Wesley went over to open it, standing so the person outside couldn't see the folders spread all over the office. After speaking in low tones for a moment, Wesley closed the door again and returned to the desk, an envelope in his hand.

"This was just delivered by hand, sir," he said, handing him the envelope. "By private messenger."

Bill raised his eyebrows and sat back in his chair, turning it over in his hand. There was no direction written on the envelope.

"Did they specify that it was for me?" he asked.

"The messenger asked that it be delivered to a senior official," Wesley told him. "You and Sir Jasper are the only two senior officials in the building at the moment."

"Are we? How is that?"

"It's a bit early yet, sir."

Bill peered at him blankly, then turned to look at the clock on the wall.

"Good God, it's only seven-thirty?" he exclaimed. "How long have we been at this, Fitch?"

"Oh, about an hour, sir."

"What the devil were you doing here so early?"

"I knew you would be back, sir," Wesley said with a grin. "I thought I'd come in and help you get settled."

Bill let out a short laugh, tearing open the envelope.

"I don't suppose you were expecting to be dragged into sorting through mounds of files with me, eh? Sorry for that."

"I don't mind at all," he replied cheerfully. "I'm rather enjoying it."

"I always said you were one of us. Your father should be very proud."

"I expect he would be if he knew what I did here," Wesley said easily. "He says you're the devil to keep up with."

"Oh, he does, does he? I'll remember that next time he needs my support for one of his bills."

He pulled a single sheet of paper out of the envelope and unfolded it, scanning it quickly. A frown settled on his face, and he read it through more slowly, falling silent. Wesley watched him for a moment curiously, then cleared his throat.

"Is anything the matter, sir?"

"What? Oh, no." Bill folded the paper and tucked it back into the envelope. "Do you know, I'm feeling a bit peckish. Go down and find us some tea, will you? And perhaps some biscuits or something."

Wesley nodded and looked at the pile of folders on the chair.

"Shall I take these back with me?"

"Yes, thank you."

Bill waited until his assistant had gathered the stack of files and left, closing the door behind him, before pulling the note out of the envelope again and reading it through once more. Shaking his head, he reached for the phone to call up to Jasper's office.

"Is that you, Manfred?" he asked a moment later when the line connected. "God, you're in early too. Is he in?"

"Yes, Sir William. He's right here."

Jasper's assistant handed off the phone, and he heard Jasper telling him to go and find some tea.

"Bill? What has you calling? You've never finished that project already?" Jasper demanded.

"No. I'm still working on that," Bill said. "I say, did you know that we're the only senior officials in at the moment?"

"Are we? Well, it doesn't surprise me. It's still early. Is that what you called to tell me? That we work too hard?"

"No. I've just had a note delivered by private messenger. It was to be delivered to a senior official." Bill looked down at the paper before him. "It claims that Lady Rothman is behind the breach in security here the other day."

"The devil you say!"

"It's anonymous, of course. Doesn't say much else."

"Read it to me."

Bill cleared his throat. " 'To Whomever It Concerns. The breach in security that resulted in an unknown person attempting to gain access to the personnel files on Friday was not at the request of Lord Halifax. Rather, the incident was orchestrated by Lady Rothman in an attempt to protect the Round Club.' It's signed An Interested Party."

"That's it?"

"That's the whole thing." Bill dropped the paper on the desk and sat back in his chair, a grin pulling at his lips. "Not very imaginative, is it?"

"Well, it doesn't need to be," Jasper replied. "How do you sugarcoat implicating someone in treason?"

"Oh, I wasn't referring to the brevity of the letter. I was remarking on throwing Lady Rothman to the wolves."

"Oh! No. I don't suppose that's very original, is it? After all, we already know she's up to her eyeballs in subversion. But why contact us at all?"

"I think he's getting spooked," Bill said bluntly. "He thinks Miss Pollack is going to give us his name, so he's giving us someone else to focus on. It's a distraction, or would be if we didn't already know about Lady Rothman and the

Round Club."

"Sorry. I see where you're going now," Jasper said after a moment. "I'm afraid I haven't had enough tea yet this morning. You're working on the assumption that he doesn't know that we know anything about the Round Club."

"Yes. After all, in the normal course of things, we wouldn't have any idea they exist. It's only because Jian was the one who stumbled upon them that we're involved at all." Bill tapped a finger on the arm of his chair thoughtfully. "He's hoping that we'll spin our wheels trying to find out about the Round Club and Lady Rothman."

"And not pay attention to anything Miss Pollack tells us in the meantime," Jasper finished. "We'd have larger fish to fry. It's a fantastic theory, Buckley, but there's one problem with it."

"Oh? What's that?"

"He doesn't know that we have her."

Bill frowned. "What do you mean? He must know!"

"Barton—you remember him, don't you? Well, he arranged it to look as though she's left London to visit a sick aunt in Bristol. He even left a train ticket trail for Henry to follow."

"And you think he's fallen for it?"

"Lord knows, but we've certainly done everything we can to make it so the Round Club doesn't know she's been taken."

Bill drummed his fingers thoughtfully, his lips pressed together while his mind spun. Jasper was silent for a moment, then he cleared his throat.

"I don't need to see you to know that you're drumming out a tattoo on the desk and scowling at the wall," he said. "What are you thinking?"

"Only that he can't believe that Miss Pollack has gone away to tend a sick aunt."

"Why not?"

"Because there would be absolutely no reason to send an anonymous tip if he did. If she had really flitted off to Bristol, he'd have nothing to worry about. Even if we discovered that someone had stolen a—"

Bill broke off and sucked in his breath.

"Now what?" Jasper sounded resigned.

"He knows damn well we have her because he doesn't have the file," Bill told him. "She wouldn't take it with her, not when she was stealing it for him. She would have handed it over, then gone off to Bristol."

"Hmph. That's true. Our elaborate ruse was for nothing."

"No, not for nothing. He may know that we have Miss Pollack, but the Round

Club doesn't, and that's more pressing, I think. As long as they believe she's in Bristol, we still have a chance to turn her and send her back to them."

"What's to say that Henry won't tell them?"

"He's just told us that Lady Rothman is part of the Round Club and was responsible for someone breaking into MI6 headquarters," Bill said dryly. "I think it's safe to assume that there is no love lost on his side, and he won't give them any information that will interfere with his own plans. No. I think we're quite safe on that score."

"He really is a conniving son of a bitch, isn't he?"

"Yes, he is, but his time is running out at last. I'll have this dummy packet finished in a few days, then we'll see just who we're dealing with."

"And that's only if Miss Pollack doesn't give him up first," Jasper said cheerfully. "We're finally closing in on the bastard!"

RAF Northolt

Evelyn finished reading the article that had caught her eye on the front page and folded the newspaper again, laying it down on the desk. She got up and went to open the window, watching as a squadron of Hurricanes came in to refuel and rearm. Fred was back up with his squadron today, and she wondered if he was one of the pilots landing now. She sent up a silent prayer for the pilots' safety, whoever they were, and turned to go back to her desk.

They had bombed Berlin yesterday in retaliation for the London bombing, targeting industrial compounds in Germany's capital city. While part of her felt vindicated for the assault on her beloved London, the rest of her was disturbed. Hitler wouldn't take kindly to bombs falling on Berlin, especially after both he and Göring had assured the German people that it would never happen. He would retaliate in kind, and round and round they'd go. What a waste it all was!

She settled back into her seat and was just reaching for a pen when the telephone rang, startling her. She reached for the receiver, pushing the newspaper out of the way.

"Assistant Section Officer Ainsworth," she answered briskly.

"Evie, is that you?" Bill's voice asked cheerfully. "Good Lord, you sound like an old battle axe!"

"Sir William!" she exclaimed. "I wasn't expecting to hear from you so soon!"

"No, well, neither was I. However, I have some news that I thought you'd be interested in."

"Oh?"

"Yes. Molly Pollack. You remember her?"

"Yes, of course. She tried to kill me. Not something one's likely to forget."

"Well, she tried to steal your file from the basement here on Friday."

Evelyn gasped, shocked. "She what?!"

"She came in with a pass supposedly signed by Lord Halifax authorizing her to retrieve an agent file for him."

"You keep our files in the basement?" she demanded.

"Good Lord, no. We used to, but we moved all of that out of London when the war started. All that's down there now are billing reports and supply lists. Don't worry. Your file is quite safe and secure."

Evelyn relaxed and exhaled in relief.

"Thank goodness," she murmured. "With Henry running amok through Whitehall, I'm afraid I don't have much confidence in. . .wait. Did you say Molly went there on Friday? Why, if the files have been moved?"

"Because she didn't know that. Only a handful of people are aware that we transferred sensitive material out of London in case of bombing and invasion." Bill coughed, then cleared his throat. "Pardon. Henry sent her, of course. He's trying everything to find you."

"Did she say it was Henry?"

"No, but who else would be looking for your file?"

"She knows my name?" Evelyn asked in alarm, her heart quickening.

"No. She was looking for Jian, your codename. The rather disturbing part is that she had the correct file number for where it used to be."

She sucked in her breath. "He knows where my file was? Has he seen it?"

"No, no. I told you that all the files were moved at the start of the war, before he even knew you existed. However, it tells us that Henry is someone who is well versed in our filing system, and how we assign numbers to our agents."

"Do you think he's one of us?" she asked after a moment.

"No. We cleared everyone in MI6 months ago. But I think he may have worked closely with someone here."

"Well, that's not very helpful. Most of the government has worked closely with someone at one time or another," she muttered. "I don't see that we're any further ahead, not unless Molly tells you his name. However, from what I know of her, I wouldn't hold your breath."

"That's why I'm calling, actually. I thought perhaps you'd have some insight as to how to encourage her to talk."

"Me?" Evelyn laughed. "I'm sorry to disappoint you, but I haven't the faintest idea. I was with her for about half an hour, and half of that time she had a gun to my back."

"What can you tell me about her?"

Evelyn frowned and thought for a moment, bringing to mind a pretty, dark-haired woman who dressed neatly and precisely.

"Well, she's fastidious in her dress, which suggests that she takes pride in her looks and presentation," she said slowly. "She's had to work hard to be taken seriously, I think, and her clothes reflect that. They're very professional, almost stark. No real hint to her personality there at all. I don't think you'll get very far appealing to her softer side."

"She's a hard woman?"

"I think so. She didn't flinch when she marched me up the hill to execute me. It was just business to her." Evelyn pursed her lips thoughtfully. "Although, I did think that she hadn't ever shot anyone at the time."

"Oh? Why?"

"It was the way she was holding the gun. Gingerly, as if she wasn't quite used to handling one." Evelyn shrugged. "I don't think she was accustomed to playing the killer."

"But she would have done it? Pulled the trigger?"

"Absolutely. There was no hesitation. It was almost as if she was proving something to that blasted club. A rite of passage, perhaps?"

"Or proving something to *someone*," Bill murmured.

Evelyn raised her eyebrows in surprise.

"Do you think she was trying to impress Henry? We don't even know for sure that they know each other!"

"He sent her to steal your file," Bill pointed out. "They undoubtedly know each other."

Evelyn rubbed her forehead, shaking her head.

"Yes, I suppose so. Now what? Henry must realize that she's been caught by now."

"He does. He sent an anonymous note round this morning claiming that Lady Rothman was behind the attempt to steal the file. Said it was to protect the Round Club."

Evelyn was surprised into silence for a brief second, then she couldn't stop the chuckle that welled up and escaped.

"Lady Rothman? Good heavens, he must not think very highly of the Round Club if he's trying to throw them under the guillotine!"

"Just so," Bill said, amused. "Are you laughing, Evelyn?"

"I'm terribly sorry, but I am," she admitted, still chuckling. "I thought he was much smarter than that. Why, it's so clearly a distraction so that you won't listen too closely to—" She broke off suddenly and sucked in her breath. "Goodness! He's afraid Molly will reveal his identity, isn't he?"

"I believe so, yes."

"But she hasn't yet?"

"No."

"But it's been three days!"

"I'm aware of that." Bill's voice was dry.

"Well, there's only one reason a woman facing the death penalty would refuse to name her handler," Evelyn said briskly. "She's in love with him."

There was silence on the line for a long moment, and she frowned.

"Bill? Are you still there?"

"How can you be sure?" he asked.

"Sir William, most women aren't willing to be hanged when they can easily save themselves by giving up information. And that would go doubly for Molly Pollack. She's no fool, nor would she be suffering from a sense of misplaced loyalty. She is very much the type of woman who would save herself before anyone else. Unless, of course, she was in love with them."

"Good Lord," he breathed.

"If you want her to talk, all you have to do is convince her that his life is in danger."

"That possibility never even crossed my mind!"

"No, of course not. You're not a woman."

"Well, I rang you hoping that you'd have some insight for us, and you certainly came through," Bill said.

"Now all you have to do is convince her. Good luck with that."

"Oh, we're not putting all of our eggs in that basket. I've almost finished assembling our dummy package. When it's ready, Gilhurst will leak it, and hopefully, Henry will fall for the bait. We'll get him, one way or another."

"You do know that if there's anything I can do. . ."

"No!" His voice was loud and emphatic, drawing a laugh from her. "You stay put right there where you're safe. I don't want you out roaming around when we've sprung the trap. There's nothing more dangerous than a cornered animal."

Evelyn made a face, but conceded.

"Very well. Will you at least keep me informed of progress? As I'm his primary target just now, I do think that it's only fair."

"As much as I'm able," he agreed grudgingly. "You just stay on the station where I know that nothing will happen to you."

London

The bell above the door jingled, causing Anthony Morrow to raise his eyes from the book he was ostensibly perusing. He lowered them again disinterestedly when a woman came through the opening, carrying her morning's shopping in one hand.

"Ah, Mrs. Robinson!" The woman behind the counter beamed. "Good morning! Your book arrived just an hour ago."

"Wonderful!"

The customer went up to the counter and the two women engaged in low voiced conversation while Morrow surreptitiously glanced at his watch. Lord Anthony Gilhurst had sent a message round to his office early that morning, requesting that they meet at eleven o'clock at the bookshop near Covent Garden. Morrow hadn't even known that this shop existed before a few weeks ago when Miss Evelyn Ainsworth had requested a meeting here. It was a small, out-of-the-way shop that boasted used books, rare first editions, and comfortable chairs for flipping through pages at one's leisure. More significantly, it also had questionable lighting and several places where two people could converse without being seen or heard. After his meeting with Miss Ainsworth, he had added the shop to his list of clandestine meeting places for his agents. Centrally located, it was easy to access, and customers were always coming and going. Amazing, really. With the war raging around them, it never ceased to impress him the number of Londoners who took mental and emotional refuge within the pages of books.

The bell jingled again, and a couple entered with a small dog trotting at their heels. He began to lower his eyes again, but someone called out and the man turned to hold the door. Lord Anthony appeared in the door frame, thanking him as he stepped into the bookshop, removing his hat. Morrow exhaled and closed his book, sliding it back onto the shelf. As the door closed, blocking out the late morning sun and sound of traffic, Gilhurst looked around the shop inquiringly. Spotting Morrow lurking in the gloom behind a row of shelving, he nodded to him before turning to go to the register.

"Can I help?" the woman behind the counter asked, looking up from the book she was wrapping in brown paper for her customer.

"Thank you, yes. I'm looking for a copy of *The Great Gatsby*, by F. Scott Fitzgerald," Lord Gilhurst told her with a smile. "I was told by a friend that he saw one here that was leather bound and in excellent condition. I want it for my library, you see."

"Yes, indeed. You'll find it in the corner, right back there," the woman pointed. "The lighting is rather poor just there, I'm afraid, but it prevents the spines from fading."

"Wonderful. Thank you very much."

Lord Anthony turned and went towards the back corner, which was out of sight from both the front counter and the door. Morrow smiled faintly and moved down the row of shelves he was in, rounding the corner and meeting Gilhurst midway.

"Why, my dear sir!" Lord Gilhurst exclaimed, holding out his hand. "What a surprise!"

"Hallo, Gilhurst," the older man said congenially, gripping his hand. "What are you doing here?"

"Looking for a book for the library. M'sister says that it's severely lacking in the literature department. I don't see it myself, but then fiction has never really appealed to me."

The two men turned to continue towards the back corner, disappearing from the view of the other patrons.

"Lady Rothman is growing more and more agitated that the package Evie recovered hasn't turned up yet," Gilhurst said in a low voice. "She's convinced that it's ended up with the Secret Service, and she's making plans, along with the duke, to organize a coup d'état. She believes that it can be executed before she's arrested."

"And how do they plan to execute an overthrow of the government without military help?" Morrow asked, his lips curling in disdain. "It's the stuff of fantasy."

"She believes the Germans will invade within weeks, and that will be when they strike."

Morrow grunted. "Yes, well, I suppose one can't fault her for believing it. Our lads are taking a right pummeling in the air," he muttered. "Much more of it and her wish may very well come true."

"I happen to know quite a few of the pilots fighting for our island, and I'd back them any day over the bloody Nazis," Gilhurst said firmly. "Wonderful chaps, you understand, but deadly when they're up against it."

"Yes, well, I hope you're right. We're asking them to do the impossible." Morrow exhaled and stopped before a case filled with leather-bound editions. "What is it that you're supposedly looking to add to your collection?"

"*The Great Gatsby.*"

Morrow nodded and began to half-heartedly scan the shelves, looking for the title.

"Where are we on the plan to find this mystery German agent?" Gilhurst asked, joining him in examining the spines of books. "I must confess that I'm at a loss as to how I'm expected to find a man whose name I don't know, and whom I've never laid eyes on."

"You've heard his voice," Morrow pointed out humorously.

"And it was familiar to me, but that's hardly surprising," Gilhurst said with a shrug. "My position in government ensures that I am familiar with most of London. It's hardly any kind of help, is it?"

"Well, you won't need to find him if everything goes to plan. He'll find you. MI6 has promised to have the package ready by the end of the week. When I have it, I'll contact you and we will proceed. This agent called Henry will find you quickly enough once he hears of it, I assure you."

Lord Anthony had turned to stare at him while he was speaking, and Morrow became aware of a look of consternation on his face.

"What is it?" he asked, glancing at him. "Don't tell me you're getting cold feet."

"Of course not, but. . .I don't understand. The package is already out there!"

Morrow felt a chill go through him and he turned to look at him, his expression suddenly grim.

"What are you talking about? It hasn't been finished yet!" he hissed.

"Then something else is out there," Gilhurst told him. "That's why I contacted you. I thought you'd already leaked it."

"No!" Morrow rubbed his forehead and took a deep, calming breath. "You'd better tell me everything."

"I have a man in a pub on the edge of the West End. He keeps his ears open, and occasionally hears something useful. Several of the Round Club drink there, you see. Last night, he overheard a conversation between two men. They were sitting in the pub garden outside. He didn't get a good look at them, though he thinks that one of them was a scientist of some sort."

"And?" Morrow prompted when Gilhurst paused.

"Well, it appears that drawings from Germany have surfaced," Gilhurst answered with a shrug. "The one who did most of the talking kept saying that they must be the missing plans taken from Germany last year."

"Did he say what they were for?"

"Some kind of weapon, but my man couldn't make out what. Their voices got very quiet for that bit. So, you see, I thought you'd already released the packet through some other means."

"No, we bloody well didn't." Morrow swore and thought hard for a moment. "And the other man? The one who wasn't doing all the talking?"

"A gentleman, and one who knew enough to keep his voice low. Quite possibly our German spy."

"If it was, then our plan is out the window, and we're up the damned creek!" Morrow said furiously. "Did your man hear anything else?"

"Yes. The scientist looking chap didn't have the papers. He said he examined them, then they were taken away again. They discussed where the plans are now."

"Well?"

"The other one said to try to arrange another viewing, and he would take care of the rest." Lord Anthony looked at him, his lips pressed together grimly. "He's going to take the papers and kill the agent who holds them."

Chapter Twenty-Nine

Evelyn shaded her eyes against the sun and watched as three Hurricanes came in to land, one pouring black smoke out behind it. It was midday, and after a relatively quiet time the day before due to rain and overcast skies, the squadrons had been up since before dawn. She'd heard them taking off, the sound of the engines waking her from an already restless sleep. When the sun rose into a bright and cloudless sky, she knew it would be a busy day of raids coming over the channel.

Evelyn stopped to watch as a fire engine sped out to meet the smoking fighter, followed closely by the ambulance. The wounded Hurricane was from Fred's squadron, but it wasn't him. None of the three coming in were Fred, and she turned her eyes to the horizon. High above, she could see multiple dogfights taking place, the fighter planes twisting and turning in deadly combat. She knew, however, that those airplanes were probably not from Northolt at all. She wondered if they were from the infamous Big Wing, and then she bit her lip. It didn't matter who they were, really. They were up there defending her airfield, and they might die doing so. Her gaze dropped to the smoke coming from the landing strip once more. Or they might return with smoke pouring out from *their* machines.

After watching the activity on the runway for a moment, Evelyn turned away resolutely. She would drive herself mad if she looked for Fred every time a Hurricane came in, or if she thought about the pilots engaged in their fatal acrobatics so high above the earth. It was one thing to know what Miles and Robbie were doing every day, but it was quite another to witness the dogfights and to see the fighter planes coming back all shot up. If she thought too much about it, Evelyn was quite sure she'd be in with Nurse Kensington with a severe state of the nerves, whatever that was, after all.

She was beginning to walk away when she spotted another figure watching the smoking Hurricane. He was standing alone, dressed in his uniform, with his hands in his pockets. After a moment's hesitation, she went towards him.

"Flying Officer Wyszynski!" she called.

The man turned and spotted her, a smile breaking over his face. He took his hands from his pockets and walked to meet her.

"Assistant Section Officer Ainsworth!" He enunciated the title slowly. "You are back!"

"I thought we agreed that you would call me Evelyn," she said with a smile.

"Apologies." Tomasz bowed slightly. "Evelyn."

"It doesn't look very good, does it?" she asked, turning to nod at the damaged airplane.

"No. Not good." He shook his head. "That is second today. I watch."

"They're still not letting you fly?"

"No." He sighed and dragged his eyes away from the landing strip. "We train. Always we train."

Evelyn felt a surge of frustration, not just for him but also for the rest of the pilots. Here they were, battling desperately against overwhelming odds, and the RAF wouldn't activate a dozen experienced pilots who were motivated and more than ready to get up there and join the fight.

"We can speak Russian?" he asked, looking down at her.

"Yes, of course."

"I practice my English all day, but it never sounds good," he confessed with a sheepish laugh.

"You'll master it. If you can master Russian and German, you can master English," she assured him. "And you aren't doing as badly as you think. I can understand you, which is more than I can say for some Londoners!"

"Thank you." He fell into step beside her as they walked along the pavement that ran parallel with the runway. "When did you arrive back? I haven't seen you before now."

"On Sunday. I've been rather busy catching up, I suppose."

"And your brother? Is he well?"

"Yes, thank you."

"Good."

"What about your family?" Evelyn asked. "Do you have a brother? Or sister?"

"I did have two brothers," Tomasz said. "One was killed with my parents when the Nazis came. I do not know where the other one is, if he is alive or dead."

"Oh, I'm so sorry," she said, stopping to face him. "I didn't know. I suppose I should have realized. . ."

He waved his hand impatiently.

"It is not your fault. It is just the way of it. Most of us lost everything when the Nazis came. Ludwig also lost his home to them. His father is dead, but his mother went missing in the chaos. He doesn't know what happened to her." Tomasz shrugged. "We have nothing left, and so we come here to help fight the Germans."

"What do you miss most about Poland?" Evelyn asked after a moment, trying to take his mind from his slain family.

A wistful smile came to his face, and he began walking again.

"I miss the food," he said. "We have a dish, gołąbki, that has been my favorite since I was a boy. It is cabbage leaves that are stuffed with pork, onions, and a little rice. They are cooked and served with potatoes and a tomato sauce. In the summer, like now, they would be filled with vegetables."

"That sounds delicious."

"It is. I haven't had it since. . .well, the last time was on my birthday, two days before the Nazis attacked."

"Two days. . .why, that means that your birthday is this week!" Evelyn exclaimed.

"On Friday," he said, smiling sheepishly.

"Well, we must celebrate," she said cheerfully. "We'll take you down to the pub. They won't have gołąbki, but I daresay we can manage to find you some boiled cabbage and potatoes."

He laughed and stopped, looking down at her.

"You said that very well," he commended her. "You got the pronunciation just right."

"I have an ear for pronunciations."

"I could teach you Polish," he offered, "and you can help me with my English."

"I don't think you need very much help with your English, but I'm quite happy to try," she said with a smile. "And your birthday? I'm serious, you know. I'm sure Fred, Flight Lieutenant Durton, would come along. And, of course, your friends from your squadron."

"Is Lieutenant Durton a friend of yours?" Tomasz asked. "He's a very good pilot. I saw him fending off two 109s while we were on a training flight, before they made us come back, away from the fighting. His squadron is something of a model for us. They give us tips when they can, and tell us about their. . .how do you call them? Sorties?"

"Have the other pilots been good to you since you've been here?" Evelyn asked.

"I mean, they haven't given you a hard time?"

"They were a little reserved to start," he admitted with a grin, "but once they got to know us, they learned that we have experience. It also helps that we have vodka in the officers' rooms."

Evelyn laughed at that. "Yes, I suppose it would," she said. "Sometimes I think—"

She broke off suddenly when an engine roared overhead. They stopped walking and looked up, staring in alarm as a Hurricane streaked across the sky, very low and seemingly right above the roofs of the buildings. Thick black smoke poured out from under a wing and the engine was screaming as the fighter flashed past them in an uncontrolled dive. Evelyn stared at the plane in horror as it went by, the inside of the cockpit covered in blood. Her brain registered that the pilot must be dead, but she couldn't seem to make her feet move.

Tomasz let out an exclamation in Polish, grabbing her arm. Then, foregoing the Russian, he yelled in English,

"Run!"

The Hurricane was heading straight for a hangar about fifty yards away and Evelyn needed no more encouragement. She started to run as fast as she could, one hand gripping the strap to her gas mask case and the other holding her hat on her head. Fear mixed with horror rolled through her as she willed her legs to move as fast as her heart was pounding.

The sound of the propellers hitting the tin roof of the hangar was ear-piercing, and Evelyn felt two strong hands grip her waist as the noise ripped across the station. Suddenly her feet left the ground, and she was flying through the air as Tomasz threw her behind a truck parked a few feet away just as an explosion ripped through the hangar behind them. The sound was deafening, making her ears throb in protest, and Evelyn's heart seemed to stop for a second. She felt a burst of searing heat before she fell behind the truck, hitting the ground hard. A second later, Tomasz landed on top of her, covering her with his body as debris slammed into the truck and rained down around them.

Then everything went black.

Author's Notes

Directive No. 16.

On July 16, 1940, Hitler issued Directive No. 16, "on preparations for a landing operation against England." This was the authorization for what became known by the German military as Operation Sea Lion, or the invasion of Britain. It is worth noting that, through the war to this point, Hitler frequently stated that England was not Germany's natural enemy. Yet, by July 13, 1940, Britain was still refusing to make peace with him, and Hitler determined that he would have to force them into suing for peace.

The following are excerpts from the actual directive:

> The Führer and Supreme Commander of the Armed Forces.
> Führer Headquarters, 16 July, 1940. 7 copies.
> Directive No. 16 On preparations for a landing operation against England.

> Since England, in spite of her hopeless military situation, shows no signs of being ready to come to an understanding, I have decided to prepare a landing operation against England and, if necessary, to carry it out.

> The aim of this operation will be to eliminate the English homeland as a base for the prosecution of the war against Germany and, if necessary, to occupy it completely.

I therefore order as follows:

1.   The landing will be in the form of a surprise crossing on a wide front from about Ramsgate to the area west of the Isle of Wight. Units of the Air Force will act as artillery, and units of the Navy as engineers. The

  possible advantages of limited operations before the general crossing (e.g. the occupation of the Isle of Wight or of the county of Cornwall) are to be considered from the point of view of each branch of the Armed

  Forces and the results reported to me. I reserve the decision to myself. Preparations for the entire operation must be completed by the middle of August.

2.   These preparations must also create such conditions as will make a landing in England possible, viz:

  a.   The English Air Force must be so reduced morally and physically that it is unable to deliver any significant attack against the German crossing.

  b.   Mine-free channels must be cleared.

    c.   The Straits of Dover must be closely sealed off with minefields on both flanks; also the Western entrance to the Channel approximately on the line Alderney-Poitland.

    d.   Strong forces of coastal artillery must command and protect the forward coastal area.

    e.   It is desirable that the English Navy be tied down shortly before the crossing, both in the North Sea and in the Mediterranean (by the Italians). For this purpose we must attempt even now to damage English

      home-based naval forces by air and torpedo attack as far as possible.

3. . . .The invasion will bear the cover name 'Seelöwe.'

a.   Army. . .

b.   Navy. . .

  c.   The task of the Air Force will be: To prevent interference by the enemy Air Force. To destroy coastal fortresses which might operate against our disembarkation points, to break the first resistance of enemy land forces, and to disperse reserves on their way to the front. In carrying out this task the closest liaison is necessary between individual Air Force units and the Army invasion forces. Also, to destroy important transport highways by which enemy reserves might be brought up, and to attack approaching enemy naval forces as far as possible from our disembarkation points. I request that suggestions be made to me regarding the employment of parachute and airborne troops. In this connection it should be considered, in conjunction with the Army, whether it would be useful at the beginning to hold parachute and airborne troops in readiness as a reserve, to be thrown in quickly in case of need.

[signed] ADOLF HITLER

"Hitler Issues Directive 16 on Preparation for a Landing Operation against England," Battle of Britain Diary (website), accessed July 7, 2024, https://battle-of-britain-diary.org.uk/1940/07/16/hitler-issues-directive -no-16-on-preparations-for-a-landing-operation-against-england/.

Adlertag (EAGLE DAY).

August 13, 1940. The first day of Göring's Adlerangriff (Eagle Attack). This was to be a two-week assault on Fighter Command's aircraft, airfields, and installations. However, poor weather and a series of blunders on the part of Luftwaffe commanders and pilots caused the day to be much less impactful than intended.

- August 13 was chosen for the commencement of the attack because weather forecasters (on both sides of the Channel) called for clear skies. Instead, the day dawned under heavy cloud cover. The operations of the Luftwaffe for the day, however, were not dependent on good weather, and so they proceeded. An armada of Dornier bombers rolled out at 5:00 a.m. to rendezvous with a mass of Messerschmidt 110s.

- The ME110s were equipped with newly issued radio crystals, but the bombers were not. However, the fighter pilots were not told that the bomber aircraft did not have the new radio crystals and assumed the bomber pilots could still hear them.

- At 6:15 a.m., Göring decided to postpone Adlerangriff until later in the day and recalled all the aircraft. The cancel order was sent out over the radio transmitter, and the ME110s turned back. Due to their outdated radio crystals, the bombers they were escorting did not receive the message and continued without their fighter escort. When they crossed over Eastchurch, Spitfire and Hurricane squadrons fell on them; five Dorniers were shot down, and six more badly damaged with wounded crews.

- After that disastrous start, England was left alone until the afternoon, when a furious Göring began the attack again.

Despite the rocky start, the Luftwaffe sent over 1,485 aircraft that day. Of those, forty-five were shot down with the pilots lost to death or captivity. In contrast, the RAF lost thirteen fighters, and only seven pilots were killed, with the rest parachuting to safety over their own land.

Martin Gilbert, *The Second World War: A Complete History*, rev. ed. (New York: Henry Holt and Company, 1989) 117-18.

Richard Hough and Dennis Richards, *The Battle of Britain: The Greatest Air Battle of World War II* (New York: W.W. Norton, 1990) 54-163.
C.B. Dear and M. R. D. Foot, eds., *The Oxford Companion to World War II* (Oxford: Oxford University Press, 1995) 4, 988.

Black Thursday.

August 15, 1940, was to become infamous to the Luftwaffe as Black Thursday. It was the first, and last, time that Luftflotte 5 (the Luftwaffe division transferred to Norway in April, 1940) attacked Britain in a daylight raid. It was also a good example of how badly Göring and Kesselring underestimated RAF Fighter Command. 520 German bombers and 1,270 fighters crossed over the Channel and North Sea to England. Seventy-five of them were shot down to an RAF loss of around thirty fighters, and thirteen pilots.

- Luftflotte 5 was destined to have a hard day due to one simple fact: the German commanders believed that there were no fighter squadrons in the north of Britain. Göring was so confident they had devastated the reserves that they believed all the fighters were busy in the south of England. What they didn't know was that Air Chief Marshal Hugh Dowding had already begun to rotate experienced squadrons who were exhausted after their battle in France and over the Channel, to the north for rest and recuperation. Those squadrons, in addition to the reserve squadrons held in 12 and 13 Group, were rested and yearning for action. They had been watching the battle rage in the south and wanted nothing more than to get into the action themselves. Luftflotte 5 flew right into their house.

- Luftflotte 5 consisted of Heinkel bombers and ME110 fighter/bombers. However, the distance from Norway necessitated the 110s fly with an extra fuel tank which it could jettison when empty. The extra weight hampered their speed and maneuverability, and made them easier targets for the British fighters than they would normally have been. Meanwhile, the Heinkel bombers were flying with a smaller bomb load than normal in order to conserve fuel. So, in addition to sustaining heavy losses, Luftflotte 5 did not inflict the damage that they expected to.

- While they were attacking the north of Britain, Luftflottens 1 and 2 (Göring's divisions in France) were scheduled to attack the south, believing that half of the RAF fighters would have gone north to defend against Luftflotte 5. However, poor weather delayed their offensives, and they were unable to commence until after noon. By the time they did attack southern England, Luftflotte 5 was well on the way to being soundly rebuffed, and the southern attack met the same number of defenders as usual.

- More significant than the number of losses the Luftwaffe suffered that day was the number of senior officers that were lost. Group Commander Hauptmann Walter Rubensdoerffer was killed when his ME110 went down, and three senior officers were among the crews of the eight Heinkel 111s that failed to return.

Martin Gilbert, *The Second World War: A Complete History*, rev. ed. (New York: Henry Holt and Company, 1989) 117-18.

Richard Hough and Dennis Richards, *The Battle of Britain: The Greatest Air Battle of World War II* (New York: W.W. Norton, 1990) 171-82.

The Hardest Day.

While August 15 was the Luftwaffe's worst day, August 18 was the RAF's. The Luftwaffe, no doubt offended by their losses so far, redoubled their efforts and attacked on the eighteenth with one focus: to destroy the airfields once and for all. To that aim, they hurtled over 850 sorties comprised of over 2,200 aircrew over Britain. For their part, RAF Fighter Command responded with 927 sorties and 600 aircrew. At the end of the day, the figures were grim for both sides. The German losses totaled between sixty-nine and seventy-one aircraft with ninety-four aircrew killed, forty aircrew captured, and twenty-five returned wounded. The RAF also experienced heavy losses: sixty-eight aircraft destroyed, only thirty-one of which were in combat; the rest were destroyed on the ground by bombing raids. Ten pilots were killed outright, with two more dying from their wounds, and a further nineteen pilots wounded – with eleven of them so badly injured that they were out for the rest of the Battle of Britain.

- Instead of spreading out their attacks across several airfields as they had been, Commanders Kesselring and Sperle agreed to change tactics and focus on only a few airfields instead. This way they could concentrate their efforts and be assured of successfully destroying the targets. They chose Kenley, Biggin Hill, Gosport, Ford, Thorney Island, Hornchurch and North Weald, and the radar station at Poling. However, they didn't succeed in destroying any of them, though they inflicted heavy damage. Kenley received the most damage that day, with all but one of the hangars destroyed, but they were only out of action for approximately an hour. In that time, two of their squadrons still in the air landed at other airfields to refuel and rearm. Biggin Hill was also heavily hit, but was never out of operation. It's a huge testament to the skill and determination of the ground crews and support personnel that the airfields continued to operate, despite heavy damage, throughout the Battle.

- A squadron of Hurricanes based at Kenley was 615 Squadron. While their airfield was being bombed 15,000 feet below them, they took on the top fighter cover alone. Outnumbered five-to-one, they fought desperately against ME109s. The Hurricanes, however, did not have the maneuverability of the 109s and were no real contest for the enemy fighters. Within a few minutes, 615 had lost four fighters in the air with one pilot killed, and six more of their fighters destroyed on the ground below. In less than ten minutes, they lost ten planes. (It's interesting to note that, by the beginning of September, Air Chief Marshal Dowding changed the battle plan to separate fighter duties. The faster, more maneuverable Spitfire was assigned the task of attacking the ME109s, while the Hurricanes were able to focus on the bombers.)

Richard Hough and Dennis Richards, *The Battle of Britain: The Greatest Air Battle of World War II* (New York: W.W. Norton, 1990) 206-12.

"The Hardest Day," Royal Air Force Museum (website), accessed July 7, 2024, https://www.rafmuseum.org.uk/research/online-exhibitions/history-of-the-battle-of-britain /the-hardest-day/.

"The Hardest Day: A Key 24 Hours in the Battle of Britain," Forces (website), accessed July 7, 2024, https://www.forces.net/news/hardest-day-key-24-hours -battle-britain.

Fighter Command Structure.

The structure of RAF Fighter Command during the Battle of Britain was pretty straightforward. It was divided into six groups: 9 Group, 10 Group, 11 Group, 12 Group, 13 Group, and 14 Group. Each group covered a section of Great Britain. Upon its formation on August 9, 1940, 9 Group covered Northern Ireland and North West England. South West England and South West Wales were covered by 10 Group; 11 Group covered South South East England and London; 12 Group covered East Anglia, Midlands, and North Wales; 13 Group covered North England and Scotland; and 14 Group (reformed under Fighter Command in June, 1940) covered Scotland.

- There is ongoing debate even today as to the exact number of aircraft Air Chief Marshall Dowding had at his disposal at the start of the Battle of Britain (July 10, 1940). After going through several different sources, I've chosen to go with the standard figure of serviceable aircraft (as opposed to aircraft still under repairs). Using those numbers, Fighter Command had roughly 591 serviceable aircraft and 1,200 pilots available on July 1, 1940. Those consisted of 347 Hurricanes (single engine fighters), 160 Spitfires (single engine fighters), 25 Defiants (single engine fighters), and 59 Blenheims (twin engine fighters).

- Counting only Luftflottes 2 and 3 (and not Luftflotte 5, stationed in Norway and Denmark) Reichsmarshall Hermann Göring had 1,935 serviceable aircraft ready for battle on July 1, 1940. Those consisted of 656 ME 109s (Messerschmidt single engine fighter); 168 ME 110s (Messerschmidt twin engine fighters, also used as a light bomber); 248 JU 87s (Junkers dive bomber); 767 combined of JU 88s (Junkers twin engine bomber), HE 111s (Heinkel twin engine bomber) and DO 17s (Dornier twin engine bomber); 48 long-range reconnaissance planes, and 46 short-range reconnaissance planes.

- At the beginning of the battle, the RAF fighter Squadrons were organized into two Flights: A Flight and B Flight. Within those flights, there were two sections each: Red Section, Blue Section, Yellow Section, and Green Section. In general, A Flight would fly with Red and Yellow Sections, while B Flight flew with Blue and Green Sections. The Squadron Leader would lead Red section, and Flight Leaders led the others.

- To begin with, all the squadrons adhered to what was known as the Vic formation. Each section flew in Vic formation, with the Flight Leader in front and his two wingmen on either side behind him (forming an upside-down *V*) However, losses were heavy as they could not see to protect each other from the German fighters when they dove down from higher altitudes with the sun behind them. Though the RAF didn't officially change the formations, the pilots took matters into their own hands and began using the German formation, which they called the four-finger formation. This formation had four planes instead of three, the Flight leader out front, with a wingman on either side, and the fourth plane covering the two wingmen. This allowed them to protect each other as well as combat the enemy, and lowered losses significantly.

- Squadrons were scrambled by Headquarters, or HQ, after they received notification of incoming raids from the radar towers and observer corps. The basic structure was Fighter Command HQ—Group Headquarters—Sector Station—Airfield (dispersal). In general, once enemy aircraft was picked up by radar, they had twenty minutes before they reached their target. Once scrambled, squadrons averaged sixteen minutes to intercept. That means that HQ had four minutes to decide how, and with what squadrons, to respond. They did this with the aid of plotters, who mapped the courses of both incoming raids and defending squadrons on a massive physical plot at Group HQ. (The movie *The Battle of Britain* shows the HQ setups brilliantly, along with the WAAFs who manned them).

- RAF airfields had multiple squadrons stationed on one airfield. In a perfect structure, each fighter squadron had sixteen total aircraft. This allowed for twelve operational airplanes while four were being repaired/serviced. Military wisdom at the time also dictated that, ideally, each squadron would have twenty total aircraft in order to account for pilots who were injured, on leave, or otherwise unable to be operational. However, the lack of machines and men prevented any squadron during the Battle from meeting the twenty aircraft threshold. In fact, going into the Battle, losses over Dunkirk and the Channel had depleted most squadrons to below the sixteen aircraft minimum. Though aircraft production was ramping up, and pilot training was being shortened, in reality, the Battle of Britain was begun with an average squadron having just twelve total aircraft.

- By August, squadrons were losing both aircraft and pilots at a rate that was not equal to the number of replacements coming in. As a result, once Adlertag arrived and the Luftwaffe was coming over Britain en masse, squadrons in 11 Group were often meeting them with eleven, ten, eight, and even four total aircraft.

Len Deighton and Max Hastings, *Battle of Britain* (London: Penguin Group, 1990) 100–101.

"Royal Air Force Tactics During the Battle of Britain," Classic Warbirds (website), accessed July 7, 2024, https://www.classicwarbirds.co.uk/articles/royal-air -force-tactics-during-the-battle-of-britain.php

For a great visual map, visit:

https://warfarehistorynetwork.com/wp-content/uploads/WW-Britain-Map -4C-Jan02.jpg

For a good visual map of all the airfields and locations, visit:

https://www.asisbiz.com/il2/Bf-109E/Bf-109E/pages/Artwork-showing-a-m ap-of-Battle-of-Britain-airfields-of-South-East-England-1940-0A.html.

Squadron Losses.

It goes without saying that the RAF losses were heavy. For some idea of the loss and chaos that the RAF fighter pilots experienced, here is a very small cross section of squadron losses taken over the course of a single five-day period (Aug 15 – 19, 1940):

- No 1 Squadron – Northolt. (Fred's squadron) Four Hurricanes destroyed, three pilots killed, one wounded.

- No 66 Squadron – Coltishall. (Miles' squadron) One Spitfire destroyed, one pilot killed. (never regained consciousness after bailing out)

- No 32 Squadron – Biggin Hill. Six Hurricanes destroyed, four pilots hospitalized – two burned, two wounded.

- No 64 Squadron – Kenley. Three Spitfires destroyed, one pilot killed, one captured (when he crash-landed in France), one wounded.

- No 615 Squadron – Kenley (mentioned above). Eleven Hurricanes destroyed, four pilots killed, three hospitalized—one burned, two wounded—1 injured in both legs.

I chose Aug 15-19 to highlight because the fighting only got worse as the Battle raged on. More crucially, as senior pilots were wounded and killed, the younger pilots coming in to replace them had no more than ten hours training in a cockpit. Many of them were seventeen years old, fresh out of school, and their first taste of combat was harsh. The lucky ones only watched one or two members of their squadron go down, but the unlucky ones only saw combat once. They went up, and never came back. It was the harsh reality that the fighter pilots of the RAF faced daily during the Battle of Britain.

One more thing to note is that, as the losses mounted, the officer corps was depleted. While it was always standard for pilots to be of officer rank (Pilot Officer was the lowest rank), as they were killed there were fewer and fewer officers to replace them. In response to this dilemma, the RAF began using enlisted pilots. These were noncommissioned pilots, and held the rank of sergeant pilot. They were not officers, and so were not allowed into the officers' mess or officers' recreations rooms.

Winston G. Ramsey, ed., *The Battle of Britain: Then and Now* (London: Battle of Britain International, 2000) 354–73.

Norman Gelb, *Scramble: A Narrative History of The Battle of Britain* (n.p.:S harpe Books, 2018).

Vichy Ban on Public Dancing.

On May 20, 1940, a ban on all public and private dances was imposed in Paris by the French government, and extended to all areas outside Paris on May 24, 1940. This was combined with a curfew, both of which remained in place until April 30, 1945. However, it is interesting to note that while the French people were prohibited from holding dances (publicly or privately), cabaret dancers were exempt from this. The cabaret patrons could not dance, but they could watch the dancers on the stage.

- While the ban was enforced in May, 1940, Marshal Pétain reinforced it on June 20, 1940, when he condemned the "pleasure-seeking" activity as having led to the defeat of France. He blamed dancing, in part, for the "corruption of the youth and society at large." He believed that bodies in close contact went against the ideal of a "pure and healthy life." Therefore, all dances were banned throughout mainland France.

- So what did the French people do? They moved their dances underground, holding them at secret locations. In cities and towns, they resorted to apartments, private houses, cellars, stores, and the back rooms of cafes. In the rural areas, people would hold dances in clearings, barns, or farmyards. The dances were often held on Sunday afternoons and evenings, word spreading by word of mouth to all the surrounding areas. The dancing would go long past curfew, after which the people would make their way home. In both urban and rural locations, absolutely no music or songs from the Pétain government or Germans were played.

- It was left up to the police (in Paris) or gendarmes (in rural areas) to enforce the law and prosecute offenders. Anyone caught and booked would be tried by a magistrate's court and, depending on the number of offenses, would be fined up to two hundred francs or imprisoned for up to three days. However, the average fine was around sixty francs, which was roughly two days pay.

- Illegal dances were widespread and continued throughout the war. They were a common meeting place for resistance members as well locals. A lookout was always posted to raise the alarm at the approach of the gendarmes, and the dancers would scatter to take cover in hiding places. Most gendarmes did not look too hard for them.

- Interestingly, though dancing was banned, dance classes were not. The Vichy government wanted to maintain dance classes to educate the French youth, and encouraged certain styles of dancing, such as traditional country dances. Dance schools were strictly regulated, but in reality, they became hotspots for illegal dances. Local enrollment was high, and the schools became a place where youth could dance as much as they liked. A lookout was posted to alert to approaching gendarmes, at which point the student pretended to be learning, and the instructor took control of their "class."

- The ban remained in place until April 30, 1945, when it was finally lifted. However, areas that were severely affected by the fighting, and in which the local authorities deemed it inappropriate at the time, the ban remained—in some instances for as long an additional year.

Geneviève Montcombroux, *WWII France: A Writer's Guide* (Solitude Publishing, 2023).

No More to the Dance You'll Go! Illegal Dances, 1939–45,
https://musees.isere.fr/sites/portail-musee-fr/files/docs/20210706_livret_tra d_bd.pdf

Also by

About the author

CW Browning was writing before she could spell. Making up stories with her childhood best friend in the backyard in Olathe, Kansas, imagination ran wild from the very beginning. At the age of eight, she printed out her first full-length novel on a dot-matrix printer. All eighteen chapters of it. Even at that tender age, her stories consisted of action scenes and ghost stories, with a little Trixie Belden mystery thrown in. The plots have improved since those days, but her genre remained true. Over the years, writing took a backseat to the mechanics of life. Those mechanics, however, have a great way of underlining what genuinely lifts a spirit and makes the soul sing. After attending Rutgers University and studying History, her love for writing was rekindled. It became apparent where her heart truly lay. Picking up an old manuscript, she dusted it off and went back to what made her whole. CW still makes up stories in her backyard, but now she crafts them for her readers to enjoy. She makes her home in Southern New Jersey, where she loves to grill steak and sip red wine on the patio.

CW loves to hear from readers! She is always willing to answer questions and hear your stories. You can find her on Facebook, X (formerly known as Twitter)and Instagram.

If social media isn't your thing, she can also be reached by email at cwbrowningbooks@cwbrowning.com and on her store at www.cwbrowningbooks.com.

Made in the USA
Coppell, TX
30 July 2024

35367898R00173